A SPY FOR HELP

Book 15 of the NEVER SAY SPY series

Diane Henders

A SPY FOR HELP

ISBN 978-1-927460-61-0

Copyright © 2020 Diane Henders

PEBKAC Publishing Inc.
P.O. Box 67, Station Main
Qualicum Beach, BC   V9K 1S7
www.pebkacpublishing.com

Books in the NEVER SAY SPY series:

More books coming! For a current list, please visit
www.dianehenders.com
Or sign up for my New Book Notification list at
www.dianehenders.com/books

Humour by Diane Henders

Probably Inappropriate

Definitely Inappropriate

Totally Inappropriate

Completely Inappropriate

Unabashedly Inappropriate

More books coming! For a current list, please visit
www.dianehenders.com
Or sign up for my New Book Notification list at
www.dianehenders.com/books

First printed in paperback June 2020 by PEBKAC Publishing
Inc.
v.4

Since You Asked...

People frequently ask if my protagonist, Aydan Kelly, is really me.

Yeah, you got me. These novels are an autobiography of my secret life as a government agent, working with highly-classified computer technology... Oh, wait, what's that? You want the *truth*? Um, you do realize fiction writers get paid to lie, don't you?

...well, shit, that's not nearly as much fun. It's also a long story.

I swore I'd never write fiction. "Too personal," I said. "People read novels and automatically assume the author is talking about him/herself."

Well, apparently I lied about the fiction-writing part. One day a story sprang into my head and wouldn't leave. The only way to get it out was to write it down. So I did.

But when I wrote that first book, I never intended to show it to anyone, so I created a character that looked like me just to thumb my nose at the stereotype. I've always had a defective sense of humour, and this time it turned around and bit me in the ass.

Because after I'd written the third novel, I realized I actually wanted other people to read my books. And when I went back to change my main character to *not* look like me, my beta readers wouldn't let me. They rose up against me and said, "No! Aydan is a tall woman with long red hair and brown eyes. End of discussion!"

Jeez, no wonder readers get the idea that authors write about themselves. So no, I'm not Aydan Kelly. I just look like her.

Oh, and the town of Silverside and all secret technologies are products of my imagination. If I'm abducted by grim-faced men wearing dark glasses, or if I die in an unexplained fiery car crash, you'll know I accidentally came a little too close to the truth.

I hope you enjoy the book!

For Phill

Thank you for being my technical advisor and the most tolerant husband ever. Much love!

To my beta readers/editors, especially Carol H., Judy B., and Phill B., with gratitude: Many thanks for all your time and effort in catching my spelling and grammar errors, telling me when I screwed up the plot or the characters' motivations, and generally keeping me honest.

To the Regina Police Service: Thank you so much for your helpfulness and patience with my myriad questions! I know how busy you are and your work is far more important than mine; so I really appreciate the time you took to help me get my facts straight. Any inaccuracies in the way I've portrayed Regina police officers and/or their procedures and attitudes are entirely my own mistakes or fabrications.

To everyone else, respectfully:
Canadian English is an unholy hybrid of British and American English, so I apologize if spellings in this book look odd to you. But if you find typos, please send an email to errors@dianehenders.com. Mistakes drive me nuts, and I'm sorry if any slipped through. Please let me know what the error is, and on which page. I'll make sure it gets fixed as soon as possible. Thanks!

CHAPTER 1

My pulse thumped a little faster than necessary as I cruised toward the building. This was probably a bad idea.

But I had to do it sooner or later, and I wouldn't be able to relax until it was over.

My craven hands steered my car past the building for a second time instead of turning into the parking lot. I did have to deal with it, but not necessarily today...

I hissed out a breath of annoyance. Make up your mind, idiot. If somebody notices you circling the building, it'll only make things worse.

One more trip around the block stiffened my spine.

Okay, I was doing this.

Now.

I steered into the lot and parked. Before my inner coward could take over, I pried myself out of the driver's seat and strode across to the building's entrance.

Confident. In control.

Not intimidated at all, goddammit.

A gust of icy wind whipped my long hair across my face as though flagellating me for a bad decision. My little Glock weighed temptingly in my ankle holster; but it couldn't help me here.

Another blast of snow-laden wind pushed me through the door. I shot a glance around the warm and silent lobby, trying not to look furtive.

"Hey, Aydan! What are you doing here?" From behind the bulletproof glass of the Sirius Dynamics security wicket, Leo gave me a smile. "I thought you were on leave until January second."

"I am." I scurried over to sign in.

Just let me get up to my office without running into Dermott...

Pasting on a smile, I added, "I'm only here to file a report, and then I'm gone until the new year. I did a verbal report yesterday, but I want to get it down in writing while it's still fresh in my mind."

I spun the turntable containing the sign-in sheet. *Come on, Leo, give me my security fob and let me sneak upstairs.*

Oblivious to my psychic plea, Leo leaned forward and lowered his voice. "I heard you had a big blowup with Dermott yesterday. Tribunal with the chain of command; the whole enchilada."

I shook my head in equal parts chagrin and admiration. "Jeez, Leo, where do you get your intel?"

He grinned. "I overheard Dermott bitching about it this morning. Sounds like you made him look like a total ass."

With a giant effort of will, I managed not to say 'No, he did that all by himself'. I also didn't point out that Dermott should know better than to shoot his mouth off where he could be overheard.

Instead, I kept my face and voice neutral. "It was just a misunderstanding. We got it cleared up; no big deal." I added a shrug that was probably a bit too casual. "Well, I'd better get that report done. The wind's picking up outside and I want to get home before dark. There's already a pretty bad ground drift on the highway."

I imagined a telepathic connection with all my might. *Hand over the fucking fob, Leo!*

"Yeah," he agreed, reaching for the control button in slow motion. "I hear it's supposed to be pretty crappy weather this week. Wouldn't you know it; right when everybody's trying to get home for Christmas. Well, that's Alberta for you. What else is new, eh?"

Suppressing my scream of frustration, I unclenched my teeth and managed a smile as the turntable delivered my security fob at last.

"Yep, no kidding." I snatched up the fob and hurried for the stairs, tossing a bright "See you later" over my shoulder.

Mistake.

As I faced forward again I nearly ran into Dermott, who had just emerged from the secured area.

His normally ruddy complexion flushed to burgundy. "What the hell are you doing here?" he barked.

Shit, shit, shit!

I stayed expressionless, hoping he couldn't hear my heart hammering. "I'm only in for a little while. I wanted to file my report while everything's still fresh in my mind."

"You're supposed to be on stress leave." His ominous tone fired another burst of adrenaline through my already-overloaded system.

Faking confidence for all I was worth, I gave him a smile. "Yep, you're right. I'll only be here long enough to file that report."

I waved my fob at the reader, but Dermott's large hand slapped onto the door, holding it closed.

"Get the hell out of this building," he growled. "Right. Fucking. Now."

My asshole-defense system spiked to DEFCON 1,

delivering a burst of rage that drove my fist forward.

Fortunately it shot toward his hand, not his throat. A sharp tweak of his thumb startled him enough to ease his hold on the door, and I yanked it open and strode through.

"*Back off,*" I hissed as I passed him.

He didn't, of course. The door had barely closed behind us when his hard grip clamped onto my arm, spinning me around.

I jerked free, snapping into a defensive position with my weight on the balls of my feet and my hands guarding my head in loose fists.

Thank you, muay thai videos. Please don't let Dermott be a martial arts expert. This defensive position was pretty much the extent of my skills.

Doing my best badass imitation, I snarled, "Do you *really* want to go there with me?"

He paled and took a step backward. Thank God.

I made my voice strong and steady. "Now, we're going to go up to your office and work this out. Without bloodshed. Move it." I jerked my chin toward the stairs.

His florid face creased into a sneer. "I'm the Director of Clandestine Operations. I don't take orders from fucking *agents.*" He spat the word as if it was a foul insult.

"You're the *acting* DCO, and only for the next ten days," I growled. "And if you want to do this here in the hallway, then fine." I lowered my guard but stayed light on my feet in case he tried to sucker-punch me. Attempting a reasonable tone, I added, "I'm sorry you looked bad in front of the chain of command. I didn't mean for that to happen. We need to be able to work together, so what can we do to fix this?"

"You can die, bitch," he gritted, and shoved past me.

"Listen, dipshit!" I snapped at his receding back. "If you

don't drop this stupid grudge and do your job, you're putting everybody at risk. Suck up your whiny-baby attitude and let's talk this out!"

Dermott's back went rigid and his hands curled into white-knuckled fists, but he kept walking without a reply. When he disappeared around the corner, I hissed out a long breath through my teeth.

"That went well," I said to nobody, and concentrated on steadying my shaking knees while I climbed the stairs.

My phone was already ringing when I arrived at my office. I hurried in for a cautious peek at the call display.

Not Dermott. Whew.

I picked up, trying for a breezy tone. "Hey, Leo. What's up?"

"Are you okay?"

"Of course; why wouldn't I be?"

"I was watching the security monitors. I saw what happened."

Shit.

He went on eagerly, "I thought you were going to deck Dermott, the way you decked Holt. You could have gotten away with it, you know. He attacked you first."

I groaned. "No, he didn't. I tweaked his thumb first, to get him to take his hand off the door. And anyway, I didn't mean to hit Holt on Monday..."

Shit, had that only been three days ago? It felt like a lifetime.

Jerking my attention back to the conversation, I finished, "...and if I had taken a swing at Dermott, my ass would be in Dr. Rawling's anger-management class so fast it would make my head spin."

I didn't bother to add 'again'. One ten-week session had

been more than enough for me; although if Rawling found out about this latest episode with Dermott, he might disagree.

Leo was talking again. Shit, I had to stop zoning out. Too tired.

"Sorry, what did you say?" I asked.

"I said, I'm saving a copy of the security footage just in case Dermott tries to make trouble for you. Don't worry, I'm on your side."

"Thanks, Leo. But we're all supposed to be on the same side here."

He snorted. "Tell that to Dermott."

I didn't have a good reply.

Twenty minutes later my worn-out brain had disgorged as much information as I could recall, and my aching heart shuddered away from shock of my mother's tacit murder and espionage confession and the horrible memory of her lifeless body hitting the floor.

Feeling every one of my forty-eight years and then some, I dragged myself up from my desk and trudged over to peek into the hallway.

No sign of Dermott. Small mercies.

Squaring my shoulders, I held my head high and strode for the stairs.

I had just sunk into the safety of my car when my cell phone vibrated. I twitched guiltily, but a glance at the call display made me relax with a smile. Hellhound.

I started the car to get some heat into the already-frigid

interior, and accepted the call. "Hi, Arnie."

"Hey, darlin'. Did ya get home okay?"

"Not yet. I went in to Sirius to file my report first. I'm just heading home now."

His momentary silence was just a fraction too long. "Was Dermott there?" he asked cautiously.

"Yep."

Another beat of silence. Then, "How'd that go for ya?"

I let out a sigh that felt like it came from my toes. "Not as well as I'd hoped. About as shitty as I'd expected." I considered. "Maybe a bit shittier. I probably shouldn't have lost my temper."

"Aw, fuck. Did ya shoot him?"

"Didn't even punch him," I said with a touch of pride.

Hellhound laughed. "Good job, darlin'." When he spoke again the smile was gone from his voice. "Anyway... the reason I'm callin', uh..."

Unease skittered up my backbone. "What's wrong?"

"Nothin'," he said hurriedly. "Nothin's wrong. I just, um... I got a... bit of a situation." He drew a deep breath. "I think I found Kathy."

CHAPTER 2

"Wh-" I bit off my first reaction of 'who?' as realization struck. "*Kathy?* Your *sister?*"

Another deep breath came over the line, and when Hellhound spoke again there was a faint tremor in his voice. "Yeah. Yeah... I think so." His voice firmed. "Hell, I know it. It's her."

"Is she...?" I couldn't finish the sentence.

"She's alive."

A potent mixture of excitement and worry stopped my voice for a moment. Could Arnie's search finally be over after thirty long years? He'd be devastated if it was a case of mistaken identity. But what if it really was Kathy and she'd been avoiding him all this time? I knew exactly how much that would hurt.

I sucked in a shallow breath. "What... how... shit, I don't even know where to start. Have you contacted her yet?"

"Yeah, I left a message on her machine, an' she called me back."

I waited, but he didn't elaborate.

"So what did she say?" I prompted.

"She said she ain't Kathy, an' don't ever call her again."

"Oh." My word jerked out on a gut-punch of disappointment on his behalf.

"But it's her, Aydan, I know it is," Hellhound insisted. "An'... an' I gotta see her. I gotta *know*. But I can't show up on her doorstep like some fuckin' stalker. 'Specially lookin' like me."

Fondly imagining his fearsome face and tattooed bulk, I agreed, "You'd scare the shit out of her. She'd probably call the police." An idea eased into my mind. Maybe I could be their go-between. "But you know where she lives, right?" I added hopefully.

"Yeah." His voice was flat. "The whole fuckin' world knows. Some asshole doxxed her. That's prob'ly why she doesn't wanna talk to me. Or anybody."

"Wait, what do you mean, 'some asshole doctor'? She's a doctor?"

Hellhound let out a breath. "No, darlin', I said 'doxxed'. Somebody doxxed her. It's a hacker thing, where they dig up all your personal shit an' put it on the internet for everybody to see. She's LaVonda Rainey."

I rested my aching forehead on the steering wheel. "Sorry, should that mean something to me?"

"Guess ya ain't been followin' social media lately."

"No, I've been a little busy staying alive and out of prison," I agreed.

"LaVonda Rainey's a psychic, an' she blogs. Up 'til last week she was nobody, bloggin' about all kinds a' shit like messages from the other side an' music an' her cat an' her recovery from drug addiction. She had maybe a coupla dozen followers. Then she wrote a funny post about how it sucks bein' overweight; an' some fuckin' idiot took it the wrong way."

My stomach clenched. "Oh, God. I know what's coming next."

"Yeah," Hellhound growled. "The fuckin' idiot quoted it outta context an' made it sound like she was fat-shamin'.

Ten seconds later it went viral an' the whole fuckin' world
started screamin' for blood. Fuckin' trolls puttin' shit on her
blog about how she oughtta be raped an' tortured; death
threats, the whole shit-a-ree. An' then some fuckin'
asshole..." His voice rose. "*...thought it'd be a fuckin' good
idea to doxx her so* EVERY FUCKIN' NUTJOB IN THE
WORLD CAN FIND HER!" The end of his sentence was a
full-throated bellow that made me yank the phone away from
my ear.

When I dared to move it closer again, I could hear him
breathing harshly at the other end. "What if somebody
attacks her?" he rasped. "What if..." The sound of his gulp
came clearly over the line. "Aydan, I can't lose her. Not now.
Not after all this time." The raw emotion in his voice tore my
heart.

"We won't let that happen." The words were out of my
mouth before I could consider their magnitude. "Tell me
everything you know. How do you know LaVonda is Kathy?
Did they publish her real name?"

"Yeah. She said they were bullshittin' an' they got it
wrong, but I read her blog an' it sounds like her. An' the
drug addiction stuff, that all fits with what I knew about her
before she disappeared; an' the timeline's about right."

"Arnie," I said as gently as I could. "I know your
memory's nearly photographic, but after thirty years do you
really think you could identify her just by the way she writes?
Zillions of people blog, and-"

"Shit, no, I didn't mean that," he interrupted with
uncharacteristic impatience. "I meant she used a word
nobody else would know. It ain't even a real word, just
somethin' we made up as kids. I'm tellin' ya, it's her."

"Okay, I believe you," I soothed. "So where does she

live?"

"Regina. An' all this shit hit the fan last week, an' I didn't catch it 'til an hour ago." His voice rose again. "By now they could be closin' in on her..."

"Slow down, Arnie. Take a breath. You said you'd just talked to her, so you know she's okay, right?"

"She was okay half an hour ago. An hour from now, who knows? I'm goin' out there. I gotta-"

"Arnie, stop!"

He fell silent, and I went on, "Just think about this for a second. You phoned her and told her who you were, and she blew you off. So if you show up there, you'll be harassing a woman who's already terrified, and who's going to think you're some crazy stalker. You'll end up getting arrested for sure. And if she actually is Kathy..." I hesitated, not wanting to hurt him.

"You're gonna say, if she really is Kathy an' she doesn't wanna see me, I oughta leave her be," he said flatly.

"Well... maybe you should give it some time, at least until the shitstorm dies down and she's feeling a little safer-"

"Or some fuckin' asshole comes after her," he snapped. "Ain't gonna happen. I already booked my flight. I was just callin' to see if you'd stay at my place an' look after Hooker. Miz Lacey can't do it 'cause she's in the Bahamas with her bridge club for Christmas."

"Of course I will, but, Arnie, if she flat-out told you not to contact her..." I trailed off.

"Yeah, just think about that for a sec," Hellhound growled. "Here's a woman that just got shit on by the whole fuckin' world. There're fuckin' wackos screamin' for her blood, an' they all know her phone number. Just think about that," he repeated. "'Cause I'm thinkin' a woman like that sure as hell ain't gonna return a call from some random shithead that phones up pretendin' to be her long-lost brother."

My jaw dropped as his words sank in. "Shit. You're right."

"I know I'm right. She wasn't tryin' to get rid a' me, she was warnin' me off. Tryin' to protect me." His voice went husky. "Just like when we were kids. Only this time, I'm gonna be there for her."

My heart squeezed. "Arnie, you were only five when you and Kathy went into foster care..." I didn't mention his brothers. Neither of us needed that ugly reminder. I went on hurriedly, "...and she was hooked on drugs by the time you were nine. You were just a kid. There was nothing you could have done."

"I know!" he snapped, frustration edging his words. His voice softened. "Thanks, darlin'. I know I couldn't'a done anythin' then, but I can now. An' I'm gonna."

"I'll help you. I'll come down right away." I switched the phone to speaker and laid it on the passenger seat as I reversed out of the parking space. "What time is your flight? I can be at the Calgary airport in two and a half hours. If you book me a ticket, I'll pay you back when I get there. John has a key to your apartment, so he can look after Hooker until we're back."

"Thanks, darlin', but ya don't hafta-"

"I know I don't have to, but I want to." I switched to a teasing tone. "Somebody has to keep your ass out of jail."

His chuckle sounded relieved. "Thanks, darlin'. The flight leaves at six-twenty."

I glanced at my watch and pressed a little harder on the accelerator. "I won't get to the airport before five-thirty.

Even with the special security screening for agents, that's cutting it pretty fine."

"Just drive safe. Don't take any chances. If ya get there in time, we'll take the six-twenty; an' if ya don't, we'll take the eight-fifteen. We're payin' full fare anyway, so it won't matter." His calm words couldn't hide the tension in his voice.

"I'll do my best," I promised, and steered my car onto the treacherous highway.

Fifteen minutes later I slithered to a stop on the packed snow in front of my house. Leaving the engine running, I scooted inside to retrieve my grab-and-go bag from the front closet. I was halfway back to the car when my cell phone vibrated again.

A glance at the call display yielded no surprise. John Kane. Of course Arnie would have called his best friend next. A small glow warmed my heart at the knowledge that he'd called me first; but it was probably only because I was the most available cat-sitter.

Sliding into the driver's seat, I hit the hands-free control and tossed my phone onto the passenger seat.

"Hi, John," I said as I put the car in gear.

"Aydan." His sexy baritone warmed me. "Arnie said he just gave you the news."

"Yes. I can't believe he's finally found her after all these years."

"Maybe he hasn't," Kane said cautiously. "You do know she denied any acquaintance, don't you?"

"Yeah, but Arnie swears it's her."

Kane's sigh carried over the line. "I can't decide whether to hope he's right or wrong. He'll likely end up getting arrested if he tries to force her to talk to him."

"I know. That's why I'm going."

Kane's reply came in a teasing tone, but the undercurrent of disapproval was clear. "So you can get arrested instead. Or as well."

I bit down on annoyance and kept my voice light. "Let's hope not. She's less likely to be intimidated by a woman."

"Aydan..." Kane hesitated. "I don't mean to question your judgement, but... you're in no condition to tackle this. In the past seven days you've been significantly sleep-deprived, come off a mission where you had a serious incident with loss of life; and you had a major emotional upheaval yesterday with your imprisonment and your mother's death. You need time to recover."

"Well, tough," I snapped. "That's not an option."

After a fractional pause, Kane said patiently, "I wasn't trying to dissuade you from going. I know that would be futile, and anyway, I'd do the same if I was in your place. I'm just saying that you need to take your mental and emotional state into account. Analyze your reactions, or call and run things by me as an impartial observer. Count to ten before you lose your temper. That sort of thing."

"One," I said dangerously. "Two..."

His laughter rolled out of the speaker. "That admonition went over about as well as I'd expected."

I relaxed. "Well, at least you're not completely delusional."

"I frequently question my own sanity where you're concerned, but I certainly don't harbour any delusions." The smile left his voice. "I wish I could come, too. This is so important to Arnie."

"I'm sure he knows you'd come if it wasn't Christmastime, but we both know your first Christmas with

Daniel is really important."

"The first Christmas with my *family*," Kane corrected. "You and Dad and Arnie and Daniel, together. Do you think..." He stopped. "Well, of course you have no way of knowing how long you'll be. I hope you can make it home in time for Christmas Eve."

His tone was matter-of-fact, but I knew how much longing was hidden behind it.

"We'll do our best," I assured him. "Today's only the twenty-second. We'll be in Regina tonight, and either this woman is Kathy or she isn't. If she isn't, we'll be home tomorrow. And even if she is Kathy, she and Arnie might have a reunion or she might tell him to get lost; but either way, I don't see us sticking around past tomorrow. Arnie won't push it if she really doesn't want to have anything to do with him. He just needs to know whether he can stop looking after all these years."

"That's true, but there's the added complication of this social media furor," Kane said. "If he thinks his sister is in danger, nothing will convince him to leave her. Even though Kathy was only nine when their mother was killed, she still tried to take care of her little brother. She was the only mother figure Arnie had left. He'll sacrifice his life for her if necessary."

My throat tightened. "I know."

CHAPTER 3

Leaving my car in short-term parking, I dashed into the Departures level of the Calgary airport at five-thirty. I cleared security mercifully fast, and jogged into the boarding lounge just as the last passenger vanished down the boarding ramp.

Hellhound rose to greet me with a smile and a kiss, and minutes later we were taking our seats on the aircraft.

As we buckled in, I joked, "You know, travelling with you is pretty much my worst nightmare." I bumped my shoulder against his. "I always get squished in the seat next to the big guy."

He chuckled and leaned down to rumble softly in my ear. "Ya could always sit on my lap, darlin'." He accompanied the invitation with a whiskery kiss below my earlobe, sending a tingling cascade of shivers down my spine.

"Mmmm. Promises, promises," I murmured. "But I'm not harbouring any ambition to join the Mile-High Club on a flight to Regina, Saskatchewan."

"Aw, come on, darlin', live a little. If ya gotta go to the armpit a' the world, ya might as well make it fun."

I settled against his leather-scented warmth with a sigh. "Regina's a nice city. Why does everybody hate it so much?"

"'Cause it's the armpit a' the world," Hellhound repeated matter-of-factly, tucking an arm around my shoulders. "I started hatin' it when I hadta ride the Greyhound bus between Calgary an' Winnipeg back in the 80s. The bus got into Regina at the ass-crack a' midnight, an' the depot was always crawlin' with hookers an' druggies. The shitters were so fuckin' filthy they made outhouses look like operatin' rooms. I used to stand four feet away from the urinal to piss, 'cause you'd get crabs if ya stood any closer."

"Ech!" I shuddered. "If you were hosing down the urinals from four feet away, it's no wonder the bathrooms were disgusting."

"I'm kiddin'," he assured me. "I didn't really." As I relaxed, he added, "I pissed in the sink instead."

I recoiled. "Gross!"

His belly-laugh made heads turn toward us, only to snap rigidly forward after a glimpse of Hellhound's forbidding bearded and tattooed presence.

"You're so much fun to bullshit," he said, snuggling me close again. "Ya know I wouldn't do that."

"You would," I protested. "You totally would."

"Okay, you're right; I would if I hadta. But I didn't."

I snickered. "So you're judging the entire city based on its bus depot."

"Nah. When I quit ridin' the bus an' started drivin', Regina pissed me off, then, too." At my raised eyebrow, he went on, "You're cruisin' along, eight hours into the drive with six to go; an' there's Regina like a big fuckin' turd in the middle a' the highway. Hit Victoria Avenue, slow down, fight the traffic... I fuckin' hate Regina. The only good thing about it is, it rhymes with vag-"

"Got it," I interrupted.

Hellhound grinned. "Ya sure do." The smile slid off his face. "Wonder how many times I drove past her," he muttered. "All those times I blew through there without stoppin'."

"You don't even know if this woman is Kathy," I reminded him. "And even if it is Kathy, she probably hasn't lived in Regina for the last thirty years."

"Yeah, but still." He fell silent, staring into the troubled past.

I woke with a start at the jolt and rumble of our landing.

"Rise an' shine, darlin'," Hellhound teased.

"Uh. Right." I twisted to rub at the incriminating damp patch on his shoulder where my cheek had rested. "Okay, I take back what I said about big guys. You make a great pillow. Sorry about your shirt."

"No problem. We're in Regina in the middle a' winter. I'll be wearin' my parka twenty-four-seven."

As we taxied toward the terminal, I squeezed his hand. "How are you doing?"

His brows drew together. "Pissed that it's already nine o'clock local. By the time we get to the terminal an' get our rental car, it'll be too late to go see her."

I concealed a small exhalation of relief. At least he wasn't going to be unreasonable.

A short time later, I dropped my backpack into the trunk of the rental car beside Hellhound's guitar case. He lowered his small duffel bag in, too, and unzipped it. Delving inside, he pulled out a tire iron and a clinking handful of objects, then slammed the trunk and headed for the driver's seat.

I slid into the passenger's side in time to see him tuck the tire iron down beside his seat. Ready for trouble.

I let out a small sigh, hoping we wouldn't find any.

The clinking objects turned out to be large rings. Bemused and a little touched by this unusual attention to his appearance, I watched him slip them onto the fingers of both hands.

He flexed his fingers, the rings clicking softly.

"Does Kathy like jewellery?" I asked. "I've never seen you wear a ring before."

Hellhound gave me a grim smile and made a fist. "Brass knuckles are illegal."

I gulped at the shiny array of grinning death's heads. "Right."

"I wanna drive by her place right away just to scope it out," he added. "Then I'll drop ya off at the hotel an' go back to watch."

"Stalk much?" I teased as gently as I could.

Not gently enough.

He scowled. "I ain't leavin' her exposed. Cops can't do anythin' unless somebody kicks down her door, an' by then it's too fuckin' late. I can protect her."

I brushed a fingertip over his scarred knuckles. "But maybe you shouldn't."

Hellhound pulled his hand away. "What the fuck? Ya think I'm just gonna sit here like a-"

"No, no," I interrupted, recapturing his hand and stroking it. "Of course not. I'm just saying that if you take down her boyfriend or the pizza delivery guy, you're going to be in deep shit."

"I do this for a fuckin' livin'," he said stiffly. "I ain't gonna fuck it up." His stony expression stabbed me in the heart, an ice-cold dagger sliding into an old wound.

"No, Arnie, I'm sorry, that's not what I meant," I blurted,

misery rising like acid in my throat. "I'm sorry, I didn't mean to-"

He stopped me with a gentle finger to my lips. "Hush, darlin'. Ya got nothin' to apologize for." He stroked my hair away from my face. "You're only tryin' to help. I'm sorry. Did I scare ya?"

"No, of course not." I couldn't quite meet his eyes.

"But I triggered ya somehow. Your ex, right?"

I shrugged and sat back in my seat, staring through the windshield. "No big deal. You're nothing like him. We'd better get going."

"Aydan, look at me."

When I faced him, he was frowning. "If ya tell me what just happened, I can make sure I don't do it again."

"Everything's fine." I leaned in to kiss him. "Don't worry."

His arms closed around me, strength tempered to gentleness as always. "I ain't worryin'. I just hate makin' ya feel bad, an' I don't wanna do it again. But it's okay if ya don't wanna talk about it."

Letting out a breath, I thumped my forehead against his shoulder. "John told me I was messed up after the last week. He was right, as usual."

Hellhound pressed a kiss to my temple. "So what happened just now?"

I sat back with a sigh. "You were angry and you shut me out for a few seconds, and I... flashed back. Thought you were furious and you hated me and you'd freeze me out and punish me for days." I shrugged again. "I know you'd never do that. It was just an old stupid reflex."

"Not stupid," he disagreed gently. "Nobody goes through hell an' comes out the same."

I squirmed. "It wasn't 'hell', just a shitty marriage. Lots of people have them. No big deal."

His face softened. "Darlin', I know what ya went through. I saw it every day when I was a kid."

"No." I squeezed his hand. "Your father was a sick vicious bastard. My ex never hit me. There's no comparison."

"Words can hurt worse'n fists," Hellhound said quietly.

"But words can't break the bones in a five-year-old's face and beat his mother to death in front of him."

"Guess you're right about that," Hellhound muttered, and put the car in gear. "Words ain't gonna protect Kathy, either."

I glanced at his grim profile, my stomach tightening. "What's her address? I'll plug it into the GPS."

"Don't need the GPS. I looked it up on the internet before we left." He guided the car expertly around a large pothole and onto the snow-packed street.

"You and your memory," I teased. "Must be nice."

"Yeah," he said seriously. "She's on the sixth floor, an' now I know all the streets an' buildin' heights around it."

"You memorized the whole..." I trailed off, shaking my head. "You know, you scare the shit out of me sometimes." As he glanced over, frowning, I hurriedly added, "In a good way. So if she's on the sixth floor, at least we don't have to worry about somebody getting in her windows."

His scowl deepened as he returned his attention to the dark street. "Hell, that'd be the easiest way in. Rappel down from the roof an' go straight through her balcony doors. Bet she doesn't even keep 'em locked, thinkin' she's safe up there. An' even if she's all locked up, all she's gotta do is walk close enough to the window to cast a shadow on the blinds an' a sniper could pick her off no problem. There's another buildin' a block away with a perfect line."

"I'm sure she's taking every precaution," I reassured him. "And maybe you could get to her easily; but you're a professional assassin. There aren't too many guys like you in the world."

Hellhound grunted. "Army's fuckin' full a' guys like me. An' the only difference between a good soldier an' a bugfuck looney-tune is one little screw loose up here." He tapped his temple.

"Maybe, but army guys probably aren't the demographic that got offended by her blog post."

"Prob'ly not," he agreed. "But ya never know what's gonna shake that little screw loose. Some guy with a wife or girlfriend that got in on the shitstorm; maybe he decides he's gonna be a fuckin' hero for the ol' lady. But hell, ya don't need special trainin' to take out a woman livin' alone. Any fuckin' idiot can do it."

A traffic light turned yellow ahead of us and he accelerated through the intersection as the light turned red.

I considered offering more reassurances, but it would be pointless. He was right.

A tension headache thumped sullenly at the base of my skull, and I blew out a breath and massaged the spot. "Do you know anything about Kathy's building? It's probably got a secured door, right?"

"Prob'ly, but I couldn't get that from the internet. That's why I wanna scope the place out first thing. But even if it's locked, most people'll hold the door for somebody that comes in behind them lookin' like they belong there. That's gonna be the weakest link."

We fell silent as he guided the car through the dark and

slippery streets.

"Comin' up on it now," he said after a while. "That's it on the left, that brown highrise."

I surveyed the neighbourhood as we cruised past. Not upscale, not a slum. Just a generic mix of apartments and grim-looking commercial buildings, all buffered by giant snowbanks the plows had pushed up. We could be in any city in Canada.

"I wanna do a quick recon around the buildin' an' through the back alley," Hellhound said. "How 'bout if I drop ya at the front to check out the entrance doors?"

"Sure." I zipped my parka up tighter.

When I stepped out of the car, the frigid air sucked an involuntary wheeze from my throat. Minus thirty at least. Probably colder.

Trying not to bend my legs so my flash-frozen jeans wouldn't touch my skin, I scuttled stiffly toward the bright glassed-in vestibule.

As I yanked the door open and slipped inside with a grateful breath, an elderly man paused halfway through the inner door.

"It's a cold one tonight," he observed genially.

"You can say that again. I only walked a few feet from the car, and I thought my nose was going to freeze shut."

He chuckled. "It's always worse when you get out of a warm car." As he turned toward the foyer, he courteously held the inner door open for me. Just like Hellhound had surmised.

I hesitated only an instant. Might as well scope out the floor layout.

"Thanks," I said as I followed the man in.

One set of elevator doors rattled open, and with old-world etiquette the man preceded me into the car. He pressed 4, then gave me a questioning look with his finger hovering over the buttons.

"Six, please," I said, and he pressed the appropriate button.

"So, are you all ready for Christmas?" he inquired as the elevator groaned upward at a glacial pace.

"I think so. How about you?"

"Oh, yes. These days we just give gift certificates." He straightened his bent shoulders proudly. "We have four kids, thirteen grandchildren, and five great-grandchildren with another one due any day. Our kids are the best thing Martha and I ever accomplished in this world. Do you have children?"

"Um... no."

When he gave me a pitying look, I added, "But I'm looking forward to a nice time with my, uh... boyfriend's family. He has a seven-year-old who's pretty excited about Christmas."

"That's nice, but it's sad when families break up. Is the mother still in the picture?"

"Yes, she'll be there, too." I managed a sickly smile. "This will be the first Christmas everyone's together, so I hope it all works out."

Dammit, if Alicia spoiled John and Daniel's first Christmas together, I'd...

I stopped that train of thought.

I'd keep my temper. I wouldn't punch her. I wouldn't even tear her a brand-new asshole. Even though she *really* deserved it.

"We'll make it work," I said with determination. "We all want Daniel to have a perfect Christmas."

The old man smiled as a 'ding' announced the fourth floor. "That's great to hear. Christmas is all about the little ones. Enjoy every minute with your adopted son! Merry Christmas!"

He stepped out of the elevator and I choked out a feeble "Merry Christmas" in return.

'*Your adopted son*'. The echo of his words encircled my throat like a noose.

As the doors closed, I gave a whole-body shudder and pulled out my phone to text Hellhound, 'Got in. Going to 6th now.' My phone had no connection at the moment, but he'd get the message as soon as I left the elevator.

Then I concentrated hard on a grubby mark shaped like the state of California on the elevator door. Anything was better than panicking about dependent children.

My contemplation was short-lived. As the elevator rose, the approaching sound of yelling filtered into the cab.

The volume increased and my pulse quickened.

Shit, that sounded like it was coming from the sixth floor.

CHAPTER 4

As the elevator slowed, shrieks of rage penetrated the cab.

"You filthy bitch-slut! You should be gang-raped by a dozen sumo wrestlers with steel cocks! And AIDS! And Ebola! But you'd like that, wouldn't you?" The screaming was punctuated by the thunder of fists on a door. "You cheap sleazy whore! I know you're in there! You're really brave when you're hiding behind your computer, but you don't have the-"

The elevator stopped and I whisked my Glock out of my ankle holster and stowed it in my pocket, heart pounding.

As I slipped out the elevator doors, a wild-haired woman continued spewing hate at the door she was battering with both fists. *"-guts to come out here and trash-talk to my face, do you, you cowardly bitch!"* She kicked the door, then shot a triumphant look at me. "I've got the bitch cornered! Come and help me!" She hammered on the door again. *"Now there's two of us! We're going to kick down this door and take you apart like-"*

"No, we're not!" I said loudly. "You need to calm down and step away from that door."

The woman gaped open-mouthed at me. "You're on *her* side?" She launched herself toward me, fingers crooked like claws, screaming at the top of her lungs. *"You bitch-loving whore-"*

In two fast steps I planted my back against the wall and snatched my Glock out of my pocket, but kept the muzzle pointed at the floor.

"Hold it!" I snapped, showing her the weapon.

The woman jerked to a halt so abruptly she fell. "*Help! Police! She's got a gun!*" she screeched, scuttling backward on her hands and heels.

Adrenaline and outrage kicked my temper into overload. "Who the hell do you think you are, calling for the police?" I roared. "How dare you-"

The doors of the other elevator opened and two uniformed policemen sprang out, their guns jerking up.

"Drop your weapon! Do it now!" they bellowed.

"Oh, for fucksakes," I mumbled as my fingers opened nervelessly and my Glock thumped to the carpet.

"Come toward me!" the taller cop barked. "Slowly!"

I eased forward, hands spread and arms away from my body. The unwavering muzzle of his gun was only slightly scarier than his taut jaw and the laser-focused gaze boring into me. Even though I knew he was one of the good guys, adrenaline gushed into my veins.

The shorter cop was dealing with the other woman, but I kept all my attention focused on the deadly gaze of the tall cop.

"Forward!" he commanded. "More! Down on your knees!"

My knees had barely hit the floor when he barked, "On your stomach! Spread your arms and cross your legs!"

I obeyed.

An instant later my hands were wrenched behind me and handcuffs bit my wrists.

"I'm a federal agent," I said quietly, and as clearly as I

could manage with my face mashed against the carpet. "I have a concealed-carry permit for the Glock, and my ID is in my waist pouch. I also have another-"

A wordless grunt interrupted me as rough hands grabbed my second ankle holster.

"Another weapon..." I continued a little louder, trying to keep my voice low enough for the cop's ears only. "...which is *classified* so please-"

He ignored me. "I'm arresting you for possession of a prohibited weapon..." He continued reciting charges and my rights as he yanked off my waist pouch and held me down, presumably stowing my weapons in his pockets or somewhere safe. At least I hoped he'd keep that classified tranquilizer pistol safe. If he didn't, I was in deep shit.

Well, deeper shit.

He finished, "...whether or not you say anything. Anything you do say may be used as evidence. Do you understand?" I managed a dazed 'yes' as he pulled me up. "On your feet. Let's go."

I stood in time to face a blinding flash of light.

"Fuck! Reporter!" I yelped, ducking my head sideways.

One look at the reporter's predatory grin brought reality crashing down on me. Within seconds my face would be all over the internet. And if the press reported that I was an agent, my cover would be hugely, fatally blown.

I launched into damage-control mode.

"Yeah!" I bellowed at the wild-haired woman who was squirming facedown the carpet, also in handcuffs. "I'm Arlene Widdenback! And if that name doesn't make you piss yourself with fear, you're even dumber than you look, you stupid twat!"

The tall cop propelled me toward the elevator, his grip

bruising my arm.

"Arlene Widdenback is my cover identity," I whispered urgently, head down so nobody could read my lips. "If my real identity gets out, I'm dead."

"Okay," the cop agreed.

He obviously wasn't taking me seriously. He hadn't even looked at my ID. A surge of anger pushed my fear aside.

I raised my voice so both cops could hear. "I was coming up in the elevator, and I heard screaming and thumping all the way from the fifth floor. When I got out on six, this woman was kicking and pounding that apartment door and screaming threats. I told her to calm down and step away from the door and she charged at me. I drew my weapon in self-defence, but I didn't point it at her."

"She pulled a gun on me! I'm the victim here!" The woman's lies ratcheted my temper up even higher. Fortunately for her, my hands were cuffed behind my back and the cop had both my weapons.

Before I could explode, the sound of an apartment door was followed by a male voice. "She's lying. She's not a victim at all. She's been raising Cain here for the past ten minutes, and it's about time somebody stopped her. That red-haired woman is a hero." The 'ten minutes' part had a tone of accusation, and the cop's hand tightened on my arm as if his temper was raw, too.

"All our units were busy with serious traffic accidents and we got here as soon as we could," the other cop replied crisply. "We'll take your statement soon. Please close your door and stay in your apartment until we knock." The click of a latch signalled the man's obedience.

The elevator door slid open at last, disgorging two more uniformed officers with their hands hovering close to their weapons.

As we stepped in and the elevator doors slowly closed, I heard a few door-knocks. "Police, Ms. Rainey. Are you all right in there?" More rapping. "Hello? Ms. Rainey, it's the police. Please open the door."

The elevator doors closed, and I asked the tall cop, "How many times has this happened in the past week?"

He didn't answer my question.

"So, Arlene, you're a federal agent," he said conversationally. "Which department are you with?"

"Department of Clandestine Operations. It's a secret branch of CSIS." His eyebrow rose skeptically as I added, "Arlene Widdenback is my cover identity. My real name is Aydan Kelly."

"Okay, Aydan. Why is CSIS involved here?"

"They're not," I said grudgingly. "I'm not officially here."

His understanding nod made it clear that he was only humouring the crazy person. "Not officially here, or not here officially?" he inquired.

Damn cops. Always trying to trip a person up. Even though I was technically part of law enforcement myself, my freakishly guilty conscience made my heart thump even faster. The handcuffs didn't help.

Don't think about handcuffs.

"I'm off-duty," I clarified. "Visiting here with a friend."

"Your friend lives on the sixth floor?"

Hands restrained. Trapped.

Panic sizzled at the edges of my mind.

"I'm not visiting a friend in the building," I said, holding my voice level. "I'm visiting here *with* a friend. My friend is LaVonda Rainey's brother, and he's here to help her until all this social media crap settles down." Before he could ask another question, I added, "Have you had to respond to a lot of disturbances at LaVonda's lately?"

"What's your friend's name?" he countered.

"You're not being very helpful," I said mildly.

"I'm not here to be helpful to you."

The elevator doors opened on the main floor and he gripped my arm tighter and guided me outside into the glare of a television crew's spotlights. Gritting my teeth, I kept my head down and face turned away from the camera on the way to the cop's cruiser.

As he opened the rear door, I said, "Would you please check my ID and take off the handcuffs now?"

"Sure, I'll check your ID. You just have a seat in the meantime." He placed a firm hand on my head and tucked me neatly inside the car, slamming the door behind me. Off-balance in the handcuffs, I toppled sideways onto the vomit-scented seat, wrenching my shoulder.

"Ow!"

"What did you call me?" the cop inquired dangerously as he slid into the driver's seat.

A dozen retorts fought to escape, but I focused on the memory of Kane's voice. *'Count to ten before you lose your temper...'*

My voice came out strangled. "I said *'ow'*."

"That's funny, because it sounded like you called me an asshole."

I might have been thinking it, but I definitely hadn't said it.

Had I?

I squirmed upright, perching uncomfortably on the edge of the seat to keep from squashing my cuffed hands behind me. "I think that was one of the reporters. Would you please check my ID now? It's in a hidden inside pocket of my waist pouch. I really am a federal agent."

He said nothing. So did I, mostly because the only other words I wanted to say were obscene.

Stay calm, stay calm...

The passenger door opened and his partner slid in. I raised my voice. "Would you please check my ID? It'll save us all a lot of time and trouble." As the tall cop put the car in gear, I added with a touch of desperation, "Just humour me, okay? What have you got to lose?"

He blew out a breath and shifted back into Park. "Fine. Mendel, get her waist pouch from the trunk."

His partner got out and returned a moment later bearing my waist pouch.

"It's in a hidden pocket at the back of the main compartment," I instructed, peering through the barrier between the seats. "There. That's it."

Mendel pulled out my ID and scrutinized it, frowning. "It looks like a CSIS ID," he said slowly. "But I don't recognize that department. Do you?" He passed it over to the tall cop.

He barely glanced at it. "Nope."

"There's a concealed-carry permit for the Glock in here, too, issued to Aydan Kelly." Mendel held my firearms license up to compare to my face. "It's her."

This time the tall cop gave my documents a longer look, then turned to frown at me.

"Where did you get these?" he demanded.

"From the Department." I pointed my chin at my ID in Mendel's hand. "I told you, I'm an agent."

He scowled. "Seriously?"

"Seriously."

"I'll need to verify that with your Department." He pulled out a cell phone. "What's your director's name?"

"Charles Stemp." Even as I said the name, my heart sank. "Wait," I added. "Stemp's my director, but he's on Christmas vacation. Brent Dermott is acting director."

My heart plummeted even lower while he dialled. This wouldn't end well, I just knew it.

"This is Constable Dennis Gould of the Regina Police Service. May I speak to Director Brent Dermott, please?" Gould said into the phone. "It's urgent." He provided his badge number and then fell silent, watching me while we waited.

It was a long wait.

In my mind's eye, I saw the hapless analyst-on-call phoning Dermott, whose usual irritable bluster would flare into rage when he discovered I was the reason he was being bothered at home late in the evening.

Oh Lord, I was completely fucked.

"Hello, Director Dermott," the cop said at last. "This is Constable Dennis Gould of the Regina Police Service. I have a woman here by the name of Aydan Kelly, carrying concealed weapons along with an unusual-looking CSIS ID. She claims to be an agent. Can you verify her identity?"

Dermott's response was abrupt, and the click of his disconnection was audible even from where I sat. The cop blinked, then lowered the phone, a frown forming on his face.

"Well, Aydan Kelly, if that is actually who you are... I guess we can add 'impersonating a police officer' to your list of charges. Director Dermott says he has no active agents by that name."

I gaped at him for an instant in sheer disbelief before hot

fury suffused every inch of my body. Even my fingers and toes tingled.

"Call Dermott back," I said, my voice level and dangerous. "Ask him if he has an Agent Aydan Kelly on leave. Not currently active."

Gould put the car in gear and pulled out onto the snowy street.

My heart rate ratcheted up another notch. "Call the Department back and ask for General Briggs. He'll vouch for me."

Gould kept driving. "I'm sure he will."

Mendel cast a cautious glance between me and Gould. "Maybe we should-"

"We'll sort this out at the P.O.," Gould said in a tone that indicated the discussion was closed.

Adrenaline pumping, I kept silent.

Hands restrained. Shoulders aching.

Flashbacks swooped down like dark merciless birds, plunging cruel beaks into my most vulnerable places.

Helpless in the hands of enemies. Soon to be brutally tortured...

My breath hitched into panicked panting.

I shook my head, fighting the terror.

Dammit, just breathe. They're the good guys. They won't hurt you.

Breathe.

In, two, three, four...

"Are you having an asthma attack or something?" Mendel's voice held an edge of concern.

"No. I'm... fine." I forced the words out, but my voice was a thready quaver.

He turned to study me. "Do you need medical

assistance?"

"No."

Dammit, I wouldn't show them my weakness. It was none of their damn business.

"Are you having chest pain?" Mendel demanded.

"No. I'm just... it's... a flashback." My voice trembled even though I tried to keep it level. "Handcuffs..." The word came out in a strangled squeak and my throat closed.

Oh shit.

Naming my fear made it worse. My breath came in choppy gasps as I fought the deluge of adrenaline.

"I'm fine," I whispered fiercely, squeezing my eyes shut. "*Fine!* Ocean waves. In, two, three, four..."

I slumped sideways on the seat, not wanting to put my face near its smelly surface but trembling too hard to sit up.

Breathe. Just breathe...

The siren came on and the car accelerated.

CHAPTER 5

By the time we got to the police station a few minutes later I had fought my way back to a semblance of composure. My heart still hammered hard enough to shake my body, but at least I had stopped hyperventilating.

I didn't register much of the trip to the interview room. When we reached it, I sank gratefully into the chair Gould indicated, my breath still coming too fast. Mendel withdrew, and the door locked behind him with a decisive click that did nothing to calm me.

The chair was hard and uncomfortable, but it was better than the smelly cruiser seat. My entire body vibrated, the handcuffs rattling in a calypso rhythm.

Gould said, "I'm sorry the handcuffs upset you. If you promise to cooperate, I'll take them off now."

"Of c-course I'll c-cooperate."

He unlocked the cuffs and I couldn't prevent a gasp of relief. I wrapped my arms around myself, rubbing my aching shoulders and trying to look as though I was only easing my muscles, not desperately trying to hold back panic.

I was pretty sure I'd failed.

Gould took a seat across from me and gave me a cop's pseudo-smile, his lips curving upward without warming the detached evaluation in his eyes. "There, is that better?"

"Y-Yes. Thank you."

"You must have a hard time doing your job as an agent if

you have such a difficult time with handcuffs."

Was he trying to build rapport, or was he taunting me? I fought back adrenaline-induced rage.

Deep breath. Let it out slowly.

"I don't have a problem putting handcuffs on other people. But I just came off a mission yesterday where I was..."

I had to stop and take another calming breath. "...in a bad situation... with handcuffs. I had a f-flashback."

"That sounds rough. Can you tell me more about your... mission... yesterday?"

I might have believed he was sympathizing with me, if not for his momentary hesitation over the word 'mission'.

He thought I was a nutjob.

And why wouldn't he? Dermott had made sure of that, the asshole.

I held my voice as level as I could. "I'm sorry, I can't share the details with you."

Gould nodded as though that was perfectly reasonable. And as though he was mentally dialling the number for the psych ward.

"Well, it sounds like we've got quite a misunderstanding here," he said mildly. "But I'm sure we can figure everything out. Let's start from the beginning. Why were you in that apartment building tonight?"

Don't get angry. He's just doing his job.

Cooperate.

"I already told you what happened and why I was there." My voice came out quite a bit higher than my normal register, but at least it was steady. "And I've told you I'm an off-duty agent, and you need to call the Department back and verify that. You can waste a lot of time trying to question me, or you can take a couple of minutes to make a simple phone call and straighten this all out."

Gould let out a small breath that was probably annoyance, but his face showed only patience. "You heard me make the call. I spoke to the man you said was your director. He said he has no agent by the name of Aydan Kelly."

"No *active* agent," I argued. "He's got a hate on for me right now, so he's just being difficult." Even as the words left my mouth I realized how ridiculously delusional I sounded, but I persevered. "If you call him back and specifically ask if he has an Agent Aydan Kelly currently on leave, he'll have to admit that he does."

I swallowed hard. Would he admit it?

"But you should probably call General Briggs instead," I finished lamely.

"Ms. Kelly," Gould said with tolerance. "Do you really think-"

"*Call him back.*" My voice cut across his, hard and level.

Gould stiffened, and I hurriedly softened my tone and added, "Please call him back. Otherwise I'm going to shut up and lawyer up, we'll be here all night, and in the end you'll still have to make the damn phone call and let me go."

We locked eyes.

Taking out his phone slowly as though he couldn't quite believe he was doing it, Gould dialled. "Director Dermott, please," he said, his tone as firm and professional as before.

The connection was quicker this time.

"It's Constable Gould again," he said into the phone. "Could you please verify that Agent Aydan Kelly is currently on leave? *Not* active?" An unreadable expression crossed his face. Then he said, "Thank you", and hung up, frowning.

Shit, Dermott had burned me. My pulse thundered in my ears.

I held my voice as steady as I could manage. "Call General Briggs from the military div-"

"Dermott confirmed your identity," Gould interrupted. He hesitated. "Is he always..."

He let the question trail off, and somehow I managed not to complete his sentence with '...that much of a prick'.

Instead, I said, "Yep. He's rude to everybody, but he's got an extra-special grudge against me right now."

"That's... extremely unprofessional," Gould said, in the understatement of the year. His voice hardened. "And he just wasted our time."

"You could lodge a complaint," I suggested, trying not to sound hopeful. "He intentionally misled you."

"I can't prove that. He apologized and said another critical call had interrupted us while he was on the line with me the first time. He said he intended to call me back as soon as possible and set the record straight."

Nothing I wanted to say was even remotely professional, so I clenched my teeth and kept my mouth shut.

Gould rubbed the back of his neck as if to ease aching muscles, letting out a sigh. "Why did you start blabbing about being an agent while I was securing the scene? No undercover cop would do that. I thought you were a psych case."

Oh, God.

My insecurities sprang up to jeer in my face. After all my tactical courses, all my hours of grinding through reams of departmental policies and procedures, I'd slipped up on something so basic that any police officer would know it.

Which was probably why it hadn't been specifically

mentioned in the damn documentation.

But hell, I should have known it anyway. If I'd been on a mission using my Arlene Widdenback cover, I would have done it instinctively. Kane was right. I wasn't in any shape to deal with this.

Gould was still waiting for my reply, frowning.

I scrubbed my face with my mercifully free hands. "I'm sorry. I'm not used to working with police officers. I'm usually deep undercover and surrounded by criminals, and I'm..."

Shit, I couldn't explain that I was really just a bookkeeper, floundering far out of my depth and completely intimidated by uniformed police.

I sighed. "I'm still a bit messed up after yesterday's mission. That's why I'm on leave." I realized I was compulsively rubbing my wrists where the handcuffs had been, and folded my hands in my lap. My face heated. "I'd appreciate it if you don't tell anybody about my little episode with the handcuffs."

Gould's eyebrows rose. "Why? Post-traumatic stress is nothing to be ashamed of. Your Department needs to-"

"*Please* don't tell anybody," I interrupted.

Gould frowned at me in silence.

"I'm dealing with it," I assured him. "I just haven't had time to process everything yet. I can't let a weakness like that get back to Dermott."

"But if he put you on leave he must already know, so... oh." His face hardened. "He does know, doesn't he? So when I called and he saw a chance to leave you in handcuffs..." His stony expression gave way to a frown. "That's just vicious."

I shrugged. "That's Dermott. But he doesn't know for

sure I have a problem. The last time he did this, I pretended it didn't bother me. So please don't say anything."

"The *last* time? This has happened more than once?" Gould's scowl deepened. "If you decide to file a complaint against him, I'm willing to provide testimony. Just let me know."

"Thanks, but-"

The ring of the phone interrupted me. Gould answered, listened for a moment, and then said, "She's free to go, and I'll be there as soon as I can." He hung up and pushed a statement form and a pen across the table to me. "Your friend is in the waiting room threatening to call your General Briggs. Let's wrap this up."

I filled in the blanks along with a description of the incident and passed it back to him. As he tore out my copy and handed it over, Mendel came in with my gear.

I accepted the weapons, automatically ejecting the magazines and the round in each gun's chamber and checking everything over. Reassembled and reloaded, I returned the pistols to my ankle holsters.

"I've never seen anything like that second firearm," Mendel said. "What's in the darts?"

"Um..." I hesitated.

"You said earlier it was classified," Gould prompted. "That's when I really thought you were..." It was his turn to hesitate, obviously searching for a polite way to say 'a complete fucking wacko'.

I saved him the trouble. "Yeah. Sorry about that."

"So what is it?" Mendel persisted. "Poison darts?"

"No. It's a tranquilizer pistol."

Both their jaws dropped.

"What's its range? How does it-"

I halted their questions with a palm-out 'stop' gesture. "Sorry. It's classified, and I have to get each of you to sign a nondisclosure agreement. You, and everybody else who saw it or handled it."

"Only Gould and I did," Mendel said. "Is it going into production soon? We could really use a better alternative to Tasers."

"I don't know, but you're right; it's much more effective and safer than a Taser." I brought up the document on my phone and showed him the screen. "These agreements need to be printed so you can sign them."

Mendel let out a resigned breath. "Email them to me." He recited his email address and I entered it and hit 'Send'.

"I can't leave until they're signed," I warned them.

"Okay, come on." Gould unlocked the door and gestured me out ahead of him. As we strode down the hall, he asked, "So if you had that other weapon, why did you draw your Glock? Shouldn't you default to non-lethal force?"

"I wouldn't have shot her," I assured him. "I was pretty sure she'd back off as soon as she saw I had a gun. But if she'd kept coming, I would have tranked her when she couldn't get a good look at the pistol."

"That's risky. What if you lost control of your Glock before you could draw the other?"

I glanced around us, but the hallway was deserted. I lowered my voice. "It wouldn't matter. I could fire the trank pistol blind. If the dart actually hit her, she'd be down for twenty minutes, but as soon as the dart hits anything it lets out a burst of tranquilizer gas. It instantly knocks out everybody within a four-foot radius and keeps them down for about five minutes. Including me, if I forget to hold my breath." Resuming my normal volume, I added, "And now that I've told you that, I *really* have to get you to sign that nondisclosure."

We halted at a small conference room and Gould gestured me ahead of him. As we took seats, Mendel continued down the hallway.

"He'll be back with your forms in a few minutes," Gould said. "If I didn't already believe you were with CSIS, the paperwork would be enough to convince me."

I gave him a sympathetic grimace, and he went on, "So... is this guy in the waiting room really your friend and LaVonda's brother, or is that just another cover story? Is he an agent, too?"

"He's really my friend and LaVonda's brother. Everything I told you was the truth. And he's a civilian..." I trailed off uncertainly. That was true, but not the whole truth.

Gould waited for a moment, but when I didn't elaborate, he asked, "What about that other name you used? Arlene Widdenback?"

"I have an ongoing cover as an arms dealer who supplies designer weapons."

He gave me a meaningful look. "*Classified* weapons?"

"Yeah. Arlene Widdenback has a reputation for handling stuff nobody else can get."

Mendel returned with the nondisclosure agreements, which they duly signed and handed over. I photographed the signed pages and sent them to the Department, stowing the hard copies in my pocket.

We all trooped down the hallway again.

"Here you go," Gould said, opening the waiting room door for me.

"I'm sorry this was such a mess," I said. "Thanks for

your patience."

He gave me a smile that was mostly grimace, and closed the door firmly behind me.

Hellhound hurried over, his worried gaze checking me as if to be sure I was undamaged.

"Okay, darlin'?" he asked, drawing me into a hug.

"Fine," I mumbled. "Let's get out of here."

"Don't hafta tell me twice." He turned us toward the door, one arm still protectively around my shoulders.

When we emerged into the bitter cold I sucked in a grateful breath of freedom, and hard shivers seized me.

Wrapping my arms around myself while my teeth clacked together, I muttered, "Okay, now I'm b-beginning to h-hate Regina, t-too."

"Go back inside," Hellhound urged. "I'll go get the car an' bring it around."

"Is it f-far?"

"Half a block."

"Let's g-go." I tightened my grip on my shivering torso and hauled ass.

The tiny bit of warmth lingering in the car's interior felt like a tropical paradise. As soon as Hellhound started the engine, I cranked the heater fan to full.

"Ain't gonna be much heat yet," he cautioned. "It's been sittin' here nearly an hour."

"It's still warmer than me." I curled my fingers in front of the heat vent.

He shot me a sidelong glance. "So what happened?"

I sighed and pressed my head against the headrest, trying to iron the headache out of my skull. "I got into the building no problem, just like you'd said. An elderly man let me in. He got out on the fourth floor, and by the time the elevator passed the fifth, I could hear banging and yelling."

The steering wheel creaked under Hellhound's tightening grip and he accelerated. "Is Kathy okay?"

"As far as I know, but I didn't see her. Her door was closed and some crazy woman was hammering on it. But she didn't get in."

Some of the rigidity left his posture, but he didn't slow down. "So that's why the cops got there so fast. I just got your text when they showed up."

"Yeah, they'd been called ten minutes earlier but couldn't get there right away. It was just my stupid luck that I showed up right before they did."

"So the cops saw ya an' grabbed the wrong woman," Hellhound deduced. His shoulders bunched again. "Shit, is that crazy bitch still there?" he rasped.

"No, don't worry." I rubbed his shoulder, his muscles tense under my hand. "She was cuffed when I left. One of the residents identified her as the troublemaker. And anyway, the cops will probably still be there taking statements."

"Right." Hellhound eased out a breath and slowed the car to the speed limit. "So what happened? How'd ya end up gettin' arrested?"

"The crazy woman attacked me. I drew my Glock and she screamed; and somebody must have been on the phone with the 911 operator and said there was a weapon. The cops jumped out of the elevator with guns drawn so I dropped mine right away. And then they found my trank pistol when they searched me; and even though I told them who I was, it, um... took a while to get straightened out." I grimaced. "And then the damn reporters showed up. They must have been monitoring the police radio. One of them got a picture of my face, so I had to pull my Arlene Widdenback cover. What a clusterfuck."

"Shit."

I sighed. "Yeah."

"Sorry, darlin'. I shoulda never dragged ya into this."

"You didn't drag me. I want to be here." I rubbed his shoulder again. "Anyway, it all worked out okay. At least neither of us got arrested, and now the police know we're here and who we are. This actually might work out for the best."

"Maybe," he said hesitantly. "Um... Aydan... I gotta tell ya somethin', an' I hope ya ain't gonna be mad."

Somehow I managed not to groan. "What is it?"

"I, uh... called Kane. Soon's the cops grabbed ya."

"Oh. Alicia must have been pissed that you phoned after Daniel's bedtime."

He shrugged, an uneasy twitch of his shoulders. "Yeah, prob'ly. But, uh... Kane's on his way. Here," he added when I gaped at him.

"What? *Why?*"

He tensed. "Sorry, darlin', I know ya can handle yourself an' I wasn't tryin' to-"

I silenced him gently. "It's okay. Of course I'm not mad. I'd have called him, too, if you'd gotten arrested." I gathered my scattered wits. "Anyway, it's no big deal. He'll have barely made it to the airport by now. I'll just call and tell him everything's okay and he can go back home." I pulled my phone out of my waist pouch and hit the speed dial.

"That prob'ly ain't gonna-" Arnie began, but before he could finish the sentence Kane's voice crackled over the speaker.

"Aydan? Are you all right?"

"Hi, John. Relax, everything's fine. It was just a misunderstanding. You can go home."

"No, I'm coming. I want to be there."

"Uh... okay... but... what about Daniel? I thought you wanted to be there for the pre-Christmas excitement. And what about your dad?"

Kane let out a short breath. "I do want to be with Daniel, but things are... complicated with Alicia. She doesn't seem to mind Dad spending time with Daniel, so Dad says he's happy to hold the fort here and handle the last-minute moving details while I'm gone."

"You're moving already? But your deal only closed yesterday!"

I could hear the smile in his voice. "The house is unoccupied and the seller is a lawyer, so she's fast-tracking the deal. I take possession on the twenty-fourth."

"Wow, that's fast!"

"Yes, that's the joy of the computer age. Anyway, we can talk when I get there. They've just called my flight. See you soon."

Feeling two steps behind, I mumbled, "Uh, yeah, okay. See you soon." I disconnected and frowned out the windshield at the dark snow-covered street. "That was weird."

"Yeah," Arnie agreed. "His first Christmas with Daniel, an' he's comin' here instead? He'd walk though fire for that kid. Somethin's wrong."

CHAPTER 6

"I need to talk to John's dad. Your dad," I corrected, remembering Arnie's status as a much-loved and unofficially-adopted son. "What's his number?"

Hellhound recited Doug Kane's cell phone number and I dialled.

When Doug picked up, I said, "Hi, this is Aydan. I'm sorry to bother you so late."

"No bother at all," he said warmly. "I've been thinking of you and Arnie. How are things going in Regina?"

"Um... okay, I guess. Kathy seems to be safe but we haven't gotten to see her yet." I didn't get into any of the details. "Arnie's with me," I said instead. "He's driving, so I'm going to put you on speaker." I pressed the button. "There, can you still hear me?"

"Loud and clear. Hi, son," Doug said.

Some of the tension went out of Hellhound's shoulders, as though Doug's voice alone was a source of comfort. "Hey, Dad. How's it goin'?"

"Everything's fine here." Doug's tone went serious. "I assume this isn't just a social call."

"No," I admitted. "We're calling because we're worried about John. Is everything okay with him? Why is he leaving you and Daniel and coming out here?"

Doug's sigh carried over the line. "I think... he's trying to do what's best for everyone. Alicia went ballistic when he told her he was moving out, and their conflict is upsetting Daniel."

"That's stupid," Hellhound rasped. "When he moved in, Lish knew it wasn't 'cause he wanted to be with her. He was just tryin' to get Daniel settled down after the kidnappin'. He told 'em right from the start it was only temporary."

"Yes, but apparently she was hoping... well, I don't know what's in her mind. Anyway, instead of including John like she did earlier, now she's forcing Daniel to choose between being with John or doing the Christmas traditions they've done together all Daniel's life."

"That bitch!" The words burst out of me before I could tone them down to something more diplomatic.

Doug sighed again. "This is hard for everybody. I think John's hoping that if he comes out to help you, you'll be able to resolve everything quickly and be back in time to have a family Christmas."

"We oughta be there with him now." Arnie's voice was tight, his conflict obvious in the whitening of his knuckles on the steering wheel.

"No," Doug countered. "He wouldn't want that. Don't feel guilty, Arnie. You can't change John's problems with Alicia. The best thing you can do is to let him help you."

"But what about you?" Hellhound demanded. "Ya flew all the way out from Winnipeg for Christmas, an' now John an' I both fucked off."

Doug chuckled. "It's a two-hour flight, not a round-the-world trek. I'm enjoying my time with Daniel while you're gone, and we'll have lots of time together after you're back. I don't have to rush home."

"But-"

"No buts," Doug said firmly. "We're all where we need to

be. I'll go over to your apartment twice a day to feed Hooker and scoop his litter box; and if there's anything else I can help with, call me any time of the day or night. Is that clear?"

"Yessir," Hellhound said, smiling. "Thanks, Dad."

"You're welcome, son. Was that all?"

Arnie and I exchanged a glance and a nod. "Yep, that's it for now."

"Both of you take care, then, and good luck. 'Bye now."

"Thanks. 'Bye," I said. I disconnected and slumped in my seat. "Shit."

Hellhound sighed. "Yeah, Lish can make things real ugly if she puts her mind to it." He made the turn into the parking lot of the apartment building and parked in a visitor's slot. "There's the news van still hangin' around."

"Those assholes never quit, do they?"

"Well, it's their job," Hellhound pointed out reasonably. "D'ya wanna lay low while I go an' see if I can get in?"

I eyed his forbidding features with a smile. "No offence, but I doubt if anybody would let you in."

He grinned. "Would ya dare slam the door on a guy like me?"

"If I thought I could get away with it, hell yeah, I would. In a heartbeat."

"Then I'll just hafta make sure they don't think they can get away with it."

We fell silent as a woman came out of the building and got into the news van. It drove away, and moments later Hellhound let out a grunt of amusement.

"Ha. Look at that. They're gonna be pissed when they find out they left too soon an' missed a cop car comin' back."

I straightened eagerly. "Hey, that's Gould and Mendel.

Maybe they'll let us in."

We sprang out of the car and hustled to the front door. We arrived just as Gould and Mendel strode up, and Gould greeted us with a small frown.

"We never did get to talk to LaVonda," I explained.

"Oh. Well, come on up, then."

When the elevator began its leisurely ascent, Gould turned to Hellhound. "So you're LaVonda Rainey's brother," he said conversationally, but I knew there was nothing casual about the gambit.

"Yeah. Well, Kathy Helmand's brother, actually," Hellhound said. "She wasn't LaVonda when I last knew her."

Gould leaned against the wall of the elevator, projecting polite interest. "I wonder why she changed her name."

If I hadn't known Arnie so well, I would have missed the faint stiffening of his posture. "Dunno," he said. "Guess she'll tell me when she's ready."

"So it's been a while since you've seen each other," Gould deduced.

"Yeah."

"How long?"

"Thirty years."

"That's a long time."

Hellhound nodded and said nothing.

"I heard she was denying that she was Kathy Helmand," Gould said. "Maybe she's not your sister at all."

Hellhound shrugged.

"What will you do if she's not?" Gould persisted.

"See if she wants my help as a private investigator; an' if she doesn't, I'll go home."

Gould kept prodding. "Are you from Calgary, too? Regina's a long way to come for nothing."

Hellhound remained stone-faced. "No big deal."

Before Gould could try again, I interjected, "Have there been a lot of disturbance calls from LaVonda's in the past week?"

If Gould was annoyed by my interruption, he didn't show it. "This is the first time I've been here, but I know there have been other calls."

"Has she reported phone harassment, too?"

"I wouldn't know. As I said, this is the first time I've responded here." The elevator doors opened, and Gould added, "I'll walk you to her door."

Uh-oh.

He motioned us ahead of him, and I adopted a decisive stride and managed not to glance worriedly at Hellhound. Shit, this was *not* how we'd hoped to make first contact.

As we arrived at LaVonda's door, Gould insinuated himself between us to knock on it. "Police, Ms. Rainey. There are two people out here asking to see you. One claims he's your brother."

No reply came from inside the apartment.

A police officer holding a sheaf of papers emerged two doors down, glancing our way. "She's probably got her headphones on again and can't hear you. Seems like she wears them all the time."

Gould thumped a little louder and increased his volume. "Ms. Rainey, it's the police. Please open the door."

"She won't," the other cop supplied. "I pushed the statement form under her door, and she filled it out and gave it back to me the same way. She doesn't want her cat to escape."

Arnie and I exchanged a frown.

"She won't open her door, even for the police?" I asked.

"How do you know she's okay in there?"

The cop shrugged. "I asked, and she said she's fine. She didn't sound upset."

Hellhound stiffened. "What if somebody's holdin' her hostage?" he demanded. "He could be holdin' a knife to her throat, makin' her say whatever he wants!"

Gould hammered on the door again. "Ms. Rainey, this is the police. If you don't answer the door, we're coming in!"

"It's all right, I'm fine." A mellifluous but breathless voice came from the other side of the door. "Thank you for checking on me."

"Ms. Rainey, open the door."

"No," she said sharply. "I told you I'm fine, and I am. Now go away."

"Open the door, Ms. Rainey. Prove to me that you're fine," Gould insisted.

She hesitated in silence for a long moment, as if deciding whether to trust him.

Or as if receiving instructions from someone holding her at knifepoint. My blood chilled.

Gould's back went rigid.

"Okay," she said at last, a tremor in her voice. "If I open the door, then will you go away?"

"As soon as we know you're fine, we'll go away." Gould's voice was deep and reassuring. Cop voice. So much like Kane's. His hand eased toward his gun.

"All right, then."

The metallic sound of a retracting deadbolt was followed by two more *click-clunks*. Apparently she was well-fortified.

Or effectively imprisoned.

My heart thumped anxiously, and I curled my fingers into Hellhound's. His hand was stiff, his gaze riveted to the door.

It eased open a crack, revealing a sliver of black garments dusted with cat hairs, the curve of a cheek, a brown eye with a delicately arched brow, and a cloud of grey hair. The eye sparkled with gold flecks exactly like Arnie's.

He jerked forward. "*Kath!*"

LaVonda tried to slam the door but Gould threw his weight against it.

"Keep them back!" he snapped.

Mendel's hands clamped around my arm and Arnie's, yanking us backward off balance.

Hellhound roared and spun toward him.

"Arnie, no!" I threw my weight against him, trying to pin his arms.

He didn't fight me. "It's okay, darlin'," he said quietly, but his breathing was ragged. "I ain't gonna do anythin' stupid."

I let go and stepped back. Mendel stood a few feet away in a battle-ready stance, his weight on the balls of his feet, his Taser in his hand.

"It's okay," I assured him. "We won't cause any trouble. You just startled us."

He nodded, but the watchfulness in his gaze didn't ease.

Gould's shoulder was jammed against the door, which was still only open a crack. "Ms. Rainey, I promise I won't let anyone else come inside. Just let me in for a few minutes so I can be sure you're all right."

LaVonda's rapid breathing was loud from the other side of the door. Terror of someone in there with her? Or only the effort of fighting Gould's pressure on the door?

She shot a fearful glance over her shoulder, and Gould seized the opportunity to push inside.

LaVonda's voice rose in a breathless squawk. "I haven't done anything wrong! Get out! You're trespassing! Get out, get out!"

"Ms. Rainey, I promise I'll leave as soon as I'm sure you're safe." Gould sounded a bit breathless himself, as though it had been a struggle to push into the apartment. "You have nothing to fear. Even if I saw something illegal in here, I couldn't charge you. I'm only making sure you're not being held hostage."

"I'm not! I'm fine! I told you, I'm *fine!*" The voice that had been so soft and beautiful earlier was clogged with tears. "Please, just *go away! Please!*"

Anguish contorted Arnie's face. "Kath, it's okay!" he called. "He's just tryin' to help! He won't hurt ya!"

"Go away!"

Gould reappeared, standing in the doorway to block the door open. "I'm sorry for the intrusion, Ms. Rainey," he said. "But we needed to know that you're safe."

LaVonda was a mere flicker of dark movement beyond him, as if she were hiding behind the door. Her only response was a sniffle.

"Ms. Rainey," Gould went on. "This man in the hallway claims to be your brother. Can you verify his identity?"

"No!"

Arnie stiffened.

Gould's voice was as calm as ever. "That's odd. He seemed to recognize you. Is he lying? Should I arrest him?"

"*No!*"

Her response came so loud and fast that Gould twitched. "So you're saying he *is* your brother," he persisted.

"Yes, all right, he's my brother! I don't want to see him, I don't want to talk to him, I just want you all to *go away!*"

Arnie caught his breath as though he'd been punched in the stomach.

"Kath," he said gently, and the heartbreak in his voice brought tears to my eyes. "That's all ya needed to say. Just that it's really you, an' ya don't wanna see me. I'm goin' now. If ya ever wanna get in touch, that phone number I gave ya will always work, an' I'll always keep that same post office box I rented for ya thirty years ago. Be safe, now. Be..." His voice roughened with emotion. "Be happy. I love ya."

He spun and strode toward the elevator.

I let him go, partly because I knew he needed to be alone, and partly because the enormity of his pain held me paralyzed.

"Thank you, Ms. Rainey," Gould said quietly, and stepped out of the doorway.

LaVonda swung the door almost shut, tears rolling down her face while she watched the elevator doors close behind her brother.

"Arnie..." Her voice was so choked I barely heard her. As I turned to call him, she added, "No! Let him go. Just..." Her voice broke. "Just... tell him..." Sobs disrupted her words. "I love him... and... if he calls... I won't answer."

The door clicked shut and the bolts shot home. The sound of weeping came clearly through the door, as though she had slumped against it with the last of her strength.

CHAPTER 7

I stood staring dumbly at LaVonda's door until Constable Gould touched my sleeve.

"Let's go," he said.

I blinked. "Right." Somehow I managed to turn away and make my feet walk down the corridor.

As we stood waiting for the elevator, Gould spoke again. "So that's it? He'll really just go away and leave her alone?"

I shook myself out of my stupor. "He won't badger her. It's just... he's been looking for her for thirty years. And all this time she was..." I trailed off, hardly able to think the words, let alone speak them.

"Avoiding him," Gould completed my sentence bluntly.

We rode down to the main floor in silence.

When we stepped out of the elevator Arnie was waiting in the lobby, expressionless, his arms crossed over his chest. My throat tightened. Even those powerful arms couldn't keep his heart from breaking. His posture was so stiff he looked as though he might shatter at a touch.

I didn't touch him.

"Ready to go?" I asked, and he nodded.

Gould held the door for us. As we stepped out into the arctic darkness, the lock clicked shut behind us with bleak finality.

Inside the car Arnie stared blindly through the windshield, his strong hands strangling the steering wheel.

"She loves you," I said softly. "She told me to tell you that."

His jaw flexed. "Thanks, but ya promised you'd never lie to me. Don't start now."

I laid my hand on his arm, the muscles rigid under my palm. "I'm not lying. She was crying her heart out. She said, 'Tell him I love him. And if he calls, I won't answer.' You were right, Arnie. She's trying to protect you from something."

He moved at last, twisting to wrap his arms around me and dropping his forehead onto my shoulder. I pressed kisses against his temple and stroked his shoulders, unable to close my arms around his bulk in the awkward confines of the front seat.

He drew back after a moment, chin high and shoulders squared. "Thanks."

"You're welcome."

"Can I ask ya a favour?"

"Of course."

"Call Kathy."

I took out my phone. "What do you want me to say?"

"Don't mention me. Just tell her ya were the one that scared off the crazy bitch, an' see if she'll let ya take her to a hotel somewhere. She's a sittin' duck in that apartment."

I frowned at him. "I doubt if that'll work. All she knows about me is that I'm armed and probably dangerous. If she remembers the name I yelled out in the hallway and looks it up, she'll think I'm an arms dealer and that's even worse."

Arnie sighed. "I know; an' even if she doesn't know any a' that shit, when she finds out ya were with me she'll prob'ly say no anyway. But we gotta try. Hell, if she won't go with ya, just try an' convince her to get the hell outta that apartment an' go somewhere else. Anywhere."

"I'll try. What's her number?"

I dialled as he recited it, and put the phone on speaker.

After four rings the call went to a generic voicemail message.

"Hi, LaVonda," I said after the beep. "My name is Arlene, and I was the one who chased that crazy woman away from your door earlier. I'm Arnie's friend, and we really want you to be safe. We understand that you don't want to see us or talk to us, and we won't harass you, but please leave your apartment as soon as possible and go to a hotel or a friend's place. If you want help or protection, please call me back at this number, but no matter what you do, please go somewhere safe right away. I hope to hear from you soon."

I hung up and faced Arnie's resigned expression. "That's the best we can do."

"She ain't gonna call."

I sighed. "No, and she probably isn't going to leave, either. If this has been going on for a week and she's still there, she's staying. And if I were her, I wouldn't trust me."

He grimaced agreement. "Neither would I. No offense, darlin'."

"None taken."

We sat in silence, watching while the first set of police officers came out and drove away. Ten minutes later Gould and Mendel emerged from the building and left, too.

"Guess that's it for tonight." Hellhound let out a breath and slouched down in his seat, staring up at the faint illumination that leaked around the curtains of LaVonda's apartment. "At least she's got blackout drapes so nobody can get a clear shot at her." He returned his attention to me.

"Okay, so let's think this through. Is she really tryin' to protect me, or is she just hidin' from me? An' didn't ya think it was weird the way she kept yellin' at the cop to get out?"

After a moment's reflection, I agreed, "Yeah. If I were a woman living alone-"

Hellhound's chuckle interrupted me. "Ya are, darlin'."

I grinned, relieved that he had recovered enough to joke. "Okay, fine; if I were a woman living alone without handguns, and if I'd just had some wacko screaming threats at me and trying to kick my door down, I'd be thrilled to see a police officer. I'd invite him in and feed him tea and cookies and hope he'd never leave."

"An' what was the first thing she said when he pushed into her apartment?" Hellhound eyed me expectantly.

"Um..." I dragged my exhausted mind back to the scene in the hallway. "...she said 'get out'."

"Nah, that was the second thing. The first thing she said was 'I haven't done anythin' wrong'."

I stared at him. "She has a guilty conscience."

"Seems like it. Wonder what she did?"

"Maybe nothing," I countered. "Maybe she's like me. I can't even be near a cop without twitching. They have that way of looking at you like you're guilty as sin; and those uniforms..." I shivered. "I always feel like I'm going to do something wrong without realizing it and get arrested." I grimaced. "And tonight didn't help a damn bit."

Hellhound's face softened into a smile. "Ya know the cops are the good guys, right?"

"I know, but... the worst the bad guys can do is torture me for a while before they kill me. That scares the hell out of me, but the police..." I let out a breath that was half shudder. "They can lock me up for *years!* The bad guys don't freak me out nearly as much. At least I can fight them."

"You're seriously fucked up, darlin'."

I sighed. "Yeah, I know."

He chuckled and reached over to squeeze my hand. "An' ya know I love ya anyway." He hurriedly added our usual codicil. "With no commitments."

I leaned over to drop a kiss on his lips. "Music to my ears."

He gave me a smile and then leaned back in the seat, staring up at LaVonda's apartment again. "So... wonder what Gould saw in there."

"What makes you think he saw something?"

"I dunno if he did; but remember what he said." He quoted Gould's words verbatim. "Even if I saw something illegal in here, I couldn't charge you."

"Now you're just showing off," I teased.

He grinned. "Yeah." His smile faded. "But still. D'ya think he was just tryin' to calm her down, or did he actually see somethin'?" His hand clenched into a white-knuckled fist. "Shit, d'ya think she's doin' drugs again?"

My heart sank. "I hope not. But with all the stress..." His heartsick expression prompted me to add, "But she didn't seem high. And anyway, here's an easy solution: I'll just call Gould and ask him if he spotted anything illegal."

Hellhound raised an eyebrow. "Think he'll tell ya?"

"He might."

A quick internet search yielded the non-emergency number for the Regina Police Service, and I identified myself and left a message for Gould.

"If he's still on shift he prob'ly won't get back to ya 'til tomorrow," Hellhound said. "Ya might as well head to the hotel now. Ya look wiped out."

"I am, but I'm game if you've got something else in mind."

"Nah. I'm just gonna hang around an' watch, so ya might as well take the car an' go."

I frowned at him. "In the first place, no; I'm not going to drive away and leave you outside all night in thirty-below weather. And in the second place, what do you think you're going to watch for? There are probably a couple of hundred people living in the building and you don't know any of them. These internet trolls probably aren't the sharpest tools in the drawer, but I can't see them being stupid enough to walk up to the building carrying an obvious weapon that you'll be able to spot."

He waited patiently until I ran down and then replied, "I ain't gonna be outside all night. I'm gonna stand in the vestibule where it's warmer. If somebody lets me into the buildin', great; I'll go up to the sixth floor an' keep watch."

"But-"

"I ain't gonna let her see me," he said, obviously anticipating my objection. "I'll stay around the corner by the fire stairs."

"And get arrested when one of the residents calls the cops and says there's a big scary guy lurking in the hallway."

"If anybody sees me, I'll tell 'em I've been hired to make sure there are no more problems. Show 'em my private investigator's license..."

"From Alberta," I interrupted. "Which isn't valid here in Saskatchewan."

Hellhound shook his head sorrowfully. "Darlin', have a little faith. I took all the provincial exams. I'm licensed everywhere in Canada."

I blinked at him. Dammit, his dumb-biker act was so

convincing that even I occasionally underestimated him; and I knew better.

I took up the argument again. "Okay, but what if they ask who hired you?"

"I'll tell 'em it's confidential. An' in the mornin' I'll call the buildin' management an' tell 'em what I'm doin'. It won't cost 'em a dime, an' they'll love the chance to make it look like they hired me to make the buildin' safer."

"But..." My aching brain refused to disgorge any more usable objections.

He patted my shoulder. "You're too tired to think straight, darlin'. Go back to the hotel an' get some sleep. Kane oughta be gettin' in around one-thirty, an' I'll get him to spell me off."

"So that's your plan?" I demanded. "Just hang around watching? For how long?"

Hellhound shrugged. "Long's it takes. The more borin' it is, the better. Kane'll get here an' see there's nothin' he can do, so he'll head back home for Christmas; an' I'm hopin' the internet idiots'll move on to their next victim pretty soon. But I ain't leavin' 'til I know Kathy's safe."

"Okay." Staring up at LaVonda's apartment, I kept my tone casual. "So, um... did you make arrangements with John about a hotel room?"

"I told him where we were stayin' an' he said he'd get a room there if he could." Arnie hesitated. "If ya wanna sleep with him instead..."

"No," I said hurriedly.

"Why not? I thought the two a' ya had worked things out."

"N... well... yeah, we worked things out; it's just, um..." I trailed off.

"He ain't pushin' ya for a commitment, is he?" Arnie inquired gently.

"No. No, he gets it. He knows that's not on the table, and I don't know if he even really wants it anymore, now that he has Daniel. It would be 'way too complicated, and anyway, my job's too dangerous. He wouldn't put Daniel at risk by having me around."

"You're freakin' out," Arnie observed.

"No, I'm not. I'm fine. Everything's fine. We talked, and everything's okay. Even when he asked me to move in with him, I didn't even freak out then." I stopped babbling by clamping my teeth firmly on my tongue. "Much," I added a moment later, prodded to truthfulness by Hellhound's skeptical silence.

"Kane asked ya to move in with him?" he asked cautiously.

"No, not really. He just said there was room in his house and his life for me if I wanted that. It's not the same thing as asking me to move in. He just wanted me to know, just in case..." I drew a deep breath and shut up.

"You're freakin' out," Arnie repeated.

I sighed and thumped my head against the headrest. "Okay, yeah. A little. But not a lot. That's progress, right? And... right after he said it..." I hesitated. "Um..." I rolled the seatbelt into a tube across my chest, smoothed it out, then rolled it up again.

Arnie took my hand, stilling my fidgeting. "Ya don't hafta tell me, darlin'. It's none a' my business."

I darted a quick look at him. "I... thought... just for an instant... I thought, '*I wish I could have that with him.*'" A shudder shook me. "And I've been freaking out ever since."

"Aw, darlin'." Arnie folded me into his arms and pressed

a kiss to my forehead. "It's good ya thought that, even if it was only for a second. It doesn't mean you're gonna get trapped in a marriage with a kid to take care of..."

My heart leaped into a panicked rhythm and I pulled back. "Is this supposed to be making me feel better? You're scaring the shit out of me!"

"Shhh, darlin', you're okay. Kane ain't tryin' to tie ya down, an' even if he did, I wouldn't let it happen unless ya wanted it. Ya know that, right?" He studied my face worriedly. "An' ya know you're safe with me, right? I'm never gonna want anythin' more'n friendship an' a roll in the hay."

I shook off my panic. "*A* roll in the hay?" I teased shakily. "Only one? As if."

I leaned into him and he chuckled, linking his arms lightly around me as though I was fragile.

Maybe I was.

"Darlin', with you, once is never enough." He sprinkled whiskery kisses across my cheek to find my lips.

As he kissed me with exquisite slowness, I sighed and pressed closer. The feather-light brush of his tongue made warm light explode behind my eyelids-

"FUCK!"

Arnie jerked away and my eyes flew open, following the direction of his gaze with horror.

Silvery shards of broken glass fell from LaVonda's window, bright edges flashing out of the darkness.

Hellish orange lit her apartment.

CHAPTER 8

Hellhound was already out of the car and charging toward LaVonda's apartment building.

I wasted precious seconds untangling myself from the seatbelt before scrambling out and sprinting after him. Treacherous snow shifted under my feet and I nearly fell, then regained my balance and poured on the speed again.

Hellhound lunged into the vestibule, swinging the tire iron I hadn't noticed him grab. Yanking his hood over his head, he barely slowed as the glass beside the door exploded into a shower of glittering rubble. He burst through, head down like a charging bull.

I caught up to him only because he had to pull open the door to the fire stairs instead of pushing through. We hammered up the stairs two at a time.

By the fifth floor we were panting in hard gasps, and I gave silent thanks for the Department's demanding fitness requirements. Still some reserve left...

As Hellhound rocketed past the fifth-floor landing he snatched a forty-pound fire extinguisher off its bracket as though it was weightless. On the sixth, he grabbed a second fire extinguisher and body-slammed the door open.

It rebounded nearly into my face. I caught the blow on my shoulder and pivoted around the corner to see a black-clad man outside LaVonda's door, only a few paces away.

The man spun to face Hellhound's oncoming bulk with a

slack-jawed expression of shock that might have been comical if not for the gun in his hand.

Hellhound pounded forward, the two big fire extinguishers swinging from his hands like toys.

The gun jerked up.

"*GET-DOWN-GET-DOWN!*" I hit the floor, grabbing frantically for my Glock.

Hellhound smashed a fire extinguisher into the man's face like a battering ram. A gunshot exploded and the bullet gouged into the wall only a few feet away, but the man was already cartwheeling backward.

His gun fell from slack fingers, his crushed head flopping at an impossible angle. The body hit the floor and bounced once before settling into limp and final repose.

Hellhound didn't spare it a glance.

"*HANG ON KATH, I'M COMIN' IN!*" He slammed the bottom of the fire extinguisher into the door with terrifying force as I scrambled up.

I had grown so accustomed to Arnie's gentleness that I had forgotten how much deadly power was coiled up in those bulky muscles. Even though I trusted him with my life, primal fear electrified my skin. He wasn't a man anymore; he was an unstoppable freight train of destruction.

The door buckled after only a few devastating blows. Hellhound kicked it open and lunged inside. I followed, sidestepping to put my back to the wall, Glock at the ready.

Across the room, smoke boiled from under a closed door and thin tongues of flame licked upward, charring the door and releasing even more smoke. Too late for fire extinguishers. We had seconds to get out.

"*KATH!*" Abandoning the fire extinguishers, Hellhound rushed to the figure huddled coughing in the middle of the smoky room.

Hunched over and panting shallowly through a fold of my scarf to limit the smoke I inhaled, I cleared the small apartment at top speed. Nobody else was there, unless they were in the burning room. Too late for that. I holstered my gun and ran to help Arnie.

Piercing yowls issued from one of the two duffel bags LaVonda clutched, and I realized it must be a soft-sided cat carrier.

Hellhound was tugging LaVonda forward, bellowing, *"COME ON! KEEP LOW!"*

"No!" LaVonda collapsed to the floor. "I... can't," she sobbed. "Take Princess..." Coughing seized her again.

"COME ON!" Hellhound tried to help her up but she kicked at him, flailing with her free arm.

I grabbed her arm, surprised by her strength.

"No, no!" She shoved the cat carrier toward me and curled around the other bag. "Leave me! Take Princess!"

Smoke abraded my throat and I hunched closer to the floor in search of fresh air. A spasm of coughing shook Arnie. He dropped to his hands and knees, dangerously close to LaVonda's thrashing feet. A kick caught him in the shoulder.

Arnie turned anguished eyes to me.

The door to the burning room glowed dull red in the smoke-darkened air. In a moment it would fail and we would die.

I yanked my tranquilizer pistol out of its holster. Arnie gave me a sharp nod of comprehension and we pressed our faces to the floor to suck in one last breath.

I shot LaVonda.

She went limp and Arnie dove toward her, ripping the

duffel bag from her lax hands and shoving it in my direction. I grabbed the cat carrier, now worryingly silent, and nearly wrenched my back when I snatched up the duffel bag.

What the hell did she have in there? It must weigh at least forty pounds.

No time.

Still holding my breath and bent double to see below the smoke, I scuttled for the door, my lungs screaming for oxygen.

A grunt of effort came from behind me and I spun to see Arnie lurching forward with LaVonda in a fireman's carry. Only his legs were clearly visible, his upper body obscured by smoke. He'd be completely blind.

I slung the bags out the door and dove back in to pull him in the right direction.

As we burst out into the hallway, I yanked the remains of the apartment door shut and dropped to my knees, gasping.

Arnie sucked in a wheezing breath that immediately came out in a wrenching cough. "Stairs," he croaked. Another fit of coughing shook him, but he staggered in that direction with LaVonda's inert body slung over his shoulders.

A grey canopy of smoke gathered on the hallway ceiling. The ear-splitting din of the fire alarm drilled my ears and white-faced residents hurried from their apartments. Cries of shock and fear pierced the smoke as the crowd eddied around the dead man's broken body.

His gun still lay beside him. Shit!

I yanked on my mitten as I shouldered people aside. Scooping up the weapon with my covered hand, I stuffed it in my pocket and yelled, "Get out! Don't take the elevator! Down the fire stairs! Go, go!"

As the residents obeyed, I shot a frantic glance around the hallway. I should bang on everyone's door and make sure they got out.

But if there were more gunmen in the building...

I grabbed the bags and made for the fire stairs.

The stairwell was blessedly smoke-free. I shouldered through the heavy door to find Arnie hunched over, elbows on knees, sucking air between coughing fits. LaVonda lay unmoving at his feet.

Dropping the bags, I punched 911 into my cell phone. I gave the emergency dispatcher the building address and rapped out, "Tell Constables Gould and Mendel that Aydan Kelly said there was a gunman on the sixth floor but he's dead. I don't know if he was alone. LaVonda's apartment was firebombed and we're getting her out." Unwilling to divert my attention from the crisis at hand, I hung up hoping they'd get the message.

Residents from the upper floors poured down the stairs, glancing fearfully at LaVonda's motionless form and our soot-smudged faces. I scanned the crowd, but they all looked appropriately worried. Maybe there had only been one gunman?

For the first time I got a good look at LaVonda and realized what a big woman she was. Even slumped on the floor, she looked at least as tall as my five-foot-ten; and she wasn't skinny.

"Can you carry her down six flights?" I asked.

"'Course," Hellhound said shortly. "Come on, let's get outta here. That asshole had a buddy with a grenade launcher, an' he's prob'ly still out there watchin'. Maybe he won't recognize Kath if I'm carryin' her in a crowd." He hoisted LaVonda into a fireman's carry again with a hard exhalation of effort. As I knelt to pick up the bags, he added, "Is Princess okay?"

Heart clutching, I peered through the mesh at the motionless white form. Oh, God, please don't let her be dead.

"She just got knocked out by the aerosolized trank," I lied with all the confidence I could fake.

"Hope it ain't toxic to cats," Arnie muttered worriedly. "Can ya see if she's breathin'?"

"She's breathing," I lied again. Please, let her be breathing... "Come on," I added. "If we don't get out of here soon, none of us will be breathing."

Fortunately the weighty duffel bag had a shoulder strap, and I slung it cross-body before picking up the cat carrier. Hellhound was already halfway down the next flight of stairs, the breadth of his shoulders with LaVonda across them blocking traffic and limiting the exodus to his pace.

I surveyed the people above us, but didn't spot anyone moving purposefully enough to be a threat.

At the third floor landing Hellhound stepped aside and leaned against the wall. He was panting heavily, but he didn't put LaVonda down. After only a few seconds' rest he tackled the next set of stairs.

His rest at the second floor was longer.

By the time we neared the main floor, sweat was pouring down his face. His chest heaved with the effort to supply oxygen to his straining muscles.

"Out the back," he gasped. "Bring the car. Keys in my pocket."

"No, go out the front with everybody else," I objected as I scooped the keys out of his pocket. "I bet the other guy's waiting out back. They would have planned to bring her out at gunpoint while everybody else was milling around."

"Or he mighta... just been gonna... shoot her," Hellhound said between gasps.

I threaded through the throng and ran out the front door, trying to look in all directions at once. Chaos. There could be a dozen gunmen in the crowd and I'd never know.

Fire trucks already clogged the driveway. Dammit, I wouldn't be able to bring the car close enough. And Hellhound couldn't make it much farther. Even his prodigious strength was almost at an end.

I turned to dash back to him, but a heavy hand descended on my arm. Spinning, I faced the firefighter gripping my sleeve.

"Ma'am, stay out of the building-" he began, but I jerked free and sprinted away.

Male shouts behind me made me redouble my speed, dodging through the crowd in a broken-field run. The momentum of the heavy duffel bag yanked me off course with every direction change, and I winced when the cat carrier slammed into my thigh.

Poor Princess. She was going to be black and blue.

If she was still alive.

Shoving through the crowd, I returned to Hellhound just as he emerged from the stairwell. "Back door," I panted.

He nodded and turned, and I pivoted and raced back the way I'd come, jostling the crowd a second time.

When I emerged, I was face to face with the scowling firefighter. "Sorry," I gasped. "Cat." I raised the carrier as a distraction, dodged out of grabbing range, and ran for the car.

By the time I got there my knees were rubber. My heart hammered and my breath came in uncontrolled gasps as I heaved the duffel bag into the passenger's seat with the last of my strength. The cat carrier went on top as gently as I could manage at top speed, and a moment later I fell into the driver's seat.

More emergency vehicles were pulling up, and the damn television van was back. Blue and red lights stained the snow, strobing over the residents huddled in shivering knots.

I eased around the crowd to get to the street, then turned into the back alley. As the car slithered around the corner, I slammed on the brakes.

"Shit!"

Another fire truck was pulling to a halt ahead of me, blocking the way.

My overstressed brain rocketed through the possibilities. If the firefighters saw Hellhound carrying an unconscious woman, they'd want to help; and he couldn't plausibly ignore them and carry her past them to our car.

But if an unseen gunman was waiting for a clear shot, this would be a perfect opportunity.

"*Fuck!*" I jammed the car into Park and ran.

As I pounded up to the fire truck, another firefighter stepped in front of me. "Ma'am please stay back-"

Hellhound staggered through the back door with his burden.

"That's my boyfriend!" I shouted, and shoved past the firefighter.

Two other firefighters hurried to Hellhound, reaching for LaVonda as I panted up.

"We've got her, sir. Easy now..."

Hellhound was clearly beyond the ability to protest. He fell to his knees as his burden lifted. The two burly firefighters struggled under the sudden weight of LaVonda's limp body.

"*Arnie!*" I skidded to my knees beside his hanging head. "Arnie, are you okay?"

"Out of the way, ma'am!" Another firefighter pushed past me with a portable oxygen cylinder. As he pressed the mask to Arnie's face, Arnie collapsed.

Sheer terror froze my veins.

"*Arnie!*" I lunged for him, but a hard hand clamped onto my shoulder, yanking me backward and spinning me around.

CHAPTER 9

Constable Gould's furious face filled my vision, only inches away. "What the *hell?*" he barked.

I twisted away from him and threw myself to my knees beside Arnie, but he was already stirring, thank God. His shaking hand came up to hold the mask to his face and he rolled over and struggled into sitting position, sucking in huge gulps of oxygen.

Dragging myself back to my feet, I faced Gould's scowl. No wonder he was pissed off. What a clusterfuck.

I gave him a fast summary and handed over the dead gunman's weapon. As soon as I finished, Gould turned away to relay the information into his radio.

I let my trembling knees drop me to the snow beside Arnie again, leaning into him to reassure myself that he was really okay.

A firefighter took his pulse, frowning. "How far did you carry her?" he demanded.

"Down six flights of stairs," I answered for him. "Her apartment was on fire and he carried her out."

"Holy crap!" The man gazed at Arnie with awe.

"Kath okay?" Arnie rasped, worriedly watching the firefighters working on her.

"She's unconscious but her vital signs are strong." The firefighter who was attending him glanced up. "Here's the ambulance."

A young blonde paramedic hurried over to us as the others deployed the stretcher.

"What happened?" she asked, pen poised over her clipboard.

"Her apartment was on fire," I supplied. "We went in to get her and then she passed out."

The paramedic scribbled busily. "Was she coughing or wheezing? Did she seem disoriented before she lost consciousness?"

"She was coughing," I began. "But she didn't seem to be-"

"She's breathin' okay now, ain't she?" Hellhound interrupted anxiously, craning his neck to see.

"She seems to be breathing well and her vital signs are strong," the woman reassured him. "But she hasn't regained consciousness. Do you know her medical information? Name? Age? Health conditions?"

"She's LaVonda Rainey," I supplied.

"Oh, the Fat Lady." The paramedic grimaced.

I was about to rip a strip off her when she added, "Those trolls are horrible. I read her blog and I can't see what their problem is. She seemed like a nice person."

I felt Arnie relax beside me.

"Do you know anything else about her?" the paramedic asked.

"She's..." I did some quick mental math. Four years older than Arnie. "Fifty-three?" I turned to him.

"Yeah," he confirmed. "She'll turn fifty-four in June."

The paramedic brightened. "You know her?"

"She's my sister."

"Oh, good." She poised her pen again. "Does she have any medical issues that might cause her to lose consciousness? Diabetes, blood pressure problems...?"

Hellhound's face fell. "I dunno. I ain't seen her in thirty years."

"Oh." The woman tucked the clipboard under her arm with a sigh. "Well, at least we have her name and age. I see she has her purse over her shoulder, so maybe she'll have her health-care card in it. Thank you for your help. We'll get her to the hospital now."

As she turned away, Hellhound laid aside the oxygen mask and stumbled to his feet. "Hang on, I'm comin' with her."

"You're not going anywhere," Gould snapped.

"I gotta go with her! She's gonna wake up soon an'-"

Gould gripped Hellhound's arm and for a precarious instant I thought Arnie would explode. I lunged toward him and Gould barked, "Settle down, or I'll cuff you both!"

It was probably an empty threat, but...

"We'll cooperate," I said hurriedly, giving Hellhound the stink-eye until he subsided with a growl. "But please send a guard with LaVonda. Somebody tried to kill her, and nearly succeeded."

Gould spoke into his shoulder mike, requesting another unit, and a moment later the lights of a second cruiser lit up the alley.

Mendel emerged from the back door of the building, and they ushered us to where the two cruisers blocked the alley behind our rental car.

We climbed obediently into the back of Gould's cruiser, and its warmth made me realize how hard I was shivering. Hellhound wrapped a comforting arm around my shoulders and I huddled close, clammy with sweat.

Gould and Mendel got into the front seats and Gould

twisted around to survey us.

"Okay," he said wearily. "Give it to me from the start."

I explained how we had been parked in the visitor's lot strategizing when we saw the firebomb smash through LaVonda's window.

Gould raised a skeptical eyebrow. "On the sixth floor. Even a pro baseball player couldn't throw that high and that hard."

"It was a grenade launcher with an incendiary round," Hellhound said.

Gould's other eyebrow rose. "Did you see it? Get a description of the person using it?"

"Nah, I only heard it. Then I was too busy runnin' for the apartment."

Gould eyed me questioningly and I shook my head. "Same here."

He blew out a breath. "Okay. So they used a grenade launcher to firebomb Ms. Rainey's apartment. Then what happened?"

"We saw the fire and ran like hell. We broke the glass in the vestibule and ran up the fire stairs..."

"Which were conveniently unlocked," Gould interrupted.

I blinked at him. "Um... yeah, I guess. Arnie? I know you're really strong, but..."

He shook his head. "Not that strong. The door was unlocked."

I frowned. "That's weird."

"Yes," Gould said crisply. "And the entire building is sprinklered, but the firefighters said the sprinkler water supply had been turned off. What can you tell me about that?"

"Shit, you're right. The sprinklers didn't kick in..." His

last question filtered through my tired brain and I straightened with indignation. "And I don't know anything about it. What are you trying to say?"

"I'm saying that you spent an unspecified amount of time in the building before we arrived the first time. You could have easily tampered with the lock on the fire stairs and disabled the sprinkler system."

"No, I didn't spend an 'unspecified' amount of time," I snapped. "I have a witness who can confirm what time he let me in, and he was with me until seconds before I arrived on the sixth floor. Look for an eightyish Caucasian man about five-foot-eight, blue eyes, white hair, balding on top. He lives on the fourth floor and has a ton of kids, grandkids, and great-grandkids with another great-grandkid due any day; and his wife's name is Martha."

"Oh." Gould's posture eased slightly. "So you ran up the stairs knowing Ms. Rainey's apartment was on fire; but you apparently still had enough time to beat a man to death, and you did a thorough job. There was nothing left of his face."

"We didn't have *any* time. I told you, we came around the corner and the guy shot at us. Arnie hit him once in self-defence."

Gould let out an incredulous snort. "With what, a Mack truck?"

"The bottom of a forty-pound fire extinguisher," Hellhound said. "I was runnin' full-out."

Gould winced, and I said, "So, yeah; basically a Mack truck. Check the outside of LaVonda's door. Arnie used the same fire extinguisher to smash her door in, so you'll probably find the guy's blood in circular patterns that match the size of the cylinder. When we got inside it was already too late for the fire extinguishers, so all we could do was get

LaVonda out."

"Why did you run away from me and try to sneak her out the back door?"

I gaped at him. "I didn't run away from you."

"You did," Gould said with a scowl. "You ran out of the building carrying two large bags, spotted me, dodged through the crowd, and fled in your vehicle. And then you ran away from me again, here in the alley."

I stared at him in disbelief. "I didn't even see you. I was watching for gunmen. I wasn't paying attention to uniforms because I knew they weren't a threat. We were afraid the gunman's accomplice would be waiting for LaVonda, that's why we went out the back." Sudden anger heated my blood. "And I wasn't *fleeing* in my vehicle! I drove around the building at about ten kilometres an hour. A crippled snail could have caught me!"

"Speed isn't-" Gould broke off as an officer tapped on his window.

He rolled the window down and the other officer shot us a glance before leaning in to murmur in Gould's ear.

Gould's shoulders stiffened. "Seize it," he snapped. "And go over it with a fine-toothed comb."

The other officer nodded and withdrew, and Gould got out of the driver's seat and came around to the back door.

When it opened, he was holding his Taser and his face was hard. "Give me your weapons and waist pouch."

"Wha..." I gaped up at him in disbelief for an instant before sheer irritation took over my mouth. "You've got to be fucking kidding me!"

"Do it now," he grated. A glance at the tension in his Taser hand convinced me he definitely wasn't kidding.

"Whoa, okay, fine!" I yelped, raising my hands. "Here."

Keeping my hands in the air, I squirmed around on the seat and stuck my ankles out. "Take them yourself. Getting tased would completely spoil this utterly craptastic evening."

"I'm detaining you both," he said grimly as he appropriated my Glock, trank pistol, and waist pouch. "If you cooperate, Agent Kelly, I won't put you in handcuffs. You..." He jerked his chin at Hellhound, who had already placed his hands on top of his head with a resigned sigh.

"I'll sit right here while ya cuff me," he said. "I ain't gonna give ya any trouble."

Gould jerked his chin at my feet and I retracted them into the car. The door slammed, and a moment later he and Mendel had handcuffed Hellhound, read us our rights, and returned to the front seats.

"What the hell?" I snapped. "You already know who we are and what we're doing here."

"Do I?" Gould asked coldly.

As he reversed out of the alley, I leaned forward and spoke to the back of his head.

"What's going on? Why are you-"

"We'll sort it out at the P.O."

Squelching my impulse to argue, I shut up. I had some thinking to do.

If he thought I'd sabotaged the building and tried to abduct LaVonda and flee, I could see how that looked bad; but I'd provided him with a full explanation. And he knew I was an agent. Why did he suddenly mistrust me? What had that other cop said to him?

We hadn't done anything wrong. With all the smoke and yelling and noise, surely there had been witnesses who could corroborate our story. And even if nobody had seen anything, the gunman's bullet in the wall would still prove that Arnie had killed in self-defence.

Cold fear washed over me. Had Dermott called with some trumped-up accusation? But what? My imagination sprang into overdrive. Was I somehow in trouble for using my Arlene Widdenback cover? Or pulling my Glock? But that was standard procedure.

Dermott couldn't possibly believe we had launched the firebomb, could he? And anyway, there hadn't been time for Gould to contact him and tell him about it...

My mind circled through increasingly wild scenarios during the silent ride to the police station. The faint scent of old vomit made my stomach churn, and the barrier seemed to be getting closer to my face with each passing moment.

Trapped...

I fought rising panic.

Stop it. Get a grip.

I wasn't handcuffed. Gould had obviously received some information that made him doubt me, but we were only being detained for questioning. I wasn't going to jail; I *wasn't*...

What if he handcuffed me again? What if...

Calm. Stay calm.

Breathe. In... two... three... four. Out... two... three... four.

Slow like ocean waves...

If Gould and Mendel noticed my quiet hyperventilation, they made no comment. When we arrived at the police station and Gould opened the back door, I sucked in a grateful breath of fresh air.

"I'm counting on you to cooperate," Gould said sternly.

"Of course we'll cooperate," I said. "Why wouldn't we?"

"I don't know," he replied. "Why wouldn't you?" I gave

him a 'what-the-hell-are-you-talking-about' frown, and he added, "Let's go."

He didn't actually grip my arm while he ushered me into the station and down a barren hallway, but I could feel his tense readiness. Mendel kept a firm grip on Hellhound, and his other hand hovered near his gun.

"In here." Gould's voice interrupted my fear.

He motioned me into the interview room again while Mendel led Hellhound away.

Gould shot me an unreadable look and withdrew. The lock clicked loudly behind him, making me twitch.

The chair was just as uncomfortable as before. I self-consciously avoided looking at the camera lens and concentrated on keeping my posture confident and relaxed while silently talking myself down from an incipient panic attack.

Time crawled by while I shivered miserably, unable to get warm in my sweat-damp clothes despite my parka.

At last I calmed down enough to take stock. A glance at my watch showed almost two-thirty AM. God, I was tired.

I stifled yawn after yawn, still shivering.

After a long fight against sleep during which I performed several embarrassing head-bobs, I finally gave up. I slumped forward onto the table, head cradled on my trembling arms.

The sound of the door jerked me awake, seemingly only seconds later. Basic interrogation tactic. They'd waited until I'd fallen asleep just so they could wake me up. Assholes.

I sat up, expecting Gould or Mendel, but a different man strode in and closed the door behind him. He took the chair across from me and eyed me in silence for a moment.

I studied him in return. Thirtyish, Asian, about six feet and one-eighty, eyes like tungsten carbide drill bits. His nametag read 'Tan'.

I'd felt intimidated by Gould. Tan scared the hell out of me.

He gave me a cop-smile that made him look like a shark. White teeth, emotionless eyes.

"I'm Detective Constable Tan," he said pleasantly enough, but his voice reminded me of a knife on a whetstone. "Please tell me everything, from start to finish."

I recounted the whole story, except for the details of how LaVonda had ended up unconscious.

Tan nodded politely throughout my recital. When I was finished, he said, "Are you sure that's exactly what happened?"

My guilty conscience kicked my pulse into overdrive. "Pretty close," I said cautiously. "Everything was happening fast, so I might have missed a few details."

Tan nodded understandingly. "Maybe little details like how you drugged Ms. Rainey before carrying her out of her apartment?"

Cold fear returned in a deluge. Dammit, I should have known he would have checked with the hospital.

"You're right, I had to give her a short-acting tranquilizer," I explained, holding my voice steady with all my might. "She refused to leave the apartment. The fire was so advanced that we only had seconds to spare. She's a big strong woman and she was fighting us with all she had. If I hadn't tranquilized her, none of us would have gotten out."

"So you injected her with something. What was it?"

"Like I said, just a short-acting tranquilizer. She should have regained consciousness without any ill effects about twenty minutes after I gave it to her."

His shark-eyes bored into me. "What was it?" he

repeated.

"Sorry, it's classified."

That netted me a long silent scrutiny. It took all my will to hold his gaze without flinching.

"Why are you on leave?" he asked.

I blinked, momentarily thrown by the unexpected question. "Uh... what?"

"Why are you on leave right now? Are you suspended? Under investigation by your Department?"

Oh, God. Dermott had been dripping poison into his mind.

"Um, no, nothing like that," I croaked through dry lips. "I, uh... I can't give you details..." I hesitated. I'd have to give him some details if I expected him to believe me. I tried again. "I was on an op last week where two agents got shot, one fatally..." A memory-flash of scarlet blood on white snow made my stomach lurch and my voice wobble. I swallowed hard and held my voice as steady as I could. "There wasn't anything I could have done to prevent it, but after any serious incident we get pulled from active duty pending a psych clearance. I got cleared for reduced duty on another mission that was supposed to be safe, but it went... a bit sideways. Nothing serious," I added hurriedly, in case he thought I'd been suspended for incompetence. "It all worked out fine, but there was a misunderstanding and I ended up being... detained for a while. And then my m-"

The word 'mother' didn't want to come through my lips, but I forced myself to say it anyway.

"Then my mother... um, died... suddenly... right beside me, during the tribunal with my chain of command." I met Tan's gaze, trying to look calmer and more in control than I felt. "So I'm on stress leave until January second."

Tan frowned. "So in the past seven days you've had tremendous emotional trauma on top of your original post-traumatic stress. Constable Gould told me about your problem with handcuffs."

Oh God, Tan was going to tell Dermott I was out of control.

My pulse thundered in my ears. "It's not as bad as it sounds," I bleated. "I'm fine, really; just a bit sleep-deprived..."

Tan's frown deepened. "You're so far from fine, you're not even on the same planet. I can't believe they let you out on the streets carrying weapons."

Panic crackled at the edges of my mind.

No, no, no...

CHAPTER 10

Summoning every ounce of control I owned, I sat up straight and looked Detective Constable Tan in the eye. "If Command had any doubts about my mental state, they would have confiscated my weapons. And the fact that tonight I've been physically attacked and then shot at, and I didn't fire a shot in return, should prove to you that I'm fully in control."

Chin high, I maintained eye contact.

A tiny muscle quivered in my cheek. Stop that, dammit.

Tan didn't look impressed. "Tell me about your conflict with your Director."

I abandoned my attempt at dignity and slumped back in the uncomfortable chair with a sigh. "He's actually the Acting Director, and we used to get along fine. He's..." Trying to come up with a tactful description, I settled on, "...a decisive, opinionated guy who's pretty rough around the edges." I couldn't help adding, "Some of the agents consider him reckless."

"And what do you think?"

With heroic restraint, I managed not to tell him. I gave him a grimace. "The Director has a tough job. If you take a big risk and it pays off, you're brilliant. If it doesn't, you're reckless. Dermott isn't always lucky with his decisions."

"And is that what caused your conflict?"

"No," I said, choosing my words carefully. "The last time

Dermott was in charge, he dropped the ball on what could have been a vital communication. I didn't mean to make him look bad, but the discrepancy showed up during my debriefing. Dermott got reprimanded. Then when things went sideways in my last mission, he saw a chance to get revenge. He made some serious accusations that could have sent me to prison for life..."

My heart made a reflexive leap of panic and I sucked in a slow breath. When I spoke again my voice was higher-pitched than I would have liked.

"...if they'd been true. But I was completely exonerated in a tribunal with my entire chain of command, and Dermott got another black mark on his record. So now he's got a vendetta against me."

"I see." Tan's words were without inflection.

Did he believe me? No way to tell what was going on behind those steel-hard eyes.

"So that brings us back to tonight." Tan gave me another shark-smile. "We've got some confusing evidence here, so I hope you'll be able to clear things up. According to you, you just happened to be present when someone firebombed Ms. Rainey's apartment, and you were fortunate to be able to rescue her in the nick of time."

His tone raised my hackles.

"That's what *happened*," I clarified, slightly louder than I should have. "Those are the facts."

"Of course." Tan probably intended to sound agreeable, but the skepticism that edged his tone heated my temper. He went on, "Now, being in law enforcement yourself, I hope you'll understand that I need to eliminate some alternate possibilities. Just being thorough, as I'm sure you'd do if you were in my place."

His courteous words didn't fool me. Those eyes said I was guilty, guilty, guilty.

I kept my tone neutral. "I'll do my best to help."

"Thank you. So, if we look at this from another perspective, you can see how it might look as though this was all just an elaborate plot to abduct Ms. Rainey."

"That's what I thought," I agreed. "I don't know whether the guy with the gun was there to shoot her or just grab her when the firebomb flushed her out of her apartment, but I'm leaning toward the kidnapping theory. If they'd been serious about killing her, they wouldn't have needed a guy with a gun. They could have just used a bigger firebomb and incinerated her."

"That's what I thought, too." Tan eyed me expressionlessly. "What I don't understand is why you would kill your accomplice."

I stared at him. "My accomp... what are you talking about?"

"You were in the building earlier to unlock the fire door and turn off the sprinkler water supply. You were caught outside the victim's apartment with your weapon drawn, so your attempt at quietly kidnapping Ms. Rainey was thwarted. Then you returned to the building and used Constable Gould to confirm that your target was actually inside her apartment. Minutes later, a firebomb was launched from approximately the location of the visitor's lot, where you were parked. And Mr. Helmand had ropes and climbing gear in his luggage. So, did you kill your accomplice to make yourselves look like heroes who were rescuing your victim instead of kidnapping her?"

My jaw dropped. "Jesus, no! That's stupid!"

"Ms. Rainey said she wanted Mr. Helmand to go away

and never bother her again. She had been hiding from him for thirty years. That sounds as though she had reason to fear Mr. Helmand. And he arrived with all the gear necessary to rappel down the building and break into her balcony doors. You firebombed her apartment, kicked in her door, drugged and abducted her, and tried to escape out the back entrance of the apartment building."

I swallowed a toxic mixture of rage and fear. "That's bullshit! Arnie's been looking for her for thirty years because he loves her. He's been worrying about her for decades, and he's only here to protect her from the internet trolls. He probably brought his ropes in case LaVonda needed to escape from her apartment. He's a climber, so he usually has them with him."

I mentally crossed my fingers as I uttered the last sentence. Arnie usually had his ropes when he was on a job. And the details of his job required a much higher security clearance than Tan's.

"Love can make people do strange things," Tan said. "And an agent like you would have the resources to plan and execute an 'op'..." His verbal air quotes sounded distinctly sarcastic. "...like this."

Somehow I managed not to thump my forehead in sheer frustration. "I already gave Constable Gould a description of the man who let me into the building the first time, and that man will confirm that I wasn't in the building long enough to sabotage anything. I have airline tickets and rental car records that prove we just arrived and wouldn't have had time to sabotage the building earlier. And I'm sure that by now you've searched our car and haven't found a grenade launcher."

Tan's expression remained impassive. "No, but we only

have your word that there was a grenade launcher in the first place. And we found the money. How do you explain that?"

I rubbed my aching forehead. "What money?"

"Give up the innocent act," Tan advised. "I've already spoken to Mr. Helmand. If you tell me your side of the story, you might be able to avoid some of the more serious charges."

I squeezed my eyes shut and reached down deep for patience.

I found none. Only stale adrenaline, bone-weariness, and a deep swell of hot fury.

"I'm going to say this very slowly in small words," I growled. "We. Did. Nothing. Wrong." I opened my eyes and gave Tan a death-glare. "And you can stop hinting that Arnie ratted me out, because there's nothing to rat about; and even if there was, he wouldn't. We're partners. He's withstood torture to protect me in the past; and he would sacrifice his life for me without hesitation, just like I would for him. So cut the bullshit. I have no idea what money you're talking about, and if you don't tell me so we can figure this out together, it's going to be a hell of a long night."

Tan met my glare head-on. "You fled from Constable Gould carrying the money. Nearly a quarter million in cash, in that black duffel bag you left in the front seat of your rental car, under the dead cat. Does that refresh your memory?"

All the air vanished from my lungs. My lips repeated 'a quarter million', but no sound came out.

A moment later I processed the rest of his words and sorrow sank my belly like a cold aching stone.

"Princess is d-dead?" My voice came out in a quaver, and suddenly I just wanted to curl into a ball and cry.

"A quarter million dollars," Tan repeated. "You sabotaged the building, firebombed Ms. Rainey's apartment, murdered a man, drugged and kidnapped Ms. Rainey, and fled with a quarter million dollars. You have motive, means, and opportunity."

All my exhaustion and misery combusted in white-hot rage.

"For fucksakes, get your head out of your ass!" I barked. "If somebody was paying us to abduct her, I wouldn't have had the money until we'd delivered her. If we'd known she had the money and we'd planned to rob her, we would've grabbed the duffel bag and left her to burn in the apartment. And if I was planning a kidnapping, I sure as hell wouldn't do it with a firebomb in front of police, emergency responders, and dozens of witnesses." I glared at him. "Arnie and I had no idea what was in the bag. We only brought it out because LaVonda wouldn't let go of it. And while you're pissing around questioning us, her real attackers are getting away."

Tan remained expressionless under my tirade. "Abusive language is unacceptable." His gaze bored into me like frozen steel.

Sudden fear evaporated my anger.

He could only detain us for twenty-four hours, but if he wanted to hold us longer he could arrest us. There was more than enough circumstantial evidence.

Don't piss him off.

"You're right," I said in a small voice. "I'm sorry. I was out of line."

He eyed me in silence, clearly intending to intimidate me.

It worked wonderfully. My courage shrivelled to the size

of a raisin and plummeted into my sweaty socks.

Which enraged me all over again.

I held onto my temper with everything I had.

After another chilly moment, Tan said, "Ms. Rainey has regained consciousness, and she denies that the money is hers."

"She's lying." My answer came out reflexively, and an instant later the obvious reason struck me. "It must be unreported income. But just for the sake of argument, let's follow that thought. If you believe the money's not hers, that would mean I brought it with me when we ran into the building. Who in their right mind would run forty pounds of cash across a parking lot, up six flights of stairs, and into a burning apartment? I hope you don't think I'm that stupid."

"I've seen dumber things."

My anger trickled away into a deep well of exhaustion. "I believe you. Look, I know you're being thorough and I see how you could misinterpret the evidence, but it's all circumstantial and I've explained how everything really happened. You know I'm an agent, and Arnie works with me. With the security clearances we've got, you can be pretty damn sure we're on the right side of the law."

"I'm sure you are." He didn't sound sure at all. "As I said, I'm just sorting through evidence right now." He got up and headed for the door, then paused with his key hovering near the lock. "Do you need a bathroom break? Or I could move you to a cell for a while so you can lie down."

Lock me in a cell?

Every muscle in my body seized up.

Don't-panic-don't-panic!

He was probably just being considerate. It probably wasn't a threat.

It sure as hell sounded like one.

"No, thanks." My voice crept weakly from my dry throat. "I'd rather stay here."

He went out, leaving me with more than enough time to regret my earlier outburst.

Dammit, why had I lost my temper like that? He had been asking the same questions I would have asked if our roles had been reversed. And my antagonistic attitude hadn't helped one bit.

'*Count to ten before you lose your temper.*' Kane's advice echoed like a taunt in my memory.

God, I was a moron. If Tan arrested and charged us, it would be my own damn fault. And Arnie was counting on me to stay calm and act like a professional. I had failed him.

I should have been working with Tan and trying to help, not throwing tantrums. I owed him a huge apology.

Lord, *why* was I such a shitty human being?

Fear coiled into an icy ball in my stomach.

Maybe I should have shut up and demanded a lawyer.

Had I just sent us both to jail?

I stifled a whimper and dropped my head onto my arms.

I must have nodded off again. The sound of the door made me jerk upright with a gasp, my hand flying to where my holster should have been.

The uniformed woman twitched in return, her hand darting toward her weapon.

I held up my hands and let out a slow breath in an attempt to calm my racing pulse. "Sorry. I guess I was asleep."

"It's okay. I'm sorry I startled you." She smiled,

crinkling pleasant laugh-lines around blue eyes that looked as though they'd seen far too much. "Hi, I'm Rosemary Whittle. I work with Constable Tan. He's gone off-shift." She extended her hand and I shook it.

The chevrons on her epaulets told me she didn't just work with Tan, she outranked him. Maybe my status as an agent rated the involvement of a supervisor.

Was that good or bad?

As she took a seat across from me, I said, "I owe Constable Tan an apology. I was rude and confrontational, and I'm sorry."

She nodded. "I'll pass that on to him. I know your stress levels are sky-high right now because you've had no time to deal with your previous work-related trauma, let alone what happened tonight." She gave me an understanding smile. "So let's see if we can get this resolved as quickly as possible."

Her voice was warm, and even though I could still see the detachment of a veteran cop in her eyes, her well-faked friendliness soothed my ravelled nerves just a bit.

"I'll do my best to help." I tried not to wince at the memory of how I'd acted right after the last time I'd said those words.

"So, we're still trying to sort out the facts," she said briskly. "Would your Acting Director confirm what you told Constable Tan about your recent missions and the tribunal that relieved you of duty?"

God, all I needed was for her to roust Dermott out of bed in the middle of the night and piss him off all over again. My aching brain struggled to find a diplomatic response.

"Um... probably not. He'd probably tell you it's all classified. But you could try talking to General Briggs. He led the tribunal, and he's a little higher in the chain of command if you need actual details."

I kept my expression bland while I pushed psychic messages across the table with all my might.

Don't call Dermott. Don't call Dermott. PLEASE don't call Dermott...

"You've mentioned this General Briggs several times tonight," Whittle observed. "Do you trust him?"

"Yes."

She smiled and rose. "Well, I'm glad you can count on one of your commanding officers. Do you need to use the bathroom? Would you like a cup of coffee?"

I hid my suspicion in a bland smile of my own. Was that the extent of her questions? What was she up to?

"No, thanks, I don't need the bathroom," I said. "And I don't drink coffee."

"Hot chocolate?"

I hesitated. "Sure. Thanks."

She nodded and left.

Staring at the door, I tried to figure out her strategy. Tan had taken a hardline approach, hammering away at me and pretending he knew more than he did in an effort to trip me up. So now Whittle would switch to pleasantness, plying me with hot drinks like a friend and hoping I'd let my guard down enough to say something that contradicted what I'd already told Tan.

But first she'd make me wait.

And wait.

My ass felt as though somebody had been kicking it enthusiastically for several hours, and my lower back wasn't much better. Dragging myself up out of the uncomfortable chair, I did some stretches, my stiffened muscles creaking with protest.

That took a whole three minutes.

Then I paced back and forth, trying to get warm. Despite my parka, I was still cold. My ankles felt like frozen sticks, my feet like blocks of ice.

The tiny room only allowed me three steps.

One, two, three.

Turn.

One, two, three.

Turn.

The room seemed to contract with each lap.

Trapped, two, three.

Turn.

Trapped, trapped, three.

Turn.

Trapped, trapped, *trapped*...

My heart rate spiked and my shivering intensified.

Stop that. Just stop.

I sank back into the butt-breaking chair, lowering my head to my arms and concentrating on my breathing.

CHAPTER 11

It seemed as though I had barely settled when I heard the door again. The tantalizing smell of warm chocolate dragged my eyes open to see Corporal Whittle carrying a paper cup.

I warily surveyed the brown beverage she placed in front of me.

"Don't worry, it's safe to drink." She smiled. "Not very good, mind you. It's from a vending machine. But it won't poison you."

God, I was losing it. This was a police station, not an enemy stronghold. They weren't going to drug my drink.

I sipped.

She was right, the brown liquid bore little resemblance to chocolate; but at least it was warm and sugary-sweet. I shuddered, and sipped again.

Whittle slid into the seat opposite me. "Ms. Rainey has confirmed your story. She was hysterical and had to be sedated after she regained consciousness, and she says she was confused by the sedative when we asked her about the duffel bag the first time. Now she claims it's really hers and that she's paid taxes on all of it." She raised a skeptical eyebrow. "Apparently the clients of her psychic services prefer to pay in cash. It looks like drug money to me."

"That doesn't seem likely," I objected. "LaVonda was an addict long ago, but according to her blog she's been clean for nearly thirty years. She wouldn't deal drugs."

Whittle nodded. "I hope that's true. Anyway, we don't have any reason to investigate her. Her neighbours have no complaints about her and have never seen her leave her apartment, and they say the only people who come to her door are delivery people from grocery stores and online shopping networks. Canada Revenue Agency might want to do a tax audit on her, but that's outside our jurisdiction."

"And she did tell you that we were trying to rescue her, right? We didn't just barge in there and drug her."

"Yes. She also made it clear that she wasn't avoiding Mr. Helmand because she was afraid of him; only because he was a reminder of a lifestyle she wanted to leave behind. She was quite adamant that he had never threatened her and would never hurt her."

Hope flickered to life. "Okay, so... are you saying you believe us now?" I asked.

"Witnesses confirmed that when you and Mr. Helmand ran up to Ms. Rainey's apartment, you were empty-handed except for fire extinguishers. They also confirmed that Mr. Helmand struck the gunman once in self-defence, and we've retrieved the bullet from the wall where you described it."

I let out a breath of relief. "Have you identified the gunman yet?"

"No."

"And... Arnie's in the clear for killing him? Because it was definitely self-defence."

"We're waiting to hear from the prosecutor."

"But it'll likely be okay, right?" I pleaded.

"I would think so," Whittle replied reassuringly, but her next words deflated my tiny bubble of optimism. "But it's not up to me. The prosecutor will have to decide."

Oh, God, what if the prosecutor was a real hardass? What if Arnie got charged with murder?

Don't think about that.

Clutching the warm paper cup for reassurance, I asked, "And did you find the man from the fourth floor who let me into the building?"

"Yes. He belongs to a bowling league, and he rides the same bus home each Thursday evening. The bus was on time, so he was able to confirm exactly what time he let you into the building."

I leaned cautiously back in my chair. Could this nightmare be ending at last?

"So, if everything works out and you and Mr. Helmand are both released, what is your next step?" Whittle asked.

"We'll go and see LaVonda in the hospital to make sure she's okay. If she still doesn't want to have anything to do with us, I guess we'll go back to Alberta."

"Mr. Helmand said he intended to ask whether she wants him to stay until she's settled in a new place and she feels safe again."

"Okay, that sounds reasonable." I gulped some more artificial hot chocolate, suppressed a shudder, and added, "I'm only here to support Arnie, so it's up to him."

"And what if he decides to stay and harass her?" Whittle asked.

"He won't." When she raised her eyebrows, I went on, "I know Arnie really well. He'll do everything he can to protect the people he loves, and if that means putting aside his own needs, he'll do it in a heartbeat. I can absolutely guarantee that he won't harass her."

Another glance at Whittle's world-weary eyes prompted me to add, "I know; that and five bucks will get you a cup of coffee. So how about this: If LaVonda doesn't want contact of any kind with Arnie, I'll make it my personal responsibility to get him to the airport and onto a plane, and make sure he doesn't come back."

She smiled and rose. "Fair enough. I have a few loose ends to tie up, and it may take a while. Are you still okay in here? If you'd like me to transfer you to-"

"No, I'm fine here," I interrupted before she could say 'cell' and freak me out all over again.

Her face softened. I hadn't fooled her.

"Okay," she said. "I'll be back as soon as I can."

She unlocked the door and let herself out, leaving me alone again in the stuffy room, reeking of smoke and desperation.

A glance at my watch didn't help. Good God, it was twenty after six in the morning.

My skin itched with the need to burst out of the room, sprint down the hall, and run screaming into the frozen darkness of the winter morning.

Just run, and keep on running until the icy air washed away the stink of smoke and fear, the memories of blood and death, the corrosive anxiety sizzling just below the surface of my mind...

Stop it.

Just stop.

I got up and stretched again, then sank back into the chair from hell and laid my head on my arms.

Breathe.

Don't think about running.

Just breathe.

I twitched when the door opened at last, my muscles bunching as if to fulfill my fantasy of fleeing.

Whittle closed the door behind her and sat opposite me again. "I'm sorry for the long detention, but we've finally sorted everything out. You'll be pleased to know that the prosecutor said Mr. Helmand can be released without charges. You'll be free to go, too, as soon as we clear up a few last items."

My heart had risen at the words 'free to go', only to sink again at her caveat. I blew out a breath. "Okay, what's left?"

"Nobody saw the person who launched the firebomb, and although Mr. Helmand insists he knows the sound of a grenade launcher, we only have his word for that. I hope we'll find evidence when the arson investigator is able to enter the apartment."

"If Arnie says he heard a grenade launcher, I guarantee there was a grenade launcher."

Whittle frowned. "You sound very sure."

"Positive."

"There's a lot you aren't telling me about him, isn't there?"

I gave her a shrug and a grimace. "Classified. Sorry."

She nodded. "Anyway, with no description of a suspect, we don't have much to go on. We'll continue to canvass the neighbourhood for witnesses this morning." She hesitated. "May I ask your professional opinion?"

I felt about as competent as a third-grader in an advanced calculus class, but I put on my best fake-confident expression and said, "Sure, of course."

"You're obviously aware that Ms. Rainey has been harassed several times this week."

"Nobody gave me the details, but I figured."

"Yes, there have been two different women who got as far as her door; and there was hate graffiti in the vestibule. Although Ms. Rainey didn't make any formal complaints, she also noted in her statement that she had been receiving harassing phone calls." Whittle's eyes narrowed. "But a grenade launcher... that's heavy-duty stuff. That doesn't feel like garden-variety internet trolls to me."

She hadn't actually asked a question, but I agreed anyway. "Me, neither."

"It's beyond what we're equipped to handle." Whittle frowned. "It's beyond what you should be handling in your current mental state, too, if you'll excuse my saying so."

I grimaced agreement, and she went on, "I called your General Briggs and he confirmed your duty status and the results of tribunal, but he wouldn't confirm or deny whether your Department is involved in this. If they're not, they should be. You should call in reinforcements."

I sighed. "They're not involved. I can call it in and ask for help, but if Constable Gould reported my, um... issues with Dermott...?" I hesitated with eyebrows raised, and she nodded. I finished, "...I think we both know how that'll go."

"Go over his head," she said flatly. "Innocent lives are at stake."

"I'd like to; but even if I did take it up the chain of command, they'd need some indication of terrorism or espionage or organized crime, or an imminent threat to the public before they could get involved. There was a lot of potential for collateral damage tonight, but it was pretty clear that LaVonda was the only target."

Whittle rubbed her forehead as though her head ached. "I hate bureaucracy. I hate the fact that there's somebody out there targeting an innocent woman and there's not a thing we can do about it. If they've got weapons like grenade launchers..."

She didn't bother to complete the sentence.

There wasn't much point. We both knew the score.

She rose. "I'll get your weapons and personal items. I'll be right back."

She returned a few minutes later with the paperwork and my gear, and handed it over. I was pleased to see that the trank pistol had been stored separately in a sealed opaque bag. Gould and Mendel had taken their non-disclosure agreement seriously.

As I rechecked my Glock and stowed it, Whittle said, "Mr. Helmand has your luggage and he's in the waiting room. You can claim your car from the impound lot; just pick up the paperwork from the front desk on your way out."

My heart sank. "Where's the impound lot?"

"It's only about five minutes away. I called you a cab. It should be waiting for you outside."

Some of the weight came off my shoulders. "Thank you. I really appreciate that."

"You're welcome. Thank you for your cooperation, and I hope this is the last we'll see of each other. No offense."

"None taken. I hope so, too." I stood, fighting the urge to dash out the door.

We strode down the corridor in silence. At the entrance to the waiting room, Whittle said, "Call me if you find out anything new." She handed me two business cards. "This is my cell number, and the other is Constable Tan's. One or the other of us will be on duty pretty well any time of the day or night for the next week or so."

"Thanks. Here's mine." I wrote out my personal cell number and handed it over. "Are you done for the night?" I glanced at my watch and sighed. Ten AM. "The day, I guess," I amended.

She shook her head. "I came on shift at zero four hundred, so I'll be here until sixteen hundred."

"That's 'way too long a shift."

Whittle shrugged. "It's the job." She opened the door, then closed it behind me as I stepped into the waiting room.

Arnie sat in the far corner. Our luggage and his guitar case surrounded his feet, and the cat carrier occupied his lap. Its mesh door hung open, revealing a motionless white paw.

Hunched over with his forehead propped on the carrier, oblivious to the rest of the room, Arnie stroked the small dead paw over and over with a gentle fingertip.

My heart clutched and tears stung my eyes. Of all the shitty things that had happened so far, Princess's death was the shittiest.

Swallowing hard, I crossed the room to lay a hand on Arnie's shoulder.

He stood, transferring the carrier to the table beside him. "Hey, darlin'. Ready to blow this popsicle stand?"

I cleared my throat, but my voice came out husky anyway. "Yeah. I guess..." I gestured at the carrier. "We'd better take it with us to the hospital. LaVonda will want to see her one last time."

Arnie's brows drew together. "Yeah, Kath'll be glad she's okay; but what d'ya mean, 'one last time'?"

I stared at him, a bright bubble of hope expanding in my chest. "Wh... She's *okay?*"

"Yeah, she's fine. See?" He lifted the carrier and I met the gaze of two luminous eyes, one silvery-blue and one green, in a sleek furry face decorated with snow-white whiskers. "She's missin' a leg so she doesn't move around much, but she's fine. Cops've been feedin' her tuna all night. You're spoiled rotten, ain't ya, sweetie?" he crooned, tickling her whiskers.

The release of tension nearly undid me. I half-fell against Arnie, flinging my arms around him and burying my face in his chest.

"Hey, darlin'." His arms came around me, warm and strong and safe. "It's okay," he whispered against my hair, rocking me gently. "It's okay. Everythin's okay."

"I th-thought she was d-dead." I sniffled into his chest. "Tan said she was dead."

"She's just fine, darlin'. Everythin's fine. Everythin's okay." He kept rocking and murmuring comfort until I got myself under control a few moments later and straightened.

"Thanks," I whispered, and gave him a fierce hug, swiping my face against the shoulder of his parka to remove the telltale moisture. "Let's go give LaVonda the good news."

As we gathered up our belongings, I paused. "Hey, where's LaVonda's duffel bag?"

Hellhound glanced around the room and lowered his voice. "I told 'em to hang onto it. Didn't wanna be luggin' that kinda cash around. Kath can come an' get it herself when she's ready."

I let out a breath. "Good idea."

The trip to the hospital passed in a blur. Lulled by the motion of the car and the warmth of the cat carrier on my lap, I let my eyelids droop.

Seemingly only moments later, Hellhound's voice roused me. "We're here, darlin'."

Yawning, I dragged myself out of my stupor and out of

the car. The frigid air and brilliant sun were an insult to decency, but at least they catapulted me into alertness. We hurried for the emergency room entrance, Hellhound cuddling the carrier to protect Princess from the cold.

At the information desk we requested LaVonda Rainey, and the nurse in charge checked her records, frowning.

"No, she's been discharged."

"*Discharged?*" Arnie and I exclaimed in unison.

"Yes, around four o'clock this morning."

"But what about the police officer that was with her?" I demanded. "She was supposed to have a police escort."

"The police officer left shortly before they did."

"*They?* Who else was with her?"

The nurse shot a harried glance at the lineup forming behind us. "I'm sorry, I don't know. We've been very busy..." She let out a small breath. "...as usual... and I wasn't the one who did the release paperwork. I only spotted them leaving because..." She hesitated. "Well, she's a big tall woman, and the man with her was even bigger and taller. But I only glimpsed them from behind. I really can't tell you any more than that."

CHAPTER 12

"*Fuck!*"

The emergency room nurse flinched at the force of Hellhound's epithet, and I hurriedly said, "Thank you for your help. We'll let you get back to work now, but is there anyone else who might be able to give us more information?"

"The nurse who did the release paperwork might know more, but, as I said, we're very busy..."

"Never mind, we'll check with the police," I assured her, and towed Hellhound away from the desk.

"What the fuck was that fuckin' cop thinkin'?" he ground out. "He was s'posed to be guardin' her, an' instead he lets some asshole waltz in off the street an' walk off with her? I'm gonna-"

"Maybe the guy was a friend," I interrupted before he could utter any threats that might get him into trouble. "Or maybe she hired a bodyguard, who knows? I'll call Corporal Whittle. She'll know." I glanced around the crowded waiting room. "Let's go to the car."

Back in the car, I extracted my phone and punched in the number, putting it on speaker so Arnie could hear.

"Whittle."

"Hi, it's Aydan Kelly calling. I'm sorry to bother you, but we're at the hospital and we've just discovered that LaVonda left without her police escort. Do you know what happened?"

"Yes, her friend came to pick her up. She said he was ex-military and a childhood friend, and he would take care of her. She didn't want a police guard and we don't have the resources for that anyway, so that was the best we could do."

"Did you get the guy's name? Do you know where they went?"

"Unless you're investigating in an official capacity, I can't tell you. Sorry."

"It's okay. Thanks anyway," I said gloomily, and disconnected. "Shit."

"Well, never mind, darlin'," Hellhound said. "We know she ain't picked up her money yet, an' she ain't gonna walk away from a quarter mil. All we gotta do is wait for her outside the police station."

"Um... don't you think that's a bit stalker-ish?"

"Hell, no. She's gonna want Princess back, so we gotta find her somehow."

I peered into the carrier, where the cat was grooming herself with languid strokes of her tongue. "She's sure quiet. Do you think she's okay? Doesn't Hooker freak out when you put him in his carrier?"

"Yeah, but Hooker hates the carrier 'cause the first time he went in it, he came home without his nuts." Hellhound grinned. "Can't blame him. But little Princess here, I'm guessin' the carrier's her safe place. She's just havin' a bath in there without a care in the world." He tickled her whiskers through the mesh. "Ain't ya, sweetie? But I bet you're gonna need a litter box pretty soon."

I groaned. "Oh, hell, I didn't think of that."

"No problem, we'll hit Wally-World an' grab some stuff for her on our way back to the hotel. Kane'll be wonderin' what the hell's goin' on, so I'll call him an' get him to go over an' take the first watch at the police station."

"I completely forgot he was coming." I slumped back in the seat. God, all I wanted was a soft bed in a quiet place.

While Hellhound dialled, I wearily consulted my phone. There were several missed calls from Kane; no surprise. He had also left two voicemails, one at two AM telling me he had just picked up his rental car at the airport; and a second one at two-forty-five: *'Aydan, this is John. I'm over at LaVonda's apartment and I can see that something has gone seriously wrong. Since I can't raise you or Arnie, I'm going to contact the police and hospitals. Call me as soon as you get this.'*

There was also a brief message from Constable Gould from about an hour ago: *'I didn't see drugs or anything suspicious in Ms. Rainey's apartment.'* But even if he had seen something, he probably wouldn't tell me.

I deleted the messages with a sigh. When I looked up, Arnie was just concluding his call.

"...'kay, Cap. When she wakes up, tell her Princess is fine. Thanks. See ya." He disconnected, looking happy for the first time since we'd landed in Regina. "Guess who Kathy's 'friend' was," he challenged with a grin.

I sagged with a sigh of relief. "John. Thank God. I'd forgotten that she would remember him from when you were young. He left me a message saying he was going to check the hospitals, so that must be how he found her. So she's okay? She went with him voluntarily?"

Hellhound's smile faded. "Yeah, she's okay... ish. Kane said she's scared to be alone, an' she finally just got to sleep about half an hour ago. No surprise there, but... there's somethin' else."

My heart plummeted. "What?"

"I dunno. He didn't wanna talk about it on the phone. He just said we need to talk."

I collapsed forward to thump my forehead on the cat carrier. "Oh, God. I can't deal with any more shit."

"Ya don't hafta." Hellhound's palm made gentle circles on my back. "We're goin' back to the hotel an' straight to bed. Kane paid for our room, Kathy's safe, an' nothin' else's gonna happen in the next few hours."

As he put the car in gear, I hoped with all my heart that he was right.

After a quick stop for fast food that I barely tasted, and an even quicker stop for a litter box and provisions for Princess, we headed for the hotel at last.

The vibration of my phone made me jerk awake from my semi-doze. A text message: 'Call home'.

I groaned. "That can't be good."

Hellhound shot me a worried look. "What's wrong, darlin'?"

"I have to call the Department." Taking a secured phone out of my waist pouch, I hit the speed dial. When the analyst-on-call answered, I said, "It's Kelly."

"Hi, Aydan. It's Spider."

"Oh, hi, Spider. I didn't know you were on call today." I hesitated, squeezing my eyes shut to brace for the blow. "What's up?"

"My web monitoring program popped up a flag this morning. Arlene Widdenback is mentioned in the Regina Leader-Post."

"Shit. That damn reporter! What does it say?"

"Not much. Just that Arlene Widdenback was arrested during a disturbance at an apartment building that was then firebombed later in the evening. There's a photo of you in the apartment building where part of your face is visible, and they have video of you being put in a police cruiser. And there's a blurry photo of you running out of the burning apartment building carrying two big bags. Your face isn't really visible in that shot or in the video, but you're wearing the same parka and jeans and your long hair's kind of a giveaway." He paused. "And the reporter must have done some digging. They didn't say anything outright, but they hinted that Arlene Widdenback was linked to organized crime. What happened?"

"Oh, shit. Dermott's going to blow a blood vessel." I folded forward to thump my forehead against my fists. "Long, stupid story. It all started with a troll..." I laid out the whole sorry tale.

"Oh," Spider said when I was finally done. "Well, it's probably not bad. The Department has been trying to kickstart your arms-dealer cover since November, so maybe this'll do it. I'll spin it that way to Dermott. Maybe that'll calm him down."

"Thanks, Spider, you're the best," I said with gratitude.

"But, Aydan... you shouldn't be involved in any active missions right now," he said anxiously. "Be careful."

"Believe me, I'm trying." I disconnected with a sigh.

"Everythin' okay?" Hellhound inquired.

"Kind of. Arlene Widdenback is in the Regina paper this morning. Spider's trying to cover my ass with Dermott."

"Think it'll work?"

"Hell, no."

We fell silent for the rest of the short trip to the hotel.

When our room door finally closed behind us I made a beeline for the bed, shedding clothes all the way. My head hit the pillow, and I knew no more.

Some sixth sense woke me. The smell of smoke filled the hotel room and an orange glow haloed the draperies.

I jerked up in bed with a gasp.

Hellhound's warm hand landed on my shoulder. "It's okay, darlin', everythin's okay."

Blinking, I parsed my surroundings and relaxed. The smoke smell came from my hair, and the orange glow was sunset. The clock radio read 4:23 PM.

"Oh." I flopped limply back, but Hellhound's strong arm stopped me before I landed.

"Careful, don't squish Princess."

I twisted to see a mound of white fur in the warm spot where I had lain only seconds before. Princess surveyed me with her bi-colored eyes, her snowy whiskers curving smugly upward.

"You little freeloader," I said, and rubbed her chin. "Who knew a three-legged cat could move so fast?"

Her purr vibrated through my fingertips as she slitted her eyes in pleasure.

Hellhound grinned. "Yeah, I thought she couldn't move around much 'cause a' her missin' leg, but I guess she was just bidin' her time. She's been bouncin' on an' off me for hours."

"Wow, you're some classy guy," I groused. "I know we promised 'no commitments', but you could have at least waited until I got out of bed before you brought in your next pussy."

He chuckled and eased his hands under Princess, lifting her in a compact bundle and resettling her beside him. I snuggled down again and laid my head on his chest. His arm came around me, his fingertips stroking feather-light caresses across my shoulder.

My eyelids fell shut as if they'd been weighted. I was drifting back into warm and glorious slumber when the ring of the hotel phone jerked me upright again.

"It's okay, I got it," Hellhound said, grabbing the receiver.

I lay down again, but my drowsy relaxation was shattered. The previous day's events crowded into my mind while I listened to Hellhound's end of the conversation.

"Nah, it's okay, we were awake ... Yeah, she's fine, just tired." Hellhound shot me a quick smile before responding to the next question. "Yeah, she's fine, too." The way his hand settled gently on Princess's back, I knew this time he was talking about the cat. "... No problem, I figured she'd wanna see her ASAP. I'll bring her over in a few minutes; just gotta get showered an' dressed ... 'Kay. See ya in a few."

He hung up.

"LaVonda wants to see Princess," I guessed.

"Yeah. Go back to sleep, darlin'. I'll take her over."

I sighed. "I'd love to, but now my brain's awake and so is my bladder. Just let me have a quick pee, and then we can take our showers and go over together."

"You'll fall asleep again if ya just lie here for a few minutes," he countered. "Go take a leak an' then come back to bed."

I rolled out of bed and padded toward the bathroom. "No, I want this smoke stink out of my hair, and I'm hungry again. I'll get showered and dressed and have some supper. And then I'm going back to bed and I'm going down for the count until morning."

I slipped into the bathroom and used the toilet, then

worked the tangles out of my hair. The mirror showed a few remaining smudges of soot on my cheek and chin. That would wash off, but the puffy dark circles under my eyes were probably going to be there for a while.

As I was adjusting the temperature of the shower, a tap at the door accompanied Hellhound's voice. "Want some company, darlin'?"

"Sure, come on in."

We stepped into the shower together and I pressed close to him, enjoying the feel of skin on wet skin.

"Gimme your shampoo, darlin'," he said.

I handed it over, happily anticipating one of his sybaritic scalp massages. As he worked the shampoo through my hair, my eyelids fell closed and I leaned against him.

Warm water cascading over my body, tiny electric tugs as he finger-combed my hair, those strong fingers making blissful circles on my scalp...

"I've died and gone to heaven," I mumbled against his chest, my muscles slack with pleasure.

His chuckle rumbled under my ear. "You're meltin', darlin'."

"Oh, yeah." I glided a hand over his hot slick skin, sliding it down between us. "You seem to be stiffening up, though."

He growled satisfaction as I stroked him. "Mmm. Funny how that happens..." His teeth closed lightly on the sensitive skin between my neck and shoulder, the whisker-tickles of his moustache stimulating every nerve. "...when I see ya naked."

"Ahh... mmhmm..." I was arching into him when a yowl jerked me upright.

"It's okay, it's just Princess." He pulled me close again.

Another yowl resounded through the tiled room, more demanding than the first. Then another and another, getting louder and more frequent.

"Shit, I shut the door," Hellhound said. "She must need her litter box."

He stepped out of the shower, and a waft of cool air indicated that he'd opened the bathroom door.

As he got back under the spray, the yowls began again.

He opened the curtain to survey the small cat making such a big noise.

"What's wrong, sweetie?" he asked. "Your litter box's right behind ya."

Princess gazed up at us, tail switching, and gave another series of piercing meows.

"It's okay, Princess. Everythin's okay, just settle down now."

She kept meowing, her tail writhing as if it had a mind of its own. Even her furry forehead seemed wrinkled in agitation.

"Awright, awright." Hellhound closed the curtain on the commotion, diminishing it not at all. "Guess she ain't gonna give us any peace." He had to raise his voice to be heard over the racket. "Sorry, darlin'. Rain check?"

"Any time."

We cycled through our ablutions as quickly as possible, accompanied by Princess's unhappy cries.

By the time we turned off the shower my nerves were frayed. As we stepped onto the bathmat, her yowls magically ceased.

"Thank God," I muttered.

Hellhound towelled off rapidly, then slung the towel around his hips and crouched. Princess bounced over with her choppy three-legged gait, uttering small purring chirrups and stropping back and forth against his knees.

"What, sweetie?" he asked, petting her with gentle hands. "What was that all about? Ya don't like the shower, is that it? Did it scare ya?"

I looked down at the extravagantly purring cat as she arched and rubbed against his stroking. "You little shit, you just wanted attention. Nice cock-block."

"Nah, I don't think it was that," Hellhound said, still petting her. "She was scared. Weren't ya, sweetie?" he crooned. "Ya thought we were gonna get washed down the drain, didn't ya?"

"Okay, now you're giving me diabetes," I teased, leaning over to kiss him and run my hand down Princess's back. "Take your new girlfriend and get out of here while I dry my hair. If the shower scared her, the blow-dryer will give her a coronary."

"She's actually doin' pretty good," he said as he rose, cuddling her against his chest. "Considerin' her whole world went up in smoke last night an' she's stuck here with a coupla strangers, not even knowin' where her main person is..." He smoothed a gentle fingertip over her head, making her squeeze her eyes shut and nose blissfully up into his touch. "...she's a brave little Princess. Aren't ya, sweetie? Don't worry, we'll get ya back to your best friend..." His comforting rumble faded as he carried her out, closing the door behind him.

Smiling, I plied the blow dryer.

A few minutes later we were on our way down the hall to Kane's room. Hellhound bore Princess in her carrier with the litterbox stacked on top, and I followed with the shopping bags containing dry cat food, extra cat litter, food and water dishes, cat treats in expensive-looking little foil packets, and a small assortment of toys. Princess held a fluffy fake-fur mouse possessively between her chin and front paw while she surveyed her surroundings through the carrier's mesh, royalty in a sedan chair borne by her adoring slave.

Safely concealed behind Hellhound's burly back, I didn't bother to suppress my smile. Big tough ugly biker, turned to mush by a six-pound ball of white fur. He was deeply attached to Hooker, his own battle-scarred Maine Coon cat, and little Princess had gotten instantly under his skin, too. What a marshmallow.

My heart did a marshmallow act of its own, going all sweet and gooey just thinking of him.

When I tapped on Kane's door, he opened it almost immediately.

Soft faded jeans hugged his muscular thighs, and a snug black T-shirt showed off his broad chest and bulging biceps. My stomach dipped with instant uncontrollable lust.

Damn this chemistry between us. I didn't need or want the kind of commitment he did; and the prospect of dealing with his child scared the shit out of me. Why couldn't I get over this insatiable attraction and just relegate him to 'good friend'?

"Good to see you," he said, and gave me a platonic hug. "Come on in."

His smile was as warm as ever, but the iron-grey of his eyes told me that all was not well.

Not even close.

CHAPTER 13

When I walked into the hotel room, LaVonda rose from a chair on the opposite side. About six feet tall and broad-shouldered, she was definitely overweight; but her bulk gave the impression of strength, not softness.

She wasn't a pretty woman. Although she had beautiful brown eyes and thick lustrous grey hair, her skin was coarse from years of hard living and she had the same flattened nose and lumpy features as Arnie. Maybe she had suffered the same brutal treatment from their father's fists; or maybe her injuries had come later during her life on the street. Maybe both.

Under normal circumstances her height and weight would have lent her an imposing presence; but as she took a small step backward, her shoulders hunching and her hand quivering at her throat, she looked frightened and fragile.

"Hi, I'm Aydan," I said, guessing that she wouldn't remember me as Arlene. "I'm a friend of Arnie's and John's."

"It's nice to meet you," she said politely, but she wasn't looking at me. Her gaze was riveted behind me, on Arnie.

"Hey, Kath," he said softly. "I brought Princess."

Kathy made a small sound and covered her mouth with her hand, tears pooling in her eyes. Then her chin came up and she straightened as if it took all her strength.

"Thank you," she said in a voice that trembled only

slightly. "But I'm LaVonda now."

The words came out in the lovely contralto I remembered from the previous day, and I smothered a smile of delight. Apparently Arnie wasn't the only one in their family with a vocal gift.

"Right. Sorry. LaVonda." Arnie moved forward slowly, as though trying not to spook her. As he passed me, I lifted the litter box off the carrier, and he gave me a brief smile of thanks.

"Here she is," he said as he placed the carrier on the table and stepped backward a couple of paces to stand beside me, giving LaVonda space.

"She's a real little sweetie," Arnie said as LaVonda unzipped the mesh panel with shaking hands. "I've got a cat, too. Hooker." LaVonda looked up with a frown, and he added hurriedly, "After John Lee Hooker, the bluesman."

Princess chose that moment to hop out of the carrier and launch off the table at LaVonda, who instantly folded her arms. In a perfectly choreographed leap, Princess gained purchase with her hind feet on LaVonda's forearm and sprang to her shoulders, where she flopped belly-down around LaVonda's neck like a living fur stole. LaVonda's face lit up as Princess nuzzled her cheek, purring and trilling little mews of happiness.

LaVonda cooed nonsense back at her, petting and cuddling the ecstatic cat.

"Guess Princess's just gonna love me an' leave me," Hellhound said, but he was smiling.

At the sound of his voice, Princess looked up and chirruped at him.

"You're welcome, sweetie," he said. "You take good care a' LaVonda, now."

Meeting Arnie's eyes shyly, LaVonda asked, "She liked you? She wasn't scared?"

"Didn't seem to be," he said. "She purred an' snuggled up like I was her long-lost buddy."

"Maybe she thought you were just a big cat, too, with all that fur on your face," I said, tickling his beard.

He grinned. "Maybe. Hey, LaVonda, is she scared a' the shower?"

"Yes. She hates water. Whenever I get in the shower, or even run a tap into the sink, she cries and cries." LaVonda's gaze flitted briefly to the floor, then back to Hellhound's face. "When she was only a tiny kitten, she was attacked by a dog. The dog killed her mother and all her littermates, but someone turned a hose on the dog just in time to save her. I'm sure she still associates water with that horrible experience. The dog mangled her front leg so badly it had to be amputated, and she nearly died. She's a tough little girl."

"A survivor," Arnie said gently. "Like you."

LaVonda blushed and ducked her head. "Thank you for taking care of her," she said to the floor. "And for buying her all that." She nodded at the bulging bags. "I'll pay you back."

"Nah, ya don't need to. It's just a few Christmas presents from her Uncle Arnie. She likes that mouse-thing. Maybe she'll remember me when she plays with it." As though realizing he'd given LaVonda an opportunity to dismiss him, he quickly added, "So you're a psychic? I never knew that about ya. How does it work?"

"I'm not really a psychic," she said, still studying the floor. "That's just how I make my living." Colour rose in her face and she darted a glance at him before dropping her gaze again. "I'm not a con woman. I never cheat people out of money. I just... it all started years ago when I was joking with a friend and I predicted the winner of a horse race. The horse won, and she said, 'Oh, you're psychic'. It was a joke. Everybody knew it."

"Yeah, that makes sense," Arnie encouraged. "So what happened next?"

I glanced at Kane, who was observing the exchange in patient silence. Knowing that we were witnessing the first shaky steps along the path to reconciliation and not wanting to make a sudden movement that might break the spell, I eased back to lean against the wall beside him. He gave me a small smile, and we stood together watching.

"Well, it was a joke," LaVonda repeated. "So when the Grey Cup came around, somebody asked me which team was going to win. And I guessed right. I got the score right, too."

"Cool," Hellhound said.

"Cool, but not psychic. I'm a football fan. I knew the stats and I'd been following the teams all season. It was an educated guess and some luck, nothing more."

"But I'm guessin' there *was* more," Hellhound prompted.

LaVonda blew out a short breath. "A few more coincidences based on my own knowledge and some lucky guesses; but somehow word got around that I was psychic. Soon people were contacting me and asking for predictions; and offering to pay. And the more I refused, the more money they offered."

She glanced at us, her expression a mixture of vulnerability and defiance. "I needed the money. I had promised myself I wouldn't go back to the street." She looked down again. "I never took money from anyone who couldn't afford it, and I never took any missing-persons cases or relationship things or anything that could hurt people. I only made predictions about things that I could research and provide an educated guess." She shrugged. "I'm a good researcher. I'm usually right. And when I'm not, people believe I'm right anyway. I once counselled a man not to invest in a small business with three of his friends. He took my advice, and the friends went on to make millions without him. I was wrong, but he refused to admit it. And when his friends were sued and lost everything a few years later, he told the world what a brilliant psychic I am."

After that long speech she seemed to draw into herself, still not making eye contact. "My clients pay in cash and I pay taxes on it all. The bag of money is what I've saved. I'm sorry I made the police suspect you by denying it."

"It's okay," Hellhound assured her. "We didn't get arrested or anythin'. They knew you'd had a sedative an' ya were a bit confused. It was no big deal. The money's still there at the police station, nice an' safe. They know it's yours, an' ya can pick it up anytime."

"Thank you." When she raised her head at last, her eyes were brimming with unshed tears. "I... I'm sorry, I'm exhausted and frazzled. Could you... just give me some time alone with Princess?"

"Sure, no problem," Hellhound said.

Kane added, "Nobody knows you're here, so you'll be safe. And I'll keep watch outside the door."

"Oh, thank you, but no. I have a psychic reading call scheduled for five-thirty, and everything I say to my clients is confidential. I wouldn't feel comfortable knowing you might overhear."

"All right," Kane agreed. He was too good an agent to display any emotion, but I sensed his relief. "Are you hungry? I could-"

"No," she interrupted. "Thank you, I'm fine. Why don't the three of you go and have supper now? An hour and half is all I need."

"All right," Kane agreed. "We'll go down to the restaurant. Remember, my cell number is on your phone's speed dial, so you only have to touch a button if you need help. We can be back here in seconds."

"Thank you." Her downcast gaze was a subtle dismissal.

"See ya later?" Hellhound asked tentatively.

She didn't answer his question. Instead, she looked him full in the face for the first time, gazing at him as though memorizing him.

"Arnie," she said tremulously. "M-may I... hug you?"

He swallowed, but it seemed the words wouldn't come. He opened his arms.

LaVonda stepped forward, cautiously at first, but then her steps quickened and she flung her arms around her brother. His arms closed around her in turn and they stood in silence, faces buried in each other's shoulders.

"I love you," she quavered. "I never stopped loving you. I will *always* love you."

"I love ya, too." Arnie's voice was rough with emotion. "Always will."

After a long moment she pulled away, turning her back to wipe her tears.

"D'ya want us to go now?" Arnie asked gently.

"Yes, please. Thank you. I love you."

She didn't say 'see you later'.

"I love ya, too." When Arnie turned to face us, his jaw was clenched as though in pain.

In the hotel restaurant, the three of us sank into chairs and regarded each other in silence. A waitress came over and poured coffee for Kane and Hellhound. I requested herbal tea, and she handed us menus and departed.

"Did you sleep well?" Kane asked me, skirting the elephant in the room.

"Like the dead," I assured him. "Just not long enough. I'm planning to go down for the count right after I eat."

"So... you're going to stay here for a while?" he asked, but he was looking at Hellhound.

Hellhound shrugged. "Prob'ly not. Looks like she doesn't wanna have anythin' to do with me." The pain behind his matter-of-fact words stabbed me in the heart.

"Maybe she's just stressed out and needs a chance to process everything," I comforted. "After all, she just lost her home and everything in it."

"Yeah, maybe." He hunched over the menu, studying it as though there might be an exam later. Since Kane and I both knew he could memorize the entire thing at a glance, his act wasn't very convincing.

I changed the subject, turning to Kane. "What's bothering you? I can tell something's wrong."

He cast his gaze down to his coffee, rotating the mug first one way and then the other. "Where should I start?" he muttered, then straightened as if getting back to business. "When I was driving LaVonda back from the hospital last night, someone tailed my rental car."

CHAPTER 14

"*What!*" Hellhound slapped his menu down so fast that his coffee sloshed across the table. Oblivious to the spreading pool, he sprang to his feet. "She's up there alone! We gotta-"

Kane gripped his arm. "No, it's all right. I lost them. She's safe."

Hellhound hesitated, obviously torn between the need to rush upstairs and the knowledge that Kane had been the top agent in the Department. If he said he'd lost the tail, there was no way that they'd been followed back to the hotel.

After a long moment Hellhound lowered himself to the chair again, but remained poised on the edge.

"Did ya see who it was?" he demanded.

"A single driver, probably male, in a dark-coloured newer-model Ford SUV. Saskatchewan doesn't require front plates so I didn't get a license number." Kane frowned into his coffee cup. "Ordinarily I would have lost the tail and then tried to follow him so I could read the plate, but LaVonda was having an anxiety attack from my evasive manoeuvres already. She was on the verge of hysteria, so I brought her directly to the hotel instead. I'm still second-guessing that decision."

Hellhound eased back in his chair and dabbed at the spilled coffee with his napkin. "Nah, ya did the right thing. She's freaked out enough as it is."

The waitress hurried over with a cloth, and conversation ceased while she cleaned up the mess, refilled the coffee, and took our food orders.

When she had departed, Kane picked up the thread again. "There's a reason why LaVonda is so on edge." He hesitated. "Well, more than one reason. Obviously anyone would be stressed after what she went through last night; but it's harder for her than it would be for most people."

Hellhound was back on the edge of his seat again, his forehead creased in concern. "Why? What's wrong with her?"

"She's extremely agoraphobic. Until last night, she hadn't left her apartment in eight years."

"Eight *years*?" Hellhound and I exchanged a look, all the pieces falling into place.

"No wonder she was just standing there in the middle of a burning apartment," I said. "She wanted to save herself but she couldn't decide whether she was more afraid of going outside or burning to death."

"She was more afraid of leavin'," Hellhound rasped. "That's why she was tryin' to get us to take Princess, an' why she fought us so hard when we were tryin' to get her out."

I shivered. "That poor woman. No wonder she had to be sedated when she woke up in the emergency room. She must have been terrified."

"Yes," Kane agreed. "I think that's the only reason she agreed to see me when I found her at the hospital. By then she was desperate enough to cling to even the most tenuous acquaintance."

"It's lucky she did," I said. "If anybody else had picked her up, they never would have noticed they were being followed."

"Maybe, maybe not," Kane demurred. "Our tail wasn't a professional."

I grinned at him. "But you are."

His face hardened. "Was."

"Are," I argued. "Just because you're not officially an agent anymore, it doesn't mean you've lost your skills. I'd still put my life in your hands without hesitation."

"Me, too," Hellhound seconded.

Kane's frown eased. "Thank you."

Hellhound leaned back and let out a breath. "Hell, I hate to say it, but I feel better knowin' Kath-, uh, LaVonda ain't gonna be chompin' at the bit to get outta that hotel room."

Kane grimaced. "My concern is that she may not be able to leave it at all."

"Maybe we can find a psychologist who makes house calls," I said. "God, the thought of her being cooped up for years gives me the heebie-jeebies."

Hellhound reached over to squeeze my hand. "Yeah, but you're claustrophobic, darlin'. Imagine feelin' the same way about open spaces that ya do about closed ones."

I couldn't suppress a shudder as my imagination took over. To feel that heart-pounding, sweat-popping, knee-trembling terror every time I approached an open door...

"I *really* hope she gets some therapy," I said. "That's a shitty way to live." Kane opened his mouth, and I spoke before he could. "And yes, I'm working on my claustrophobia."

Hellhound coughed behind his hand. It sounded a lot like *'bullshit'*.

I turned to him. "Smartass. Just because I'm not spilling my guts to Dr. Rawling, it doesn't mean I'm not working on it."

"Sure, darlin'," he said, patting my hand. "Whatever ya say."

Fortunately the waitress arrived to deliver our food. After she left, I steered the conversation back to LaVonda's plight.

"So. A firebomb through the window to flush her out and a gunman waiting at her door. Those assholes weren't messing around."

"No." Kane frowned. "The woman pounding on her apartment door and yelling threats is what I'd expect from an internet troll. Last night's attackers were well-organized and well-equipped."

"Military gear," Hellhound mumbled around a mouthful of his burger. "Grenade launcher with incendiary rounds."

Kane's frown deepened.

I swallowed a bite of my chicken quesadilla. "But that gunman didn't look military, did he, Arnie?"

"That weedy little shit? Nah. Mighta been one a' those fuckin' wannabe paramilitary assholes that can't cut it in the real army."

"LaVonda is an odd target for a paramilitary group, though," Kane objected.

Hellhound sucked back some coffee as though it held the key to eternal life; or at least temporary alertness. "Maybe, maybe not. Ya never know what's goin' through their fucked-up heads. Maybe they watch the internet for shitstorms like this an' go vigilante, thinkin' they're fuckin' heroes."

"That sounds disturbingly possible," Kane agreed.

I pulled out a secured phone. "I'll call Moonbeam and see whether she and Karma and Skidmark have heard anything. They'd know about any paramilitary groups operating in western Canada." I found the number in my personal cell phone and punched it into the secured unit.

Moonbeam answered after only one ring. "Yes?"

I smiled. Of course a seasoned agent wouldn't identify herself to an unknown caller.

"Hi, Moonbeam Meadow Sky," I said.

Her voice warmed. "Storm Cloud Dancer! How lovely to hear from you. But since you're calling in the middle of the night, I presume this is not a social call?"

"Ohmigod, I'm sorry! I forgot about the time zone..." I thumped my forehead.

"It's quite all right, dear." Her voice was as serene as ever. "I can tell by your voice that all is not well. How can I help?"

"I'm so sorry," I repeated. "It really wasn't that important, but since I've woken you anyway... have you heard of any paramilitary groups operating anywhere in Canada recently, particularly in or near Saskatchewan? Maybe a group that might take vigilante action against someone who's been villainized on social media?"

"I'm not aware of any, but let me check into it and call you back. Can I reach you again at that number?"

"For now. If I have to ditch it, I'll call you back on a different one. But it isn't that urgent. Go back to sleep, and call me tomorrow. I'm *so* sorry to have woken you."

"Nonsense, dear, it's quite all right. I can easily check, and I'll return your call as soon as possible. May the Earth Spirit guide and protect you."

"You, too," I said, and disconnected. I sank my head into my hands. "I'm such an idiot."

"So she an' Karma an' Skidmark are still overseas with Stemp," Hellhound said.

"Yes. I forgot it's nearly two o'clock in the morning over there." I hesitated. "I hope she doesn't say anything to Stemp."

"Why?" Kane eyed me warily. "Are you doing something that could get you in trouble with the Department?"

"No..." My denial came out sounding uncertain, and I sighed. "I don't think so; but with Dermott breathing down my neck, I'm afraid to even fart in case he makes up some accusation about how I'm misappropriating Department resources."

"Yeah," Hellhound said, straight-faced. "Ya know damn well ya oughta be savin' all that gut-bacteria action for the Department."

I snickered. "Have you got a hose and some mylar underpants? I could pipe it all into a flask for Dermott and give it to him when we get back."

Hellhound guffawed. "Can I watch?"

"The collection process, or Dermott opening the flask?"

"Both."

Kane observed our childish sniggering with a long-suffering expression, but the corners of his lips were twitching. "Getting back on topic..." he prompted. "Did Moonbeam know anything?"

"Not off the top of her head. She'll check into it and call me back." I smiled. "Probably within a few minutes. She's so..."

I trailed off, not quite sure how to finish the sentence. I loved Moonbeam like the mother I wished mine had been. Kind, brave, dedicated and loyal; with a steely will, a fondness for deadly weapons, and decades of experience as a field agent. How could I encapsulate all that into a single adjective?

Hellhound finished my sentence. "She's Moonbeam."

Of course he understood.

"Yeah." I smiled at him, then sighed. "So if we all agree that this is more than random internet trolls, we need to figure out a way to keep LaVonda safe. She can't hide forever."

"She did just fine for thirty years," Hellhound muttered.

My heart contracted with sympathy and I reached over and squeezed his hand. "Maybe I could ask Spider to use his uber-geek skills and circulate some fake news articles reporting that LaVonda died."

"Except that we were followed out of the hospital," Kane pointed out. "So they know she survived the fire and the gunman."

"We could get Spider to report that she died in a car crash, and describe your rental car. They might believe you'd had a fatal accident in your hurry to escape."

"Maybe." Kane's voice was laden with doubt. "But I'd rather find out who these people are. If they're a paramilitary group, they may have quite a few members. And if I had a big team, I'd send them around to check all the hotel parking lots and see if they could spot the rental car."

Hellhound stiffened. "We gotta take Kath-, shit, LaVonda, an' get the fuck outta here. Leave your car here an' take ours."

"My car isn't here," Kane replied. "After I got LaVonda settled in the room last night, I drove the car over to another hotel and parked it illegally. It wouldn't take long for it to be ticketed and towed away, and even if someone did spot it there last night, they'd be looking for us in the wrong place."

Hellhound's shoulders eased. "Thanks, Cap. I'll pay your parkin' ticket an' impound fees."

"You're welcome. But I'm not convinced it was the right move. If we had kept the car, we'd have some bait."

Hellhound scowled. "Yeah, I wouldn't mind havin' a little talk with one a' those assholes."

"One of them, sure," I pointed out. "But if they're a gang, we're probably better off avoiding them altogether. This is still best. LaVonda can disappear just like she did before, and we can help her relocate."

Kane nodded agreement. "Her apartment was gutted, so she has nothing to tie her here. We can have her halfway across the country in a day or two without anybody knowing."

My burner phone vibrated, and I snatched it up. "Yes?"

"Agent Kelly." Director Charles Stemp's emotionless voice made my heart plummet.

"Y-yes?" I stammered.

He hadn't sounded accusing, but my guilty conscience went into overdrive anyway. Why the hell was he phoning me? Was I in trouble again?

I shivered as his cool precise voice chilled my ear. "Mother has informed me that you are asking questions about possible paramilitary activity. It was my understanding that you were on stress leave until the new year. Has that changed?"

"Um, no. I'm still on leave." My voice came out small, and I stiffened my spine and strengthened my voice. "I'm on vacation in Regina. Arnie Helmand's sister was attacked, and we're trying to figure out who did it."

A beat of silence on the line provided more than enough time for my blood pressure to skyrocket.

"Helmand located his sister after all these years?"

Shit, I should have known Stemp would have everyone's

dossier memorized for instant recall.

"Yes." I didn't offer any details.

"What makes you think she might have been attacked by a paramilitary group?"

"They used a grenade launcher to firebomb her apartment."

"Ah." Stemp hesitated. "And... did she survive?"

"Yes, we got her out uninjured."

"I'm glad to hear that. Who is 'we'?"

Oh, God, the more questions he asked, the heavier my sense of impending doom grew. But lying to him would be a fatal mistake.

"John Kane, Arnie, and me," I answered reluctantly.

"I see. Need I remind you that unless the Department specifically assigns you to the case, this is a matter for the local police?"

"You don't need to remind me," I muttered. "But the local police asked for the Department's help."

"They made an official request?"

"N-No..."

There was a moment of silence on the line and I squeezed my eyes shut, waiting for the axe to fall.

CHAPTER 15

When Stemp spoke again, his tone was slightly less formal. "Since you and I are both on vacation, technically I have no authority over you. However, I would like to offer a..." He hesitated. "...recommendation. If the Department becomes officially involved, you will not be assigned to the mission due to your inactive duty status. Therefore, I strongly *recommend...*" He emphasized the word. "...that you cooperate with the agent in charge but do not involve yourself directly in the mission. I further recommend that if the Department does not become officially involved, you should defer to Kane's expertise and abide by his decisions."

He wasn't telling me to stay out of it.

My mouth fell open. No words came out.

As if he had heard my thoughts, Stemp added, "I realize the futility of forbidding you to protect Helmand's sister. However, I am counting on you to show sufficient professionalism and self-awareness to acknowledge that you are not mission-ready at this time. A wrong decision or delayed reaction could cost lives, including your own."

I managed to croak, "Thanks, I, uh...", but Stemp was already speaking again.

"To answer your earlier question to Mother: Neither I nor my parents are aware of any recent paramilitary activity in the area. Mother asked me to express her regret that they were unable to help."

I finally managed to coordinate my brain and mouth. "It's okay, tell her thanks anyway. At least that'll help us eliminate some possibilities. I'm really sorry to have woken you, and her." I hesitated. "And thank you for your recommendations. I'll do my best to follow them."

"I am glad to hear that. Is Kane with you now?"

I shot a glance at Kane, who was watching me intently. "Yes."

"May I speak with him?"

"Um... sure. Hold on." I passed the phone to Kane. "Stemp wants to talk to you."

Kane's eyebrows went up, but he accepted the phone and spoke with his usual decisiveness.

"Kane here."

Stemp's voice was only an indistinct crackle, but I listened to Kane's end of the conversation with trepidation.

"Considering the events to date, I'd say it's likely." Kane's gaze flicked over me, assessing. "I don't have the professional qualifications to evaluate that." His brow furrowed. "As I said, I can't judge that, but..." He let out a small breath that might have been irritation. "Generally not, but..." His frown deepened and his words came out sounding stiff. "I trust her with my life, in any situation. No question." He leaned back in his chair, pinching the bridge of his nose as if to stave off a headache. "I realize that ... Yes ... No, I don't ... Yes, absolutely. Helmand will, too."

Hellhound frowned and leaned forward as if to protest, but Kane gave him a small headshake and finished the conversation. "Agreed." He disconnected.

Hellhound and I demanded in ragged unison, "What did he say?"

Kane handed the burner phone back to me. "He asked

whether I thought this was likely to be dangerous, and I told him it probably was. He reminded me that Aydan has been under a lot of stress lately and that she isn't cleared for active duty. He said he's holding me directly responsible for her safety. He also..." He hesitated with a sidelong glance in my direction. "...put me in charge of any tactical or strategic decisions we might need to make in order to protect LaVonda."

"Perfect," I said.

Kane let out a breath, his shoulders easing. "That's a relief. I was bracing for an explosion."

"Nope. It's going to be a treat to let somebody else call the shots for a change. Well, somebody I like and trust," I clarified. "I'd be choked if I had to take orders from somebody like Holt The Magnificent."

Hellhound snickered, but Kane frowned. "Holt is a good agent."

"Yeah," I agreed. "And he's an okay guy most of the time, too, but he loves to be in charge. When he starts doing his action-hero thing, I could just-"

Kane interrupted with a grin. "In the interests of plausible deniability, it's probably better not to complete that sentence." I chuckled, and he went on, "For the record, I did tell Stemp that no matter how stressed you might be, I had no doubts about your competence."

My face heated. "I heard that. Thanks."

"Yeah, I heard my name, too," Hellhound put in. "What was that about?"

Kane shrugged. "When I told Stemp I would trust Aydan with my life, he asked if I was prepared to sacrifice my life if I was wrong. I said yes, absolutely; and that you felt the same."

Hellhound gave a satisfied nod. "Good."

Warmth swelled in my chest. "Thanks, guys. That means a lot to me." I hesitated. "While scaring the shit out of me."

They laughed even though I wasn't actually joking.

Hellhound turned to Kane. "So that was it?"

"Yes, that was the end of the conversation."

"Awright. Then that's as far as we're gonna get with LaVonda's case for now. So... spill, Cap. Dad said Lish's fuckin' ya over. What's goin' on?"

Kane let out a breath and slumped back in the chair, cuddling his coffee mug as if hoping to find comfort in its warmth. "It's... complicated."

Hellhound theatrically checked his wristwatch. "Well, we got time."

"Come on, John." I laid a hand on his forearm, somehow managing a concerned-friend touch instead of a full-on fondle. Looking into his troubled grey eyes, I prompted, "Talk to us. Maybe we can help."

"I doubt it." He drained his coffee, and the waitress hurried over to top up the mug. Earlier I had noticed her gazing dreamily at him whenever she had a momentary break in her duties. The woman had excellent taste. He was well worth a dreamy gaze, and then some.

I heroically rerouted my dirty mind and kept my attention on his face.

"Even if we can't help, at least we can listen and commiserate," I encouraged.

"Yeah," Hellhound seconded. "So what's up? Dad said Lish went ballistic when ya told her ya were movin' out, but a few days ago ya said she agreed ya couldn't live together."

Kane grimaced. "In our family counselling sessions, we

were working through the issues that had caused our divorce in the first place, and I thought we had agreed that there was no future for us together. Apparently I was wrong."

"So what changed?" I asked.

Kane's knuckles whitened on his coffee mug. "I don't know. Alicia said right in front of the counsellor that she didn't think a relationship with me could ever work. But when I told her I was moving out, she screamed at me like a madwoman. Saying that my only reason for marrying her in the first place was because I wanted a child, and that she had never been anything to me but a brood mare. That now she'd given me the son I'd always wanted, and I was sacrificing everything for him that I should have sacrificed for her."

"Shee-it," Hellhound rasped. "She's jealous of her own kid?"

Kane gave a helpless shrug. "I don't know. I tried to explain that it was never about her; that I quit the Department because I'm turning fifty in a few months and I thought it was best to step down before I lost my edge..."

I winced. "Ouch."

"What?" Kane frowned at me. "Please tell me you can explain."

"You pretty much just said it yourself. It was never about her."

Kane scrubbed a hand through his hair, frustration tightening his face. "That's what I just said. I'm not trying to blame her for our original breakup, and I'm not trying to hurt her by leaving now. I regret that I wasn't there for her during our marriage, but I can't change the past. And it's not fair that she's punishing Daniel for the bad feelings between her and me!"

His voice had risen, and he pressed his lips together as if to silence himself. "Sorry," he added. "It's just... she stole six years of Daniel's life from me. I want to be with Daniel for our first Christmas together, and Daniel wants me there. And Alicia is making us all miserable by forcing Daniel to choose between us. She even threatened to take me to court and fight for sole custody, even though we'd already agreed that Daniel needs full access to both of us. I just... why is she doing this?"

"'Cause she's a spoiled brat that never grew up," Hellhound growled.

Kane blew out a short breath between his teeth. "It's too easy to blame her for everything. There has to be something I can do, or not do, to make this better." He turned to me. "Aydan, you said you could explain. I'm listening."

"Well..." I hesitated, carefully nudging my knife and fork into alignment on my empty plate. "You'd be better off to talk to your family counselor about this. I'm no expert."

"But your opinion is important to me."

I sighed. "I think Arnie's right; Alicia just never grew up enough to put anyone else's needs ahead of her own."

"But that can't be true," Kane argued. "She puts Daniel first in everything. She took parenting courses, she volunteers at his school, she-"

"Deprived him of his father," I interrupted. "She flat-out lied and told him you were dead. She knew Daniel needed and wanted a father and she knew you'd always wanted a child, but she couldn't put aside her own desire for revenge even though she knew you'd be a great dad."

"She didn't know that," Kane said quietly. "I was a lousy husband. Why would I be a great dad?"

"That's not fair." I frowned at him. "Okay, so your

marriage didn't work. You were in the Forces when you married her, and she should have known what came with that. And after you transferred out and went into police work, she had to know there would be irregular hours and dangerous situations." I raised a hand to forestall his objection. "I'm not blaming her. Military and police service is notoriously hard on marriages. I'm just saying that you don't have to shoulder all the responsibility for the breakup."

He shifted impatiently. "Fine, but why did you wince earlier when I said I had tried to explain to her?"

"Because I see how she must have felt. Remember when you saw her for the first time after you found out about Daniel and his kidnapping? Within minutes, she was yelling at you because you didn't fight to stay married after she kicked you out seven years ago. Even after all that time, she was still furious that you hadn't given up your job to stay married to her. And now..."

Kane's face twisted into a pained grimace. "All right, I see it. By refusing to quit years ago, I as much as told her that my job was more important than she was; and I focused on the job again when I said I was quitting because of my age. Instead, I should have explained that I would have quit at any age if we'd had a child."

"And if you'd said that, she'd have torn you a new one, too."

Kane frowned at me, then clutched his head as his expression cleared to comprehension. "*That's* what she meant about being nothing more than a brood mare! But... it was only coincidence that our marriage ended soon after the doctor told her she would likely never conceive. I had never intended to leave her. I was completely blindsided when she threw my things out of the house and told me not to come back."

I squeezed his hand, my heart hurting at the thought of him coming home shattered after witnessing the murder of ten helpless hostages, only to be kicked out of his house and marriage.

"She'd just lost her dream," I said. "She was too wrapped up in her own misery to think about what she was doing to you."

Which was no excuse as far as I was concerned, but I didn't say that out loud.

Kane stared at the tabletop, speaking quietly as if to himself. "When I didn't fight to stay, it must have seemed as though I had discarded her because she couldn't give me a child. And now that we have Daniel, it looks to her as though I'm quitting my job for him when I wouldn't quit it for her." His face went blank and his hands fell to his sides. "Dammit. That *is* what I'm doing."

"Don't start beating yourself up," I said. "It doesn't mean you're a bad person or a lousy husband. It just means that you weren't the right husband for her, and she wasn't the right wife for you."

"Amen," Hellhound seconded.

"So when I moved in with her..." Kane muttered. "...for Daniel... and then I moved out and bought the house down the street to be close to Daniel..."

"It reminded her all over again that she's not even a distant second place to the child you have together," I added. "And she's furious."

Kane sank his head into his hands. "Good Lord. How can I fix this?"

"Ya can't." Hellhound leaned back in his chair, stretching out his legs. "It's her problem, not yours. She's just gonna hafta get over it on her own."

"But... Christmas with Daniel..." The pain in Kane's face made my stomach twist with sympathy.

I was searching uselessly for something comforting to say when my cell phone vibrated.

Saved by the phone. I snatched it out of my waist pouch with relief and accepted the call.

"Hello?"

"Detective Constable Tan here. Do you know a John Kane?"

"Yes, he's right here. Would you like to speak to him?"

Tan let out a breath. "I just spent the last half-hour tracking him down, only to find out that you probably knew each other. If Ms. Rainey is with you, then I don't actually need to speak with him."

"She's not with us right this second. We're having supper downstairs and she's up in the hotel room."

"Oh. I have a few more questions for her. Where are you staying?"

I gave him the hotel name and room number, and he promised to arrive in fifteen minutes and disconnected.

"What was that about?" Hellhound demanded.

"Tan has a few more questions for LaVonda. He'll be here pretty soon, so we should probably go and knock on the door so LaVonda has a bit of advance warning."

"Awright." Arnie hesitated. "Think I oughta come up with ya?"

"Of course. She didn't tell you to go away."

Hope brightened his face. "Guess you're right."

We paid the bill and trooped up to the room.

Kane tapped on the door. "LaVonda, it's John. We're finished dinner and we'd like to talk to you. Is it all right if we come in now?"

No sound or movement came from inside.

"She's prob'ly got her headphones on," Hellhound said. "Cop said she wears 'em all the time an' can't hear a thing."

Kane knocked again and called louder. "LaVonda! It's John! Are you awake?"

Still no reply.

A chill gripped my heart. "She doesn't have her headphones. Everything in her apartment burned. She's got nothing but her purse, phone, and the clothes on her back."

Kane's brows snapped together and he whipped out his cardkey. I held my breath as he swiped it.

"Stay here," he said, and opened the door.

Ignoring his instructions, Arnie pushed in behind and I followed.

Princess bounced over, meowing and weaving between our ankles.

No sign of LaVonda.

CHAPTER 16

I stared around the hotel room, unbelieving. The bed was made. The bathroom door stood open. There was absolutely no place a six-foot-tall, two-hundred-and-fifty-pound woman could hide.

I swung the door shut and gaped at the empty closet alcove behind it. Hellhound dove into the bathroom, checking futilely around the open shower curtain and the bathroom door. Kane strode forward, yanking up the bedspread to reveal nothing but the enclosed bedframe, built to the floor. Then he stilled, his gaze going to a notepad and pen on the table.

"She's gone," he said hollowly.

"*What?*" Arnie's voice cracked. "What the *fuck?*" He slammed the bathroom door and stomped over to the table, his face creasing into a scowl. "Ya said she was agoraphobic! Ya said she couldn't leave the fuckin' room!"

"I..." Kane gestured at the paper, looking stunned. "She must have lied to me. I never thought..."

I managed to uproot myself from where I stood. I crossed the room and stared at the notepad Arnie now held in shaking hands.

LaVonda's handwriting was neat and precise.

Dear Arnie,
Thank you so much for rescuing me. I have to leave

now, to keep you safe. Please don't try to find me, and please don't tell James or Don or Dad that you saw me. I hate leaving Princess behind but I know she'll be safe with you. I love you.

LaVonda

Arnie turned the pad over, then riffled the pages, but there was nothing more.

"She left," he muttered, staring blindly at the message. "She fuckin' fucked right off."

"I'm sorry," Kane repeated, his voice strained. "I believed her..."

"Are you sure she left under her own power?" I asked, hating to voice the thought and wondering whether it would be worse or better if she had been coerced.

Hellhound tossed the notepad back onto the table, where it landed with a slap of finality.

"Yeah, she left on her own," he growled. "No sign of a struggle, an' Princess is fine. If anybody'd attacked LaVonda, they woulda hurt Princess; or she'd be upset an' hidin'." A sigh escaped him. "Nope, LaVonda just moved the fuck on." He dropped into a chair and stared at his boots. "Guess we're done here."

A tap at the door made us all swing around. Arnie's eyes widened and he lunged up out of the chair to jerk the door open.

Detective Constable Tan stood in the hallway, just as intimidating as ever. I suppressed the impulse to hide behind Kane.

Arnie let his forehead fall against the open door with a thump. "Aw, fuck."

Tan's eyes narrowed. "What's that supposed to mean?"

"It means..." My voice came out in a croak, and I cleared my throat and tried again. "LaVonda lied to us. She told John she was agoraphobic and couldn't leave the room. Then she told us she needed some time alone; and while we were eating supper, she left."

"Voluntarily?" Tan demanded.

"Looks that way." I gestured to the table. "She left a note."

Tan strode to the table and snatched up the pad. His gaze flitted across the short message, his brows drawing together.

His lips moved and I was pretty sure he was mouthing obscenities, but when he spoke a moment later his voice was level. "She picked up the duffel bag full of cash nearly an hour ago."

Tan spoke into his shoulder radio, giving instructions to check the security cameras outside the station to find out whether LaVonda had arrived and left in a taxi. When the conversation concluded, he hooked the radio back into place with a short breath that sounded like frustration.

His intensity seemed out of proportion to the situation. My gut clenched.

"What's wrong?" I asked.

"Confidential. It's an ongoing investigation." His words were clipped.

"It seems pretty important for you to talk to LaVonda," Kane observed. "If you tell us why, maybe we can help."

"If you have any information regarding her whereabouts or her destination, I need to know it now," Tan said levelly. "Withholding information or hiding her could have legal repercussions for you."

"Whoa, relax," Hellhound said. "What's the big deal? If

ya need to know more about the fire last night, we're right here. Ask whatever ya want."

"It's not about the fire," Tan said tersely.

We regarded each other in silence. My mind raced. This didn't sound good.

"If you can give us some more details, we'll be in a better position to help you," I offered. "We all have top-level security clearances, so you know you can trust us."

"Can I? You have a personal connection to Ms. Rainey." Tan's gaze raked up and down Hellhound's bearded face, shitkicker boots, and tattoos.

"Looks like it ain't much of a connection," Hellhound rasped. "Considerin' she lied to us an' fucked off."

"Or maybe you helped her escape and now you're lying to me," Tan countered.

"For fucksakes!" Hellhound lunged to his feet, only to freeze as Tan's hand dropped to his weapons belt. "Take a fuckin' pill, would ya?" Hellhound snapped. "I'm just gonna let the cat take a shit."

He detoured around Tan and strode across the room to open the bathroom door for Princess, who had been pawing at the bottom of the door and emitting small anxious mews.

I shot Hellhound a warning glance as he went by, then turned back to Tan. "Look, we want to help if we can. If this isn't about the fire last night, what is it about?"

Tan hesitated for a long moment. Then he let out a breath. "If I find out you're hiding anything from me..." He didn't finish the threat and none of us responded. He sighed again. "I was reviewing LaVonda Rainey's case this morning, and I looked up Kathy Helmand. That name brought up a flag in some old records. She was a person of interest in a murder investigation about thirty years ago." He shot a glance at Hellhound as if expecting an explosion.

Hellhound sank wearily into the chair. "Drug-related?"

Surprise flickered across Tan's face, quickly suppressed. "The police suspected so."

"You said 'person of interest', not 'suspect'," Kane observed. "What was the situation?"

"The victim was Bradley Percival Montmorency the Third. Thirty-one years old, the only son of rich and influential parents. He was stabbed to death in a run-down house in Winnipeg, near the University of Manitoba."

"Abducted?" I asked.

"Unlikely. He was your typical entitled rich kid who never grew up and figured he was above the law. Word on campus at that time was that if you wanted to score some designer drugs, he was your man. There were also whispers that he was connected to organized crime and that a lot of drug money had gone missing the night he died, but none of that was ever substantiated. He had a number of arrests related to drugs and violence against prostitutes, but no charges ever stuck. The house where he was killed was a known hangout for party animals and prostitutes."

"Sounds like the asshole got what he deserved," Hellhound said.

"Nobody deserves to be murdered," Tan retorted.

Hellhound's face froze.

I couldn't divulge that Hellhound was basically a government-sanctioned murderer, so I prodded the conversation forward. "So Montmorency was a high roller who led a risky life. Why was Kathy a person of interest in his stabbing?"

"Well..." Tan shot another unreadable glance at Hellhound. "She was a known drug addict and prostitute."

Hellhound nodded. "And...?"

"Rumour was that Montmorency was her drug supplier. And her pimp."

"Pretty sure she couldn't afford any designer drugs," Hellhound said mildly. "An' a snob like Montmorency wouldn't a' wanted to pimp her. She'd been livin' on the street since she was fifteen, an' she was pretty much used up by the time she was twenty. Last I saw her she was twenty-three, nothin' but skin an' bones. Needle tracks an' open sores an' missin' teeth. By then she could only get the johns that didn't mind scrapin' the bottom a' the barrel."

Tan's lip curled. "This is your *sister* we're talking about."

"I fuckin' *know* that!" Hellhound gave him a murderous glare. "Listen, when she started turnin' tricks I was eleven, livin' in a foster home an' tryin' to scrape together enough cash so she didn't hafta fuck every scum-suckin' asshole that came along. An' every fuckin' cent I gave her went up her nose or in her veins. Even when I brought her food, she'd sell it an' use whatever she got for drugs." His chin went up, his hard stare never leaving Tan's face. "She was still a good person. Kind-hearted. Always lookin' out for me. I loved her then, an' I still do."

Tan dropped his gaze. "Sorry."

Hellhound's scowl eased. "Forget it. What I was tryin' to say was, Kath prob'ly didn't run with the same crowd as Montmorency."

"So how did she end up being a person of interest?" I asked Tan.

"Her fingerprints and some personal belongings were found in the house where Montmorency was killed, so there was a connection. But there were so many fingerprints there, including those of other prostitutes, it didn't prove anything.

Montmorency's body wasn't found for a couple of days..."
Tan grimaced. "Or, more likely, nobody reported it.
Anyway, by the time the medical examiner got
Montmorency's body, the time of death could only be
narrowed down to a window of a few hours. And during that
time, Kathy Helmand was miles away in downtown
Winnipeg, being beaten nearly to death." A spasm of pain
twisted Hellhound's face, and Tan's expression softened.
"Sorry," he said again.

Hellhound shook his head. "It's okay. That's how it
usually ends for girls like Kath. That or an overdose."

Tan gave him a sympathetic look, one that actually
reached his eyes. "But it didn't end that way for Kathy.
When she recovered enough to be questioned, she said she'd
been soliciting downtown at the time that Montmorency was
killed. She claimed her date had attacked her, and a
passerby called 911. The police report corroborated the
details and the timeframe. Kathy claimed to know nothing
about Montmorency's murder, and she was so ill and
emaciated that nobody seriously considered her as a suspect.
She would have been barely able to walk, much less
overpower a man in his prime."

I frowned. "Okay, so she answered all the investigators'
questions, and they decided she couldn't have done it. So
why are you so wound up about questioning her after all this
time?"

Tan gave me a measured look. "The duffel bag full of
cash."

Slow dread chilled my guts. "Yes...?"

"It was niggling at me, and I realized what was bothering
me about it when I came back on shift this afternoon. Did
you notice anything unusual about the money in that bag?"

"We never saw the money," I reminded him.

He nodded, and the flicker of satisfaction on his face tipped me off. He'd been testing me, the bastard, just to see if I'd keep my facts straight.

"Right," he agreed smoothly. "Well, I realized it was all old money."

"What d'ya mean?" Hellhound asked. "Like, rich people's money?"

"No. *Old* money." Tan gave us a significant look. "About thirty years old. The design of those bills hasn't been used in decades. Remember, a lot of money went missing the night Montmorency was killed. And if the money in that duffel bag was really cash payments from LaVonda's psychic business, there should have been modern bills in there, too. There weren't any."

CHAPTER 17

Silence blanketed the hotel room, broken only by the sound of Princess scratching industriously in the litter box.

Hellhound scowled at Constable Tan. "Did ya check through all the money in LaVonda's duffel bag?"

"Yes, it was inventoried when it was checked into the lockup."

Hellhound leaned back in his chair and crossed his arms over his chest. "'Course it was all old. She'd been savin' it for years. She prob'ly has newer stuff somewhere else."

"Quite likely. That's what I want to ask her." The humanity that had softened Tan's eyes earlier was gone. He gave Hellhound a shark-smile that was probably meant to be reassuring. "It would only take a minute to clear this up. So if you know where she is..."

"Sorry, no idea," Hellhound said, not looking sorry at all. "An' I'll never know, 'cause she ain't comin' back." He flicked the notepad with a dismissive fingertip.

"Or maybe you know exactly where she is, and she's splitting the cash with you in exchange for helping her disappear," Tan replied.

I tensed for Hellhound's explosion.

It didn't come.

He blew out an impatient breath. "If you're gonna arrest me for somethin', get on with it. If ya ain't, then stop fuckin' around."

Tan stiffened.

Kane spoke up hurriedly. "Sorry, this has been a difficult time, and we're all exhausted and on edge. We've told you everything we know. Maybe the staff at the front desk noticed LaVonda leaving, or called her a taxi."

"I'll check with them," Tan said curtly. "And if you hear from Ms. Rainey or get any new information, no matter how unimportant it may seem, please call me or Corporal Whittle immediately."

"We will," Kane promised. His sincere expression wavered, then smoothed into an inscrutable mask.

"What are you hiding?" Tan snapped.

The reason for Kane's uncharacteristic lapse struck me full force an instant later, when an unbelievably foul stench invaded my nasal passages.

Unlike him, I wasn't nearly polite enough to ignore it. I clapped a hand over my nose. "Princess, you little pig! That's disgusting!" Eyes watering, I hurried over to turn on the exhaust fan and shut the bathroom door on the sinus-searing reek.

Just before the door closed, Princess scampered out, her upturned whiskers making her look as though she was smirking.

Tan's nose twitched. "That tiny little cat did... *that?*"

Hellhound burst into laughter. "Aw, c'mere, sweetie," he said, leaning over to pick her up. "It's okay. A girl's gotta do what a girl's gotta do."

She nuzzled his beard, preening under his caress.

"Call me if you learn anything new about Ms. Rainey," Tan said in a slightly strangled voice, and hurried out.

Hellhound snickered. "That's my girl," he crooned to Princess. "Chased that fuckin' cop right outta here, didn't ya?"

"That cat has serious digestive issues," Kane said. He shot a mischievous look at me. "Since Arnie's her keeper, I guess she'll be rooming with you. Don't forget to take her litterbox with you."

I must have paled.

Hellhound raised a mocking eyebrow. "Yeah, you're a coupla real badass agents; can't even deal with a little cat shit." He rose. "Fine, I'll go get rid a' the scary turd for ya."

He placed Princess on the floor and slipped into the bathroom. A moment later the toilet flushed.

When he came out, Kane said, "I thought cat litter was bad for plumbing systems."

Hellhound shrugged. "I got the flushable kind. It ain't great, but I figured it'd do for a day or two, 'til LaVonda could get her usual brand..." He trailed off, his expression turning grim. "Guess I got myself another cat. Hope she'll get along okay with Hooker."

"It was shitty for LaVonda to dump her on you," I said.

He grimaced. "If she's on the run, it's prob'ly best for Princess to stay with me."

"But not best for you. How are you supposed to take a cat home with you? Will you rent a car?"

"Nah, the airline'll take her. I'll call 'em."

"Are you thinking of going home right away?" Kane asked, hope brightening his voice.

Hellhound slouched against the door frame and frowned at his boots. "I... dunno."

Kane and I exchanged a glance, but neither of us offered an opinion.

Hellhound scuffed at an invisible spot on the carpet. "The note said she wants me to leave her alone. But... I dunno if I oughta do what she wants, or what she needs."

"You mean, what you *think* she needs," Kane corrected gently.

Arnie blew out a breath. "Yeah. I tried doin' what I thought she needed thirty years ago, an' look how that turned out. Ya can't save somebody that doesn't wanna be saved..." He trailed off, his scowl deepening.

We waited in silence while he glared at the floor, his fingers flexing into a fist.

Several long moments later he added, "If she'd said she wanted to forget the past an' me along with it, I'd know I hadta just let her be. I wouldn't like it; but I'd know."

He gave us an anguished glance. "What's buggin' me is the part about how she hasta leave to keep me safe. If she's just blowin' sunshine up my ass to make me feel better, that's okay; but what if she really thinks she's gotta take on these assholes by herself, to protect me?" His knuckles whitened. "She ain't got a fuckin' chance." His chin rose and he glowered at us. "An' I ain't walkin' away an' leavin' her! *Fuck* that shit! Fuck that shit all to hell!"

Kane's shoulders slumped almost imperceptibly. I could practically hear his heart sinking, but when he spoke his voice was as firm and decisive as ever. "All right. So what's your plan? How can we help?"

Arnie sank onto the edge of the bed, hunching forward to stare at the floor and clenching his hands behind his bowed neck. "I ain't got a plan. Hell, I ain't got a fuckin' clue." He looked up, his eyes imploring us. "Can ya think of anythin'?"

Kane let out a long breath and plodded across to sink into the chair. I sat beside Hellhound on the bed and put an arm around him.

After a moment, Kane broke the glum silence. "All right,

let's start at the beginning. Arnie, you know what Kathy's life was like around the time of the murder. Do you honestly believe she couldn't have killed Montmorency and stolen his money?"

"'Course she couldn'ta..." Hellhound began hotly, but the sentence trailed off into uncertainty. He stared at the floor again. "I dunno. She was an addict. They'll do anythin' for a fix."

"But she was so weak and sick," I protested. "You said she was just a walking skeleton, and the police obviously didn't think she was capable of killing someone. If they had, they'd have arrested her back then."

"She was nothin' but skin an' bones," Hellhound mumbled, staring at the carpet as though it held the ghosts of the past. "But she was always strong. An' she's tall. Good reach, if she had a knife. She couldn't'a fought for long, but if she got lucky an' hit a big blood vessel..."

I stared at his bent head. "You think she did it?"

He looked up, giving me a twisted smile. "I don't wanna think so, but I can't say it'd never happen." He sighed. "It's the cash that's buggin' me. Tan's right, she oughta have newer bills if it was from her clients. An' if it's Montmorency's drug money, she either killed him herself or she was there when somebody else offed him. That kinda cash wouldn't lie around long in a place like that."

"That fits," Kane said thoughtfully. "And if Montmorency owed money to a gang; and if the gang thought Kathy had taken the money; some longtime members might still be holding a grudge."

"But that doesn't make sense," I argued. "Tan said she was beaten half to death. She was in the hospital, and she obviously didn't have the money with her there. If she had, the police would have treated her as a suspect then. And if a gang was after her, surely she never would have made it out of the hospital alive."

Hellhound rose decisively. "Whoever killed Montmorency did the world a favour. If it was Kath, she musta had a good reason, 'cause she was still a good person even when she was completely fucked up on drugs. So fuck it. None a' that shit matters now. How're we gonna find her?"

"Our first stop will be the front desk to find out whether anyone saw her getting into a cab," Kane said.

I stifled a cavernous yawn and knuckled my gritty eyes as I stood. "Okay, let's do this."

Kane and Hellhound exchanged a glance.

"Tell ya what, darlin'," Hellhound said. "Tan'll already have asked 'em, so why don't ya call him an' see if he'll give ya any intel?"

My suspicions flared instantly. What were they up to?

"Okay," I said, dialling. "I'll do that right now."

Listening to the ringing of phone, I frowned at them, but their expressions were unreadable.

"Tan."

I transferred my attention to the call. "Hi, it's Aydan Kelly. We're going to try tracking Kathy. Have you had any luck finding out whether she got a cab?"

A short silence hovered on the line.

"I'm sorry, that information is part of an ongoing investigation," Tan said formally.

I pulled the phone away from my ear and gave it a 'what-the-fuck?' glare, then repositioned it and kept my tone neutral. "So you've decided you don't want our help?"

"Any assistance you can provide is appreciated."

"We'll be able to assist you better if you share some information," I said with my best show of patience. "Otherwise we'll be wasting time and duplicating your efforts. So, did you find the cab company?"

"I'm sorry, that information is part of an ongoing investigation," Tan repeated.

Clamping my teeth on my tongue so I wouldn't say something we'd all end up regretting, I sucked in a deep breath and let it out slowly.

Count to ten...

"Thanks for your help," I snapped, and disconnected. "*Asshole!*"

Kane's eyes widened.

"Relax, I already hung up," I grumbled, and stowed my phone back in my waist pouch.

"So I take it that he chose not to share any information," Kane said.

"Yeah. He said it was part of an ongoing investigation."

Kane shrugged. "It's all right. We'll check with the front desk; and even if they didn't notice anything, there aren't that many cab companies in town. It won't take long to contact all of them."

"What if Tan's already arrested her an' he ain't tellin' us?" Hellhound demanded.

"Unlikely," Kane replied. "He'd have no reason to keep that information from us. More likely he's hot on her trail and has decided to keep us out of the loop in case we warn her." A small grim smile quirked his mouth. "That was a poor choice on his part."

I sighed. "I guess we're going to do this the hard way, then."

Kane gave me a cautious smile. "May I make a

suggestion?"

"Of course."

"I think it would be best for you to stay here and rest while Arnie and I do the legwork."

Irritation stiffened my spine. "You think I'm-"

"We won't go anywhere important without you," Kane interrupted hurriedly. "But we need to get my rental car from the impound lot, and we can ask at the front desk to see if they noticed LaVonda getting into a cab. After that, we'll likely be phoning cab companies trying to trace her movements. We might hit it lucky right away or it could take hours, but if you can sleep in the meantime, you should."

I swallowed my pride along with my irrational objections. They made an unwieldy bundle in my throat, and my voice came out slightly choked despite my best efforts. "You're right. Thanks. Arnie, you should sleep, too. You were up all night along with me."

"Nah, I'm good," Hellhound objected. "Ya know I'm usually up half the night anyway." When I began to protest, he added, "An' I wasn't sleep-deprived to start with. So we'll move Princess to our room, an' I'll drive John over to the impound lot to pick up his rental car." He picked Princess up from her comfortable nest on the bed and tucked her back into her carrier. "Pack up, sweetie; you're movin' again." He zipped the mesh shut and handed the carrier to Kane. "You carry Princess, Aydan can bring the bags, an' I'll get the litter box."

Kane turned to me. "If you'd like to nap without feline interference, you can stay here."

"No, it's okay. I like cats." I gave him an innocent smile. "And since she just finished polluting the air in here, I know I'm safe for a while."

"So you think," Kane said darkly. "Cats are inherently evil. She'll wait until you're asleep and then use the litter box again and asphyxiate you."

"Christ, you'd think ya never smelled shit before," Hellhound snapped. "What d'ya do, stick an air freshener up your ass every time ya take a dump?"

Kane shot me a worried look before turning back to Arnie. "I was only joking. You know I like cats."

Arnie blew out a breath. "Yeah. Sorry, Cap. I'm just..." He shrugged, letting his arms drop to his sides.

"I know," Kane assured him. "It's all right."

We trudged down the hall bearing our various burdens. After reinstalling the litter box in our bathroom Arnie washed his hands, accompanied by a cacophony of wails from Princess.

"It's okay, sweetie, it's okay," he reassured her, but her cries didn't stop until the water was safely turned off. "It's okay," he repeated as he picked Princess up and cuddled her. "Nothin' bad's gonna happen to ya here."

"Well, nothing other than having her home firebombed and being abandoned by her mistress," Kane said with perhaps a touch of sarcasm.

Hellhound shot Kane a scowl and turned back to Princess. "Nothin' *else* bad's gonna happen to ya. You get nice an' comfy with Aydan an' have a nap now." He placed her on the bed and turned to me. "See ya later, darlin'."

"Wake me right away if you..." A huge yawn interrupted my words. "...find out anything. But you might have to come in and shake me. I might be dead to the world."

He chuckled. "No chance. When the housekeepin' cart went by in the hall earlier, ya had your gun in your hand before I was even half awake."

I stared at him. "You're joking, right?"

"Hell, no."

Worry tensed my gut. "I don't remember that. Maybe I shouldn't sleep with my gun for a while."

"Nah, you're fine." He planted a whiskery kiss on my forehead. "Ya weren't aimin', ya were just ready for action. Get some sleep, an' don't worry."

"But..."

"Your instincts are good, Aydan," Kane reassured me. "Trust yourself. We do."

"But what if I'm dreaming and one of you comes through the door?" I demanded. "If I was having a nightmare..."

Kane took my shoulders in his big warm hands and looked into my eyes. "Aydan, I was an agent for a long time. Before that, I was a police officer, and before that, a soldier. My life has always depended on knowing whom to trust, and I know for a fact that you would never fire without identifying your target. Even in your sleep. If you won't trust yourself, trust me."

I let out a breath. "Okay. Thanks."

They said their goodbyes and left.

A few minutes after the door closed behind them, I realized that despite his confident assurances, Kane had completely misread someone very recently indeed: LaVonda.

And Alicia, too, come to think of it.

Shit.

CHAPTER 18

Despite my exhaustion, sleep didn't come easily. Princess prowled around the room, jumping on and off the bed with plaintive mews and pressing her nose to the crack under the door. After the third time she marched across my stomach, I captured her gently and cuddled her.

"It's okay," I reassured her. "He's coming back, I promise. Arnie's not like everybody else. He'll always be there for you, no matter what."

She squirmed and I let her go, but kept petting her. After a few minutes of treading circles on the bed and leaning into my stroking, she let out a tiny sigh and settled into a compact cat-loaf tucked into the curve of my waist. As her nearly-silent purr thrummed against my hip, my eyes drifted shut.

Seemingly only seconds later, the vibration of my phone on the bedside table jerked me upright, heart pounding and gun in hand. My sudden movement startled Princess into a frantic leap off the bed, her hind claws ripping lines of pain across my hip.

"Ow-*fuck!*" My involuntary bellow sent her hurtling across the room and into the safety of her carrier. "Shit, sorry, Princess..." I put down my gun and snatched up the phone. "Kelly." The phone vibrated again and I realized I'd missed the 'Answer' button. "Fuck!" I smacked the button again. *"Kelly!"*

"Don't yell in my fucking ear!" Dermott's irritable snarl did nothing to improve my humour.

A glance at the glowing numerals of the clock-radio added confusion to my annoyance. Eight-fifteen PM, which made it seven-fifteen in Alberta, on a Friday night two days before Christmas. Why was Dermott still working?

"What do you want?" I demanded.

"What the hell do you think I want? Why did you tell the fucking Regina Police Service we'd help them?"

"I didn't. I told them they could ask, but you probably *wouldn't* help."

"Damn right we won't. It's their problem, not ours. Bunch of pansy-ass whiners."

What an asshole.

Somehow I managed not to say that out loud. "So why are you calling me?"

"You need to get your ass back here."

I clenched my teeth so the obscenities wouldn't leak out. "Yesterday you gave me shit for being at the office. I'm supposed to be on leave, remember?"

"And you're still on fucking leave. I don't want to see your face again until after New Year's." Fortunately he kept talking, preventing me from ever-so-politely pointing out that he was a dick-headed goat-humping moron. "The Department needs you to get back here and call off your mother's fucking lawyer."

"My moth... *what?* What lawyer?"

"The lawyer that's trying to overturn the proceeds-of-crime seizure that took Sirius Dynamics out of your Mommy's greedy murdering hands. Now that your old lady is worm food, the lawsuit is being continued by her estate. And you're the executor of her estate. So get your ass back here and make this bullshit go away!"

He disconnected, leaving me sitting in bed with my jaw dangling.

My sleep-fogged mind ground slowly through the ramifications of the short but unpleasant conversation.

Why had my mother named me her executor? Until a few days ago, she hadn't seen me in decades; and I hadn't even known she was alive.

That raised another interesting question: If I was her executor, who were her heirs?

A slow and evil smile tugged at the corners of my mouth. If Sirius were returned to my mother's estate and then passed on to her heirs, the Department would have to suck up to a new owner.

My grin widened.

And if that new owner happened to be me...

Oh. My. God. No wonder Dermott had a wild hair up his ass.

A laugh bubbled up. It got bigger and bigger until I was drumming on the mattress with both hands and cackling with glee.

I was making so much noise that I didn't notice the small sound of the cardkey. Hellhound slipped into the room, a smile spreading across his face.

"What's up, darlin'?" he inquired.

I let out a whoop and sprang up, using the bed as a trampoline to bounce off the end and land in front of him. Seizing him around the middle, I danced him around the room, still laughing.

Chuckling, he pulled us to a halt and swept me into a dramatic dip, planting a smacking kiss on my lips before pulling me upright.

"Okay, darlin', spill," he demanded. "Did ya win the lottery or somethin'?"

"Nope, even better!"

Hope flared in his eyes. "LaVonda called?"

"Oh." My wicked joy deflated, leaving my chest hollow with guilt. "No. It's not that good. I'm sorry I got your hopes up."

"It's okay." He kissed me again, summoning up a smile with a visible effort. "So what's the good news?"

"I just heard from Dermott."

He grimaced. "An' you're *happy* after talkin' to that dickless fucktard? Why, did he tell ya he's dyin'?"

"No, this is even better." I flopped onto the bed, pulling him down beside me. "Did I ever mention the proceeds-of-crime thing with Sirius?"

"Nope."

"Okay, well..." I hesitated. "There's a bunch of classified stuff I can't tell you, but the simplified version is that Sam Kraus... the guy who owned the civilian research branch and all the buildings and infrastructure of Sirius Dynamics... was secretly married to my mother. And he left everything to her when he died."

"An' now that your mother's dead..." Hellhound's eyes widened. "You're kiddin'. She left it all to you?"

"I don't know. I just found out that she made me her executor, so there's a chance that I might get at least part of it. Except that the government seized the whole thing as proceeds of crime last year after they found out Sam was crooked."

"Oh." Hellhound frowned. "So ya ain't gettin' anythin'. The way ya were jumpin' around, I thought..."

I raised a finger. "But..."

He grinned. "But what?"

"But before she died, my mother hired a lawyer who was sure she could overturn the seizure, because Sam was never convicted. He died before his trial started. And the legal action doesn't end just because my mother died. Her estate takes over."

His grin widened. "An' you're the executor of her estate."

I gave a gleeful bounce on the bed. "And Dermott is shitting bricks. Even if I don't get a penny out of the estate, at least I get to watch him sweat."

Hellhound chuckled. "Enjoy, darlin'."

"Oh, believe me, I will!" I sobered, finally realizing there was probably a reason why he'd been returning to our room. "So did you get John's car? Did you find out where LaVonda went?"

"Got the car. Kane's sweet-talkin' the cab company right now. We know which company picked her up, but they ain't admittin' it, an' they ain't tellin' where they dropped her off."

I sighed. "I'm glad, actually. It's a pain in the ass for us, but if John can't get them to give out that information, nobody else will be able to get it, either."

"Yeah." Hellhound glanced at me, then looked away. "They'd hafta tell the cops if they asked, though."

His meaning wasn't hard to decipher.

"I could call the cab company and tell them I'm officially investigating," I said, suppressing a shudder at the thought of Dermott's wrath if he found out. "But they might ask for a warrant before they'll release the records, and I don't have one. I could bluff..."

"An' if they don't buy it an' they call the cops instead, you'll be up Shit Creek," Hellhound said. "I really wanna find LaVonda, but I ain't gonna get ya in trouble to do it."

"Let's ask John," I suggested, hiding my relief at being able to defer responsibility to somebody else for a change. I got up and grabbed my hairbrush. "Who knows; maybe he's already told them he's investigating in an official capacity," I added as I yanked out some tangles, then abandoned the hairbrush to strap on my waist pouch.

"Don't think so," Hellhound said as he rose and followed me to the door. "Kane's by-the-book. He wouldn't take a chance on impersonatin' a police officer."

"Yeah, I guess you're right."

We completed the short walk to Kane's room in silence.

When I tapped on his door, Kane opened it immediately.

"How'd it go?" Hellhound asked before the door had even closed behind us.

"They refused to tell me LaVonda's destination," Kane said. "And I didn't press the point. We'll find another way."

"What did you tell them?" I asked.

"I said my sister was supposed to have met me an hour ago and I was getting worried because she hadn't shown up. I told them I knew she had some errands to run and she was going to stop in at the police station; but I didn't know where she might have gone from there and she wasn't answering her cell phone. When they wouldn't give me any information, I told them I had called the police, and asked if they'd gotten a call from an officer yet." He grimaced. "They had. Tan is ahead of us."

"Did they say whether they'd told him anything?" I asked.

"They didn't say specifically, but I expect they did."

"*Shit!*" Hellhound's fists clenched, shoulders bunching. "Tan's gonna find her an' arrest her!"

"Which might be okay," I pointed out cautiously. "She'd be safe from the wackos then. And at least she shouldn't be claustrophobic, if she didn't leave her apartment in eight years." I glanced at Kane. "Or do you think she was lying about that, too?"

Kane shook his head, frowning. "I would have staked a bet that she was telling the truth. She showed all the physiological signs of extreme anxiety; and she had no tells to indicate she was lying."

"Hard to believe she changed that much," Hellhound said. "She was always a shitty liar. She'd blush like crazy an' she could never look me in the face..." He stopped. "Aw, shit." He dropped onto the bed and sank his head into his hands. "She was lyin' her ass off."

"To me?" Kane demanded. "I swear she wasn't. She made eye contact-"

"Not to you," Hellhound interrupted. "To me, when we brought Princess over. I thought she was just... I dunno, shy or somethin', 'cause we hadn't seen each other for so long. But... the whole time she was tellin' us about her psychic business..." His fists clenched. "She never looked me in the eye."

In the silence that followed, I replayed the scene in my mind.

"You're right," I said. "I don't have your photographic memory, but I did notice that she seemed uncomfortable making eye contact. I just assumed it was because..." I trailed off, not wanting to say anything hurtful.

"'Cause she didn't wanna have anythin' to do with me," Arnie said gloomily to the floor. "Yeah, me, too. Maybe that was part of it, but I can pretty much guarantee she was lyin' about the psychic business."

Kane frowned. "But if you're right, her actions don't make sense. If she was telling the truth about the severity of her agoraphobia, there's no way she should have been capable of leaving this room alone."

Arnie sighed. "Ya don't know Kathy. Hell, LaVonda. Whatever." He glanced up at Kane. "I never really told ya much about... when we were kids."

"No," Kane said gently. "I assumed that if you wanted to talk about it, you would."

Arnie stared at the floor again. "The first stuff I remember that makes sense, I woulda been about two years old. An' I got a complete record of everythin' for the next forty-eight fuckin' years. Right there in my head like movies I can play back anytime."

I shuddered and sank down on the bed to take his hand. "What a horrible curse."

He grimaced agreement and went on, "For a long time I never played back the movies from when I was kid. But after Kathy disappeared, I hadta do it. I was tryin' to figure out what mighta happened to her. Where she mighta gone, if she was still alive. So I watched those fuckin' movies in my head, over an' over."

I put my arms around him, my heart quailing at the horrors he had witnessed.

"It was my fault Mom died," Arnie said.

"No, it wasn't!" I hugged him harder, wishing I could protect him from the pain. "You were five years old. You couldn't have changed anything."

He squeezed my hand. "Nah, I didn't mean that. I meant, I'm the reason she died. If she hadn't been tryin' to keep the ol' man from whalin' on me, he wouldn't'ta killed her."

"I doubt that," Kane said. "As a cop, I saw quite a few domestic violence situations. Your father's violence would have continued to escalate. Even if he hadn't killed her that time, he would have soon after."

"Maybe, maybe not." Arnie shook his head. "Doesn't matter now. What I'm sayin' is, right from the very first thing I can remember, Mom always kept Kathy close. Prob'ly tryin' to protect her, but I think it fucked her up worse. Kath saw every beatin' Mom got, an' she saw every time Mom took the hits for me. An' when Mom was hurt too bad to move, she used to tell Kathy to look after me. An' I think..."

He heaved a sigh. "Fuck, she was just a little kid. I think Mom taught her, without meanin' to, that I was more important than both a' them. It got so that when the ol' man was on a rampage, Kathy'd push me behind her to protect me, same as Mom. This poor damn little kid, standin' up to that fuckin' big scary asshole..."

I shivered, my throat tightening. I had faced his father's rage once. Even in his mid-seventies, he'd been terrifying. I couldn't imagine what it had cost little Kathy to face him in his prime.

"So where I'm goin' with this..." Arnie said into the silence, "...is that LaVonda was so scared to leave her apartment that she'd rather burn to death; but if she thought leavin' this room was gonna protect me..." His voice wavered and he swallowed. "I think she'd make herself do it," he said hoarsely. "An' I don't even wanna think about what she's goin' through if she's that fuckin' scared."

CHAPTER 19

As Arnie's words sank in, an idea formed. "I need to talk to Tan again," I said, and punched in his number.

He answered on the first ring. "Tan."

"Hi, it's Aydan Kelly again."

His tone was still formal. "Do you have information to share with me?"

This time his standoffishness didn't annoy me. If he'd recently requested help from Dermott and gotten slapped down, I didn't blame him for being prickly.

"Maybe," I said. "I have a question for you first."

"I told you before, I can't-"

"Yeah, I know," I interrupted. "I'm not asking for any details of your investigation. I just want to know whether you personally handed LaVonda's money back to her."

"No."

"Damn."

His voice sharpened. "Why does that matter?"

"I was hoping you might have noticed whether she looked anxious when she picked it up."

He hesitated as if weighing his reply. "I reviewed the security footage afterward, and I interviewed the clerk who released the duffel bag to her. And... yes, she seemed extremely anxious. Elevated respiration, sweating, trembling, stammering. Why?"

I let out a breath. "So she wasn't lying to John. She

really is agoraphobic."

"Or she has a guilty conscience," Tan countered.

"Maybe, but John was certain that she was telling the truth when she told him she was severely agoraphobic."

"So what?" Tan challenged.

"So I bet she'd go to ground as fast as possible. We'll start checking hotels right near the police station."

Silence blanketed the line.

"Hello? Are you still there?" I demanded.

"I'm still here. I'm thinking."

I waited.

"I guess I can tell you this," Tan said reluctantly. "You're right, that's exactly what she did. The taxi dropped her off at a hotel a few blocks away from the station, and she checked in there."

"*What?* You found her?"

Hellhound jerked upright at my exclamation, his eyes wide.

"No." Tan sounded testy.

I shook my head regretfully at Hellhound, and he sank back onto the bed.

"What do you mean, you *didn't* find her?" I asked Tan. "You just said-"

"I said she checked in. And sometime before we caught up with her, she left again."

"What the hell?" I demanded. "She wouldn't leave. She'd just gotten to safety, and she'd be completely messed up. She'd hole up in her room and order room service..." Even as I spoke the last sentence, my heart sank with realization. "Oh, shit. She didn't leave voluntarily."

John and Arnie stiffened and Arnie surged to his feet, fists clenching. I flung up my palm to keep them silent.

Tan still hadn't replied.

Maybe he was deciding whether to share more information with us. My heart thumped with hope and fear.

"You're right," Tan said at last. "She didn't leave voluntarily. We just got the hotel's security footage. It looks as though she was quietly abducted by three men. Professionals, I'd say. Would you and your friends come down to the station and watch the footage? See if you can identify the men?"

"We'll be there as soon as we can," I said, and disconnected before he could change his mind.

"What's happenin'?" Hellhound demanded.

"LaVonda checked into a hotel right near the police station, but she was followed. Her attackers must have been watching the station and waiting for her to pick up her money, just like we were going to do. I don't think Tan was going to give us the whole story, but when I guessed right..."

Hellhound was already heading for the door, and as we hurried out behind him I added, "Wait, I have to grab my parka." As we strode down the hall toward our room, I lowered my voice. "Tan said she was abducted from her hotel by three guys who looked like professionals."

"*Fuck!*" Hellhound looked as though he was about to punch something.

I squeezed his rigid hand. "We'll get her back. This is what we do, remember?"

"Have they identified the men yet?" Kane demanded as I pushed my cardkey into the reader and yanked the door open.

"No. Tan wants us to look at the footage and see if we can help." I shoved my feet into my hiking boots and snatched up my parka. "Let's roll."

"We'll take my car," Kane said as we double-timed down the hall. "If her enemies are still watching the station, we don't want them to be able to identify both our vehicles."

When we got to the car, Kane slid behind the wheel and Hellhound climbed into the back, leaving me the front passenger seat. Moments later we were on our way.

We had only been driving for a few blocks when Kane stiffened.

"Don't look now," he said. "But we've got a tail."

I wasn't sure whether 'don't look now' was a figure of speech or a command, so I dipped my chin only fractionally to peek into the side mirror.

"Same vehicle as last night?" I asked, scanning the array of headlights behind us.

"No. It's an older-model beige sedan." Kane maintained his speed. "Fell in behind us right after we left the hotel parking lot."

I eyed his grim profile. "But nobody followed you back from the impound lot, did they?"

"Not that I spotted."

"Then nobody followed you. This will be a new tail." I peeked in the mirror again, but couldn't see the other car. Damn, I was glad Kane was driving.

"So what do you want to do?" he asked.

And the responsibility was back on my plate. Shit.

"I vote we grab him an' find out who these assholes are," Hellhound growled before I could speak.

"Aydan?" Kane raised an eyebrow in my direction.

"Me, too," I said.

"Agreed. I'll pull over and let the two of you get out so he has to decide which of us to follow." Kane glanced at Hellhound in the rearview mirror. "What does your miraculous memory tell you about this area? I want a place to drop you where I can drive for another two or three blocks and park. Whoever he follows, the others can come up on foot and box him in."

"Hmmm..." Hellhound hesitated, and I imagined him paging rapidly through his mental files.

"Awright," he said after a moment. "Four blocks ahead, deke to the right like you're gonna turn, but instead pull over to the curb right before the light. Aydan an' I'll jump out there. Then keep drivin' for two blocks, hang a right, an' there's a multi-level parkade on the right. He'll hafta follow ya in there if he doesn't wanna lose ya, an' we can hoof it there in a few minutes. Or you can hoof it back, if he follows us instead."

"Perfect." Kane changed lanes unhurriedly. "Get ready."

Heart thumping, I poised on the edge of the seat, my finger on the seatbelt release button.

"If you're gonna lead him outta the parkade on foot, turn right," Hellhound commanded. "There's an alley that joins up to another alley. We'll be comin' up from the right, so turn left into the second alley."

"I will if necessary. But I'd rather do it in the parkade if we can. I'll move slowly." The car swung to the curb and Kane braked hard. "Go!"

I was already scrambling out of the car. Hellhound's and my doors slammed almost in unison, and we scurried onto the sidewalk.

I nudged Hellhound toward the buildings. "Guilty people stay close to buildings and doorways," I whispered, sneaking a glance over my shoulder as though I was afraid of being observed. In the reflection of a large window, I watched the beige sedan drive past. The driver's head snapped around to look at us, but he didn't stop.

Turning away as though I hadn't a clue we'd been followed, I pulled out my phone and hit the selfie camera app. A rotation of the phone showed the beige car behind us, following Kane into traffic.

"And... we're clear," I muttered as a truck blocked the view.

We broke into a jog. Letting Hellhound lead the way, I pulled my scarf up over my nose and mouth to warm the frigid air a bit before I sucked it into my lungs.

"Do you have a plan?" I panted.

"Take the fucker down," Hellhound growled.

"Okay..." I yelped as my foot skidded on a patch of ice, then righted myself and sped up to jog beside Hellhound again. "I'll tap him with a trank dart."

"Don't want him out that long."

Hellhound was setting a fast pace, and my words came out in bursts between my gulps of air. "I won't inject him. Just break the dart. He'll be out for five minutes."

"'Kay." Hellhound was beginning to breathe heavily, too. "Almost there." He dodged into an alley and slowed to a brisk walk.

"Parkade's in half a block," he said, halting at the corner of a building. After a moment to catch our breath he added, "This's where we gotta be careful we don't run into Kane an' our mark." Taking out his phone, he switched to the camera app and eased the lens around the corner.

The display showed a deserted alley, and he hissed, "Go!"

We dashed around the corner and sprinted to the rear entrance of the parkade. As we reached the outdoor stairwell, Hellhound glanced at the phone he was still clutching. His face creased into a predatory grin that sent a chill down my spine.

"Third level." He turned the phone toward me so I could read Kane's text message.

"Split up," I decided aloud, and jogged across to a stairwell I'd spotted on the other side. Unzipping my parka, I let it fall to either side of me as I crouched. If there were surveillance cameras, the parka would conceal my actions while I took my trank pistol out of my ankle holster and liberated a single dart before tucking the weapon into my pocket for easy access. I straightened and gave Hellhound a nod.

He replied with a single jerk of his chin, and ran up the stairs. I did the same on my side, pulse hammering. Panting open-mouthed in an attempt to stay silent, I concentrated on keeping my footing.

The stairs were coated with sand and salt-eroded slush, icy in some places and liquid in others. My boots splashed loudly through the muck, and I sent up a short plea to the patron saint of action heroes, if there was one. Please let the traffic noise hide our footsteps...

Just before the third level, I stopped and used my phone as a periscope, checking the view through the open stairs.

Nothing but car tires. Dammit. I'd have to go all the way up. And if our mark recognized me...

I yanked my hood up and wrapped my scarf tighter around my face, then climbed the remaining stairs at a casual pace. Don't act suspicious...

Stepping as softly as possible, I rounded the corner onto the landing.

A single glance made me stifle some particularly vile obscenities. Kane was walking away, nearly at the other stairwell. In seconds, he'd come face to face with Hellhound.

The mark was lurking well back, concealed between two cars.

I couldn't sneak up on him. As soon as I came out of the stairwell, he'd see me in his peripheral vision. And when he spotted Hellhound, he'd realize it was a setup.

I only had time to whisper, "Shit..."

Hellhound emerged.

The mark stiffened and snapped a glance around the parkade.

He spotted me, *dammit!*

Adrenaline exploded into my veins as he ducked down between the cars. I yanked out my trank pistol and shot the car where he'd disappeared.

The tiny *'pfft'* of the propellant was lost in the traffic noise, but the dart struck the bodywork with a high-pitched ping.

Kane and Hellhound dove in opposite directions, disappearing behind parked vehicles.

I stared at the place where the mark had vanished. Was that a dark huddled shape on the ground? Or only a murky shadow between the cars?

I thought he had collapsed.

But if I was wrong...

Kane and Hellhound were on the move, slipping from car to car to bracket the mark's last known position.

I scooted around the next parked car.

Dammit, it was now or never. The mark would have collapsed instantly if he had gotten a breath of the aerosolized tranquilizer, but he might not stay down for long. Five minutes was the absolute maximum, and if he hadn't gotten a full dose it might be a lot less.

Muttering a fast three-word prayer, I lunged around the last intervening parked car, trank pistol at the ready.

A flicker of movement catapulted my heart up into my throat. My finger snapped to the trigger, only to fall away as I sucked in a breath of relief. The mark was unconscious. The movement had been Kane.

An instant later Hellhound appeared, too.

"I'll get the car," Kane said, and ran.

"Got hand restraints?" Hellhound asked, crouching beside the fallen man.

"Dammit. In my grab-and-go bag, but not with me." I snapped a glance around us, looking for a substitute. "Here." I jerked a lace out of the mark's boot and handed it to Hellhound.

He trussed the man's wrists while I bound his ankles with the other bootlace.

Kane pulled up beside us and got out to open the rear door of his rental car. Hellhound and I manhandled the mark's limp body into the back seat, and moments later we were driving out of the parkade.

"Where are we going to take him?" I asked.

"Nowhere," Hellhound growled. "He's gonna tell us what we wanna know as soon's he wakes up." He seized the back of the man's neck and doubled him over with his head crammed against the back of my seat, then leaned his elbow on the man's back and gave me a feral grin.

Kane shot him a warning glance in the rearview mirror. "Remember, this isn't Department business. You'll be held responsible if you commit any crimes."

The mark groaned. Regaining consciousness already.

"*Any* crimes?" Hellhound's wolfish grin widened. "Hell, I'm plannin' on *many* crimes."

"John's right," I cautioned. "Let's not-"

"Get carried away?" Hellhound interrupted. "Fuck that.

If this asshole..." He drove the point of his elbow into the man's back. "...doesn't tell me what I wanna know, *he's* gonna get carried away. 'Cause he's never gonna walk again."

The man twitched and groaned.

"Ain't that right, asshole?" Hellhound elbowed the man once more.

Despite his threatening words, he was only striking our captive in soft-tissue areas and not using full force. Fortunately. One well-placed blow at that angle could leave the man a paraplegic.

The mark was mumbling now, frantic incomprehensible words muffled by his awkward position and the remainder of the drug in his system.

"What's that?" Hellhound mocked. "I can't hear ya." He jerked the mark upright.

Purple-faced, the clean-cut young man twitched and jerked against his bonds while jumbled words spilled from his mouth. I couldn't understand most of them, but one slurred phrase paralyzed me in my seat.

"Hang on," I quavered. "Did you just say, 'I'm a cop'?"

CHAPTER 20

Our captive nodded vigorously. "Cop."

"Search him," I snapped, but Hellhound was already rifling the man's pockets. Yanking out a wallet, Hellhound flipped it open and shuffled rapidly through its contents.

"Unn'r-cuv," the young man slurred, shaking his head. "Unn'r-cuv cop."

"Undercover? What's your name and badge number?" Kane demanded.

"'Tecv Cons'b Airk Reeis. Reeis," he repeated, his voice rising as if frustrated by his inability to speak clearly. "*Airk... Reeis.*" A garbled number followed, but he hadn't regained full control of his tongue yet and I didn't bother trying to decipher it.

I hit the speed dial for Tan.

"Tan."

"Who's Airk Reeis?" I demanded.

"What? Who is this?"

"It's Aydan Kelly. Who's Airk Reeis? He says he's an undercover cop."

"Underc..." Tan's voice hardened. "Do you mean Eric Regis?"

"That might have been what he said." Anger boiled up, but I kept my voice under control. "Did you assign him to follow us?"

"If you've harmed him..." Tan said dangerously.

"He's fine. Did you or didn't you assign him to follow us?"

"Let me speak to him."

"He can't talk right now." My rage erupted. "Do have *any* idea how much danger you put him in?"

"*Did you harm him?*" Tan's hard voice sent a shiver through me despite my anger.

"I told you, he's fine," I said in a voice as cold as his. "He's recovering from a tranquilizer and he should be able to talk in a minute or two. Why the hell did you have him follow us? You had to know we'd spot him, and we had no way of knowing which side he was on."

"I didn't know you'd spot him. And regardless of which side you thought he was on, you have to go by the book just like we do."

I had to stop and take a calming breath. When I spoke again, my voice sounded scary even to me as I repeated the words Kane had said to me long ago.

"*Sometimes we use a different book.*"

A short silence hovered on the line.

When Tan spoke again, his tone was mild. "May I speak to Eric now? It's okay if he's not quite coherent."

I sighed. Extracting my jackknife from my waist pouch, I passed it back to Hellhound. "Undo him."

The sharp blade sliced easily through the bootlaces, and I handed my phone to Regis. "Tan wants to talk to you."

He took the phone with both hands as though he didn't trust his muscle control yet, and spoke into it.

"Reejs." He listened for a moment, then slurred, "Yeah, fine. No... 'Kay. Later... 'Kay." He extended the phone to me. "He wantsa talk t'you again."

I accepted the device. "Kelly."

"Will Regis be impaired for long?"

"No. He'll be completely back to normal in another minute or so."

"Would you please take him back to his car and drop him off there?"

A glance at our surroundings told me that Kane had summed up the situation and reacted with his usual decisiveness. We were just rounding the corner onto the parkade's street again.

"We're already there," I said. "Do you have anybody else following us?"

"No."

I took that with a grain of salt. Tan obviously didn't trust us, so he could be lying. But probably not. I was pretty sure this little episode had given him a good scare.

Not as much of a scare as I'd had, though. My pulse was still galloping.

"Okay," I replied. "We'll drop him off and see you at the station in a few minutes." I disconnected and fell back in the seat, trying to dissipate my adrenaline with some calming yoga breaths.

Kane double-parked behind Regis's car and turned to face him. "How are you feeling?"

"Okay." Regis rolled his shoulders, wincing. "A little bruised."

"Sorry," Hellhound growled.

Regis eyed him as though questioning his sincerity, but apparently decided not to push the issue.

"We really are sorry," I said. "We thought you were one of the guys who'd attacked LaVonda. We weren't expecting the good guys."

"No harm done." He hesitated. "When did you spot

me?"

"When you ran that yellow light a few blocks from hotel," Kane replied. "And I caught you craning your neck to keep us in sight when those tall vehicles moved between us."

Regis grimaced. "I knew I was taking a chance, but we didn't have any other cars available to lead or trail you."

"And we're about as cautious as they come." Kane gave him a smile. "Stay safe out there."

Regis nodded ruefully and let himself out.

As we drove away, I drew a deep breath and eased it out slowly. "God, that could have been bad."

"Not really," Kane disagreed. "We only wanted to question him. You wouldn't have shot him with real bullets; and you..." He made eye contact with Hellhound in the mirror. "...wouldn't have injured him without giving him a chance to identify himself and explain."

Neither Hellhound nor I responded. Kane might be right about Hellhound, but I was afraid his faith in me was misplaced.

We arrived at the police station without further incident. Hellhound still hadn't spoken, and when we got out of the car he strode ahead of us, shoulders hunched and hands sunk deep in his parka pockets.

Kane and I exchanged a worried glance, and I trotted ahead to link my arm through Arnie's. He gave me a brief smile that didn't reach his eyes.

"Okay?" I asked softly.

He nodded, but didn't reply.

We had only a short wait in the station before Tan ushered us into a small conference room. As soon as the door closed behind us, Hellhound burst out, "When did they take her?"

"Around nineteen hundred," Tan replied. "You'll see the timestamp on the security footage." His voice tightened with frustration. "We got there half an hour too late. Then, by the time we got access to the security camera footage..." He trailed off, pressing buttons on a projector. "Here we go. She checked in at eighteen-oh-five."

Security footage rolled, showing the timestamp in the lower left corner. LaVonda hurried into the hotel lobby, duffel bag slung on her shoulder. Her movements were jerky and she repeatedly wiped her palms on her thighs as though drying sweat, even though she wore no coat in the frigid temperatures.

As she moved toward the front desk, Tan paused the playback. "The first man came in right behind her. Recognize him?"

I squinted at the grainy image. "No. John? Arnie? Do you?"

They both shook their heads, and Tan restarted the footage. We watched the well-dressed thirtyish man take his place behind LaVonda, giving her the usual space one would allow a stranger in a lineup. He was towing a small piece of luggage, like the ones airline personnel used.

"Any identification on the luggage?" Kane asked.

"The picture quality isn't good enough," Tan replied.

Posture relaxed, the man waited quietly, letting his gaze roam around the lobby as though bored.

"Here's the next one," Tan said as a younger man wandered in. With his attention riveted to his cellphone, he meandered over to one of the large upholstered chairs and sank into it, ignoring everyone.

LaVonda appeared to be having a discussion with the clerk, tension vibrating in every line of her body.

"It's hard to check in with cash," Tan said. "They wanted a credit card; but she told them she'd lost everything in the fire. The desk clerk had heard about the apartment fire the night before; and LaVonda said she needed a place to stay long-term. She paid cash in advance for a month, so they made an exception."

Despite her obvious discomfort, LaVonda had thought ahead. When the time came to pay, she withdrew a wad of cash from the pocket of her sweatpants, not from the duffel bag.

"Okay, here we go," Tan said. "Just as she's getting her cardkey, the third guy walks in. I think the guy with the phone must have cued him so he could arrive at exactly the right moment. LaVonda gets her cardkey and moves off to the elevator, and the third guy follows her like he belongs there. The guy with the luggage steps up and engages the desk clerk, and the guy with the phone stays on lookout."

He toggled to a view of the hotel corridor and we watched LaVonda step out of the elevator and hurry down the hallway almost at a run. The man behind her maintained a brisk stride but didn't try to catch up. When she let herself into her room, he walked by without glancing in that direction.

"Confirming her room number," Kane murmured. "You're right, these guys are professionals."

The man continued to the end of the hall and stepped into the vending machine alcove. A few moments later he emerged with a bag of chips and strolled back down the hall.

Tan toggled back to the lobby view. "It worked out perfectly for them. The hotel fills up rooms in sequence. So the guy that comes in immediately after LaVonda gets the room beside her."

The first man finished checking in and accepted his cardkey. Without a glance at his co-conspirator with the cellphone, he headed for the elevator.

Tan paused the footage. "He met up with the guy with the chips and they both went into the room he just rented. The guy with the phone rented his own room right afterward, and got placed across the hall from LaVonda."

He fast-forwarded through some footage. "Okay, here we go. They're all in their rooms, probably listening for the sound of her door. LaVonda orders room service just like you guessed..."

We watched a porter wheel a white-draped cart down the hall. I tensed and leaned forward, dreading what was to come.

The porter knocked on LaVonda's door. After exchanging a few words through the closed door, he unloaded a tray and placed it beside her door before wheeling the cart away.

"She's smart," Hellhound muttered, his gaze glued to the screen. The tension in his shoulders was visible even under his bulky parka. "Waitin' for him to leave."

"As it turned out, she would have been better off to trust him," Tan replied.

The footage advanced, showing the empty hallway and the loaded tray outside LaVonda's door.

"She waits for the corridor to clear..." Tan's play-by-play was beginning to drive me nuts, but I clenched my teeth and watched in silence. "...and as soon as she opens her door, bam!"

The door across the hall flew open and a man lunged out,

hitting LaVonda's half-open door and shoving her inside.

"*Asshole!*" Hellhound barked, making me jump. "I'm gonna-"

I grabbed his clenched fist, silencing him before he could utter the intent to commit a crime.

Tan eyed us without comment before returning to his play-by-play. "...And thirty seconds later, he's out of there. He must have injected her with something." His voice went just a little too casual. "Like your fast-acting tranquilizer."

I shot him a hard look, but he was watching the security footage with seemingly intense concentration.

Transferring my attention back to the footage, I watched the man step out of LaVonda's room, pick up the tray, and return to his own room with it.

"He took her cardkey," Tan said. "And whatever he gave her must last for a while, because they took their time getting back to her."

"Or he might have restrained her," Kane said, earning a black look from Hellhound.

Tan nodded, fast-forwarding footage. "Okay, this is twenty minutes later. Guy One and Guy Two go outside. They must get Guy Two togged out in a parking lot outside the range of the cameras, because we don't have any footage until Guy One brings his car around."

He switched to a view of the entrance. "Guy One gets out a wheelchair and transfers Guy Two into it."

The footage showed Guy One struggling to transfer a tall bulky blanket-wrapped figure from the front seat of the car into the wheelchair. The figure looked limp, but when Guy One tottered during the transfer, the not-so-helpless figure's foot shot out to save them. Moments later they came through the lobby, the blanket-wrapped figure anonymous in sunglasses and a colourful tuque, head lolling forward.

"Meanwhile," Tan said, "Guy Three goes into LaVonda's room and meets them there." He toggled the camera view. "They put her in the same getup Guy Two wore, and a few minutes later... there they go."

We watched Guy One wheel out the motionless blanket-swaddled figure wearing the distinctive tuque. Guys Two and Three disappeared into the stairwell carrying LaVonda's duffel bag and Guy One's luggage.

"There's no surveillance camera in that stairwell so we lost them there," Tan explained. "But it's an exit. The access doors to all the floors in that stairwell are locked, so the only place they could have gone is outside."

"That's not as secure as the hotel would like to think," Kane observed.

"True," Tan agreed. "But I'm willing to bet they left. They got what they came for." He toggled the camera views again so we could watch Guy One wheel LaVonda calmly out through the hotel lobby and transfer her limp body into his car.

"Did ya get their plates?" Hellhound demanded. "They hadta have at least two cars."

"No," Tan said regretfully. "They didn't use the hotel's parking so they weren't on camera; and you saw how the car that picked them up in the portico had its license plates obscured by that corner of the blanket hanging out of the trunk. At least we got the rental sticker, though. We're following up with the rental company, but it's taking a while because we don't know when they rented the car."

"And they wouldn't have used their real names," Kane said.

Tan nodded. "You're right; the credit cards they used for

their rooms were stolen identities, and there was no match in any of the car rental depots anywhere in Regina. I even checked with the Moose Jaw depots. So they must have used a different set of stolen identities to rent their cars."

"They weren't worried about showing their faces on the security cameras, though," I added. "I wonder why. They had to know they'd be under surveillance."

"They likely thought nobody would ever check," Kane said. "Except for the two seconds it took to push into LaVonda's room, they didn't do anything suspicious on camera. And they likely guessed that nobody would miss LaVonda, or know where to start looking if they did."

"Enough with the fuckin' theories!" Hellhound snapped. "They got LaVonda! They've *had* her for..." He consulted his watch with an angry jerk of his wrist. "...three an' a half fuckin' hours!" As I reached over to take his hand, his shoulders seemed to shrink and he stared at the tabletop. "Maybe I oughta hope she's already dead. With what those fuckin' trolls were threatenin'..."

I clutched his hand, my throat tightening. What would be worse? Losing his sister to death only hours after finding her; or finding her alive but horribly tortured?

CHAPTER 21

"Are you sure you don't have any idea who LaVonda's kidnappers are?" Constable Tan asked.

"Positive," I said, and Kane and Hellhound concurred. "But we're pretty sure they're professionals," I added. "Probably not random internet trolls."

"Right," Tan agreed. "I think this has nothing to do with LaVonda Rainey's blog post, and everything to do with Kathy Helmand's past. A quarter of a million dollars is a lot of money even now. Thirty years ago it was a lot more. If she's got their money, I'm betting somebody has been holding a grudge for a long time."

"But it might be her own money, just like she says," Hellhound protested. "An' those guys weren't even born thirty years ago."

"No, but they may have bosses who were," Kane said.

"And we need to find out who they are," Tan said grimly. "Since there was no evidence left in their hotel rooms, we're pinning our hopes on the car rental agency. Frankly..." He hesitated. "I don't have a lot of hope for that. Of course I've got a BOLO out on LaVonda, the men, and the car, but..."

A grim silence settled.

Tan spoke first. "Agent Kelly... I'd like to ask you a question. Off the record."

"Okay..." I said slowly.

"When you said you use 'a different book'..." Tan's gaze

searched my face. "Until last night I'd never heard of your Department. Is its mandate really that different from the police?"

I glanced at Kane, hoping he'd field the question.

He said nothing. I was on my own.

"Um... yes and no." I met Tan's intent gaze. "As the police, you're the face of law enforcement for the public. Your mandate is to keep the peace and catch criminals so they can receive due process through the judicial system. The Department..." I hesitated, trying to find the right words. "Well, we also keep the peace and bring criminals to justice. It's just that... sometimes we *are* the justice."

Tan frowned. "Judge, jury, and executioner."

I didn't have a response to that, but fortunately Kane spoke up. "Only in extreme circumstances. It does happen that way sometimes, but there are checks and balances to ensure that agents uphold the law with as little collateral damage as possible."

I held my best poker face, trying not to think of my body count.

Tan digested our explanation for a few moments. It didn't seem to be sitting well.

"I called your Director," he said.

The apparent non sequitur sent a tingle of foreboding down my spine. "I know," I replied.

"The Department won't get involved."

I nodded, bracing myself.

"Do you have access to any other resources personally?"

And there it was.

I wasn't surprised. My mind had already gone down that path, and the naked pleading in Arnie's eyes wrenched my heart.

I sighed. "Send me the footage. And we'll issue some fake news saying that LaVonda was hospitalized after the attack on her apartment and later died of her injuries. The guys who have her will know we're lying, but at least it'll take the rest of the internet trolls out of the equation." I gave Tan an email address I could access with my phone, and a moment later he looked up from his laptop.

"Done."

We eyed each other in silence for a moment.

"So why did you really have Regis follow us?" I asked. "Do you still think we're trying to harm LaVonda?"

Tan blew out a breath. "I don't know. The men who abducted her were professionals. So are you. I believe that you're an agent, but you're currently barred from duty and we're getting mixed messages from your superiors. And apparently your idea of justice is quite a bit different than mine." He shot a wary glance at Kane and Hellhound. "Plus, I have no assurances about your companions other than your word that they used to be agents..." His gaze coasted over Hellhound's disreputable appearance. "...or something. Your Department wouldn't say anything about either of them, except that they're civilians."

I hid the tightening of my shoulders. Kane was right. The Department wouldn't protect us.

Tan met Hellhound's expressionless gaze. "And as a civilian, you just committed assault on a police officer, kidnapping, and forcible confinement. You uttered threats of bodily harm and admitted the intent to commit, and I quote, '*many crimes*'." Tan's eyes narrowed. "Seems like you're well on your way to achieving that goal."

Cold fear froze me to my chair.

I was opening my mouth in the hope that something

useful would come out when Kane's smooth baritone broke in. "It was my understanding that Regis wasn't going to press charges."

Tan's lips tightened. "He isn't."

"So, do we have a problem, then?" Kane inquired mildly.

"How should I know?" Tan snapped. "You could be as well-meaning as you say, or you could be completely snowing me; and if you're as good as I think you are, I won't know until it's too late." His hand squeezed into a fist. "But I'm out of options. You're LaVonda's best hope."

My throat closed.

When I didn't respond, Kane spoke again. "We understand and sympathize with your situation. For what it's worth, our only goals are to help you solve this and protect LaVonda. So... can you let us search the hotel rooms?"

Tan hesitated, frowning at the table.

Still trying to decide whether to trust us.

He sighed. "Only if I accompany you; and only if you report any new findings to me immediately."

"Of course," Kane said, his voice deep and reassuring. "Can we go over right away?"

Tan rose. "I'll meet you there in ten minutes."

I hid the trembling of my knees as best I could while we walked out.

As soon as we were back in our car, I checked my watch. "It's nearly ten PM in Alberta with the time zone difference. I want to get Spider working on this ASAP."

Arnie touched my shoulder. "Are ya sure about usin' the Department, Aydan? Dermott's gonna crucify ya when he finds out. If ya wanna step back, I'll understand."

"Hell, no." I gave him a twisted smile. "You're right, the

shit's probably going to hit the fan; but I don't see any other way to do this. The police have done all they can, and it's stupid to not use the Department's resources when we know they're so much better. I couldn't live with myself if I didn't try."

"Thanks, darlin'. I owe ya." Hellhound turned to Kane. "Cap, same goes for you. Ya got Daniel to think about. Even if ya don't do anythin' wrong yourself, you'll go down with us if this goes to hell. Ya oughta get out now, while ya still can."

"You already know the answer to that," Kane said. "You're my brother. I'm in."

Arnie cleared his throat but his voice came out husky anyway. "Thanks."

I tapped Spider's secure email address into my phone. "I'll send the footage to him right away and see if he can run it through the facial-recognition database. And maybe he can get something from that luggage tag." I pressed the 'Send' button. "Done."

"He prob'ly ain't there," Arnie muttered. "It's Friday night an' he'll be on Christmas holidays."

Hiding my misgivings, I shook my head. "Are you kidding? Even when he's not in the office, he always monitors his email."

We hadn't even made it out of the parking lot when my phone vibrated with an incoming call. I flashed the screen at Hellhound with a smile.

"See? There he is already." I hit the 'Accept' button. "Hi, Spider."

"Hi, Aydan." His voice was edged with worry. "It sounds like things are getting complicated out there."

"They are. But this is all unofficial, so it's okay if you don't want to get involved."

"Of course I'll help; I'm just afraid that you're doing something dangerous. I don't want anything to happen to you."

"It's okay," I assured him. "John and Arnie are with me, and I already talked to Stemp. He's okay with it."

"Oh, thank goodness. How can I help?"

"Arnie's sister has been abducted."

"Ohmigod, that's awful! What happened?"

I explained as concisely as I could. When I had finished, Spider repeated, "That's *awful!* Poor LaVonda. And poor Hellhound. Tell him I'll run the men through the facial recognition program right away. I'll call you the instant I get a hit. And while I'm waiting, I'll get the car rental company's records; and run image enhancement on that luggage tag. I probably won't get anything from it; but you never know. And I'll start a firestorm on social media about how internet trolls killed LaVonda. It'll go viral for sure. Oh, and I'll start calling hotels in Regina to see if they have any wheelchair-bound guests tonight. If these guys are still in the city, they might try to bring LaVonda into a hotel the same way they took her out."

"Thanks, Spider. I hate to make you go back to the office tonight-"

"No problem," he interrupted blithely. "I'm still at the office. I was supposed to clock out at eight, but I was following a hot lead. I can easily stay a bit later for your stuff."

I let out a breath of relief. "Oh, that's great. Dermott will be long gone so you should be able to fly under the radar."

"Um... no." Spider lowered his voice. "He's still here. There's something big going on. That's why I was working late."

"Oh." I hesitated. "Well, he's probably too busy to bother you, then. But if he finds out about this, tell him I didn't give you any details so you assumed it was official business."

"I'm not going to let you take the blame! And anyway, it shouldn't be an issue if Stemp said it was okay."

"That was unofficial. Stemp could get in trouble, too, if anybody finds out. Dermott can't hate me more than he already does, so I've got nothing to lose. But I don't want you to go down with me."

"Aydan!" I imagined Spider's boyish features flushed with indignation, and I couldn't help smiling as he lectured me. "I take responsibility for my own actions! This is one hundred percent my choice. And Dermott can't say I'm wasting Department time or resources, because I've been officially off-shift for nearly two hours and I was about to go home for the holidays anyway. So he can just..."

Spider hesitated, and my smile widened while I waited to find out whether he could overcome his innate niceness and say what he really meant.

"...deal with it," he finished lamely, making me suppress a chuckle.

"You're the best," I said warmly. "Thank you."

"You're welcome. Talk to you soon." He disconnected.

I eased back in my seat as we pulled into the hotel parking lot. "Well, that's in good hands. Now let's hope we can find something Tan missed in these hotel rooms."

We found nothing.

A water-spotted bathtub and damp towel in LaVonda's

room indicated that she'd had a shower. The pillows were propped against the headboard as though she'd tucked herself into bed to watch TV while waiting for her meal; but there was no sign of a struggle. Tan was right; her kidnappers must have given her a fast-acting sedative.

The men's rooms showed even fewer signs of occupancy. Someone had sat on the bed in one room, barely wrinkling the bedspread. In the other, the only thing out of place was LaVonda's empty food tray on the table.

"He ate her supper," I muttered. "Talk about adding insult to injury..." Inspiration struck, and I said, "Fingerprints" at the same time as Kane.

We turned expectantly to Tan.

"We seized the glass and cutlery," he said. "But now we have to eliminate the fingerprints of the kitchen staff; and of course nobody remembers who prepared this meal so we're fingerprinting them all. It'll take a long time." He sighed. "We've also swabbed for a DNA sample, but it'll take weeks to process. At least it'll serve as evidence if we can arrest a suspect." He glanced at his watch. "Have you finished here? I need to get back to the P.O."

"Yes. Thank you for your time," Kane said.

We followed Tan out into the hallway. "Let me know as soon as you find out anything from your other sources," he said. "And I mean *anything*; any time of the day or night. Call me or Corporal Whittle."

"We'll keep you updated," I promised.

He turned away, then turned back. "By the way, we've identified the gunman from the apartment fire. Leroy Marcus Ullman, twenty-five years old, from Winnipeg. Prior convictions for weapons, assault, and a laundry list of lesser charges. Word was that he was a prospect but nobody knows which gang he was courting. Does that ring any bells with you?"

We all shook our heads, and he gave us a resigned nod and strode off down the hallway.

As soon as the elevator doors closed behind him, Hellhound said, "I wanna question the staff. See if anybody saw anythin'."

Kane and I exchanged a meaningful glance.

"That's a good idea," Kane replied. "I'm sure Tan spoke with quite a few of the staff already, but there might be others he missed. Let's split up so we can accomplish more. Aydan and I will go down and talk to the manager and start coordinating interviews, and you check the hotel layout and that exit stair."

Hellhound eyed him from under lowered brows. "Cap..." he growled warningly. "Don't try an' *handle* me."

I took his arm and hugged it to me. "Arnie, we're not trying to handle you, I promise. We really do need to check out the rest of the hotel. You're good at that, and you're a little too intimidating to do staff interviews. We want people to relax and talk to us, not lose sphincter control and shit their pants."

His scowl faded. "Ya sure got a way with words, darlin'." He dropped a kiss on my forehead. "Awright, I'll do the recon, an' you go work your people-magic. Meet ya in the lobby when I'm done, prob'ly 'bout twenty minutes. If ya ain't there, I'll call your cell." He strode down the hall.

As he disappeared into the exit stairwell, Kane turned to me with a smile. "Well done."

I grinned. "Sometimes tactlessness works. Come on, let's go talk to the manager before Arnie changes his mind."

When we reconvened in the hotel lobby twenty minutes later, my own frustration was mirrored on Hellhound's face.

"I got nothin'," he growled. "You?"

I blew out a breath. "Nothing. The shift changed at eight. Everyone on the earlier shift has gone home, and of course we don't have the authority to get their home addresses or phone numbers. We'll have to come back tomorrow."

"*Tomorrow?*" Hellhound's voice rumbled with the suppressed violence of a volcano about to erupt. "That's too fuckin' late! They've had her four an' a half fuckin' hours already, an' who knows what they're doin'-"

My phone vibrated, and he bit off his incipient tirade as I turned the screen toward him to show Spider's caller ID.

I hit the 'Accept' button. "Hi, Spider."

"Hi, I've got names for you," he said rapidly. "Guy One is Andrew Walter McKenna, Guy Two is Brandon Alastair Karsten, and they're both from Winnipeg. I haven't found Guy Three yet."

I repeated the names aloud for Kane's and Hellhound's benefit, then added, "What's the connection? Who are they?"

"Nothing definitive. They've both been arrested multiple times for various offenses ranging from theft to assault but they've never been convicted. Right now I'm chasing a rumour..." Spider's voice faded as though his attention had been diverted. A moment later he lowered his voice and talked faster. "...they might be connected to Richard Fitzgerald and the family in Winnipeg."

"Which family?"

"The Family, with a capital F. They're like Winnipeg's

very own mafia; all kinds of shady deals and organized crime that never seems to be successfully prosecuted. Richard Fitzgerald has been the head of the Family for over thirty years, since the previous head died. Rumour was that Fitzgerald killed the previous head and took over, but no charges were ever brought."

"Shit. That's bad news, but it probably fits with what we've found out. Anything else?"

"Fitzgerald owns several companies and Karsten and McKenna are both managers, but the companies are squeaky-clean and *oh-crap!*" The line went dead.

Worry boiled up like a threatening cloud as I lowered the phone, frowning at it.

"What?" Hellhound demanded. "What's wrong?"

My voice came out as tight as the knot in my guts. "I think Spider just got busted."

CHAPTER 22

"What do you mean?" Kane snapped. "What did Webb say?"

I repeated the conversation and its abrupt ending. "It sounded like somebody had just walked in on him."

"Somebody like Dermott," Kane clarified.

"Yeah." My word came out on a sigh. "I hope Spider's okay."

"We can't do anything to change that situation," Kane said. "We'll just have to hope for the best."

"I guess. I just feel awful about it." I sighed again and refocused. "Okay, so, you guys grew up in Winnipeg. Have you ever heard of Richard Fitzgerald or the Family with a capital F? Mafia-type family?"

Both men shook their heads. "We were too young," Kane said. "Even if I had heard something as a teenager, I wouldn't have paid attention. And after we joined the army at eighteen, we were shipped all over for training and deployment. I didn't keep track of local news."

"Arnie, anything in your memory?" I asked, turning to him.

He frowned, closing his eyes, and we waited in silence. His frown deepened. "Fuck, I dunno. Like Kane says, we were too young; an' then we were in the army. The name Fitzgerald ain't ringin' a bell; an' I'd hafta replay every single fuckin' movie to find a word like 'Family'. How many times in your life d'ya hear that word?"

I slumped. "I guess you're right, it's too generic."

He opened his eyes, still frowning. "I'll keep thinkin' about it, though. Somethin' might come up."

"Thanks." I squeezed his hand. "I guess I'd better call Tan right away, just in case this is all the information we're going to get."

I punched in Tan's number and updated him, my spirits lifting slightly at his gratified tone. Maybe he wouldn't be quite so suspicious of us now.

When I hung up, Hellhound demanded, "So what're we gonna do? Now we know who these assholes are, but how the hell are we gonna find 'em?"

"Spider will call me back, I'm sure of it," I said, even though I wasn't sure at all. "He'll find a way to trace them."

"You're right," Kane agreed. "Let's give him some time. Meanwhile, it's nearly midnight and both of you look exhausted-"

"I'm fine," Hellhound interrupted.

"Aydan is exhausted," Kane said firmly, invoking the only argument that was likely to sway Arnie at that moment. "And she likely needs to eat again. We don't know when Webb will call back, or if he even will tonight; so we should get something to eat and then go back to the hotel. When Webb calls we might have to move fast, and we need to be as rested as possible."

Arnie let out a breath. "Guess you're right. We oughta go back to the hotel an' feed Princess, too. She'll think everybody's abandoned her."

Guilt squeezed my heart. I had completely forgotten about Princess.

We stopped at a 24-hour Subway restaurant, where Kane

ordered a healthy veggie-laden roast beef sandwich on whole wheat while Hellhound indulged in a foot-long pepperoni pizza sub with double meat, double cheese, and a heart attack thrown in for free. I hit middle ground with ham on multigrain and all the veggies, plus hot peppers, sub sauce, and extra mustard.

As we were heading for the door with our loaded bags, my phone vibrated again.

I nearly dropped my sandwich in my hurry to answer. "Spider? Are you okay? What happened?"

"Hi again. I'm fine. Sorry about that." Just as I was beginning to relax, he added, "Dermott caught me."

Tension seized me all over again. "Shit! What happened?"

"Oh, the usual. He yelled and swore and kicked me out of the building." Spider was trying to sound breezy, but his voice trembled.

"And what else?" I demanded.

"And nothing else. I just hate it when he yells at me..." He sighed. "I'm such a wimp; I hate conflict. But at least he didn't fire me this time."

"So you're okay? Nothing bad happened?"

"I'm fine. And I can log in from my command centre at home, so as soon as I get there I'll get back to work."

"Are you sure you want to do that? What if Dermott catches you again?"

Spider laughed. "As if. I *created* the network security at Sirius. Nobody's going to catch me unless Dermott actually barges into my house and reads over my shoulder. And even then he probably wouldn't know what he was looking at."

I smiled. "I would never question your computer skills. But if you give us information and we act on it, it'll be pretty easy to trace the source back to you. I just don't want to get you in trouble."

He hesitated, but when he spoke again his voice was firm. "Thanks, Aydan, but I honestly don't see how anything I'm doing would violate the Department's ethics policy or security protocols. The Regina police asked for your help, you're working with them, and I'm not jeopardizing any other missions to help you. This is all on my own time. I'll have to drop your job if something urgent comes up in the Department and I get called back in, but I'm not doing anything wrong by helping you."

I let out a breath I hadn't realized I'd been holding. "You really are the best," I assured him. "Thanks. Oh, and they identified the dead gunman from LaVonda's apartment. Maybe you can find a connection between him and the other guys you found." I gave him the gunman's details and added, "When you get home, tell Linda I'm sorry we're monopolizing you on your holidays."

"No problem, she'd be mad at me if I *didn't* help you. Talk to you soon."

When we got back to the hotel room a few minutes later, Princess met us at the door with disconsolate yowls. Her complaints subsided to conversational mews and purring when Hellhound filled her bowl with kibble and stroked her while she ate, murmuring extravagant compliments.

I laid my sandwich bag on the table and made for the bathroom, only to stop short. "Oh, for..."

Hellhound looked up. "What, darlin'?"

"I guess somebody got bored." I cocked a thumb at the bathroom, which was completely paved in shredded toilet paper. Only a few sad tatters clung to what had once been a full roll.

Hellhound came over and surveyed the destruction. "Guess she made her point. That ain't too bad, though. We're just lucky she didn't decide to take a piss in the middle a' the bed."

"I'm sure she's saving up some lovely surprise," I muttered, and waded into Toilet-Paper Wonderland.

A few minutes later we sat around the table munching on our sandwiches. Hellhound looked over at me with a smile that looked forced, but at least he was trying.

"Now I know why ya hadta wash your hands before ya got started."

I slurped a dribble of mustard-infused sub sauce off my wrist. "Yep. I'm going to need a shower after I finish this. The best things in life are messy."

His voice coasted down into a deep sexy rasp as he watched me lick my fingers. "Ya got that right, darlin'. I'm gonna need a cold shower after watchin' ya eat that."

"If you two would like to be alone..." Kane was smiling, but I wasn't sure whether I'd heard or imagined an edge in his voice.

Jealousy? Uh-oh.

"Yeah, I need to be alone with my sandwich," I quipped. "We're having a short but extremely passionate affair."

Both men chuckled and my tension eased.

Kane affected an expression of grave concern. "Just remember, those short impulsive affairs usually end in heartburn."

"Argh!" I threw a wadded-up paper napkin at him.

A faint buzzing sound emanated from Kane's direction, and he took out his phone and accepted the call. "Kane."

At the caller's first words, he tensed, motioning us closer and toggling his phone to speaker.

An unfamiliar voice crackled through the speaker. "...and Kathy won't get hurt."

Ice flooded my veins.

Kane's knuckles were white on the phone, but his voice was steady. "Who is this, and how did you get this number?"

"Never mind who. We know you have the bag of money. Bring it to a drop point and we'll trade you for Kathy."

My hand found Hellhound's, his fingers stiff in my grasp.

"Let me talk to her," Kane demanded.

Rustling floated over the line, followed by a rough command from farther away from the speaker. "Talk, bitch!" A moment of silence was followed by a slap and a cry of pain. "I said, *talk!*" the man snarled. Another slap was echoed by a whimper.

"*STOP!*" Hellhound bellowed, and Kane made a sharp gesture to silence him.

"She doesn't wanna talk," the kidnapper said. "You want me to make her?"

"No!" Kane said hurriedly. "Just hold the phone so I can talk to her."

Another rustle preceded the man's voice, speaking as though from a distance. "Go ahead."

"LaVonda," Kane said gently. "This is John. I know you're scared right now, but I need to know it's really you. Will you please talk to me?"

"I tol' them... they've already got... all th'money... but they... won' b'lieve me." Despite the slurring and the breathy hitches of suppressed sobs, there was no mistaking LaVonda's beautiful voice.

Hellhound's grip nearly crushed my hand.

The kidnapper came back on the line. "Bring the bag to the northwest corner of Broad and Saskatchewan in half an hour. Come alone. No cops, no tricks, or she's dead."

Just before the connection clicked off, LaVonda's voice rose in a frantic shout.

"*Don't come!*"

In the silence that ensued, I wasted only a second staring wide-eyed at the other two before yanking out my phone and punching in Spider's number.

As soon as he answered, I blurted, "It's Aydan. A ransom call just came in on John's personal cell but the number was blocked. Can you trace it?"

"Did he hit #57?"

I shot a look at Kane. "Did you hit-"

"Yes," he snapped.

"He did," I told Spider.

"On it! It'll take a while..." The high-speed clicking of computer keys took over the line.

"How long?" I demanded.

"I don't know, could be hours..." He trailed off, still typing at warp speed.

"But last summer when you tracked John's cell phone, you got back to us in minutes," I protested.

"That was the Department's locator for agents' personal cell phones," he said, his voice tight with stress. "This time I have to go into the records available to law enforcement, find the call, trace it back to the provider, get access to their database, cross-reference the number to the SIM card-"

"It's okay," I interrupted. "Sorry, I'll let you work."

"I'll call you as soon as I have something." The line went dead.

Kane had been entering our destination in his phone while Spider and I talked.

"Dammit!" he exploded. "We have ten minutes' travel to

the drop point from here. Call Tan."

"*No cops!*" Hellhound's voice was just below a shout. "They said no cops, so don't call the fuckin' cops!"

"Tan will be discreet," Kane snapped. "And we need the manpower. Hurry up and call him, Aydan."

Hellhound's hand pinned mine. "No! I ain't riskin' it!"

"Arnie," Kane said gently. "We can't expect the kidnappers to negotiate in good faith. You know how-"

"No! No fuckin' cops!" He locked eyes with Kane. "We're gonna do this the way they want."

Kane tried again. "Arnie, listen. We need more people. Tan could have a team in place-"

Hellhound interrupted, "An' if the kidnappers spot 'em, or even hear a siren, they'll kill her. No fuckin' way!"

"They won't kill her," Kane snapped. "If they intended to kill her, they would have already. They need her as a bargaining chip for the money they think we have."

"Why the hell would they think we got money?" Hellhound demanded. "They got the cash when they grabbed her. An' where the hell are we gonna get a bag a' money this time a' the night? They didn't even say how much they wanted!"

His voice was rising in agitation, and Princess flinched and scurried into her carrier.

Inspiration flared in my mind. "They didn't say how much, because they don't know. They're fishing. The grenade-launcher guy must have been watching when we brought LaVonda out of the apartment, and we had two bags with us."

"Shit, Princess's carrier! They think we got another quarter mil." Hellhound groaned. "Fuck, they ain't gonna believe it was just-"

"We don't want them to," Kane interrupted. "As long as they think there's more money, they'll keep LaVonda alive. We'll stuff the carrier with something and put some cash on top where it's visible in case we have to show it to them. We'll keep control of the bag until we can secure LaVonda."

I jumped up and hurried over to rummage through my grab-and-go bag. "I have one of those little bugs that doubles as a locator. We can stick it in the cash so we'll be able to track them after they take the bag."

"As long as we control the bag, LaVonda will be fine," Kane said. "The biggest risk is if they get the bag from us. Then they have no reason to keep her alive." His voice rose. "And going to the drop zone without backup is a sure-fire way to lose control of the damn bag!"

"They said 'no cops'," I argued on Arnie's behalf. "It's a big risk-"

Kane gave an inarticulate growl. "Not you, too! That's emotional thinking! Be logical, Aydan! You know I'm right!"

I clenched my fists in my hair. "No, I *don't* know you're right! I don't have a clue! LaVonda might end up dead no matter what we do, and you can't know what the kidnappers are thinking. Are you really willing to take a chance and end up with LaVonda's death on your conscience?"

I had expected an angry reply, but when Kane spoke again his voice was quiet. "If LaVonda dies, it will be on my conscience regardless of whether I'm right or wrong."

"We're outta time." Arnie's voice was cold and hard, and when I glanced over at him, the personality I had named 'The Killer' stared out of his eyes. "No cops, an' that's final."

As Kane opened his mouth to argue again, Arnie added, "I get it, they might kill her anyway. But it ain't gonna be because I didn't do what they said. I'll carry the bag."

Kane's shoulders sagged. "All right, we'll do it your way. But we still need to call the police, to get them to route all units away from the area. Aydan, call Tan."

This time Arnie didn't argue. He and Kane began strategizing while I hit the speed dial.

"Tan."

"It's Aydan. We've had a ransom demand for LaVonda, and we have to make a drop at the northwest corner of Broad and Saskatchewan in..." I checked my watch. Time was ticking away. "...twenty minutes. The kidnappers said no police, so would you please keep all cars and uniforms away from the area starting now?"

"I'll try, but that's only two blocks away from the P.O."

"Shit!"

"We'll try to stay away, but we'll still have to respond if we get any calls in the area. Let me know as soon as you're clear."

I hissed out a short breath. "I will." I hung up and faced Arnie and John. "The drop zone is only two blocks away from the police station. They'll do their best to avoid it, but they can't promise anything."

Kane nodded grimly. "We saw that on the map. Here's the plan. We'll take both cars to the Casino Regina..." As he laid everything out in a few short sentences, my stomach churned with fear.

"But what's stopping them from just driving up, shooting Arnie, and grabbing the bag?" I demanded. "That's what I'd do." Both men frowned at me and I hurriedly amended, "I mean, if I were them. Why would they even bother trying to trade for LaVonda? Arnie's a sitting duck out there on the street corner."

"I got my vest," Hellhound growled. "If they're gonna do

a driveby, they'll be shootin' for centre a' body mass, so I'll be fine. An' when they stop to grab the bag outta my cold dead hands, you'll nail 'em."

"But if they had a grenade launcher, there's a pretty good chance they'll have fully-automatic weapons, too," I argued. "And your vest won't protect your head and neck. They'll kill you, then they'll find out we faked the money, and then they'll kill LaVonda, too. And what if they don't even have her with them?"

"Then they're gonna wish they did. Come on, we're outta time. Let's get that carrier stuffed an' hit the road."

CHAPTER 23

When we reconvened on the main level of the parkade south of the casino, I tried one last appeal.

"Arnie, just let me park across the street with you so I'm closer. What if they attack you before I get there?"

"I'll drive the long way around," Hellhound promised. "I won't get there before you're in place. An' I got the trank dart right here." He slipped his hand out of his pocket to display it. "Even if I can't stab 'em with it, I'll bust it so everybody around me passes out. That'll give ya enough time to get to me."

"I should carry the bag," Kane objected. "They'll be expecting me, and they know my voice. We don't want them to get suspicious."

Hellhound's chin went up. "No. I'm doin' this. An' I ain't gonna talk to 'em on the phone, you are. We're both wearin' parkas with hoods an' we're close enough to the same size. They'll never know."

"But-" Kane began.

"Too late to change the plan." Helhound's face was stony, his jaw jutting. "Do the phone check."

Kane handed his cell phone to Hellhound along with two burner phones, and we each dialled one of them. With the connections open between us and tested, Hellhound turned to me.

"Don't use your phone while you're walkin' unless it's an

emergency. They'll be watchin' for people talkin' on the phone."

"I won't. But people are always on their phones anyway, so it likely won't matter." I flung my arms around him, causing a burst of static from the phone speaker. "Be safe." I kissed him. "I love you."

"Love ya, too, darlin'. You be safe, too." He held me for a moment before disengaging to offer his hand to Kane. "Thanks."

Kane gripped his hand, his jaw taut. "You're welcome. Be safe."

"You, too." Hellhound got into his car and drove off.

I watched his car turn the corner before turning to Kane. "I'd better go."

He pulled me into his arms, holding me tightly. "Be careful."

I managed a shaky smile. "I will."

His lips met mine in a short hungry kiss. "I love you," he murmured against my cheek.

"I love you, too." I gave him one last squeeze and got into his rental car. It only took a couple of minutes to drive across to the second parkade east of the casino, but it felt like hours.

Striding along the pedestrian overpass toward the casino, I fought to keep my pace casual while scouring the darkness for Arnie's car. Unless I'd missed it, he hadn't appeared on Saskatchewan Drive yet.

Two minutes to drop time.

My hand tightened on the trank pistol in my pocket. Dammit, if only it was my Glock. But I couldn't risk live ammo with so many innocent civilians around; and both Kane and Hellhound had made me promise I'd use non-lethal force.

But if something happened to Arnie, I might break that promise.

His car drove up Saskatchewan Avenue and turned into the casino parking lot. My heart lurched. I was nearly across the pedestrian bridge. Did I need to slow down or speed up to be near him at the drop time? My gaze flicked back and forth between the street corner and Arnie's slowly-moving car.

The casino parking lot was in full swing on a Friday night. What if he had to drive around for a while before he found a parking spot? He'd be late for the drop. And I'd reach the corner before him and have to keep walking. Away from him. Dammit!

I slowed, trying to keep the change of pace gradual so I wouldn't attract attention in the sparse flow of pedestrians.

Arnie solved the timing issue by driving directly to the southeast corner of the lot and double-parking.

Shit.

I sped up a bit. Then slowed down. What if the kidnappers weren't on time? Should I loiter for a while? But that would be too obvious. Nobody loitered on the street in the middle of the night at thirty below. I could blow the whole thing.

Dammit, dammit...

Arnie stepped onto the street corner, bag slung over his shoulder.

"And... time." Kane's quiet voice came over the open phone speaker.

I was still a hundred feet away.

"No sign of them yet," Kane said. "Speed up a bit, Aydan, you're looking conspicuous."

I did my best to maintain my pace. They were late, dammit.

Arnie's face was rigid as I walked past him.

"Go west," Kane snapped.

It took all I had to turn my back on Arnie and keep walking.

Kane's voice was tight. "Still nothing."

"I'll go into the casino and change my parka so I can make another pass," I muttered.

Look casual. Don't tense up.

My legs felt as stiff as two-by-fours and my shoulders ached from tension.

Maintain the pace.

Dammit, I was so far away from Arnie now...

Inside the vestibule of the casino I stepped away from the glass doors and yanked off my parka, balling it up and stuffing it into the bag I'd concealed under it.

The light windbreaker from my grab-and-go bag took its place, and I yanked the hood over my head and hurried back to the exit just as the ringtone of Kane's cell sounded through the open phone connection.

I jerked as though I'd been hit with a cattle prod, but fortunately I wasn't outside yet. Holding a casual pace with all my might, I went through the exit doors in time to see Arnie raise Kane's phone to his ear.

Kane spoke over the open connection. "Hello?"

Shit, I had to get closer.

I cut across the parking lot diagonally, heading for Arnie.

"I said 'no cops'." The kidnapper's voice sent an icy chill down my spine that had nothing to do with the inadequate insulation of my windbreaker. "You just cost Kathy her left thumb."

"NO!" Kane's shout came through my phone's speaker far too loudly, and an incoming pedestrian gave me a worried look. "I didn't call the cops!" Kane insisted. "The casino is right beside the police station so if you saw-"

"Left thumb." The kidnapper's voice was implacable. "You'll find it at the cenotaph in Victoria Park. Screw around again, and she'll lose the other one, too."

"*NO, DON'T!* I didn't call them, I *didn't*-"

"Wait for my next call." A bloodcurdling scream in the background was cut off as the connection closed.

My heart froze.

Somehow my legs were still moving.

Arnie stood like a statue on the corner, the phone still pressed to his ear.

A car horn blared inches away and I stumbled aside, realizing I'd blindly stepped out in front of the slow-moving vehicle. I raised my hand in a feeble apology to the driver, but I couldn't tear my gaze away from Arnie's desolate figure on the corner.

I had to get to him.

Nobody spoke. The only sound was the crackly rustle of my windbreaker feeding back through the open phone connection.

As I hurried closer, Arnie moved at last. Like an old man, he plodded stiffly toward his car.

"Hotel," he said in a hoarse rasp. The connection went dead.

He got into his car and drove away.

"Keep walking," Kane said harshly. "They're watching."

"R-Right." Hard shivers shook me. "G-Going b-back inside," I said through chattering teeth. "I'll ch-change and come p-pick you up."

He said nothing, and I forced my wooden legs to carry me back to the casino.

Inside, I walked blindly through the building toward the east doors. The flashing lights and noise lashed my raw nerves like whips. Brain frozen, body shivering helplessly, I kept putting one numb foot in front of the other.

Oh God.

They'd cut off her *thumb*.

My guts wrenched and I lurched into the nearest bathroom, barely making it into a stall before my stomach turned inside-out.

When I emerged trembling long minutes later, the face that confronted me in the mirror was bone-white and glistening with tears and clammy sweat. I avoided my own gaze, stooping to splash water on my face over and over.

Trying to wash away the horror and guilt.

Impossible.

I rinsed my mouth and spat, then straightened to grope my way toward the paper towel dispenser.

"Here." A woman's voice from close range made me jump. My eyes popped open to find a kind-looking middle-aged woman watching me with concern as she extended a wad of paper towels.

"Thanks," I mumbled, patting my face dry with shaking hands.

"Are you all right?"

"Fine. Thanks. Just... ate something that didn't agree with me."

"Oh. I was afraid you'd had a bad loss."

I flinched. "That, too." The words came out in a bare whisper.

She gave me a sympathetic smile. "Well, I can't do

anything to help with your food poisoning, but..." She handed me a small card. "Here's the number for the problem gambling helpline. Just give them a call. They can help."

I stared at her in silence until a ghost of my social skills returned.

"Thanks." I took the card and left.

When I arrived at the parkade where I'd left Kane, I was still shivering uncontrollably.

The harsh lighting cast black shadows over his eye sockets and cheeks, turning the paleness of his face into a macabre deaths-head. I got out of the car and flung myself into his arms.

His embrace was painfully tight, his body rigid. We stood locked together in silence. I wanted to burst into tears, but my emotions were frozen. Every part of my body was cold.

"Did you call Tan?" Kane's voice was a dry husk.

"N-not yet."

"Call him."

Nodding, I stepped back from our comfortless embrace and hit the speed dial.

"Tan."

"It's Aydan. You can cancel the alert now."

"Did you make the exchange?"

"No. They thought we'd called the police. They cut off her thumb." The words fell like stones from my mouth.

A muffled word that was probably an expletive floated through the line. When Tan spoke again, his voice was hard. "Did you see her?"

"No. They s-said they'd leave her thumb at the cenotaph in Victoria P-Park."

"We'll check it."

I had no more words, so I hung up.

Kane and I got into his rental car without speaking. I took the passenger seat, mainly because I didn't feel capable of driving. Or even breathing. My chest hurt with a wooden pain that made each inhalation feel like more effort than it was worth.

As we pulled out onto the street, my phone vibrated. The sight of Arnie's number on the call display made my heart cringe.

Somehow I managed to speak. "Hi, Arnie."

"Come an' pick me up." His voice was flat.

All my alarm bells went off.

I toggled my phone to speaker so Kane could hear. "What happened? Where are you?"

"Eastbound Victoria at Cornwall. Assholes ambushed me an' stole the bag."

Kane accelerated hard and my voice came out in a shaky yelp that was part fear and part g-force. "Are you okay?"

"Yeah. Cops're here."

"We're on our way."

He hung up without a goodbye.

"Dammit!" Kane barked. "It was a trick! They never intended to make an exchange, they just wanted to flush us out so they could grab the money. I *told* you-"

He bit off the words, apparently realizing it was too late for recriminations. A light turned red in front of us and he jammed on the brakes, breathing hard. *"Dammit!"*

The light changed, and we drove in tense silence. As soon as we turned onto Victoria Avenue, the red and blue flashing lights made our destination obvious.

Kane signalled and pulled over to the median to park

behind the traffic hazard cones that had been placed behind Hellhound's rental car. It was stopped halfway through the intersection, leaking fluids from its crumpled nose. An SUV with a correspondingly large dent in its side sat in front of it.

"A dark Ford SUV, just like the one that followed me," Kane said grimly. "That's not a coincidence."

A police officer in a reflective vest gestured for us to move along, but I had spotted Hellhound's bulky figure.

"Pull ahead and park," I said. "I'll go to Arnie."

Kane nodded and I jumped out. After identifying myself to the cop, I hurried over.

"Arnie!"

He turned, his face set like stone. "Hey, darlin'," he said, but his voice was expressionless.

I flung my arms around him. "What happened?"

He gently disengaged himself from my embrace and turned to gesture at the intersection. It was a kind attempt to spare my feelings, but I wasn't fooled. He was shutting me out.

"I was drivin' eastbound," he said without inflection. "They musta followed me from the casino. Didn't see 'em." Self-loathing leaked into his tone. "Wasn't fuckin' payin' attention."

I hugged his arm. "It's not your fault."

He ignored my platitude, but at least he didn't pull his arm away. He jerked his chin at the SUV. "Asshole was waitin' in the oncomin' left-turn lane. Soon's I got close enough, he turned in front a' me. Slid on the ice. Hit him." His voice roughened with anger. "An' what's the first thing any fuckin' idiot does when they're in an accident? They get outta the fuckin' car. An' that's just what *this* fuckin' idiot..." He jerked a thumb at himself. "...did. Left the car unlocked with the bag on the front seat."

"You're not an idiot-"

He talked over me. "The other driver's gettin' outta the SUV yellin' an' wavin' his arms, an' then he starts runnin' at me. I'm gettin' ready for a fight, but he runs right past me. That's when I figured out he was just distractin' me. That rental car was behind me, the same one they used to grab LaVonda from the hotel. The driver'd already grabbed the bag outta my car an' he was gettin' back in his own. Couldn't identify either of 'em 'cause they were wearin' ski masks. I ran after 'em but they hit me on the way by, so I was down an' didn't get their plate."

"They *hit* you?" Fear turned my voice to a squeak and I pulled away to examine him worriedly.

"I'm fine."

"You're not fine, you got hit by a car! Where are you hurt?"

His gaze focused on me at last. "It's okay, darlin', they didn't hit me with the car. They shot me."

"*WHAT?*" My voice came out in a high-pitched squawk. "How is that better than getting hit by a car?"

"I'm wearin' my vest. All I got is a bruise. If they'd run me over, it woulda been a lot worse."

"But if they'd gotten a good shot..." I wrapped my arms around him, holding him with desperate strength against what might have been.

He let out a small grunt. "Easy there, darlin'. My gut feels like I got nailed with a baseball bat."

My arms flew open. "I'm sorry! Oh, God, Arnie..." I caressed his face, needing to touch him. "I'm so glad you're okay!"

Kane strode up, necessitating another round of

explanations.

As Arnie finished, my phone vibrated. The display said 'Private Caller', and I answered with a wary 'hello'.

A familiar steel-edged voice asked, "Is this Aydan Kelly?"

"Yes."

"Tan here. Is that your party over on Victoria Avenue?"

"Um, yeah."

"I'll be there in a minute." He disconnected.

"Okay...?" I said to dead air.

"Who was that?" Kane demanded.

"Tan. He said he'd be here in a minute."

Kane eyed the park beside us and I followed his line of sight. There seemed to be a lot of activity and bright lights near its centre.

My blood went cold. "Is that... a cenotaph?"

"Yes." Kane's arm came around me.

A tall figure strode out of the lights, headed in our direction.

"That's Victoria Park," Hellhound said in a dead voice.

I clutched his hand, and we stood in silence until Tan closed the distance between us.

CHAPTER 24

Constable Tan's face was grim. The streetlights rendered his eyes empty black holes.

"Did you find anything?" Kane's voice was level, and I was glad he had spoken. I couldn't.

"A human thumb in a plastic bag."

My knees tried to collapse, but Kane's strong arm held me up. Arnie was squeezing my hand so tightly that arrows of pain shot up to my elbow.

I welcomed the physical pain. Better than the agony in my heart.

"Maybe it's not hers," I blurted.

Tan gave me a sympathetic look. "I'll let you know as soon as I hear from the medical examiner. What happened here?"

Arnie told his story again, his voice completely flat.

"They shot you?" Tan demanded. "Do you need medical attention?"

"Nah."

"Did you retrieve the bullet?"

Hellhound blinked. "Never thought of it." He unzipped his parka and twisted cautiously to eye the vest over his stomach. "Aydan, ya got your flashlight an' knife?"

"Y-Yeah." The shivering had started again. I unzipped my waist pouch, but Tan was already shining his powerful flashlight on Hellhound's vest.

"We'll need that for evidence."

"Take a picture an' dig out the bullet if ya want," Hellhound said. "But I ain't givin' up my vest."

Tan grimaced. "Understandable. Here, hold this." He handed the flashlight to Kane and turned to me. "You have a knife?"

I handed over my folding knife and Tan went to work on the vest, carefully extracting the bullet and dropping it into a bag.

As he pocketed the bag, he said to Hellhound, "Have you given a written statement yet?"

"Yeah, I-"

Sudden realization burst into my brain. "*Shit!*" I hissed, fumbling frantically for my phone and smacking my finger on the speed dial. "The tracer bug! Idiot, idiot..."

Spider's tense voice issued from the phone. "Hi, Aydan, nothing on the phone call yet-"

"Trace this bug ID, right away!" I snapped, and reeled off the code for the bug. "Is it transmitting?"

I switched to speaker so the others could hear. The rapid-fire clicking of computer keys came through, followed by Spider's voice.

"Yes, but I'm not getting much audio, just kind of a staticky-"

"Where is it?" I interrupted.

"Hold on..." More clicking. "It's in Regina, on Victoria Avenue between Osler Street and Halifax Street."

"That's just a few blocks away," Tan said, his radio already in his hand.

"Is it moving?" I demanded.

"No."

"Can you tell if it's in a building?"

"Hang on, I'm overlaying satellite imagery... I don't think so. It looks like a parking lot. The locator is only accurate to about six metres, but I'm guessing the bug's near the south side of Victoria Avenue, probably not in the parking lot itself."

Kane's arm was still around me, and I felt him slump. His voice came out weary. "They've ditched it already."

"There's a car rental agency there. We'll check it." Tan turned away and spoke into his radio.

"Aydan, what's going on?" Spider asked.

I couldn't summon the energy to explain. "We don't know yet. Thanks for your help. Just keep hunting for that phone."

"Okay." He sounded worried, but he didn't demand answers. "'Bye."

Kane stiffened. "I've got a call."

We all clustered closer as he pulled out his phone.

He switched to speaker and answered.

"Kane."

"Who needs thumbs anyway?" The kidnapper's voice was savage.

"Don't hurt her!" Kane implored.

"Too late. You should have put the money in the bag like you were told." Another horrifying scream twisted my guts.

The connection went dead.

Arnie staggered and I wrapped my arm around him. His arm landed heavily across my shoulders and Kane dropped the phone and grabbed his free arm to support him.

The three of us stood in a circle around the silent phone, holding each other up.

Slowly, as though learning to move again after a devastating injury, Arnie straightened. Kane released him, but I kept an arm around both men. Kane was rigid. Arnie was trembling.

Kane snatched up his phone and tapped #57, then hit speed dial. "Webb, I just flagged another number." His voice was devoid of expression. "Trace it ASAP. And I have a license number for a charcoal gray Ford Escape rented from Avis. Get the renter's name." He recited the plate number while I stood paralyzed.

Tan's steely voice finally penetrated my frozen horror. "There was a soft-sided cat carrier stuffed with towels with some cash on top, lying beside the street where your guy said. I need a complete update."

Somehow I managed to speak, my voice issuing in a dry croak while I briefed Tan.

"...so there wasn't any additional money in the first place," I finished. "And even if there was, we couldn't let them have it. It's the only thing keeping LaVonda alive."

Tan glanced at Arnie's white face and hesitated.

"Say it." Arnie's voice was as bleak as frozen bones.

Tan sighed. "You're probably right, they're keeping her as a bargaining chip for the money. But she may not survive the amputations. If she goes into shock or gets an infection..." He didn't finish the sentence.

"It's the only chance we've got," Kane said grimly. "They said they'd call again with another drop location. We're hoping to have a trace on that phone call before then."

"How did they get your cell phone number?" Tan's face hardened with renewed suspicion.

"I programmed it into LaVonda's phone when I left her in the hotel room alone the first time," Kane replied. "They must have gotten it from her."

Tan's shoulders relaxed fractionally, and he grimaced.

"Okay. Keep me up to date. I'm on shift until four AM, and I'll make sure Corporal Whittle is briefed before I leave." He eyed us with sympathy. "You're free to leave here as soon as you fill out your statements. Try to get some rest."

As we trudged back to Kane's rental car, I realized that Tan didn't feel like an adversary anymore.

God, I couldn't imagine doing his job. Mine was fairly clear-cut, but he had to crack down on criminals while supporting victims, and, hardest of all, figure out which were which.

"Ms. Kelly!" A call from behind made me turn to see Tan holding Princess's carrier. "Do you want this?"

"Oh. Yeah." I plodded back. "If you don't need it for evidence."

He shrugged. "They had it for all of thirty seconds. Mr. Helmand said they were wearing ski masks and gloves, so there's no point in looking for physical evidence on it. The cat probably needs it more than we do."

Somehow that warmed my frozen heart just a bit.

"Thanks." I took the carrier from him.

"And you can tell Mr. Helmand he was right about the grenade launcher. We found it in the back of the SUV." Tan jerked his chin at the intersection, where a tow truck was hooking onto the wreck. "We'll have to confirm that it matches the cartridge found in the burned apartment, but there probably aren't too many grenade launchers in this city." He grimaced. "At least I hope not."

"Me, too. Thanks again." I dragged myself back to our rental car, shivering.

As I placed the carrier in the back seat beside Hellhound, he glared at it as though it was the cause of all our problems.

Which it was.

When I got into the passenger's seat, Hellhound said, "They didn't even take the cash."

I sighed. "It was only a couple of hundred bucks."

"Still, you'd think they'd'a taken it."

"They probably figured it was marked." I slumped lower in the seat. "Or it just wasn't worth the trouble to them. These guys really are professionals. Oh, the police found the grenade launcher in the back of the SUV. So there's that, at least."

Neither of them replied, and I wrapped my arms around myself and concentrated on shivering in silence.

Kane's voice made me start, and I realized I had been staring blindly through the windshield for a while. We were in a Tim Horton's drive-through, and he had ordered three hot chocolates.

From the back seat, Hellhound rasped, "Get me coffee instead."

"No, you need sugar." Kane pulled forward to pay at the window. "We all do."

He accepted the cardboard drink tray and handed it to me, pulling out onto the dark quiet street again.

I passed a hot cup back to Hellhound and another over to Kane, then hugged the third to my chest. My body was still vibrating with fine shivers, and I sipped gratefully.

We drove in silence for a while.

"This was a setup," Kane said at last. "Professionals wouldn't stage a ransom drop two blocks away from a police station. They did that on purpose, knowing it would give them the opportunity to claim they'd seen a police presence."

Hellhound's voice came hard and cold from the back seat. "Or they *didn't* see any cops an' they knew they should, so they knew we'd called the cops an' warned 'em off."

After a moment of sick silence, Kane persisted. "Regardless, they did it on purpose to keep us off-balance. They used the drop to draw us out so they could follow-"

"Don't fuckin' remind me," Hellhound growled.

I twisted to look at him. "It wasn't your fault."

"Aydan's right," Kane agreed. "They purposely put on that show, knowing we wouldn't be thinking straight after hearing it. I wouldn't have noticed a tail at that point, either." He let out a small breath of frustration. "I *didn't* notice a tail. And it was my responsibility to be watching for one when you left. I'm the one who dropped the ball."

"It's not about whose fault it was," I said firmly. "What matters is what we do next."

"We wait for their call, an' then we do exactly what they say," Hellhound said.

"That's how they want us to react," Kane replied as he pulled into our hotel lot and parked. "But no matter how much we might want to comply, we can't; because we don't have another quarter million dollars."

"I can get it." Hellhound's voice was grimly determined. "I got a home equity line a' credit on my condo, an' I got savings."

Kane glanced at him, and I could tell he was about to argue. Instead, he pressed his lips together as though silencing himself before replying, "I have savings I can contribute, too. But we can't get to a bank before tomorrow morning, and maybe Webb will get a trace on that phone by then."

"Hope so," Hellhound growled as we got out of the car. "Come on back to our room an' let's figure out a plan."

Back in the warmth of the room, I shed my parka and appropriated a blanket, shivering afresh from my short exposure to the frigid outdoor temperature. I was just taking my seat at the table when my phone vibrated.

Oh, God. Now what?

I took it out and eyed the display with a sinking heart. "Shit, it's Dermott, and it's nearly one AM in Alberta." I caught the call on the third ring and tried for a confident tone. "Kelly."

"Dermott here." He sounded as cranky as usual, but surprisingly not rabid. "I'm sending Holt out there to cover your ass, since you can't fucking take care of yourself and you're so fucking *special* to the Department. Meet him at the airport at 09:25." He disconnected before I could reply.

My jaw sagged as the phone drifted down from my ear.

"What did he want?" Kane demanded.

"He's sending Holt for backup," I said, my mind whirling with suspicion. "Why would he-"

My phone vibrated again, and the call display showed 'Private caller'.

Adrenaline surged into my tired veins. Did Tan have an answer from the medical examiner already?

Did I want to know?

I hit the Accept button with a trembling finger. "Kelly."

"Holt here."

What the hell?

"Hi, Greg," I said cautiously.

"Having fun out there in the frozen Vagina of Hell?" he inquired.

"All the fun you can possibly imagine. I just got a call from Dermott. Is he really sending you out here to help?"

"Yeah, since you're determined to meddle with dangerous shit while you're supposed to be on leave."

"Bullshit. He already told the Regina police that the

Department wouldn't help, and he sure as hell isn't sending you here out of love and concern for me."

Holt barked out a short laugh. "He's pissed about it, all right. But he really is sending me out to babysit, in case your Arlene Widdenback cover pulls something out of the woodwork and puts you at risk. I'll be there in the morning, so don't go getting yourself killed in the meantime."

I could well imagine how pissed Dermott was. My decryption abilities made me more valuable to the Department than any other agent, and it was a never-ending source of irritation for him.

"Well, that sucks for you," I commiserated. "Sorry to spoil your Christmas."

"No big deal. My friends and family are all back in Toronto so I wasn't doing anything. Anyway, I just wanted to let you know I'll be there soon." He adopted his Holt-The-Magnificent tone. "I told you Dermott was an okay guy. You need to let go of your grudge."

I froze.

Oh.

Shit.

Keeping my voice light with a superhuman effort, I replied, "Damn, I guess you're right. So you're getting in at 09:25 local?"

"Yeah."

"Okay, I'll meet you at the airport. And, Greg?"

"Yeah?"

"Thanks."

"No problem." He disconnected.

I slapped my phone down on the table. "Shit, shit, *shit!*"

"What?" Kane and Hellhound demanded.

"Holt's coming to arrest me."

CHAPTER 25

"*What?*" Hellhound barked at the same time Kane demanded, "When?"

"His flight gets in at 9:25 AM." I glanced at my watch. "We've got seven and a half hours to vanish." I hesitated. "Assuming he was telling the truth about his arrival time. But he probably was. I don't think there are any flights into Regina this time of night."

"Why the hell would ya go meet him if he's gonna arrest ya?" Hellhound demanded.

"I'm not going to meet him. And he won't expect me to be there."

"Start at the beginning," Kane said. "Why is Holt coming to arrest you?"

"Because, Dermott," I replied succinctly.

Kane acknowledged that with a dip of his chin. "I expected Dermott would be looking for any reason to cause trouble for you; but what reason have you given him?"

"He told me to come back to Silverside immediately and deal with my mother's lawyer." I glanced at my watch. "Nearly six hours ago. So that's obviously insubordination."

Hellhound frowned. "No, it ain't. He ain't got any say over your personal life."

"Arnie's right," Kane agreed. "Dermott's not stupid. After the chain of command slapped him down for false accusations against you only two days ago, he wouldn't go after you with such a thin case."

"It's not that thin. He officially refused to involve the Department, and then I went behind his back to help the police, too." I shrugged, hiding my fear. "Even though he didn't actually give me a direct order to stay out of it, that won't stop him."

Kane frowned. "That doesn't make sense. It's too flimsy." His frown deepened. "And Holt just risked his career by warning you. Is there... something going on between you and him?"

"Good God, no." I shuddered. "Bite your tongue. No, Holt didn't tell me he was coming to arrest me. He just called to confirm that Dermott is sending him out to protect me."

"Oh. That makes more sense." Kane's voice softened. "It's understandable that you don't trust Dermott, but I think you're being needlessly paranoid this time."

"I know it sounds paranoid; but right after Holt said Dermott was sending him out for backup, he used a code-phrase that told me he was lying."

Kane jerked forward. "What did he say?"

"He said 'I told you Dermott was an okay guy' and 'you should let go of your grudge'."

"Of course he'd say that. They're friends. And Holt can't resist an 'I-told-you-so'."

"Except that he never told me that." I gave Kane a thin smile. "What he actually said when we were alone, and this is in strictest confidence..." I eyed them both and was rewarded with impatient nods. "Holt said Dermott is a vindictive son of a bitch and he holds grudges forever."

Kane blinked. "Oh. That's... unexpected."

"Holt really is an okay guy most of the time," I said.

"Dermott's definitely up to something, and if Holt didn't think it was serious he wouldn't have given me a heads-up." I grimaced as another realization hit me. "And now that he's warned me, he'll do everything he can to nail me."

Kane's lips turned up in a grim smile. "That sounds like Holt. He wouldn't stab you in the back, but he'll relish the challenge of a fair contest." The light in Kane's eyes told me Holt wasn't the only one who liked a challenge.

"An' he's gotta cover his ass with Dermott," Hellhound added. "So he's gonna be pullin' out all the stops."

"Not only that, but he knows John's working with me," I said glumly. "And Holt would *love* to claim he beat the Department's all-time top agent."

Hellhound sank his head into his hands. "Fuck. How're we s'posed to dodge him an' get LaVonda back at the same time?"

I slumped. "We can't." Doing my best to keep the fear out of my voice, I went on, "I'll meet him at the airport. Maybe John's right and I'm just being paranoid. We can't help LaVonda if we're busy trying to avoid Holt. If he arrests me..." Unable to complete the sentence without whimpering, I threw up my hands and faked courage. "Whatever. It might as well be now. I'm not going to hide for the rest of my life. I have to go home sometime."

"But Holt knows that, and so does Dermott," Kane said thoughtfully. "Holt wouldn't have bothered to warn you unless there was some reason why you should be avoiding him right now. It would be easier for Dermott to arrest you when you get home in a few days; or even when you're back to work in the new year. Sending Holt out here is a lot of unnecessary expense for the Department."

"Maybe the call about my mother's lawyer was an

attempt to lure me back. I didn't come, so he figures I'm making a run for it."

Kane shook his head. "That doesn't make sense. Dermott knows you're hunting LaVonda's kidnappers. You're not running anywhere."

"So that's why he's sending Holt. He knows I'll be here for a while."

"Well, fuck it!" Hellhound burst out. "I ain't gonna shove ya under a bus just to get LaVonda back." He reached over and took my hand. "We'll figure out a way to avoid him. What d'ya figure he'll do first?"

"He'll try to find LaVonda," Kane said. "He'll expect us to drop off-grid right away, so he won't even bother hunting us directly. He'll know that wherever LaVonda is, we'll soon be."

Hiding my abject gratitude for their support, I added, "And he'll have the police and all the analysts in the Department to help him. I have to call Tan before he gets here."

Kane sighed. "And I have to call Daniel and explain that I won't be home for a while."

Hellhound looked stricken. "No, Cap," he said gently. "Time for ya to go home now."

Kane gave him an affronted look. "Not likely."

"Go," Hellhound repeated. "Ya ain't thinkin' straight. If Aydan an' I go to jail, ya can come an' see us whenever ya want. If you end up in jail, you'll never see Daniel again. An' soon's ya start aidin' a fugitive..." He gestured at me. "Like, right fuckin' *now*... you're goin' to jail. So get the hell outta here."

"Go, John," I urged. "You know damn well that if you get convicted, or even charged with something, Alicia will go to court for sole custody of Daniel, and she'll win. You promised Daniel you'll always be there for him, and you need to-"

"*Stop right there.*" Kane straightened, eyes blazing grey fire. The steel in his tone sent a shiver down my spine and my arguments died in my throat.

"In the first place," he said in an implacable voice, "Neither of you gets to dictate my priorities to me. This is my choice, and mine alone. And in the second place, I'm working with an off-duty agent and the local police to solve a kidnapping case, and we're about to be joined by another highly-qualified agent who is coming to help us. If it so happens that we're forced to drop off-grid before he can meet us, that's not a crime; and Aydan is not a fugitive." The corner of his mouth quirked in a grim smile. "As far as we know."

Hellhound spoke into the short silence that followed. "I guess that's true..."

"It's true *now*," I argued. "But who knows how it's all going to shake out? John, are you really going to risk Dan-" His jaw muscles bulged and I rapidly changed my approach. "We're not trying to dictate your priorities. You're right, that's none of our business. It's just that we both know how much Daniel means to you, and we don't want you to have regrets later."

Kane sat very still.

I wasn't sure whether he was thinking about what I'd said or trying to get his temper under control, but either way it didn't seem like a good idea to rush the process. We sat in silence.

Kane exhaled. "Thank you for your concern," he said evenly. "But no matter how I choose, I'll have regrets. What if I put Daniel first? What if I leave now, and something terrible happens to one of you, or to LaVonda? How could I live with myself, wondering if I could have prevented it? As important as Daniel is to me, his life is not at stake. Yours and LaVonda's are. It's a painful choice, but it's not a difficult one."

"But *your* life-" I began.

"Is mine to do with as I see fit," Kane interrupted with finality. "And I'm staying. This discussion is closed."

Try as I might, I couldn't think of a rebuttal.

Arnie sat without speaking, too. Then he let out a breath. "Thanks, Cap. I owe ya big."

"You don't owe me anything." Kane gave him a smile. "Now, if you'll excuse me, I have a phone call to make. I can't call Daniel in the middle of the night, so I'll call Dad and ask him to tell Daniel in the morning."

My heart plummeted. John had just given up his first-ever Christmas Eve with his son. Would he have to sacrifice Christmas, too?

Kane rose, his impassive cop face firmly in place. "We'll have to move to a different hotel and check in under assumed names."

"I've got a couple of fake IDs in my grab-and-go bag," I volunteered.

"Department-issue?" Kane asked.

"One of them. The other's just a fake driver's license and a valid credit card, but the Department doesn't know about it. That's the one we'll use."

He smiled. "I knew you'd be prepared. I've got one, too."

"An' I got my Al Hamlin ID," Hellhound contributed. "So we're good to go."

"Excellent. I'll be back in ten minutes."

My voice came out sounding as gloomy as I felt. "I'll make my call to Tan."

As Kane went out the door, I dialled. When Tan answered, I said, "Hi, it's Aydan again. It looks as though we'll have to drop off-grid for a while. I just wanted to let you know that you won't be able to contact me at this number."

Suspicion edged his voice. "Why do you have to go off-grid?"

"We'll be able to track the kidnappers better that way." I tried to make the lie sound regretful. "Sorry. I'll keep in touch as best I can. Did you make any progress with those names I gave you?"

"No." His tone told me that even if he had new information, he wouldn't share it.

"Okay. I'll talk to you later, then." I hung up.

"How'd it go?" Hellhound asked, looking up from packing Princess's gear.

"Shitty. Now he's back to wondering if he can trust us. If he can get somebody here before we leave, we'll probably be followed again." I rose and headed for the bathroom to collect my hairbrush and toiletries.

"Fuck. It woulda been a whole lot easier if we'd'a gotten some half-assed cop that didn't give a shit." Hellhound zipped up his guitar case and placed it tenderly next to the door.

I put my bag down beside it with a weary sigh. "Yeah, but at least we can count on him to stay on top of things and protect LaVonda no matter what."

"Guess that's true." He gave me a tired smile. "Lie down for a few minutes, darlin'. Ya look bagged."

"I am." I trudged toward the bed. "Come and join me. You look exhausted, too."

That was an understatement. He looked far beyond exhausted, grey and grim with hard lines carved deep in his face.

I fell onto the bed. "God, I wish we could just stay here. A few days in a nice anonymous hotel room, eating and sleeping and reading and getting bored out of our minds..."

The bed dipped under Arnie's weight and he brushed a whiskery kiss on my cheekbone. "When this's all over, I'll take ya to the spa in Moose Jaw."

My eyes popped open on an incredulous laugh. "*Moose Jaw?* The spa capital of the world?"

He chuckled. "They've actually got a helluva nice spa. Big mineral pool, great food, massages..." His strong hands found the knots in my shoulders, rubbing gently.

"Mmm... yeah..." My eyes drifted closed again.

A rap at the door cut my moment of relaxation short, and I hauled myself reluctantly upright. "I'll let John in. You get Princess into her carrier."

When I peeked out the fisheye lens, Kane stood in the hallway, duffel bag in hand. I opened the door for him and headed for the table, pulling out my cell phone.

"I'm going to leave my phone here, along with all my secured phones from the Department," I said. "I don't want them tracking us."

"Good point," Kane agreed. "But I think I'd rather leave the phones in the rental car. We'll have to ditch it anyway. The GPS system is too easy for Holt to track. Let's leave it at the parkade where we took Regis. We can pay for several days' parking; and it will make Tan suspicious that we went to the same place twice. They'll waste time searching for something significant in that area."

"Okay, that's a better idea." I sighed. "I guess I'd better call Spider and tell him we're going off-grid. I was counting on his help for this, but Holt's probably already got him tracking our phones. I don't want to put Spider in a conflict of interest."

As I poised my finger over the phone, Kane snapped, "Wait."

I froze. "What?"

"Let's think this through." He sat down and waved a hand at the chairs, indicating that we should do the same. "A few extra minutes of planning won't make a difference in evading Holt, but it could make a big difference in the way we proceed. What makes you think Dermott and Holt will put Webb on this?"

I shrugged and sank into the chair opposite him. "Spider's the best. Everybody knows that."

"True, but Dermott just finished kicking Webb out of the building with a big show of force. And someone as insecure as Dermott wouldn't want to admit he'd made a bad decision."

"Insecure?" I stared at Kane. "Shit, you're right. That's what his problem is. I never bothered to think it through. I thought he was just an asshole."

"He is," Hellhound growled.

"Well, yeah; but that's *why* he's an asshole. And that makes sense, because Holt told me Dermott was a bully when they were in grade school. Bullies are almost always insecure."

Kane nodded. "So he won't want to reverse his decision. Plus he knows you and Webb are friends, and he already caught Webb helping you. Even if Dermott could swallow his pride, I don't think he'd trust Webb. I think he'll use the analyst-on-call, whoever that happens to be tonight."

I sagged in the chair with a breath of relief. "You're right. Thank God for..."

I almost completed the sentence with '...Dermott's non-existent balls', but a sudden flash of empathy silenced me.

I knew exactly how Dermott felt.

Never good enough. Balanced on a fraying tightrope with no safety net, with innocent lives depending on my ability to use skills I didn't have.

Poor bastard.

"Aydan?" Kane's voice brought me back to the present. "You look as though you just thought of something."

"Um. Ye... no. Just thinking about what you said. So... I guess I'll phone Spider and let him know what's going on."

"Are you going to tell him about your suspicion of Dermott?"

"Yes... Or..." I hesitated. "I don't know. If I tell him the whole story and he helps us anyway, he could get in trouble. If I don't tell him, he'll be able to swear under the lie detector that he didn't know." Another thought hit me. "Oh. And if I tell him Holt's coming to arrest me, I won't be able to tell him why I know that, because I can't risk getting Holt in trouble. But... shit." I sank my aching forehead into my hands. "I don't feel right about *not* telling him the whole story. Help me out here, guys. I'm too tired to think straight."

"Tell him Holt is coming to back you up, but you have to drop off-grid and you won't be able to meet him," Kane said. "Webb doesn't need to know the details."

"But if I tell him that, he has to tell Holt," I objected. "If he doesn't pass that on, he could be charged for withholding information."

"Guess ya got your answer, then." Hellhound sprang to his feet as though incapable of sitting still any longer. "Call him an' tell him we're goin' off-grid, an' don't tell him why. If he doesn't know Holt's involved, he doesn't have any reason to call him; an' if Dermott keeps him outta the loop, he'll be able to say he didn't know any better."

I sighed. "Or we could be completely wrong about all this. Holt would expect Spider to be helping us. He might have already called Spider and given him a direct order to report any contact we make. If he has, we're sunk. And so is Spider."

A short silence greeted my gloomy pronouncement.

"It's true that we have a problem if Holt has already gotten to Webb," Kane said. "But if you're right about Holt's coded warning, I'd guess he's allowing us a head start. He wouldn't contact Webb until he arrived at the Regina airport and 'discovered'..." He made air quotes around the word. "...that you weren't there to meet him."

I blew out a breath. "Right. Well, I'll call Spider and see what he says. Unless Holt told him the whole story and specifically ordered Spider not to say anything, Spider will tell me if he's been in contact."

I punched in Spider's number with a sinking sensation.

So many ways this could go wrong.

And for every moment we delayed, LaVonda's chances grew slimmer.

CHAPTER 26

Spider answered on the first ring. "Hi, Aydan. Sorry, I still don't have anything on that phone. I've traced it back to the provider, but I have to wait for them to give me access to their database. I'm working on the other stuff in the meantime."

"That's okay, Spider, I'm not trying to rush you..." I trailed off as his words registered. "You have to wait for the phone service provider? I thought you could just hack into their database."

"I can if you want me to."

The hint of uncertainty in his voice made me pause.

"No, I trust your judgement," I assured him. "What are you thinking?"

"It'll take me nearly as long to hack in as it'll take for them to provide it freely with the warrant I've got. Since this is a civilian case, I didn't think you'd want me to do anything that would make the evidence inadmissible in court."

I let out a breath. What would I do without Spider covering my ass?

"Thanks, Spider. You're right, as usual. That wasn't actually what I was calling about. I just wanted to let you know we're probably going to have to drop off-grid."

I held my breath. His next words would confirm or dispel my fears.

"Okay. Are you going to use burner phones?" He

sounded completely normal, and I let out a breath of relief. Spider was the world's worst liar. If he was hiding something or being coerced, I'd know.

"Yes, but I won't want to contact you because it'll show up on your phone records."

"Oh, that's okay," he said. "I've got a couple of burners here. I'll give you a number so you can reach me."

My eyebrows tried to climb to my hairline. "What? Why do you have burner phones?"

"I use them for testing my security protocols. Here you go..."

He read off a number and I repeated it aloud, secure in the knowledge that it would be instantly stored in Arnie's infallible memory until I could program it into my phone.

"Do you have your burners yet?" Spider asked.

"I have a couple, but I'll probably get more. Here are the ones I'll use first." I gave him the numbers.

"Okay, got them. So in the meantime I've been tracking down everything I can find on Guy One and Guy Two. I've passed their names on to the Winnipeg police and they'll check to see if their vehicles are still in Winnipeg. I've also initiated a trace on their personal cell phones, but if they're as professional as I think they are, they probably won't be carrying them. And I'm digging into Richard Fizgerald as well. I don't know if there's a solid connection yet. I'm expecting more results soon, so I'll call you back in a little while. Let me know when you're going off-grid."

"I will. Thanks."

"Oh, and, Aydan?" He hesitated, and when he spoke again, worry vibrated in his voice. "Stay safe, okay?"

"I will. Thanks."

I hung up. "We're all set. Let's get out of here."

"Slow down," Kane advised. "Let's plan our strategy first. We'll need to choose another place to stay, and we need a way to get there that doesn't use the rental car."

"Right." I failed to stifle a cavernous yawn. "Sorry. How do you like my tonsils?"

Kane gave me a tired grin. "They're lovely."

"Good to know, since I had them out when I was four." I yawned again, this time managing to cover my gaping cake-hole.

Kane eyed the fine tremor of my fingers. "You need sleep."

"You have no idea," I agreed. "So let's get this done. Arnie, does your marvelous brain have any record of sleazy no-tell motels in Regina? We'll need someplace cheap enough that they don't have video surveillance. Or wide-awake receptionists."

He shook his head. "Sorry, darlin', I wasn't plannin' on sleaze this trip. Lemme see what I can find." He pulled out his smartphone.

"We should be able to take transit from the parkade," I added to Kane. "And in the morning we can rent a truck from Home Depot instead of getting another rental car, just in case Holt circulates a description of us to the car agencies. He won't likely think to check at Home Depot, and the staff changes so often that even if somebody remembers us, Holt won't likely find them."

"Good idea," Kane said, focusing on his own phone. "I'll get the transit routes..." He studied the device, tapping and swiping. His brows drew together. "Oh."

Somehow I managed not to fall to the floor and curl into fetal position. "I don't like the sound of that."

"No," he said absently, still tapping at the phone. "I'm

afraid transit isn't an option." He surfaced with a pained smile. "This isn't Calgary. The buses stopped running over an hour ago."

"All of them?" My voice came out sounding shrill.

"All twenty-one routes in the big city of Regina."

Despite my best attempt to suppress it, a despairing whimper escaped me.

Kane's face softened. "It's probably for the best. We have seven hours left before Holt's plane arrives, and probably another half-hour or more after that before he gets his luggage and his rental car and starts tracking us. We're fine here tonight." He rose. "Go to bed. If we leave by eight tomorrow morning, we'll have enough time to vanish. That gives us five and half hours of sleep. Not enough, but better than running around trying to go somewhere else tonight."

"But-" The vibration of my burner phone interrupted me and I pressed the Accept button without looking at the call display. "Hello?"

"Hey, it's Spider. I've got another name for you."

My heart lifted with hope. "Great. I'm putting you on speaker now so John and Arnie can hear." I toggled the call over. "There, can you hear me?"

"Yep. Hi, guys." Without waiting for a response, he went on, "Guy Three is Randall Gordon Letz; and he's the same as the other two. Works as a manager for one of Fitzgerald's companies in Winnipeg, where he has a spotless work record; and he's had quite a few unrelated arrests, but he's never been convicted. All three of them are professionals, and they're definitely bad news. I haven't found a connection with the gunman from the apartment yet. He seems like just a small-time thug-for-hire, but I'll keep digging."

He hesitated. "Sorry I don't have better news, but... I couldn't get a name off the luggage tag, and so far none of the hotels have noticed any guests in wheelchairs. And I'm still combing through the rental car records. If I can figure out what names they used when they rented the cars, I'll be able to get the VIN numbers of the cars and trace the navigation software."

"How long will that take?" I asked.

He sighed. "Even if I luck out and find the names in the next few minutes, it'll still take a while to get access to the nav systems. They're all proprietary to the manufacturers, so that's another whole round of warrants. And if the kidnappers didn't rent the cars in the Regina area..." He trailed off. "Sorry. I really don't know how long it'll take."

"It's okay. I know you're doing your best."

"Thanks, Aydan. Oh, I do have a bit of good news! My social media firestorm is going great; everybody's outraged now that they think LaVonda's dead. There's a big backlash against the guy who doxxed her. Everybody's calling him a murderer."

"They know who doxxed her?"

I could hear the evil smile in Spider's voice as he replied, "Yeah, somebody doxxed *him*."

"Anybody we know?" I asked, my face creaking into a smile for the first time in what felt like days.

"Hard to say," he said in innocent tones. "The guy who did it must be some kind of uber-hacker. He's a ghost. Mist. A rumour."

"Remind me never to piss you off."

"You could never make me that mad."

"Thanks, Spider. I'll let you get back to work."

"Wait," Kane interjected. "Webb, if you get anything

tonight, call me, not Aydan." He recited his burner number and went on, "Aydan needs sleep, and so does Arnie." At our respective growls, he gave us a placating grimace and added, "I'll wake them if it's important, but at least this way you don't have to decide whether to call."

"Okay, no problem," Spider replied. "Get some rest, you guys. This will probably take a while."

"I'm sorry you have to stay up so late," I said.

"No problem," he replied cheerfully. "You know me; I'm usually up most of the night gaming anyway. And I'm on holidays now. I can sleep as long as I want when I'm done here."

"Thanks, Spider, you're the best!"

Hellhound added, "Thanks, Webb. I owe ya."

"Of course you don't."

We said our goodbyes and I disconnected.

Kane headed for the door, picking up his duffel bag on the way. "I promise I'll call you if there's anything important. Plan to leave at eight if you don't hear from me before then."

He slipped out, closing the door soundlessly behind him.

Hellhound got up and went over to release Princess from her carrier, then returned with my bag. "Here ya go, darlin'. You're up for the bathroom first."

"Thanks." I accepted it and plodded to the bathroom, my eyes already half-closed.

I made short work of my bedtime routine. When I emerged, all the lights had been extinguished except the bedside lamp. Hellhound sat in one of the chairs, his guitar on his lap. He usually held it like a lover, but tonight he gripped it like a lifeline, his knuckles white.

"You're next," I said.

"'Kay."

As he headed for the bathroom, I shed my clothes and crept gratefully between the sheets.

I must have fallen asleep instantly. The opening of the bathroom door woke me, and I blinked groggily as Hellhound turned off the lamp and resumed his seat in the darkness.

"Come to bed," I coaxed.

"Can't."

I turned the lamp back on and eyed him worriedly. He was clutching his guitar again, one hand tight on its neck while his other hovered over the strings, alternately opening and closing into a fist.

"They cut off her *thumbs!*" The words burst out of him as though beyond his control. "What kinda fucked-up sickos cut off somebody's *thumbs?* Don't they ever watch the fuckin' movies? They're s'posed to cut off the tip of her little finger or her earlobe or somethin' she doesn't need. Not her fuckin' *thumbs.*" His fingers opened and closed convulsively again, as if imagining the loss. "She won't even be able to..."

His voice broke and he hugged the guitar.

"Oh, Arnie..." My throat closed and I slid out of bed and hurried over to wrap my arms around him and his beloved guitar.

The kidnappers' brutality sickened me, but my trauma was nothing compared to Arnie's. Music was his lifeblood, and his hands were its conduit. To even think of losing his ability to play...

"They're bluffing," I murmured, rocking him. "They didn't actually cut off her thumbs. They *didn't.*"

Arnie barked out a laugh that sounded like a sob. "Yeah, that thumb in Vic Park right where they said it was gonna be;

that was just a random fuckin' coincidence."

"No, it was faked."

"Yeah, 'cause the cops wouldn't recognize a fake thumb." He pulled away. "It was a real thumb. They cut off her fuckin' thumbs."

"I didn't mean it wasn't a real thumb. I meant, it's not *her* thumb. They probably got it from a corpse or something."

"Yeah, 'cause corpses are just lyin' around everywhere. Easy to get a thumb in five minutes." Arnie let his head fall back with a despairing sigh and stared at the ceiling. "Cut the bullshit, darlin'. Ya don't believe that any more'n I do. An' ya promised you'd never lie to me, so just..." He swallowed and his voice wavered. "Just... don't."

"I'm not lying," I lied with every ounce of acting ability I owned. "Seriously, Arnie, think about it. You know as well as I do that hostages are a liability. They take a lot of resources. They're 'way more trouble than any professional wants, so that means these guys must really need her alive. And like Tan said, amputations are risky, especially something as major as thumbs. I don't think they'd take a chance. I think they're just messing with us."

"Well, it's workin'."

I tightened my hug. "But it doesn't have to. They haven't harmed her; I know it in my gut."

Even though I said it with as much certainty as I could muster, I still couldn't believe it. I suppressed my shudder and stroked the knotted muscles of his shoulders.

"Come to bed," I entreated again. "I'll give you a massage. I know you don't feel like you can sleep, but maybe you can relax a bit."

His hand closed over mine. "How the hell am I s'posed

to relax?" His grip tightened. "There's gotta be somethin' else we can do."

"I wish there were." I wrapped my arms around him again. "I'm sorry. I can only imagine how hard this is for you, but you can't help her by keeping yourself exhausted. When Spider gets something, and you know he will, maybe soon... you'll need to be rested so we can kick ass."

His growl vibrated against my chest. "I fuckin' *know* that. An' it ain't fuckin' helpin'."

"I know." My words came out on a sigh.

"Go on to bed," Hellhound said. "I'm just gonna sit up an' play for a while. An' then I'll lie down, too. Promise."

This time his guitar would bring him pain instead of comfort.

"No. Come and lie down now." I tugged him gently to his feet and nudged him toward the bed. "Even if you're just lying awake, you'll still be more comfortable than in the chair."

"Guess you're right about that," he conceded, and leaned his guitar against the chair. As he stripped off his T-shirt and undid his jeans, fear chilled me.

"Ohmigod, Arnie!"

CHAPTER 27

Hellhound glanced down at himself without interest as he dropped his jeans and stepped out of them. Even his extensive tattoos couldn't hide the purple bruise that marred the left side of his abdomen, and the leakage of blood under the skin had created a dark purple stain that extended to the top of his thigh.

He shrugged. "Yeah, that looks about how it feels."

"You need to see a doctor," I said. "Right away."

"Nah, it's just a bruise." He eased into bed, obviously in pain.

"You have internal bleeding," I argued. "You can see where it's been leaking under the skin."

"It's just the skin, nothin' deeper." As I hovered anxiously over him, he added, "Trust me, darlin', this ain't my first. If I had internal bleedin', I'd be passin' out by now. It's just a bruise. Nothin' to worry about."

"I'm worried."

He sighed. "I know, but I'm tellin' ya-"

"Arnie..." I sank onto the bed beside him, careful not to jostle him. "Look, it's not that I don't believe you or I don't trust you. It's just..." My voice quivered, and I had to swallow hard. "...I'm so messed up right now and... if anything happened to you... I... I just..."

Incipient tears closed my throat and I pressed my lips together and looked away, blinking back the embarrassing moisture.

"Aw, darlin'. Come here." Arnie pulled me gently down beside him, wrapping me in his arms. "It's okay. I promise I'm fine." When I couldn't reply, he added, "Tell ya what. Would it help if Kane came an' looked at it? If he told ya it was okay, too?"

Feeling like a stupid child but afraid to let it go, I nodded wordlessly against his shoulder.

"Awright. Go ahead an' give him a call, then." He touched me under the chin, raising my face to kiss me. His lips curved up. "Ya might wanna put on some clothes before he gets here, though. Remember the last time we all got naked, an' Moonbeam an' Nichele walked in?"

A shaky giggle escaped me despite my anxiety. "That was *so* embarrassing! But I was the only one naked. At least you had pants on, even though your dick was hanging out. Orion just had his shirt open, and John was fully dressed."

He chuckled. "With that sheet wrapped around ya, nobody got to see anythin' good. I was the only one flashin' the world." He nudged me gently. "Hurry up an' call Kane before he goes to sleep."

I kissed him again and grabbed my phone.

I had just pulled on my T-shirt when a tap at the door announced Kane's arrival. I checked the peephole, then let him in.

He strode over to the bed, his forehead wrinkled in concern.

"I told her I'm fine, an' I am," Hellhound said. "But she wants a second opinion."

"She's a smart woman," Kane said, studying the bruise. "If you didn't have so many tattoos it would be easier to see what's going on."

"Get over it."

Kane ignored the comment. "Are you feeling lightheaded? Any numbness or tingling in your legs? Pain in your back or chest or arms?"

"Nah, I'm fine."

"If you're lying, I'll punch you so hard on your other side that you'll have a matched set."

Hellhound grinned. "If I'm lyin', I'll be dead by mornin', so fuck ya."

Kane turned to me with a smile. "He's fine."

Planting my fists on my hips, I glared at them. "Not funny."

Kane sobered. "Seriously, Aydan, I don't think there's anything to worry about. He's conscious and oriented, there's no indication of nerve damage, and it's been almost two hours since he was shot. If he had internal bleeding he'd be losing consciousness by now."

"But what if it's a slow bleed? And what if something happens and it turns into a gusher in the night?"

Kane frowned.

"And don't tell me it can't happen," I added.

He sighed. "You're right, the only way to know for sure is with imaging at the hospital."

Arnie crossed his arms over his chest. "I ain't goin' to the fuckin' hospital."

"I know you have a phobia, but-" I began.

Kane gripped my shoulder gently and interrupted my futile argument. "Aydan, I'm not dismissing your concerns, but I have seen a few people shot in the stomach while wearing a vest, and none of them had complications. The impact point is below his liver and spleen and he's not having any other symptoms. It's a bad bruise and it's going to hurt for a while, but I'm pretty sure that's all it is. You've been shot while wearing a vest. You know what it's like."

I grimaced. "Yeah. Half my chest turned black and purple, and I could barely move my arm for a week."

"So unless he shows signs of shock or passes out, don't worry." The corner of Kane's mouth quirked up. "And if you can get him into a hospital while he's still conscious, I'll be forever impressed."

"There ya go, darlin'," Hellhound said heartily, evading the hospital topic. "Two professional opinions, plus ya been through it yourself. Ya can stop worryin'."

Begging Kane to stay just to reassure me some more would be beyond childish.

I forced my lips into a smile. "Thanks. I know I'm being a Nervous Nellie."

"No, you're not." Kane drew me into a gentle hug. "You're exhausted and stressed and dealing with a lot of trauma. I'd be shocked if you *weren't* feeling anxious."

Pressing my face into his shoulder, I somehow managed to resist the urge to wrap my arms and legs around him and cling until all my problems dissolved.

"Thanks," I said instead, and pulled away. "I'm sorry I bothered you. Go get some sleep."

"You didn't bother me. I'm glad you called." He dipped his chin and gave me a soft kiss. "Otherwise I wouldn't have gotten my goodnight kiss."

As I knew he expected me to do, I laughed and pushed him away. "Okay, but that's all you get. My reputation still hasn't recovered from that time Moonbeam and Nichele caught me with you, Arnie, and Orion."

Kane grinned and made for the door. "Moonbeam and Nichele were impressed."

"Well, duh," I agreed. "Three gorgeous guys at the same time? What woman wouldn't be impressed?"

"Who was the third guy?" Hellhound inquired. "'Cause if he was gorgeous, I know ya ain't talkin' about me."

"With your pretty pink and silver aura?" I teased. "Of course it was you."

"Shut up."

"Goodnight," Kane said, and let himself out, still grinning.

I blew out a long, tired breath.

"Come to bed, darlin'," Hellhound said.

Before he could try to get up again, I stripped off my clothes, doused the lights, and eased in beside him.

"C'mere." He lifted his arm, making room for me to cuddle against his uninjured side and lay my head on his shoulder. "Comfy?"

"Yeah..." The word vanished in a giant yawn.

"Just relax, then." He stroked my hair in gentle passes that turned my bones to mush. "Just relax..."

"Aydan." A quiet voice dragged me to near-wakefulness.

I managed an interrogative groan. "Uhhh?"

"Time to-"

A piercing beep galvanized every muscle in my body and I jolted upright, snatching my Glock from under the pillow.

The beeps continued, and Hellhound grimaced and reached over to silence the clock radio. "Sorry, darlin', I was hopin' to wake ya a little easier than the alarm."

"Jesus." I fell back on the pillows and massaged my chest in an attempt to convince my heart to stay put. "Thanks for trying. It wasn't quite as much of a shock as it could have been." Sitting up, I studied him. "How are you feeling this morning?"

"Like somebody shot me in the gut. Other than that, fine."

I folded back the covers to examine his injury. The bruise had spread, forming an unflattering purple background to his tattoos, but it didn't seem quite as scary now that he'd made it through the night.

"Did you get any sleep?" I asked.

"Yeah. Didn't think I would, but-"

My phone vibrated and I pounced on it, checking the call display. "Hi, John."

"Good morning. Is Arnie with you?"

"He's right here, hold on."

"No, it's all right," Kane said hurriedly. "Put me on speaker. I just wanted to be sure you could both listen."

Fear seized me, and my voice came out tight. "Okay, you're on speaker."

"Webb traced the phone that was used for the ransom call."

Hellhound and I rolled off opposite sides of the bed and grabbed our clothes.

"Don't panic, it's handled," Kane said urgently, obviously hearing the frantic rustle of our movement. "Are you still there?"

"We're here." I perched on the edge of the bed. "Go ahead."

"They used LaVonda's phone, then ditched it along with the bag. The phone had sunk into some fresh snow so the police missed it in the dark last night. Webb tracked the phone's GPS. When I found out it was at the same location where the bag had been, I called the police and they retrieved it. They'll check it for fingerprints or any other evidence."

Hellhound sank onto the bed with a groan, clutching his jeans. "Fuck. So we still got no way to track 'em."

"That phone is eliminated, but there was still the second call. It came from a different number and Webb's tracing it now."

"Did he make progress on anything else?" I asked.

"He's narrowed the rental cars down to a couple of possibilities. He'll have something soon. I told him to use burner phones to contact us from now on."

"Shit!" Hellhound's bark of consternation made me jerk around to face him.

"What?" I demanded.

"We can't drop off-grid."

"Why not?"

"'Cause if the kidnappers are gonna make another ransom call, the only number they got is Kane's cell. We gotta keep it with us."

We stared at each other in dismay.

Kane's reassuring voice came through the speaker. "Don't worry, I'll get Webb to monitor the number. He can intercept any incoming calls and then call us on a burner."

That would work for a couple of hours, until Holt started tracking us. Then he'd call Spider and we'd be busted.

I kept that thought to myself.

Hellhound let out a breath. "Okay. They oughta be callin' pretty soon." His voice tightened. "Shit, they shoulda called already. What're they waitin' for?"

Neither Kane nor I replied.

The colour drained from Arnie's face, his hands clenching hard on the jeans he still held. "She's dead. They got nothin' left to bargain with."

"You don't know that," Kane said firmly. "There are lots of reasons why they might be delaying their call. They want us to be panicky. And they'll want to make sure they get the money this time, so they're probably setting up a foolproof ambush for us."

"They might have even followed us here," I said with chagrin.

"I don't think so," Kane replied. "I didn't notice a tail last night; but just in case they have the resources to track my phone, we'll need to wear our vests and be alert when we leave here. I'll come to your room at eight."

"Okay, see you then." I disconnected and glanced at the clock. Twenty minutes left. "Guess I'm not washing my hair this morning."

Hellhound still hadn't moved. He sat staring blindly at nothing, his fists contorting the denim.

I reached over and touched his knuckles, the skin stretched so tightly that the tendons stood out like cables.

"Arnie?"

"D'ya think she's dead?" His voice was hollow. "Tell me the truth."

My heart clenched. LaVonda had already told the kidnappers they had all the money. If she'd also told them that the other bag we'd carried out of her apartment was a cat carrier, they might have believed her after we brought the carrier to the drop.

We might have signed her death warrant.

CHAPTER 28

A lie rose to my lips, but I bit it back. It wouldn't work this time.

I stroked Arnie's knuckles. "Until we know for sure, we have to assume she's alive. We have to keep our heads in the game."

He let out a breath and squared his shoulders. "You're right." He rose cautiously, wincing. "I'll feed Princess an' pack up her stuff while ya go through the bathroom."

When Kane's tap sounded at the door on the dot of eight o'clock, I checked the peephole and then let him in.

He raised an eyebrow at the pile beside the door. "That cat has more luggage than all three of us put together."

I sighed. "Yeah, we're not exactly travelling light."

As Hellhound came over to put on his parka, Kane eyed the bulletproof vests we both wore. "I'm glad we all have vests. I checked outside and didn't see any threats, but stay alert just in case."

We both nodded and reached for the luggage. After a short wrangle, John and I persuaded Hellhound to carry only his small duffel bag and guitar, while we divided Princess's gear between the two of us. Hellhound pretended offence at our coddling, but the stiffness of his movements belied his insistence that he was fine.

When we stepped cautiously outside, the crystal-clear sky was brightening and the arctic cold stole my breath.

"Holy shit," I wheezed, half-expecting my words to freeze solid and fall with a clatter at my feet. "Lucky you had the car plugged in."

As we hurried out to the parking lot, I realized that not only had Kane plugged the car in the previous night, he'd also started it this morning. Clouds of exhaust vapour wreathed the vehicle, hanging in the still air like a miniature fog bank.

We rapidly loaded the trunk, put Princess's carrier and Arnie's guitar in the back seat, and took our places.

"Omigod," I groaned as I slid into the passenger side. "You turned on the seat heater. I'm totally in love with you."

As I glanced over at Kane, a flicker in his expression made my stomach twitch.

Shit. Me and my big mouth.

An instant later Kane hid his reaction in a grin. "If I'd known a seat heater was all it took..." He let the sentence hang as he reversed out of the parking spot.

We all kept eyes on the surrounding traffic as we got under way, but a few evasive manoeuvres convinced us that we weren't being followed. Yet.

A fast food drive-through furnished us each with our breakfast of choice, and we ate in silence on the way to Home Depot.

In its parking lot, Kane turned to me. "You'll be too memorable, so Arnie and I will rent the trucks. As soon as we've got them, we'll follow you over to the parkade." He handed me the keys to the rental car.

I nodded and reluctantly got out of the vehicle to switch to the driver's seat. It was toasty warm, and I snuggled into it as I watched the two men stride across the frozen parking lot to the building.

Long minutes later, I identified the drawback to our plan: I was far too warm and comfortable. Despite the anxiety that gnawed at me, fatigue settled like a leaden blanket. God, I needed to sleep for a week.

My eyelids drooped.

A tap at the window jerked me upright, adrenaline gushing and hand rocketing toward my holster.

When I realized it was Kane outside, I aborted my grab for my gun. "Idiot," I muttered, and powered the window down.

He smiled. "I'm sorry to wake you. You looked so peaceful."

"Too damn peaceful. I can't believe I was stupid enough to fall asleep on the job."

"You wouldn't have fallen asleep if it had been important for you to stay awake." He reached in and squeezed my shoulder, giving me a serious look. "Don't beat yourself up. You weren't on surveillance and you knew you were safe here. Grabbing a nap was smart." He smiled. "We're ready to go. Lead on."

"Oh. Um..." Cringing at my own incompetence, I asked, "Can I follow you instead? I can't remember exactly where that parkade was. I wasn't driving, and then Arnie and I came up on foot through the back alley."

"Oh, that's right. No problem." Kane cocked a thumb at the building. "We're parked in front of the store. Just pull up behind us and I'll take point."

Grateful that he never treated me like an idiot no matter how stupid I felt, I mumbled, "Okay, thanks."

As he strode back to the orange and white truck bearing the Home Depot logo, I reversed out of the parking stall and circled around to come up behind him. Hellhound was behind the wheel of an orange Home Depot panel van, and our little caravan moved off.

Trailing them through the light morning traffic, I glanced at the dashboard clock. A quarter to nine. In forty-five minutes, Holt would get off the plane and onto our trail.

Maybe I should just drive to the airport and meet him after all. What if our cat-and-mouse game jeopardized our ability to find LaVonda's kidnappers?

What if we couldn't save her?

My greasy breakfast weighed in my belly like a cold stone. Maybe it was already too late. Maybe Arnie was right, and LaVonda was dead.

My throat tightened at the thought of her dismembered body lying cold and alone in the bitter winter. Arnie would be devastated.

No, dammit, I couldn't think that way.

LaVonda *wasn't* dead. She wasn't even injured. She was fine. Somehow we would figure out where she was and rescue her unharmed, and the kidnappers would be arrested.

Then LaVonda would prove that she wasn't a murderer or a thief, and she and Arnie would have a loving reunion and live happily ever after. And Holt would laugh and say he'd only been joking; and Dermott would buy me a thoughtful Christmas gift and apologize profusely while swearing eternal friendship. And flying pigs would flutter gracefully above the frozen ski slopes of hell.

I groaned and concentrated on driving.

Anxious mews from the back seat alerted me to the next problem. A glance at the cat carrier showed a small white paw prodding insistently at the mesh.

"You can hold it, Princess," I encouraged without much hope. "Your litter box is in the trunk and I promise you can use it just as soon as we get to the parkade. Just don't shit in your carrier, there's a good girl. Just hold it for a few more minutes, *please*."

The vibration of my phone interrupted my entreaties. Muscles bunching with renewed tension, I signalled right and braked hard, slithering around a tight corner into the parking lot of a convenience store. A glance at the phone's call display accelerated my pulse.

I hit the Accept button. "What's up, Spider?"

"I have a trace on the second phone."

"*Where?*" I snapped. My phone vibrated again. "Hold on, John's calling." I toggled to the other call. "Hello?"

"What happened? Why did you turn off?" Kane demanded.

"Spider traced the second phone. Call Arnie and come back here." I hung up without a goodbye and toggled back to Spider's call. "Go ahead."

He fired out a machine-gun burst of words. "It's in a semi-industrial area, near a little strip mall where there are a couple of stores and a restaurant. The signal should be accurate to about six metres, so I'm guessing it's in the restaurant, but I could be wrong." He rattled off the name and address of the restaurant. "The phone's not moving right now. I'm trying to narrow down the location. Call me when you're ready to move." He disconnected.

I punched the address into my phone's GPS and calculated our route. Ten minutes away.

My pulse picked up. Could this be it?

As the two Home Depot vehicles turned into the parking lot, I got out of the car and hurried over. Kane did, too, and we convened at Hellhound's van before he could get out. He powered the window down, his face taut.

I repeated Spider's information and showed them the route I'd plotted on my phone. "Maybe we're going to get lucky," I added. "If they're eating, they'll be there for a while. I'll go in-"

"No, I'll go," Hellhound interrupted.

"You can't; you're dead," I said firmly. "The driver last night got a good look at your face before they shot you. And they knew you weren't John, because they called him right afterward. That means they can identify both of you. So I'm going in."

Hellhound shook his head and opened his mouth to argue, but Kane overrode him. "She's right. You and I will cover the front and rear exits. Aydan, you're only going in for recon. If you see LaVonda or recognize any of the kidnappers, get out immediately. If not, Hellhound can call their cell phone. They don't know his voice."

"Perfect," I agreed. "I'll stay long enough to see who answers their phone, and then I'll leave and we can figure out our next move."

"But if they got her there in the restaurant..." Hellhound began.

"If they're sitting in a restaurant surrounded by innocent people, there's too much potential for collateral damage." Kane's tone was final.

Hellhound's knuckles whitened on the wheel, but he didn't argue. "Awright. Let's move."

Seconds later we were driving again. Princess's increasingly agitated mews formed a suitable counterpoint for my thumping heart. Maintaining the speed limit was more than my nerves could bear, but I managed to stay only ten kilometres per hour over. Kane and Hellhound did the same.

My mind raced, considering and discarding strategies. If only I knew the layout of the restaurant, I could plan better. I needed to be able to see all the other diners, but I could hardly roam up and down aisles peering at people. Would I be lucky enough to find someplace with a view of all the tables?

Ignoring the distracted-driving laws with a pang of guilt, I hit the speed dial for Spider.

"It's still not moving," he said without a greeting. "And I'm pretty sure it's in the restaurant."

"Good. We're on our way there. John and Arnie are going to cover the exits from outside, and I'm going in. If I see any of the kidnappers, I'll leave right away and we'll figure out a plan. If I don't recognize anybody, Arnie will call their phone number and I'll watch to see who answers."

"Okay, I'll text the number to Hellhound." Spider hesitated. "Good luck. And be careful."

"Thanks. I will." I disconnected.

So many ways this could go wrong. Our whole plan hinged on the hope that the kidnappers hadn't gotten a close look at me at LaVonda's apartment.

If they recognized me...

An icy chill crept down my spine. If they were armed, this could turn into a deadly situation.

My hands trembled on the wheel. I was a good shot, but I couldn't take out three of them that fast. If they opened fire it would be bloodbath. Dozens of innocent people could be injured or killed.

Oh God, no. There had to be a better way.

Minutes ticked away. I drove on autopilot, my brain spinning in a frantic attempt to come up with a plan that wouldn't risk more lives.

My mind was still blank when the turnoff appeared.

No choice.

I parked near the side of the restaurant. As I tucked my gun into my parka pocket, Hellhound's van circled around the rear of the mall while Kane parked a few spaces away from the front of the restaurant. The load of two-by-fours in the back of his truck fit right in with the battered contractor-type vehicles that occupied the small parking lot.

I drew a deep breath. Then another. Princess meowed every few seconds, winding my nerves up even more.

The vibration of my phone made me twitch, and I snatched it out and accepted a call from Kane's number.

"Ready?" I asked.

"We're in place. I have a good view of the restaurant. I should be able to see you inside if you stay near the front window. If you need Hellhound to call the number, unzip your parka."

I held my voice level. "Okay. I'm going now."

"I love you."

"I love you, too," I said absently, and hung up.

CHAPTER 29

Pulling my hood over my head, I got out of the car and did my best to walk casually to the front of the restaurant.

My heart hammered. Out here in the bright sun, I was impossible to miss. I might not even make it into the restaurant before everything went to hell.

The familiar texture of my pistol's grip reassured my palm, but my knuckles ached with tension. I eased my hand, blowing out a small breath.

The squeaking of my boots on the snow sounded loud enough to alert everyone inside. Despite the stiffness of my bulletproof vest under my parka, I had to force myself not to flinch as I pulled open the door.

No gunshots greeted me.

The tiny restaurant was dim compared to the outdoor brilliance of sun on snow. Blinking, I raked a glance across all the tables in the room without recognizing any faces.

A stout middle-aged man in a white apron gave me a friendly wave from behind a half-wall that divided the restaurant from the kitchen. "Go ahead and sit anywhere, I'll be right with you."

Shit, I hadn't wanted to attract attention. Now everybody was looking at me.

Somehow I managed a smile. "Thanks." Half-turning toward the window, I lowered the zipper on my parka a few inches, then sidled to the nearest vacant table and let my trembling knees drop me into a chair.

Hellhound should be phoning any minute...

The white-aproned man hurried over. "Hi, would you like coffee? Or something else to drink? Here's a menu for you."

A ringtone sounded from the kitchen.

Shit! We'd been fooled by the rental cars and the connection to Winnipeg. We hadn't even considered that one of the kidnappers might be working here.

Shit, shit, shit!

The phone rang again, then again. The waiter was eyeing me, a small frown forming while he waited for me to respond.

Another ring.

I jerked my attention back to the waiter. "Um. Sorry. If it's okay, I'll just look at the menu first. My husband is on his way, and he's a really picky eater so if there's nothing here he'll want to eat, we might not be staying."

"Oh." The man summoned a forced-looking smile. "Sure, that's fine. I'll be back in a few minutes."

The phone had stopped ringing.

Had someone answered it?

"Thanks," I said, trying to be unobtrusive about peering into the kitchen as he turned away.

I couldn't see anybody in there, and the murmur of conversation in the restaurant blurred my hearing.

Dammit!

The white-aproned man was almost back to the kitchen when the phone rang again.

Then again.

He rounded the corner into the kitchen and bent to retrieve something from under a counter. The phone stopped mid-ring, and he straightened, a phone to his ear.

Looking directly at me.

A deluge of adrenaline sizzled through my veins. I forced myself to stare down at the menu.

Get out. Now.

Catching his eye, I gave him a regretful smile and a headshake, and rose unhurriedly. The distance to the door seemed interminable.

Ten steps. Nine. Eight. Seven...

"I'm sorry you didn't find what you were looking for." The voice from behind made me freeze.

Was that a taunt?

Swallowing hard, I turned.

The waiter gave me a smile. Nothing in his hands.

"I'm sorry, too." Somehow my voice came out sounding sincere. "Your food looks great. I'm going to come back some other day when I don't have Mr. Picky with me."

He smiled. "I hope you do. Have a good day."

My phone vibrated, and I jumped. "Oh. That'll be my husband." I turned away and headed for the door again as I answered. "Hi, honey."

"Pull out." Kane's voice was expressionless.

"No, they didn't have anything you'd like," I said. As I reached for the door handle, I added, "Okay, fine. If you really want to go to McDonald's, we can." I rolled my eyes at the waiter, who returned a sympathetic grimace as I stepped out the door to safety.

As soon as the door closed behind me, I made for the car, lowering my voice. "What's happening?"

Kane sounded tired. "Nothing. The phone was ditched. The man who answered it was the owner of the restaurant. Somebody had found the phone lying in the parking lot, and handed it in to lost-and-found."

"Oh, for *shit's* sake!" I didn't quite wail, but it was close. "Another dead end! And now it's twenty after nine and Holt will be tracking us in minutes!"

"Yes, we'll have to leave the rental car here. Hellhound will take Princess and our luggage in the van, since there's no extra room in this truck cab."

My heart sank. "Oh, shit. Princess."

"What's wrong?" Kane's voice was tight.

"Nothing, I hope..." I unlocked the car, inhaling cautiously. "Nope, nothing wrong yet, but I think she really needs her litter box."

My words were nearly drowned out by Princess's incessant meowing. The carrier rocked with her attempts to paw her way free.

As Hellhound pulled up behind the car, I hurried around to open the trunk and get the litter box. Balancing it awkwardly on one drawn-up knee, I wrenched open the side door of the van and set the box inside the cargo bay.

"Litter box emergency," I threw over my shoulder as I rushed back to the car. "Hang on, Princess, hang on..."

Grabbing the carrier, I scurried back to the van and yanked the sliding door shut behind me. When I unzipped the carrier Princess bounded out, meowing frantically, but she didn't get in the litter box. Instead, she fixed Hellhound and me with what could only be a feline glare and meowed even louder, her tail switching.

"What?" I demanded. "What do you want? Don't tell me you're hungry again." A few more ear-piercing meows convinced me to slip out of the van again, careful to block the door so she couldn't escape.

When I returned with her food and bowl a few seconds

later, her cries had reached a crescendo and her tail lashed so violently I almost expected it to detach and fly across the van.

"Here! Food!" I put the bowl in front of her.

She ignored it and kept yowling.

Nerves stretched to breaking, I barked, "What the hell is your problem?"

"Come on, darlin', time to get outta the van," Hellhound said gently.

"What?"

"Let's go." He eased out of the driver's seat and closed the door behind him.

Head throbbing, I exited via the side door and rolled it shut behind me.

He rounded the vehicle and came over to put an arm around my shoulders. "Take a breath, darlin'."

Some benevolent patron saint of self-control somehow prevented me from screaming obscenities and kicking the hell out of the van. Afraid to speak in case I completely lost it, I drew a deep breath and exhaled slowly, my entire body vibrating.

"It's okay," Hellhound soothed, rubbing my shoulder. "You're just too tired to handle adrenaline the way ya usually do. You'll be okay in a minute."

His compassion quenched my blaze of temper, and tears prickled the backs of my eyes. I stared fixedly at the white wisps of cloud sailing across the blue sky. Breathe. In. Out. Slow like ocean waves.

An icy breeze stirred my hair, making me shiver.

"Okay?" Hellhound asked.

"F-Fine. S-Sorry." I pressed closer, shivering in earnest now. Partly cold; mostly nerves and exhaustion.

"No problem, darlin'." He sounded weary beyond words.

Shame twisted my guts. After all the fear and frustration and pain he'd been through, I should have been comforting him.

I slipped my arm around him and laid my head on his shoulder. "How are you doing?"

He sighed. "Just tryin' to keep my head in the game."

"Well, we don't need to stand out here in the cold." I nudged him in the direction of the driver's seat.

He didn't move. "Actually, we kinda do." Something in his voice made me glance up to see the ghost of a twinkle in his eye.

I straightened. "Why? What do you mean?"

"I mean Princess is shy. She can't use the litter box while we're watchin'."

I let my forehead fall against his shoulder. "You're kidding, right?"

"Nope." He pressed a kiss to the top of my head. "How'd ya like it if somebody watched ya takin' a dump?"

"My butt's puckering just thinking about it."

He chuckled. "That's why she was freakin' out. Betcha there's a helluva stink in that van right now."

Kane's truck pulled up and he frowned out the open window. "Why are you standing there? We need to clear the area. Holt could be tracing that rental car already."

"Go get in the truck with Kane, darlin'," Hellhound encouraged. "I'll wait 'til Princess is done an' then follow ya."

"Follow us where?" I threw a questioning look at Kane. "Any ideas?"

He made a wry face. "We might as well go and check into that motel. Until Webb gets us more information, we're at a standstill."

Unless Holt had already shut Spider down. Then we were dead in the water.

"Okay," I agreed, and gave Hellhound a hug and kiss. "Enjoy your bathroom-attendant duties. Don't inhale too deeply when you open that door."

He chuckled and kissed me back, but his eyes were bleak. I wasn't the only one reading the handwriting on the wall.

I hesitated. Maybe I should stay with him.

"Get goin', darlin'," he said, giving me a nudge toward Kane's truck.

"I could wait with you."

"Nah. You're the one Holt's trackin'. Hurry up, now."

I sighed. "Okay. Time to ditch our phones."

Hellhound gave me his and I went over to collect Kane's, then dumped them into the trunk of the rental car along with my own before climbing into the passenger side of Kane's truck.

As we pulled out of the parking lot, I said, "I wonder if I should have stayed with Arnie. I can guess what's going through his mind right now."

Kane sighed. "I can, too, but at least this way he only has to worry about LaVonda instead of both of you. That will make him feel better. As much as he can, anyway."

"I guess." I pulled out a burner phone and dialled Spider's burner.

"Nothing yet," he said by way of a greeting. "I researched the renter of the Ford Escape that ambushed Hellhound and he looks like another small-time thug. He's from Winnipeg, too. I don't know why the professionals would be working with him; they're not in the same league at all. I've got access to the major auto-makers' navigation systems and all I need is a VIN number to track that other rental. I've spotted a stolen identity that was used to rent a car at the airport yesterday morning and I should have it any minute now..."

He sounded run off his feet, and I hurriedly said, "It's okay, I'm not pushing you. I just wanted to let you know we're off-grid now."

"Okay, thanks." He hung up without a goodbye.

I stowed the burner phone in my waist pouch. "It sounds like he's getting really close." Trying to ease the tension, I threw a pointed look at the stack of two-by-fours in the truck bed before giving Kane a teasing glance. "Those'll be a bit tricky to take home on the plane."

His mouth quirked up. "I'll return them for a refund when I take the truck back, but I didn't want to attract attention by renting a truck without having a load for it. Two-by-fours are unremarkable. The guy at the counter will have forgotten me by now."

"Good thinking." I settled more comfortably in the seat, letting out a breath. What a relief to be able to depend on his expertise.

"Have a nap," Kane said. "I don't think there's a scenic route to the motel, so you might as well rest while you can."

I nodded and closed my eyes.

Despite the weariness of my body, my mind raced. Why were the kidnappers taking so long to call us?

Over eight hours had passed since they'd mutilated LaVonda's hands. What if she had died of her injuries?

And what if Spider's trace on the rental car didn't pan out? How long would we keep looking, hoping to find a clue?

My stomach clenched. We'd keep looking until LaVonda's body was found. After thirty years of fruitless searching, poor Arnie would suffer another heart-rending vigil. One that might not end until spring, if the kidnappers had dumped her body somewhere on the endless expanse of winter-barren prairie.

And what if her body were never found?

The police would eventually locate the kidnappers and question them, but even if they were charged, there wouldn't be enough evidence to convict them.

They'd get off scot-free...

My phone vibrated and I snatched it out of my waist pouch.

As soon as I said 'hello', Spider's triumphant cry filled my ear. "Got them! They're at the airport!"

CHAPTER 30

"The *airport?*" My voice came out in a squawk. "Shit, we're on the other side of the city!"

Kane slammed on the brakes and hooked an illegal U-turn.

"Get Arnie on a conference call," I barked into my phone.

"On it."

A few seconds later a ringtone sounded over the line, answered almost immediately by Hellhound's gravelly voice. "Yeah?"

"We're on a three-way call with Aydan," Spider said rapidly. "I just traced the kidnapper's rental car to the airport. They returned it five minutes ago."

"*Shit!* We're on the-"

"Other side of the city, I know," Spider interrupted. "But it's okay. Holt's still at the airport, and I sent him photos. He hasn't spotted the kidnappers yet, but it's a small airport so he won't miss them. The police have a car on the way over there, too. I'm contacting airport security now..." His voice faded as the sound of clicking computer keys floated over the line.

"We've got them," Kane said. "They can't clear security in the airport and get on a flight before Holt or the police corner them."

As I processed Spider's earlier words, my heart sank. Spider knew Holt was at the airport. That meant Holt had already contacted him.

"Spider, did you tell Holt where we were?" I asked.

"No, when he called and said you were late, I told him you were tracking down the kidnappers' phone and you'd be there as soon as you could. Do you want me to-"

"No, it's okay," I interrupted. "We'll see him at the airport."

Thank God I hadn't mentioned our avoidance of Holt. At least Spider's innocent cooperation would keep him out of trouble with Dermott.

"This is weird," Spider said worriedly. "It's just a tiny little airport. If they returned the car five minutes ago, they should be in there. Holt couldn't miss them."

A blinding flash of inspiration hit me, banging my heart against my ribs. "*Fuck!* Spider, you said you'd traced their personal vehicles! Did the Winnipeg police confirm that *all* their vehicles are still in Winnipeg? Including Fitzgerald's?"

"Oh *crap!* I confirmed theirs but not Fitzgerald's, hang on..." Frantic key-clicking took over the line. "I'm checking all vehicles registered to Fitzgerald and his businesses now!"

"Dammit!" Kane snapped, braking and swerving into a left-turn lane. "You're right, Aydan! They have another vehicle. That's why there are so many players. Some of them flew in and rented vehicles so they could act fast to grab LaVonda, while at least one other drove in from Winnipeg. It's probably a cube van or some other large vehicle with no windows so they could hold a hostage..." He accelerated around the corner. "Arnie, we're heading for the TransCanada Highway eastbound. They're taking her back to Fitzgerald in Winnipeg!"

"Fuck!" Hellhound rasped. "He ain't just after the money, he wants revenge, too! Webb, ya got anythin' yet?"

Spider was still clicking keys. "Not yet. Do you want me to contact the RCMP to set up a roadblock?"

"No." Hellhound's refusal overrode my 'Yes'.

"*NO!*" Hellhound repeated loudly. "If they see a roadblock, there's only one way this ends. They kill her."

"Why would they do that?" I argued. "Then they're up on murder charges instead of just kidnapping."

"If Fitzgerald's as bad as we think, these assholes are dead meat if they show up without LaVonda an' the money," Hellhound ground out. "An' as far as they know, they already killed me. So they got nothin' to lose."

"Arnie could be right," Kane said. "And if the police stop them with a roadblock, we'll have a hostage situation..." He trailed off.

I glanced over at him, my heart sinking. His jaw was clenched, his knuckles white on the steering wheel. I could practically hear the ghosts screaming in his head. Ten helpless hostages murdered in cold blood while he watched, unable to prevent the slaughter.

He wasn't going to offer a voice of reason here.

"But we don't know whether we'll be ahead of them or far behind," I argued. "We don't know what they're driving, so all we can do is watch for Manitoba license plates. And even if we catch up and identify them, how are we going to stop them safely when they're driving at a hundred kilometres per hour? If they get to Winnipeg before us, I bet Fitzgerald has a huge stronghold. If they're only keeping LaVonda alive so he can take his revenge on her personally, we won't get inside in time to save her."

Or we might arrive in time to retrieve the torture-ravaged shell of a woman for whom death would have been a more merciful end.

I didn't say that out loud.

"If they only left the airport five minutes ago, we'll be ahead of them," Kane said with certainty. "Or we'll be close enough behind to catch them. As to the rest..."

"We'll figure somethin' out," Hellhound finished. "But we ain't riskin' a police roadblock. Webb, tell the Regina cops an' the RCMP that we're in pursuit, an' they gotta stay the fuck outta this."

Kane offered no objection.

Dammit.

I took a short breath and dove in. "Arnie... you've driven that highway for years. You know there are side roads every mile or so. How are we going to stop them with only two vehicles? They can just drive around us."

"We'll figure somethin' out," he repeated obstinately. "You're right, there're a shitpile of mile roads, so the RCMP can't stop 'em with roadblocks, either. They ain't got enough units. An' I ain't gonna roll the dice with LaVonda's life. Webb, call 'em off!"

Spider's voice was small and hesitant. "Sorry, Arnie, I know how you feel but I can't really take orders from you. Aydan? What do you want me to do?"

Oh, God. Another life-or-death choice.

I sank my head into my hands. I could feel Kane's gaze boring into the side of my head but I didn't turn to meet his eyes.

"Aydan..." Arnie's rasp was soft and full of pleading.

My guts twisted.

I had no right to decide. And I wasn't brave enough to live with my choice if I guessed wrong.

My voice came out thin and defeated. "Call them off, Spider. And let us know as soon as you get any hits on

Fitzgerald's vehicles. We'll be driving eastbound on the TransCanada and watching for Manitoba plates. Keep this conference call open."

CHAPTER 31

"Thanks, darlin'." Even over the poor phone connection, Arnie's voice was rough with emotion.

I didn't deserve his thanks.

"You're welcome," I mumbled. "We need a plan. Spider, can you get a fix on our phones so you know exactly where we are?"

"Are you carrying your personal cell phones?"

I sighed, already knowing the answer to my question. "Nope, we're off-grid. So you'd have to go through the same process as you did to find the other burner. It'll take too long. And we need all your attention on the vehicle search."

"I could ask the analyst-on-call to trace your phone."

"But it'll still take hours."

"No, it'll be fast because you can give me the SIM card information and I've already got access to the carriers."

"Okay, I'll give you John's so I don't have to disconnect from this call." I extracted my reading glasses and squinted at the phone Kane handed me, reading off the data. So much for our attempt at staying off-grid.

When Spider had everything he needed, I let out a long breath. "We're probably going to be on the road for hours. Damn, I wish I'd peed at that restaurant."

"Um..." Spider said bashfully.

Imagining his blush almost made me smile.

But not quite.

"I'll leave this line open while I call the police and the office," he said. His voice faded as though he'd gone across the room.

"Remember, guys, this is only a hunch," I cautioned Kane and Hellhound. "They might not have a Manitoba vehicle at all. And even if they do, they might not be leaving Regina. We could get all the way to Winnipeg only to find out they're holed up in a hotel here. We'll be wasting hours."

"It's a chance worth taking," Kane said. "Your theory makes sense; and even if it's wrong, Holt and the police can cover Regina until we're back. We're not leaving any loose ends here."

"Right," Hellhound agreed. "Now, how're we gonna stop these assholes?"

"If we don't want anything that looks like an official roadblock, we'll have to stage an accident," Kane said.

I shot him a look. "Any accident that's spectacular enough to stop both lanes of traffic on the TransCanada is going to be dangerous, and it'll probably leave us with at least one vehicle out of commission."

"An' if we drive into the ditch an' try an' wave 'em down like we need help, they won't stop," Hellhound added.

"I wasn't talking about a vehicular accident," Kane said.

I caught his glance at our load of two-by-fours, and hope straightened my spine. "That's it! That'll work."

"What?" Hellhound demanded. "What'll work?"

"We've got a load of two-by-fours." I thought out loud. "If we can get far enough ahead to scatter them across both lanes, I could run back waving my arms to stop traffic. It would look completely natural. Then, while you guys are picking up two-by-fours, I can just walk up to their vehicle, looking apologetic. They'll roll down the window and I'll say

I'm sorry for the inconvenience and we'll have the road cleared as quickly as we can. Before they roll up the window, I can fire my trank pistol into their cab. Even if I don't hit anybody, they'll all pass out for five minutes. That's all we need."

"Unless they recognize you as you walk toward them," Kane pointed out.

I held my voice steady so the fear wouldn't leak out. "Well, I'm wearing my vest, and they'd have to roll down a window to shoot at me. I only have to hit close to their open window with one dart."

"Their range with a bullet is a helluva lot better than yours with a dart," Hellhound said.

"Yeah, but they won't recognize me until I'm close enough to take the shot," I argued, wishing I could believe my own words. "Then they'll be rushing to get their windows rolled down and stick their weapons out and shoot one-handed, and all I have to do is take a simple two-handed shot from a solid stance, and hit somewhere close. Piece of cake."

"Or they'll stay cool like the professionals they are," Kane said. "They'll wait for you to walk up to their window, they'll roll it down pretending not to recognize you, and then they'll gun you down at point-blank range."

"Thanks," I muttered. "If you've got a better idea, I'd love to hear it."

Both men were silent.

"So we have a plan," I said.

"Not yet. I'm still thinkin'," Hellhound growled. "There's gotta be a safer way."

"Well, neither of you can get close to them. They'll recognize you for sure. They only glimpsed me in the dark with all the chaos of the apartment fire."

"Or they got a real fuckin' good look at ya when we walked outta the cop shop in broad daylight," Hellhound rasped.

A chill trickled down my spine. "What do you mean?"

"I mean, I been wonderin' how the hell they knew LaVonda was gonna go back to the cop shop to pick up her duffel. An' the only thing I can think of is, they watched us get picked up by the cops at the apartment carryin' both bags, an' they watched us comin' outta the cop shop with only one."

My heart plummeted. "Oh. Shit."

"An' they didn't bother to follow us then, 'cause they wanted LaVonda an' her money together," Hellhound went on. "Besides, they figured they'd be able to suck us in later by usin' her for bait. An' it worked."

"Keep your eyes peeled, Aydan," Kane interrupted as he turned onto Victoria Avenue. "They could be anywhere, although I think we'll likely be ahead of them."

"Where are ya?" Hellhound asked. "I'm still on Park Street, just passin'..." He paused as though reading an upcoming road sign. "...Tenth Ave."

"We're on Victoria Avenue just passing Home Depot."

"So you're well ahead a' me. I'll slow down. Might as well open up the gap an' give us a better chance of bracketin' them."

"If we manage to spot them at all," I said gloomily, eyeing the traffic. "It's Christmas Eve, and a Saturday. Everybody in Canada is driving somewhere today to get home in time for Christmas. I can see three Manitoba license plates from here."

"They're all passenger cars or half-tons," Kane countered. "We have a clear view of the occupants. None of them are the kidnappers."

"I'm back," Spider announced over the open connection. "I've got a list of all vehicles that are registered to Richard Fitzgerald and his businesses. The police can't search his garage, though, because he hasn't done anything wrong."

"Nothin' we can prove," Hellhound said darkly. "Yet."

"Well, yeah, but we don't have any evidence that points directly to him," Spider said. "We're only guessing that LaVonda stole his money. If it's actually hers, then there's no connection at all. These other guys might be random internet trolls, and Fitzgerald might be innocent."

Hellhound snorted. "A guy like that ain't innocent. He just ain't got caught yet."

"Never mind that," I said. "Could any of his vehicles be used to transport a hostage?"

"Well, I guess any of them could, if they put her in the trunk..."

My stomach lurched at the thought, but fortunately Kane spoke up.

"I think we can safely ignore that possibility. It's thirty below. If they want her alive, they can't leave her in a trunk for six hours."

"Oh, right." Spider's small release of breath indicated his relief. "Okay, then, we're looking at panel vans and delivery trucks."

"*Plural?*" My voice cracked.

"Yes, a couple of his businesses are courier companies. Guys One, Two, and Three are all managers in the courier businesses."

"Ain't that handy," Hellhound muttered.

"What are the business names?" I asked. "And what colour are the logos? And how big are the vehicles? Are we talking passenger-sized vans or big moving trucks, or what?"

"Some of each."

"Oh, for shit's sake!" I yanked a couple of handfuls of hair, fear and frustration coiling in my belly like poisonous snakes. "Could this get any harder?"

"Just give us the plate numbers and vehicle descriptions," Kane said in his calm cop voice. "And give us Fitzgerald's personal plates, too, just in case."

I scribbled them down as Spider reeled them off, but my tired brain failed to retain even one of the license numbers. Thank God we had Arnie's infallible memory on our side.

"All right, thank you," Kane said when he was done. "We'll be watching all Manitoba plates just to be safe, but the courier trucks and vans should be easy enough to spot. Have you got a fix on my phone yet?"

"Just give me a minute..." Computer keys tapped. "...okay, I've got you moving eastbound on Victoria Avenue at Coleman Crescent."

"That's us."

"Aydan..." Spider's voice was hesitant. "Do you want me to see if I can access the navigation systems in Fitzgerald's vehicles?"

Hellhound responded instantly. "Do it."

"Aydan?" Spider repeated.

"I assume you have qualms?" I asked gently.

"Well, um... maybe..." Spider blew out a short breath. "We're in the clear if I go after the courier vehicles, since we know three of the kidnappers work for the courier companies. But if I access Fitzgerald's personal vehicles, we could have legal issues."

"Go after the courier vehicles, then," I said. "They're our most likely option anyway."

"Okay."

We all fell silent and I concentrated on watching license plates, accompanied by the clicking of computer keys over the open phone line.

As we reached the highway, Kane settled the speedometer at fifteen kilometres over the speed limit. Not fast enough to be conspicuous, but we slowly overtook most other vehicles.

When Hellhound's voice came over the phone, I startled out of my absorption.

"Awright, I'm on Victoria Avenue now, too. I'm gonna step it up an' start closin' in on ya. If they're between us, I'll shout out."

"Okay," I replied. "Drive carefully."

"How's the highway?" he asked.

"Bare and dry, with just a bit of ground drift here and there. 'Way better than the city streets."

"'Kay, good."

We drove in silence again. White City fell behind us and the highway swung north, opening out onto endless snowbound prairie. Traffic thinned, leaving me far too much time for gruesome imaginings.

Hellhound's voice jerked me out of my unpleasant reverie. "Where are ya now?"

"Just coming up on Balgonie."

"I'm just about to White City."

"Wow, you're really picking up the pace."

His voice was grim. "If they're between us, the sooner I catch 'em, the better."

Unease slithered down my spine. I had assumed he was unarmed, and I hadn't noticed any weapons in his luggage when we were at the hotel. But he might have hidden something in his climbing gear.

If he spotted the kidnappers and did something rash...

Spider interrupted that worrisome thought. "Holt checked in. None of the kidnappers showed at the airport. The police seized their rental car, but the way LaVonda was bundled up when we saw her in the video footage, it's unlikely that any of her DNA is in there. Holt's questioning the rental lot attendants to see whether anybody noticed the kidnappers getting in a private vehicle or a cab after they dropped off the car."

"Any luck on the courier trucks yet?" I asked, knowing it was a stupid question. If he had anything, he would have told us.

"Not yet. I've moved three down the list because I don't have access to the manufacturer's navigation systems. The others-"

"*I got 'em!*" Hellhound's voice knifed across Spider's. "Just east a' White City, a passenger van with Manitoba plates. I'm catchin' up to 'em now."

"Don't do anything!" Kane snapped. "Just drive by and see if you can identify any of them. Don't be obvious about it."

The Killer spoke, hard and remote. "I ain't gonna fuck this up."

"I know you won't." Kane accelerated. "I'm going to open up some space. Webb, I want at least three minutes between us and that van so we can set up. Tell me where to stop."

"Hellhound, how fast are they going?" Spider demanded. "And exactly where are they?"

"They're goin' about a hundred, an' we're just past that angle on the highway where it swings north after White

City."

"Okay... Kane, you're about three minutes ahead right now."

Kane eased off the accelerator. "All right, we'll maintain this lead and look for a good place to set up. I want to be far from populated areas in case there's gunfire. Hellhound, let us know if they speed up."

"Just got past 'em. Karsten's drivin' an' McKenna's in the passenger seat. I'm gonna make a bit a' space between us an' then drive at their speed."

Despite the anxiety ravelling my nerves, I relaxed just a fraction at Hellhound's cold emotionless tone. Arnie might act impulsively, but The Killer never would. This had just turned into a military operation.

Spider's voice came over the speaker again. "Kane, there's a tiny town called Saint Joseph's on the south side of the highway about five kilometres from where you are. If you drive another couple of kilometres you'll be halfway between it and Balgonie."

"Too close," Kane objected. "What's our next opportunity?"

"Between Saint Joseph's and the next little town, McLean, there's about eight kilometres of open prairie. From McLean to Qu'Appelle-"

"We'll do it four kilometres past Saint Joseph's," Kane interrupted. "Is there any cover on that stretch of road? Trees that might block the view while we set up?"

"Um, I don't think so." Spider sounded apologetic. "It's Saskatchewan."

"There's fuck-all but prairie," Hellhound broke in. "But if you're three minutes ahead, they shouldn't notice anythin' if you're quick."

"All right..." Kane began, but Spider interrupted.

"Aydan, I just got a message from Corporal Whittle. She says to tell you they found a thumbless body..."

My heart froze.

CHAPTER 32

"*It's not LaVonda!*" Spider yelped. "Sorry, sorry! I shouldn't have said it that way, I was just reading the message and I-"

"It's okay," I croaked, sucking in a slow breath and feeling my ribs crackle with releasing tension. "What was the whole message?"

"They found a *man's* body..." Spider emphasized the word 'man'. "...with its thumbs missing. They think it's the guy who originally rented the Ford Escape that ambushed Hellhound. The other thug-for-hire."

Kane hissed out a breath. "The professionals are cleaning house."

"Thank God." My words came out weak and breathless. "Arnie, did you hear that? It wasn't her thumb. *It wasn't hers!*"

Silence hovered on the line for a moment.

"Heard it," he rasped. His voice was unsteady and he said nothing more.

My entire body vibrated with reaction. I could only imagine how he must feel.

"Now we just gotta get her back." The Killer was in control again.

"We'll get her," Kane vowed.

I didn't bother to point out that we didn't even know if she was in the van.

"Dammit," Kane muttered.

I glanced over, wondering if I'd spoken aloud without realizing it.

"There's too much traffic behind us," he said. "We can stop, but we won't have enough time to arrange the lumber across the road before the next car arrives."

"What're ya sayin'?" Hellhound demanded.

"I'm saying I can maintain a safe gap between us and the vehicle behind us, but as soon as I slow down or stop, the timing will be too tight to safely block the road."

I twisted to peer behind us. "So we'll have to push the lumber out while we're moving." Sizing up the rear window of the cab, I added, "I can probably get through this window into the box."

"And do what?" Kane demanded. "I absolutely forbid you to try to open the tailgate from inside the box at highway speed. It's certain death if you lose your footing."

I shuddered. "No, I wasn't thinking that. But I could toss armloads over the side."

"At a hundred and twenty kilometres per hour." Kane's voice was flat.

"Well, yeah. As soon as I get the two-by-fours out of the shelter of the cab, the wind should just grab them out of my hands."

"Which is dangerous in itself. And you won't be able to dump the load fast enough," he objected. "How many can you handle at once?"

"Well, I can easily carry four at a time when I'm building stuff, so if I only have to dump them over the side... maybe six or eight. They're not that heavy; it's just that I can't get my hands around them. If you slowed down a bit so they didn't get scattered over such a long distance..."

We both fell silent, calculating.

"It won't work," Kane said flatly. "It's dangerous for you, and even if I slow down to thirty kilometres per hour, the lumber will still be scattered over nearly half a kilometre. You can't plausibly run back that far and confront them. We need to lose the whole load at once."

"Then we need the tailgate open."

"Aydan, no!" Hellhound's rasp rattled the speaker. "That's suicide."

"It's okay, I have no intention of taking a header onto pavement at a hundred and twenty klicks. But we're three minutes ahead, right? And you just said we've got too many vehicles between us and them, right?"

Kane's lips turned up. "Right. Webb, put us on the clock... now. Give us a mark every thirty seconds." He braked and pulled over to the shoulder.

"You're on the clock," Spider confirmed.

I stuffed the phone in my pocket and Kane and I bailed out of the truck. Hurrying around to the back, I opened the tailgate and Kane vaulted into the box.

Bracing his back against the cab, he planted his feet against the bottom of the load. "If we get the load just at its balance point hanging over the tailgate..."

As I took my place beside him, Spider's muffled voice said, "Thirty seconds" from my pocket.

While we shuffled the load toward the back of the box, Kane went on, "We can put one stud perpendicular across the end closest to the cab, and you can hold it down with a stud through the cab window. It'll provide a bit of stability until I can get back on the highway."

We shifted the two-by-fours a couple more feet, repositioned ourselves, and eased the pile backward again.

My pocket spoke again. "One minute."

I resumed the conversation with Kane. "That'll work. And when it's time to dump the load, I should be able to push the whole thing off using the two-by-four from inside the cab. Ease off, we're getting close." The tailgate creaked ominously as it took the weight of the stack.

I applied myself cautiously to it again. "As long as you don't get fully up to speed it should work fine."

"There, stop!" Kane straightened and carefully removed a couple of two-by-fours from the pile. It wasn't exactly teetering, but the ends nearest us hovered just off the surface of the box. "All right, go and get in the cab," he added.

As I obeyed, the load shivered as though dreading what was to come.

It wasn't the only one.

Inside the cab, I opened the rear window and accepted the end of the two-by-four Kane passed through.

Spider gave us another mark. "Ninety seconds."

"Ninety seconds," I said to Kane.

"Almost done." He placed a two-by-four crosswise on top of the stack and laid the opposite end of my two-by-four on top. Kneeling backward on the seat, I got both hands under my end and used the top of the cab window as a lever to exert downward pressure on the pile.

Kane nodded. "That'll work. Hold tight."

"Wait, I want to put my trank pistol in my pocket." I rapidly completed the transfer and returned my grip to the two-by-four.

Heart thumping, I kept upward pressure on my lever to stabilize the load while he eased out of the box and into the driver's seat. My arms trembled with fear and fatigue.

Dammit, if I used all my strength to hold the two-by-fours, my accuracy would be shit when I had to take that all-important shot...

"Time's up," Spider said tensely.

"We're moving," Kane replied, and the truck rolled forward.

"I'm fallin' back to come up behind 'em," Hellhound reported. "Be safe, you two."

My only reply was a yelp of dismay as the truck bumped over the frozen shoulder onto the pavement. *"Fuck-it's-going!"*

A car rocketed by us in the passing lane, horn blaring and passenger gesticulating.

Kane swerved. The load tipped and my two-by-four smashed down, far beyond my ability to hold. The rough wood ripped my palms, slamming into the bottom of the window frame like a sledgehammer.

Two-by-fours scattered across both lanes and Kane braked hard.

Already off-balance, I toppled backward, grabbing frantically at the window frame to save myself. The perfidious two-by-four reversed its course, pistoning forward to smack into the palm of Kane's outstretched hand.

Wide-eyed and panting, I stared at his hand where it had stopped the two-by-four only inches from my face.

"Thanks," I quavered, and sprang out of the truck.

Stumbling on the snowy shoulder and frantically waving my arms, I ran toward the oncoming van.

Shit, this had seemed like such a good idea at the time. But I had already used most of my strength and adrenaline on the load of lumber. Already I was puffing like a steam engine.

Gasping, I waved my arms harder and ran closer. My

heart was going to hammer right out of my chest and flop around like a beached fish by the side of the highway...

The van slowed.

Pulled to a stop.

Would they shoot me?

I waved feebly again and slowed to a jog, huddling into my hood and jamming my hands deep in my pockets as though fighting the cold.

The trank pistol's grip was hard in my trembling hand.

I risked a glance. Close enough to make out their faces.

They weren't rolling down the windows or aiming weapons yet.

My heart beat even harder and nausea twisted my stomach. Kane was right, they were waiting to shoot me point-blank.

Head down to keep them from getting a clear look at my face, I hurried closer on shaky legs.

The bumper of the van appeared in my peripheral vision.

I slowed and trudged to the passenger side.

Don't shoot, please don't shoot...

A power window hummed down and I looked up wearing my best apologetic smile. It wasn't going to be a good look for me if I ended up in a coffin.

"Hi, sorry," I panted. "We'll have the road cleared as soon as we can..." I jerked my head toward Kane's figure ahead of us, busily slinging two-by-fours off the road.

LaVonda's kidnapper eyed me without expression. "No problem."

As his hand moved toward the window control, I jerked the trank pistol out of my pocket and fired two fast shots.

The passenger slumped instantly. The driver managed to get his hand halfway to his holster before he collapsed forward against the steering wheel.

Swivelling, I fired a shot back into the cargo area of the van. I couldn't see anyone there, but...

The van eased forward.

Terror jolted my already-thundering heart.

It was still in gear, *fuck!*

I yanked the door handle but it was locked. The handle jerked from my grasp as the van rolled away.

Toward Kane.

I sprinted ahead of it, spun, and dove through the passenger window. The van's momentum slammed the window frame into my ribs and belly, punching the air out of me in a painful bark.

Don't-inhale-*don't-inhale!*

I flailed in, grabbing frantically for the steering wheel.

Caught it with one hand-

CHAPTER 33

"Aydan! *Aydan!*"

"Ow." My voice was only a mumble. Everything hurt, and my tongue didn't seem to be working right.

"Don't try to move." Kane's voice, tight with worry.

"M'okay," I slurred. "Trank."

"Yes, you probably inhaled some tranquilizer, but you're at a bad angle and you might have been injured when the van went into the ditch. Can you feel your feet?"

I twitched one, then the other. "Uh-huh."

"Where do you have pain?"

I groaned. "Bettr queshn'd be 'Where *doan* I have pain'." As he began to speak again, I added, "S'okay, nevr mine," and dragged my eyelids open to take stock.

I was sprawled across the knees of the unconscious passenger, my back and hips jammed against the dashboard and my lower legs and feet still stuck out the window. The console shifter was inches away from my nose, but by some miracle I seemed to have wedged my head between it and the front console without smashing my face.

Kane was leaning in across the unconscious driver, his hands braced on my head and right shoulder to hold me still. "Don't try to move," he repeated. "You might have injured your neck or back."

"No, think 'm okay..." Moving slowly and cautiously, I determined that all my body parts were still attached and working.

Accompanied by my own vile profanity and Kane's anxious cautions, I untangled myself and crept painfully to my knees on the passenger's lap. When he regained consciousness, he'd wonder why his balls felt as though somebody had knelt on them. He was lucky I was too tired to do any more damage.

"I'm okay," I repeated with a bit more confidence.

The front of the van was in the snow-filled ditch and the rear wheels were still on the shoulder, tilting the vehicle nose-down. The driver and passenger were already beginning to twitch and moan. Behind me in the cargo area...

My heart stuttered at the sight of Hellhound kneeling beside LaVonda's body.

"Is she..."

"Unconscious," Kane supplied.

"Just comin' outta the trank now," Hellhound corrected, rising and shuffling down the slope to help me to my feet. When I winced, he turned my palm up to eye an ugly splinter surrounded by scraped and blood-smeared skin.

"Yeah, that smarts." Hissing through my teeth, I pulled the splinter out, then curled my fingers to put pressure on the small bleeding wound. "How long was I out?"

"Coupla minutes. Ya sure you're okay?" He gently touched my forehead, activating an ache. Apparently I hadn't completely avoided the shifter after all.

"Just bruised," I assured him. "Lucky I was wearing my vest. Even at about ten kilometres an hour, that window frame packed a hell of a punch."

"Damn lucky. Ya coulda broken your back." Hellhound tossed Kane a roll of duct tape that must have been used on

LaVonda, judging by the shredded discards lying near her. "This oughta hold 'em 'til the cops get here."

Kane caught the roll one-handed and yanked the semi-conscious driver out onto the ground.

As I turned toward the passenger, Hellhound stopped me with an arm around my shoulders. "Let Kane do it. Come an' sit with me an' LaVonda for a while."

As I lowered myself painfully to the canted deck of the cargo bay, I noticed the third kidnapper crumpled on the floor against the back of the passenger seat. Apparently Hellhound had been generous with duct tape and rage.

"Owie," I remarked, surveying the contorted groaning form.

Hellhound let out a growl. "Hope he's fuckin' crippled for life."

"Well, I'm sure he's miserable."

The kidnapper was coatless, shivering in the icy current of air from the open doors. Hellhound had laid the man's parka over LaVonda.

She moaned and he took her hand, his voice softening to a warm rough rumble. "Hey, LaVonda, it's okay. You're safe now."

She opened unfocused eyes and whimpered.

"You're safe now, everythin's okay," Hellhound repeated.

"Not safe," she mumbled. "Not safe. Arnie."

"It's me. It's Arnie." He stroked her hand. "I'm here, an' we're both safe."

She blinked sleepily up at him, her pupils so dilated that her irises were only a thin ring of colour around the blackness. Drugged with something much stronger than my tranquilizer.

"Never safe," she murmured. "James knows. He always

knows."

Arnie frowned. "What's James got to do with anythin'?"

"Sell you. Unless I..." Her eyelids fluttered closed.

"LaVonda." He rubbed her hand. "Stay with me, now. LaVonda."

She didn't respond.

"Kath." He patted her cheek. "Talk to me, Kath."

Her eyes popped open and a smile spread over her face. "Arnie. Love you..."

"I love ya, too." He smiled back at her, but his face was taut. "I need ya to keep talkin' to me, okay?"

"Okay." Her voice was breathy and childlike.

"Ya were talkin' about James," Hellhound encouraged.

"He always knows." LaVonda blinked up at him worriedly.

Arnie frowned. "What does he know?"

"Where Arnie is."

"Why does it matter if he knows where I am?"

"Men *like* little boys. I have to..." We waited, but she didn't complete the sentence. Her eyelids drooped.

"Ya hafta what?" Arnie prompted.

"Do what he says," she whispered.

"What does he say ya hafta do?" Arnie's hand was gentle on hers, but the voice that came from his lips was The Killer's.

LaVonda's voice dropped into a passable imitation of their eldest brother James. "Fuck Mr. Fitzgerald or else."

I reached for Arnie's free hand, a chill invading my belly. His grip clamped down hard enough to make me wince, but when he spoke his tone was soft.

"So James told ya he was gonna sell me to pedophiles if ya didn't fuck Richard Fitzgerald, is that it?"

"Mmhmm."

His grip tightened on my hand. "When ya were only fifteen?"

A faint frown wrinkled her forehead. "Thirteen."

"Thirteen." The Killer's voice made me shiver.

"Mmhmm. Bradley when I was fifteen. Too old for Mr. Fitzgerald then." LaVonda blinked up at him, her frown deepening as if recognizing his turmoil. "Don't worry. Didn't hurt. Wasn't a virgin."

Arnie went still. "When did that happen?"

"Mr. Rutherford. Eleven."

Arnie's outrage erupted in a bellow so sudden that LaVonda and I both flinched. *"That fuckin' waste a' skin raped ya?"*

Tears puddled in her eyes. "I'm sorry..."

"Aw fuck," Arnie choked out, and gathered her into his arms. His voice came out in a broken rasp. "Don't be sorry, Kath, it ain't your fault. None a' that shit was your fault. *None* of it, ya hear?"

"Bradley was my fault." LaVonda pushed Arnie away, managing to sit up for a few seconds on her own before slumping to the floor again. "I killed him."

Arnie froze. "Ya killed Bradley Montmorency?" His tone was neutral, but his face was bone-white.

"Killed him." LaVonda's hand flopped at her side in a feeble stabbing motion. "Killed..." Her eyelids drifted shut again.

"Stay with me, Kath." Arnie patted her cheeks again. "Come on, open your eyes an' talk to me."

"No." Her eyes stayed closed.

"It's okay, we don't hafta talk about scary stuff. Let's talk about happy stuff, okay?"

Her eyes opened. "Took his money."

"He owed ya," Arnie said quietly.

"Was going to kill me. Told James."

Sirens swelled in the distance.

Arnie shot a hunted look over his shoulder but his voice stayed unhurried. "Ya told James that Montmorency was gonna kill ya?"

"Bradley told."

Arnie hesitated, frowning as he puzzled it out. "Ya heard Montmorency tellin' James he was gonna kill ya?"

"Mmhmm." LaVonda closed her eyes again.

"So ya killed him in self-defence?"

LaVonda didn't respond, and Arnie gave her a gentle shake. "Come on, Kath, this's important. Did ya kill Bradley Montmorency in self-defence?"

The sirens were nearly on us.

"James was so mad," she said dreamily.

"At Montmorency?"

"Mad at me. So mad at me." Her voice fell into a singsong. "James was so mad. Beat me so bad. But I never told him where I hid the money."

"*James* is the one that put ya in the hospital?" Arnie's face darkened, his fists clenching.

"Mmhmm..." LaVonda's eyes popped open and she clutched Arnie's wrist. "Not safe. He knows. He always knows."

"He's dead, Kath."

She blinked at him.

Outside, the sirens stopped and the slam of doors and a burst of radio static indicated that police or paramedics were incoming.

"Kath," Arnie said urgently. "Listen. James is dead.

You're safe."

"Dead?" She stared up at him without comprehension.

"James is dead," Arnie repeated. "You're safe. We're both safe. An' don't tell anybody what we just talked about, okay? Don't say anythin' to anybody, got it?"

As the van door opened, LaVonda dipped her chin in a nod and closed her eyes.

Arnie turned to face the police and paramedics. "Doesn't look like she's hurt, but they gave her some kinda drug. She's talkin' but she ain't makin' sense." He moved aside as two paramedics headed for LaVonda. "An' ya need to look at Aydan, here, too."

"I'm fine," I said hurriedly. "Just some bruises." I opened my hand, which was still sluggishly oozing blood. "And I could use a Band-aid."

Hellhound turned to the paramedics and tattled on me. "She hit her head, an' she mighta hurt her back an' neck." Turning back to me, he added, "Come on, darlin', let's get ya out where they can have a look at ya."

I shuffled reluctantly out of the van, trying not to flinch at the sight of the RCMP officers.

It turned out that interactions with the police were greatly simplified by Spider's expert coordination. Questions and explanations were minimal, and Kane handled most of them while one of the paramedics gave me a once-over.

When he was done, Kane asked, "How is she?"

"Just bruised and shaken, I'd say. Maybe a mild concussion, but nothing that needs hospitalization. Of course, if you have any worsening symptoms; dizziness, a severe headache..." He went on with the usual caveats and I tuned him out, nodding and agreeing automatically while I watched Arnie with concern.

The paramedic headed back to the ambulance, and I leaned close to Kane and lowered my voice. "Did you hear the conversation between Arnie and LaVonda?"

He frowned. "No, I was securing the prisoners and clearing the lumber off the highway."

The ambulance doors closed and the vehicle pulled away.

Arnie stood rigidly, fists clenched. His gaze tracked the ambulance, but his haunted eyes stared back through the years at a past far worse than he'd realized.

"I'd better ride back with him," I whispered to Kane. "He shouldn't be alone right now."

Kane's face hardened. "That bad?"

"Worse."

Hellhound roused himself from his trance and strode over. "They're takin' her back to Regina. They wouldn't let me go with her in the ambulance, so I'm gonna follow."

I slipped my hand into his. "I'll come with you."

"Thanks, darlin'. Let's go."

CHAPTER 34

When I opened the door to Arnie's van, the pungent aroma of cat shit still lingered. Placid again, Princess lounged in her carrier belted into the passenger seat.

"Here, I'll put her in the back," Hellhound said, reaching in to unbuckle the carrier.

"Let me get it," I offered. "You shouldn't be doing any heavy lifting."

He snorted. "The day a little bitty thing like Princess is heavy liftin', just shoot me, 'cause I'm done."

"You already got shot. That's my point."

My argument fell on deaf ears as he lifted the carrier out and opened the side door of the van. "An' you were in a car accident. Ya might feel okay now, but tomorrow you're gonna feel like ya got hit by a bus."

Bowing to the inevitable, I let him finish securing the carrier while I got into the passenger seat.

When we were under way, I settled into silence. At least half an hour to Regina. No need to rush this conversation.

I didn't have to.

"So, did ya get all that?" Arnie asked tightly.

"You mean LaVonda's story?"

"Yeah."

"I got the gist, but there's a lot I don't know about her childhood." I hesitated. "Who's Mr. Rutherford?"

The steering wheel creaked as Arnie's hands clenched.

"Foster parent."

"Oh, no. Yours or Kathy's?"

"Social worker talked 'em into takin' both of us. When I was a kid, I was so glad Kathy an' me were together." His swallow was audible. "But now..."

I reached over to rub slow soothing strokes on his shoulder. "That is so shitty."

"Lucky for that asshole he's dead." His muscles tensed under my hand. "Can't believe I went to his funeral. Thirteen *years* I lived with that fucker an' I never fuckin' knew..."

I kept up my slow stroking. "You were just a kid. You couldn't have known. And even when you were older... men like that know how to hide what they do."

"But maybe I'd'a seen it if I hadn't been gone mosta the time. No wonder they didn't complain when I was basically livin' over at Kane's. Rutherford was glad to get rid a' me so he could..." He trailed off, swallowing again.

I gripped his shoulder. "Arnie, you couldn't have changed anything. You were only seven when it happened."

"But I damn well coulda changed somethin' later!" He slammed the heel of his hand against the steering wheel. "Ya know how many fuckin' foster kids they had over the years? How many *girls?*" He shot a glare at me before returning his attention to the road. When he spoke again, his voice was ragged. "Eight. That's how many. Eight fuckin' helpless little girls." His chest heaved and he dealt the steering wheel another vicious blow. An alarming crack sounded from the steering column.

"Don't wreck the rental," I said softly.

"Fuck the rental," he growled, but his words held no heat.

We drove in silence for a few minutes.

"No wonder she ran away when she was thirteen," Arnie said quietly. "Poor kid. When Montmorency showed up an' pretended to love her, she musta thought somebody was finally gonna take care of her."

"I didn't quite get that part," I prompted. "When you first told me about your family, you said when Kathy was thirteen she'd started dating a guy who'd gotten her hooked on drugs. But LaVonda said..." I hesitated, not wanting to say the horrible words.

"She said James made her fuck Richard Fitzgerald when she was thirteen," Arnie said flatly. "An' that makes sense."

"Sorry, I'm not getting it."

"Remember how I told ya James was into gangs even when he was young?" At my nod, he went on, "When Kath was thirteen, Montmorency woulda been twenty-one an' James woulda been seventeen. Perfect age for a young punk to be lookin' to get into a gang. An' ya know James was all about status."

I swallowed nausea. "Montmorency was in the same circle as Fitzgerald. If James was trying to impress them..."

"The ol' man taught James early that women were just meat. He woulda offered up Kath in a heartbeat if he thought it'd get him points. But a guy like Fitzgerald wouldn't do his dirty work personally. So Montmorency pretends to be Kath's boyfriend an' sets her up in a nice apartment an' introduces her to drugs..." Arnie fell silent, his hands strangling the steering wheel.

"She had a nice apartment?"

"Yeah. When she was thirteen, fourteen. She was so happy then..." He swallowed. "Well, now I know she was fakin' it to protect me. But she used to say she liked bein' a grownup an' livin' the good life in a fancy apartment."

"Where Fitzgerald could visit her in privacy and comfort," I said, the words tasting like vomit in my mouth. "And James kept her under control by threatening to sell you the same way he'd sold her. And she knew damn well he'd do it."

Arnie's chin jerked down in bitter agreement. "An' when she hit the ripe ol' age a' fifteen, Fitzgerald kicked her out on the street an' moved on to some other poor kid, an' Montmorency pimped Kathy. He controlled the drug supply so she always owed him, an' James kept her in line by threatenin' me. An' she just kept hangin' on an' takin' it 'til I was eighteen an' in the army. Then she musta figured I'd be safe, an' she got the hell out when she got the chance."

"Hell of a chance. Your pimp tries to kill you, your brother beats you within an inch of your life, and a crime boss swears a lifelong vendetta."

"Yeah." Hellhound glanced over at me, his face set. "Remember ya asked if I remembered anythin' about Fitzgerald or The Family?"

I nodded, afraid to hear what he was about to say.

"I just figured it out. Remember when James was gonna sell ya to Fuzzy Bunny, an' he had us tied up an' was beatin' the hell outta us?"

I shuddered, remembering the pain and terror. The vicious bite of the ties around my wrists...

My heart rate spiked and I fought back the panic attack.

"Beating you, mostly." My voice came out unsteady despite my effort to control it.

Arnie reached over to take my hand. "Sorry, darlin', I hate to bring it back for ya. But remember when James said he'd let me live if I'd come an' work in the fam'ly business?"

I froze. "The Family. With a capital 'F'."

"Yeah. So James didn't give a shit if Montmorency killed Kath, 'cause she wasn't worth anythin' to him anymore. But when he found out she'd killed Montmorency an' fucked off with the money, he lost it on her."

"He wasn't just mad," I said thoughtfully. "He was ruined. His sister, the one he'd supplied as a..." I couldn't think of a word that didn't turn my stomach, so I went on, "...had killed Fitzgerald's dealer and walked off with a huge pile of Fitzgerald's money. James would be in deep shit. I'm surprised Fitzgerald even let him live."

Arnie nodded. "That musta blown it for him. He spent a lotta years clawin' his way up the ranks before he finally hit the big time. Fitzgerald musta made him start at the bottom again." He scowled. "Knowin' how these assholes think... to Fitzgerald, girls like Kath are dirt. He prob'ly figured he was doin' her a favour settin' her up in that apartment an' givin' her drugs. An' then to have her fuck off with his money... he'd never forgive that."

"What I can't understand is how she ever made it out of the hospital alive. If Fitzgerald thought she'd stolen his money, wouldn't he have just had somebody grab her as soon as she was released? How could she have escaped?"

Hellhound shrugged. "Maybe James told Fitzgerald she couldn't'a stolen it. He prob'ly thought she'd tell him anythin' to keep him from beatin' the hell outta her." His lips twisted bitterly. "He shoulda known better. After what she went through with the ol' man..."

"And maybe somebody helped her disappear," I supplied. "Fitzgerald wouldn't risk killing her while she was in the hospital, so he was probably waiting for her to get released. And instead, she somehow got away. That would explain why he's still hunting her after all these years. And as soon as he saw her name and got her address..."

I trailed off and we exchanged a sick glance.

"She's still not safe." My words came out flat.

"She's never gonna be safe. Fitzgerald's gonna hunt her 'til the day he dies. An' he's got the money an' power to do it." Hellhound accelerated. "We gotta keep a guard on her. Soon's Fitzgerald finds out his guys blew it, he'll send another batch."

Another thought trickled into my tired brain. "Maybe that explains the two thugs-for-hire. He didn't send his best guys right away. Like you said when all this started, how hard is it to grab an unarmed woman living alone? He probably farmed it out to some lower-level minions. Maybe it was a test." I sat up a bit straighter. "And that explains why they didn't shoot me on sight back on the highway there. The second batch of guys had never actually seen me before."

Hellhound nodded. "That makes sense. That whole grenade launcher thing's been buggin' me 'cause it was so over-the-top. Who uses a grenade launcher for a kidnappin'? Talk about attractin' attention. I bet..." He hesitated as though working his way through the logic. "Yeah, you're right. I bet the first two guys hit the road soon's LaVonda got doxxed an' Fitzgerald recognized her name. So one guy flies in an' rents the SUV so he can get her under surveillance right away, an' the other guy brings Fitzgerald's van from Winnipeg so they got a way to bring her back. An' then they wait."

"And wait, and wait," I agreed. "But LaVonda never left her apartment. Probably Fitzgerald was pressuring them; and like you said earlier, they'd be dead meat if they didn't deliver. So they got desperate and decided to drive her out of hiding. And since they weren't the brightest lights in the sky..."

"They fucked it up bigtime," he finished. "So Fitzgerald sent the pros to get the job done an' get rid a' the idiots."

I shivered. "I hate to think who he's going to send to get rid of the pros."

CHAPTER 35

When we arrived at the hospital, I said, "Just pull up to Emergency. You can go in while I park the car."

"'Kay, thanks." Hellhound dropped a quick kiss on my lips and strode into the building. Parking was easy at the small hospital, and soon I was hurrying into Emergency.

LaVonda had just been wheeled into a cubicle, and I joined Hellhound beside the stretcher. Only a few minutes later a scrubs-clad woman arrived bearing a bundle of vials and other equipment.

She gave us a sympathetic smile. "I'll have to ask you to wait in the corridor for a few minutes."

"We're stayin'," Hellhound said. "She's my sister."

The nurse's lips firmed. "Your sister needs a few minutes of privacy. We'll be changing her into a gown, and we'll be taking samples with a rape kit." Arnie flinched and his hand found mine. Her voice softened. "We'll be done in a few minutes and then you can come back in. I promise we'll take good care of her."

He nodded jerkily and the pain in his face tore my heart. I towed him out to the corridor and put my arms around him.

"They're just being thorough," I comforted. "She had all her clothes on, and I bet Fitzgerald gave orders to bring her back without hurting her. He'd want to..." I pressed my lips closed before I could finish, '...torture her himself.'

Hellhound didn't reply, just tightened his arms around me.

We stood in silence until the nurse emerged.

"How is she?" Hellhound rasped.

"It doesn't look as though she was raped, but we did the kit just in case. A doctor will be in to see her soon, and you'll get more information then." She eyed the mountain of tattooed intimidation that was Hellhound, and must have seen the gentle soul suffering within. Her voice softened. "She's breathing well, her vital signs are strong, and she seems generally healthy. She was probably drugged with something like Rohypnol..." She hesitated. "You might know it as 'roofies'. If that's what it is, she'll be very sleepy and forgetful for several hours, and it should wear off with no ill effects. Try not to worry."

His shoulders eased. "Thanks."

She smiled and hurried away, and we filed back into the cubicle. LaVonda lay peacefully under a light blanket, eyes closed.

Feeling uncomfortable watching her while she was so vulnerable, I whispered to Arnie, "You sit with her for a while. I have to pee so badly my back teeth are floating, and John should be here any minute. I'll go and fill him in, and then come back."

"'Kay," he murmured. "Thanks, darlin'."

I kissed him and withdrew.

After an extremely relieving trip to the bathroom, I went back to the Emergency waiting room. Poking my head around the corner, I scanned for Kane, but he wasn't there.

Holt was.

I jerked back, heart hammering, but he'd already seen me.

For one panicked instant my body tensed for flight, but common sense overcame the reflex a moment later.

Even if I somehow managed to lose Holt by dashing through the hospital, I had nowhere to go. Evading him for a few more hours wouldn't make a difference.

Feeling the ache of defeat in my bones, I waited for him to cross the waiting room.

His brows drew together as he walked up, surveying me. "You look like shit."

"Fuck you very much."

Holt grinned. "So you got LaVonda back."

"Yeah, but she's not safe yet."

"I thought the perps were all arrested or dead. You think there are more?"

I nearly blurted out the whole story. Shit, I was too tired to think straight.

"Well?" Holt prompted. "Come on, Kelly, spill. I'm supposed to be protecting you. If there's more shit happening here, I need to know about it."

Why wasn't he arresting me?

"I don't know for sure yet," I equivocated.

"You think she stole Fitzgerald's money?"

Dammit, between Spider and the Regina police, Holt knew almost everything we did. How were we going to get LaVonda out of this?

"I have no idea," I lied. "She's only semi-conscious so we don't have the whole story. The nurse thinks they roofied her, but they won't have test results for a while and the doctor hasn't seen her yet."

"Roofies?" Holt leaned a shoulder against the wall, frowning. "Shit, she won't remember anything. It might be tricky to get charges to stick to these assholes."

"We have a video of them kidnapping her, and we caught them with her tied up in the back of their van."

Holt grimaced. "I've seen guys get acquitted with more evidence than that against them."

"Great."

I eyed him warily, but he didn't make any move toward me. When was he going to pull out the handcuffs?

God, I couldn't take it anymore. Anything was better than this horrible not-knowing.

I lowered my voice. "So why are you really here?"

"Let's walk." He strode toward the exit doors, then paused and frowned back at me when I didn't follow. "Come on, step it up."

Was he going to knock me unconscious again as soon as we were out of the building? When I woke up, would I be back in prison?

Kane and Hellhound wouldn't even know what had happened to me...

Holt blew out an impatient breath. "Come *on!*"

My fingers wrapped around the stand of a hand sanitizer station as though it might save me if Holt tried to drag me away by main force. It wouldn't; I knew that. He was stronger, and I was exhausted.

So exhausted.

"Having some trust issues here." My voice wavered.

"Oh, for..." Holt stomped toward me, and my hand clenched on the stand.

He stopped, his steely eyes softening as he surveyed my white knuckles and rigid stance. "Okay, I deserved that. Relax, I'm not here to shanghai you."

"Then why are you here?"

He threw up his hands. "Because Dermott sent me to

protect you!"

"Bullshit."

"It's true!" His theatrical indignation vanished as he leaned in and lowered his voice. "And also because I'm supposed to watch you and document every single time you don't dot your 'i's and cross your 't's. Dermott's planning to build an airtight case this time."

"That's all?" I couldn't keep the suspicion out of my voice.

"That's all. I just figured..." Holt leaned casually against the wall again, but his gaze evaluated our surroundings for potential listeners. "...she's family, right? I sure as hell wouldn't be going by the book if somebody'd grabbed my sister. I thought you might need a bit of elbow room."

Every muscle in my body loosened and my knees nearly buckled with relief.

"Th-thanks." A moment later I added, "But she's not my sister."

"No, but she's your boyfriend's sister. Dermott would love to catch you turning a blind eye if Hellhound does something sketchy."

My guts clenched. Dermott had already tried to convince my chain of command that they couldn't trust me. If I failed to report even the smallest misdemeanor, he'd have irrefutable proof.

"Or, hell," Holt went on. "Dermott would be happy to take down your boyfriends just to hurt you, too. He'd rather nail you, but he'll take anything that'll make you suffer."

My spine turned to ice. Holt was right. Suddenly I was very glad that Hellhound and I had been detained and questioned so thoroughly by the police, and that the prosecutor had cleared Arnie. If I had just glossed over his killing of the gunman, both of us might be on our way to jail right now.

"Thanks for letting me know," I whispered.

"No problem." Holt took another quick appraisal of our surroundings. "So now that I'm here, you'd better behave. I like you, but not enough to put my own ass on the line with Dermott."

My mouth blurted out an inappropriate joke before my tired brain could censor it. "Damn. I guess I should have slept with you after all."

Holt let out a guffaw that turned heads in the waiting room. "*Nobody's* that good in bed. I'd throw my own mother under a bus to stay in Dermott's good books."

I was pretty sure that wasn't true; but what the hell, maybe he didn't like his mother. And if that was how he wanted to play it, that was fine with me.

"You're such a prick," I said.

"You better believe it." He raised his voice slightly. "But if you're *really* that desperate to sleep with me, you'll have to buy me drinks and dinner first."

Certain that we'd just acquired an audience, I rolled my eyes at him and turned. Sure enough, Kane had arrived.

The two men exchanged a look, both wearing their cop faces. Holt straightened, hooking his thumbs in his pockets and spreading his elbows in a classic alpha-male posture. Kane did nothing, but somehow he seemed to grow a couple of inches. Testosterone filled the air.

Holt gave him a cocky grin. "Your girlfriend just propositioned me."

The corner of Kane's mouth quirked up in a pitying smile. "Aydan doesn't belong to me, or anybody. And if she propositioned you and you didn't seize the opportunity, you're stupider than I thought."

Holt's lantern jaw hardened. "*Some* of us aren't desperate enough to take somebody else's sloppy seconds."

I shoved his shoulder. "Oh, give it up. You'd take dirty thirds and be grateful."

Holt leered. "Well, since you're offering..."

"In your dreams."

"In my nightmares, maybe." Holt dropped the banter. "So what's our next move here?"

I sighed. "We need to keep a guard on LaVonda 24/7. I'm guessing nothing more will happen in the next few hours, but I could be wrong. We have no idea how many people Fitzgerald might have sent. If these guys have backup here..." I completed the sentence with a poorly-concealed shiver.

"So you're sure Fitzgerald is behind this?"

"No way to tell right now."

Holt frowned. "Maybe the guys you just arrested will say something useful. Are you going to get in on the questioning?"

Shit, I hadn't even thought of that. My brain was as sluggish as a sloth in a vat of molasses.

And wasn't that a revolting image. My mind recoiled at the thought of all that long sticky hair...

"Earth to Kelly!" Holt waved a hand in front of my face. "Somebody roofie you, too?"

I blinked. "Um. No. I'm just really sleep-deprived. I don't even know where those guys ended up."

Kane gave me a smile. "I handled that while you were getting checked over by the paramedic. The RCMP picked them up at the scene, but they transferred them here to the Regina police station. Corporal Whittle said you could question them, but I told her you couldn't blow your cover. You can watch through the live video feed, and if you have any specific questions you can give them to Detective Constable Tan before he begins the interview."

"Tan? I didn't think he came on shift until later."

Kane grimaced. "The kidnappers' lawyer has to travel from Winnipeg. His flight arrives around seven o'clock tonight. Whittle will be off-shift by then and Tan will take over."

"Seven o'clock?" I shot an incredulous glance at my watch. "It's only noon. The lawyer could *drive* here faster than that."

Kane nodded. "Yes, but he won't. It's a risky drive in winter, and the last part of it would be in the dark. And it's Christmas Eve, so most of the flights are full. He was lucky to get a flight today at all."

My heart sank. If the lawyer arrived at seven, it would be at least seven-thirty by the time the questioning started. And Kane would be sitting there in that miserable grey room along with me, missing the magic of Christmas Eve with Daniel.

"You should fly back to Calgary now," I encouraged. "Now that Holt's here, we can manage..."

Kane was already shaking his head. "In the first place, this situation is still dangerous. Maybe even more so than before, if Fitzgerald is getting desperate. And in the second place..." He let out a small breath that was probably a sigh. "...all the flights to Calgary are full. I already checked."

My heart clenched. "Oh, no! But... you could still drive back, it's only eight hours..." I trailed off. Even if he left immediately, he wouldn't arrive until after Daniel's bedtime.

"I thought of that, too," Kane said ruefully. "But there's a storm front coming in from the west. It's not predicted to hit Regina until tomorrow morning, but Calgary's just seeing the beginning of it now. The drive could end up being a lot longer than eight hours if the weather turns bad; and if they close the roads, I might be stranded somewhere for who knows how long. At least if I stay the night here, there's a chance that I might be able to fly back on Christmas Day. The airlines usually have seats available then."

Because by then it was too late.

I didn't point that out.

CHAPTER 36

"Anyway," Kane went on, "It doesn't matter, because I'm staying until everyone's safe here." He gave me a smile that didn't hide the sadness in his eyes. "It's lunchtime, and you need to eat. Let's get something at the hospital cafeteria."

I glanced back toward the cubicles. "We need to keep a guard on LaVonda. Holt, can you-"

"Where you go, I go," Holt interrupted. "Department orders."

Blowing out a short frustrated breath, I gave him a 'come on, work with me' look.

He shook his head. "If you want two people on LaVonda, it'll have to be Kane and Hellhound. I'm your shadow from here on in."

I scowled. "Lucky I went to the bathroom before you got here."

"I can't tell you how grateful I am."

I flipped him a half-hearted bird before turning to face the much more enjoyable view of Kane. "I'll check in with Arnie before we go to the cafeteria." Kane nodded, and I jabbed a finger at Holt. Not my middle one this time. "And *you*... stay here. LaVonda doesn't need you violating her privacy, and nothing's going to happen in the fifty feet or so between here and her cubicle."

Holt shook his head. "I can think of half a dozen things that could happen between here and there. You don't leave my sight."

Somehow I managed not to tell him to stick it up his ass.

"Fine, but stay back so LaVonda can't see you. She's had enough trauma in the last few days without having to look at your face." Ignoring his fake-wounded expression, I went on, "Her cubicle is around the corner, the second on the right. I'll stay in your line of sight the whole time."

"Okay. But..." Holt eyed me without a hint of humour, his steel-blue eyes hard as knives. "...if anything goes sideways here, I will personally see to it that you go down hard. Got it?"

Hiding the chill that trickled down my spine, I nodded. "Fair enough."

I headed back into the cubicle area with Kane at my side and Holt drifting behind. At the corner of the corridor, Holt took up a position that gave him a sightline to LaVonda's cubicle.

As soon as we were out of his earshot, Kane leaned down and spoke softly. "Was he serious about that?"

"Yeah. He can't afford not to be. His official assignment is to protect me, and he's taking that seriously; but Dermott also secretly assigned him to document my every move. From here on in I have to do everything exactly by the book."

Kane frowned. "You would anyway, wouldn't you?"

Right, I'd forgotten about that by-the-book part of his personality. The part that made him such a good agent.

Not like me.

Somehow I managed a smile. "Well, yeah, I try; but I have a terminally guilty conscience even when I haven't done anything wrong. I'm going to be twitching the whole time."

"But you have no reason to." Kane smiled back at me. "You're a good agent. You won't do anything wrong. You have nothing to worry about."

Somehow I managed not to twitch.

The afternoon wore on at the hospital, a strange combination of boredom and sharp-edged fear.

The doctor came and went, confirming the nurse's original hunch that LaVonda had been given Rohypnol but unable to predict when it might wear off.

Every time someone came near LaVonda's cubicle I tensed, studying them for weapons or other potential threats. Every time a staff member fiddled with LaVonda's IV bag or came near her with a syringe, Hellhound loomed behind them until they nervously completed their task and left.

When the cubicle curtains opened yet again, we both spun to face the potential threat, only to relax at the sight of Kane.

"How is she?" he asked softly.

"'Bout the same," Hellhound replied. "Maybe a bit better, but she's still out of it."

Kane squared his shoulders. "All right. I'm going to find us a hotel for the night, take back the Home Depot truck, and pick up my rental car from where we left it at the restaurant this morning. We'll hang onto the Home Depot van for now in case we need an extra set of wheels. We can return it on Boxing Day when the store reopens."

My heart sank. He had given up on Christmas.

"But what about Dan-" Hellhound began.

Kane halted him with a palm-out 'stop' gesture. "We'll talk about it later. This is my priority now. It doesn't make sense to wait here for hours, running the van every half hour to keep Princess warm. And I'd rather leave this in a safe place." He patted LaVonda's bag, slung over his broad shoulder.

"Awright," Hellhound agreed. "Thanks."

"You're welcome."

After Kane had left, Hellhound turned to me. "Hey, darlin', can I ask ya a favour?"

"Of course."

"Can ya go get some clothes for LaVonda before the stores close? She ain't got a thing but the clothes she was wearin'. She ain't even got a parka."

"Oh..." I hid my chagrin. "Sure, no problem. I'll just check the labels in her clothes so I know her size." I got up and dug through the plastic bag the hospital had supplied for LaVonda's personal effects. Fortunately the tags were still in her clothes, and I noted the sizes along with her preferences for underwear, feeling embarrassed on her behalf. If I was in her place, I'd hate the thought of a stranger poking around in my skivvies.

Then again, if I'd been living in the same clothes for a couple of days, I'd really appreciate a clean set; so maybe she wouldn't mind too much.

Summoning a smile, I dropped a kiss on Hellhound's lips. "Okay, I'm off. Call me on my burner if you think of anything else she might need."

"Toothbrush an' nightgown an' deodorant an' all that kinda shit."

I gulped. "Um... I'll do my best, but most women are really picky about stuff like that."

"It's okay, darlin', it's just to tide her over. She can buy what she likes on Boxin' Day. Can ya put it on your credit card? I'll pay ya back."

"Sure, no problem."

When I emerged from the cubicle, Holt detached himself from the wall across the hallway. "Where are we going?" he demanded as I trudged over.

I didn't bother to suppress my sigh. "Shopping. Arnie wants me to pick up some stuff for LaVonda."

Holt groaned. "On Christmas Eve? At three in the afternoon?"

"I know," I agreed glumly. "Walmart is going to be a madhouse."

"Walmart?" Holt recoiled as though I'd suggested popping out for a shit sandwich. "You're not going to buy her clothes there!"

I drew myself up. "What's wrong with Walmart?"

"Christ, Kelly, you're a walking crime against fashion. Hang on." He whipped out his smartphone and scrolled for a few seconds. "Okay, let's go."

"Um... where are we going?" I ventured as I trailed him toward the doors.

"Pennington's. They'll have her size, and their clothes are nice."

"But she was wearing sweatpants," I pointed out. "Walmart has-"

"She wasn't wearing *Walmart* sweatpants, idiot." Holt grabbed my arm before I could step outside. "Stay alert. We don't know who's out there." As we emerged cautiously, heads swivelling, he added, "Come on, we'll take my car."

For once I was glad of Holt's insufferable know-it-all attitude. I picked out a nightgown and some underwear for LaVonda while he blitzed through the rest of the Penningtons store, rapidly assembling a few casual outfits that cost more than my entire year's clothing budget.

Standing at the checkout desk, I made a face as he laid a parka on top of the pile.

"It's pink," I objected. "I hate pink. Don't they have anything else?"

"Not unless you count that monstrosity." Holt jabbed a contemptuous finger at a perfectly nice-looking brown parka. "That would look like shit on her."

"How do you know?" I challenged. "You haven't even met her."

"I saw her in the hospital bed. It's not her colour. And we're not shopping for you, so shut up."

I was clearly outclassed. I shut.

"She needs a suitcase, too," Holt said as we left the store. "She's too conspicuous with that duffel, and she'll need somewhere to store her clothes and toiletries, too."

We found a luggage store in a nearby mall and selected a good-sized rolling suitcase. I abdicated responsibility entirely in the Shopper's Drug Mart, letting Holt show off his knowledge of designer skin care while I collected a humble toothbrush, toothpaste, deodorant, and dental floss.

In less time than I had dreamed possible, we were on our way back to the hospital. I briefly considered teasing Holt about his fashion sense and asking him to be my personal shopper, but I was afraid he might take me seriously.

I settled for a simple, "Thanks, Greg. LaVonda will really appreciate everything you picked out, and I really appreciated you making the decisions."

"No problem."

We lapsed into an awkward silence. When my burner phone buzzed, I pulled it out with relief.

"Hello?"

"This is your bank calling."

I tensed at the Department code-phrase. After a quick check of my bug detector, I replied, "Kelly here. Go ahead."

"Hi, it's Trish Belling. I'm the analyst-on-call today. Is Greg Holt with you?"

"He's here, but he's driving. Can he call you back?"

"No, that's perfect. I want to talk to both of you. If you're secure, could you put me on speaker, please?"

"Hold on..." I toggled the phone button. "Okay, Holt and I are both listening. Go ahead."

"A call came in for Arlene Widdenback this afternoon on one of the burners."

My gut clenched.

CHAPTER 37

Before I could reply, the analyst went on, "I'll play the message for you. Hold on..."

A moment later a nondescript male voice issued from the speaker. "Good afternoon, Ms. Widdenback. My name is Ted Walker, and I got your contact information from a mutual acquaintance. I noticed in the newspaper that you're currently in Regina, and I would like to meet with you today to discuss a business opportunity. Please call me at your earliest convenience." He left a phone number, and the recording ended.

Somehow I managed not to groan aloud or shrink to the size of a cowering mouse and hide under the seat.

I held my voice steady. "Okay, thanks, Trish. I'll call him."

"Have you got anything on Ted Walker?" Holt demanded.

"No flags in the database," she replied. "It's a pretty common name, probably an alias. We're tracing the call, but it looks like a burner. That might have been an electronically modified voice, too. We're analyzing it."

"Okay, keep us posted." Holt gave me a nod, and I closed the connection.

Leaning my head back, I stared at the roof liner. "I knew that damn Arlene Widdenback thing was going to come back and bite me in the ass. What are the chances that somebody in the arms business would bother to read about an apartment fire in the Regina Leader-Post?"

Holt shrugged. "With your luck? Pretty much a hundred percent."

"No kidding," I growled. "And I wonder who this so-called 'mutual acquaintance' is. I thought all Arlene Widdenback's contacts were dead."

"Guess not. Think you can handle a simple meeting?"

I scowled, ready to retort; but he was studying me with genuine concern.

I sighed. "A simple meeting, sure. But are they ever simple?"

"A first meeting should be, but only if that's all it is." He grimaced. "If somebody's trying to draw you out for some other reason, it could go to hell fast. And you're not cleared for active duty. Call him back and tell him you're too busy-" He broke off. "Shit, I've got a call coming in."

Steering into a small parking lot, he braked and pulled out his phone. "Holt."

As his caller spoke, Holt's gaze flicked to me.

"Yeah." He listened for a moment, then responded, "No, we should defer it. She's not-" His brows drew into a frown. "Well, yeah; but-" His shoulders stiffened, his chin jerking up. "Of course I can fucking handle it!" He scowled. "Fine." He disconnected without waiting for a response.

My heart had been sinking while I listened. "Dermott, right?"

"Got it in one." Holt drove out of the parking lot, still scowling.

"So we're going ahead."

"Yeah. Call Walker and set up a meet. Tell him it'll have to be after supper because you're busy. That'll give the analysts a few hours to dig a little deeper. And tell him it'll be short. And don't give him a location yet. Tell him you're not sure what part of the city you'll be in, and you'll call him later and let him know where and when. That'll give us time to secure the site and prevent him from setting up anything of his own."

I nodded in silence, memorizing his instructions and trying to summon some courage.

Holt glanced over, his frown deepening. "Why aren't you busting my balls for telling you a bunch of shit you already know?"

"Because I'm glad you're doing it," I admitted. "I don't have two brain cells left to rub together."

Holt groaned. "We're so fucked." He gestured at my burner, letting his hand drop back onto the steering wheel in a gesture of futility. "Well, then, make the call."

I drew in a deep breath that was supposed to be calming and let it out slowly. Then I activated the burner's speaker and dialled.

It rang a couple of times at the other end before the nondescript male voice spoke. "Ted Walker."

"It's Arlene Widdenback returning your call."

The voice betrayed no emotion. "Are you available to meet today?"

I kept my voice as flat as his. "Maybe. I'm pretty busy. I might have time after supper, but only a few minutes. I can call you later with a time and place."

"That will be fine. I'll wait for your call." The line went dead.

I stowed the burner in my waist pouch again with a shaking hand. "We're on."

Holt grunted, and we didn't speak again for the rest of

the trip.

He was probably planning a strategy. I was just trying not to panic.

Back at the hospital, LaVonda was responding with more alertness at last, and her pupils slowly returned to normal. In between stints at her bedside, I briefed Kane and Hellhound about the meet with Ted Walker. Nobody looked happy when I was finished.

By the time LaVonda was released at five o'clock, we were all jumpy.

"Too fuckin' many people around here," Hellhound muttered. "Ya never know when somebody's sneakin' up on ya."

I rubbed a soothing circle on his back. "I know how much hospitals freak you out. Don't worry, we're almost out of here."

"Can't be soon enough for me." He turned to LaVonda, his voice softening. "How ya doin'?"

We studied her as she stood fully dressed at the entrance of the cubicle. As the Rohypnol had worn off she had become increasingly agitated, and now she wiped trembling hands down the sides of her thighs and swallowed hard.

"I can do this." She didn't sound sure.

"Ya got the Ativan the doc gave ya," Hellhound reassured her. "If ya get too anxious, ya can take one."

LaVonda's chin lifted. "I'm not going to start solving my problems with drugs again."

"But if ya need it..." he began.

"When I was addicted, I *needed* cocaine and heroin." Her lips twisted. "I only *want* Ativan. Let's go."

"Awright. We'll make sure ya get back to the hotel safe an' sound."

Her eyes widened. "Which hotel?"

"Not the one you used before," I hastened to reassure her. I shot a smile at Kane. "John got everything set up this afternoon."

"Don't worry," Kane said. "I booked the rooms on both sides of you and directly across the hall. We'll have you surrounded. You'll be safe."

Holt The Magnificent swaggered up in time to add a codicil. "And I'll be watching the corridor all night." He gave me a look that might have been reassurance or threat. "Nobody will get by me."

LaVonda gave him a timid glance.

"This is Greg Holt," I said. "He's here to help us. Greg, this is LaVonda."

"Nice to meet you," he said, and offered his hand.

LaVonda wiped her palm on her sweatpants before accepting his handshake, and her gaze flicked over him again. "Are you police, or military?"

There was nothing in her tone to indicate she would believe any other categorization. Apparently her cop radar was finely tuned.

Holt didn't hesitate. "You've got a good eye," he said pleasantly. "Military. I'm one of Hellhound's old army buddies."

"Hellhound?" LaVonda cast a puzzled glance between Kane and Arnie. "Which one of you is that?"

Arnie flushed. "That'd be me. Guess I got that nickname after we lost touch."

"Oh." She eyed him seriously. "It doesn't suit you."

His flush deepened and he studied the floor. "Suits me

better'n ya think."

LaVonda touched his hand. "I may not have seen you in thirty years, but some things don't change. You definitely aren't a 'Hellhound'."

Arnie's jaw clenched, and I could practically feel the waves of self-hatred rolling off him. No matter how often I reassured him, he could never see the good in himself.

LaVonda must have sensed that she'd touched a sore point. She turned to Holt instead. "Anyway, it's nice to meet you, Greg. Thank you for helping."

"My pleasure." He gave her a smile, and her cheeks went pink.

I could see why. Despite my earlier gibe about Holt's appearance, he was actually attractive in a rough-hewn way if he bothered to smile. With his smart designer clothes, hard-muscled martial artist's physique, and alpha-male posture, he could turn a few female heads.

Although they'd probably lose interest fast when he opened his mouth.

"Is Princess okay?" LaVonda asked. She turned an imploring gaze on Hellhound. "You didn't leave her out in the cold car all this time, did you?"

"Nah, 'course not. She's safe an' sound, waitin' for ya in your hotel room. An' so's your bag."

LaVonda's shoulders sagged with relief. "Thank you. And Aydan, thank you so much for buying me all these beautiful things." She stroked a hand down the pink parka she wore. "I love this. It's so pretty."

Holt gave me a triumphant smirk, and I rolled my eyes at him.

"All right, LaVonda, let's get you out of here," Kane said. "Aydan and Greg will take you to a different exit while Arnie and I bring my rental car around. You won't be exposed for more than a few seconds while you go from the hospital door to my car. On the way to the hotel, Aydan will lead us in the Home Depot van, and Greg will follow in his own rental. We might drive around quite a bit before we get there, so don't worry. If we're attacked, I want you to instantly obey whatever any of us tells you. If we say run, you run to the nearest safe place and call 911. Don't hesitate, and don't try to help us."

She gave him an uncertain nod, and our small entourage split up.

My heart thumped fast as we approached the hospital doors. The kidnappers' lawyer would have alerted Fitzgerald as soon as he received their call. That had been nearly six hours ago. Who knew what Fitzgerald might have arranged by now?

Even if he hadn't had any other men here this morning, more could have driven here. Or if Fitzgerald had a private jet, his men might have been here for hours already. They could have set up an ambush somewhere along our route, or even in the darkness right outside the hospital doors. It wasn't a huge hospital. If they had enough men, they could cover all the exits.

Holt glanced over at me and I stiffened my spine and gave him a nod.

As the doors opened, I stepped outside trying to look in all directions at once. We hustled LaVonda into Kane's rental car without incident, and Holt and I split off to our assigned vehicles.

The drive to the hotel left my shoulders aching with tension and my eyes gritty from trying not to blink while I stared into too-bright headlights in the blackness. I made random twists and turns, creating a convoluted route that became even more complicated when I realized I was lost. It took me a long time to find the hotel, but I salved my embarrassment with the thought that the others would only think I was being thorough about losing any potential tails.

At the hotel, we all pulled up under the portico and entered the hotel en masse.

When we crammed ourselves into the elevator and the doors closed behind us, I drew a short breath of relief but didn't relax. As the indicator counted up to the fourth floor, my tension increased.

What if Fitzgerald's men had somehow figured out where we were staying? When the elevator doors opened, they could shoot us like fish in a barrel. Nowhere to run.

Trapped...

My breath accelerated, and I fought it back to normal. I couldn't lose control now.

I couldn't burst out of the elevator screaming. I couldn't run until I outdistanced all the fear and pain. Run until my heart finally burst, releasing me into merciful death...

The elevator dinged and the doors rolled open.

A man lunged at us.

CHAPTER 38

Kane exploded into action so fast he was almost a blur. As Hellhound shoved LaVonda behind him, Holt and I sprang out of the elevator behind Kane, backs to each other to cover the corridor with weapons at the ready.

In seconds the man was whimpering on the carpet in Kane's submission hold.

The corridor was deserted. Holt and I holstered our weapons and Holt dropped to his knees beside the man, frisking him expertly.

"Take my wallet, it's in my back pocket," the man babbled, tears rolling down his cheeks. "My watch, my phone, take whatever you want, just don't hurt me, please don't hurt me!"

Holt completed his search and made a disgusted face, shaking his head.

"I'm sorry," Kane said as he eased his hold. "There's been a terrible mistake. We thought we were being attacked." He stepped back a pace, holding his hands out in a non-threatening gesture. "Please accept our apologies."

The man rolled over slowly, gaping up at Kane's muscular six-foot-four looming over him. Come to think of it, Holt was just over six feet and I was just under. And Hellhound and LaVonda were standing in the elevator holding the doors open, too. We were all looming.

I took a couple of steps backward and crouched to

decrease the intimidation factor.

"Are you okay?" I asked.

"*Okay?*" The man let out an incredulous half-laugh, half-sob. "I... I..."

"I'm very sorry," Kane repeated.

"Who *are* you people?"

"We're, um..." My adrenaline-saturated brain refused to disgorge anything useful.

Holt slid smoothly into the gap. "...Special Forces, here for a training conference. We just got back from an exercise, so we're still a little keyed up. And when you jumped at us like that..."

I put on my most abjectly apologetic face. "We're really sorry. I hope you aren't hurt."

"N-No. I..." He scrubbed his hands over his face, wiping away the tears. "I was j-just... late. In a hurry." His voice took on a tinge of indignation. "I didn't *jump* at you."

"Yeah, ya did," Hellhound said in none-too-friendly tones. "What if there'd been some little old lady gettin' outta the elevator? Ya woulda knocked her right on her ass. Coulda broken her hip or somethin'."

"I... I..." The man gulped, staring up at Hellhound's forbidding face with unconcealed fear. "I'm sorry. I'll be more careful next time."

Hellhound gave him an approving nod. "See that ya do." He extended a hand to the man, who gripped it as though afraid to refuse. Hellhound pulled the man to his feet without apparent effort. "There ya go. Saved the elevator for ya." He stepped out into the corridor, bringing LaVonda with him, and propelled our unintended victim into the cab with a hearty backslap that made the man flinch. "Have a nice night, now."

"Y-You, too," the man quavered. "And thank you for your s-service."

We all mumbled acknowledgement as the elevator door closed.

"LaVonda's room," Kane said grimly. "Now."

When her door closed behind us, I propped my trembling self against the nearest wall. "Jesus. That guy just about gave me a heart attack."

Hellhound snorted. "Just about gave himself a one-way ticket to the boneyard. Stupid asshole."

"Nice guilt trip about the little old lady, though." Holt snickered. "That shut him up before he could get all lawsuit-y."

Kane quelled him with a glance. "Don't get smug. He may still decide to press charges."

Holt shrugged. "He won't dare."

Hellhound grunted agreement. "In ten minutes he's gonna be tellin' all his buddies how he took on five Special Forces personnel an' had 'em all apologizin' an' suckin' up. Gonna be the highlight of his pathetic life."

LaVonda had detached herself from our group as soon as we got inside the room. Cocooned in her own little world, she sat on the bed with her back to us, Princess draped around her neck. LaVonda stroked the soft white fur over and over, murmuring fond nonsense and receiving purrs and trilling mews in reply.

Kane glanced over at her but apparently decided she needed some time. He returned his attention to me, reaching into his pocket.

"Aydan, here's your phone." He handed it over. "I put your luggage in the room on this side..." He nodded to the left. "...and I'm on her other side. Holt, you can take the room across the corridor."

Holt shrugged. "Doesn't matter which room I get. I'm going to be up all night anyway."

"Why?" Hellhound gave him a puzzled look, playing his dumb-biker role to the hilt.

"Because Dermott assigned me to help with your sister's case and protect Aydan," Holt said impatiently. "Didn't she tell you?"

"Oh. Yeah." Hellhound turned back to me. "Ya gettin' hungry, darlin'?"

"Starving." I held out a hand to gauge its tremor.

"Shit, you're about six on the Richter scale." He turned to Kane. "Is the hotel restaurant any good?"

Kane smiled, the first expression of happiness I'd seen on his face since he'd arrived. "Yes, it's supposed to be."

Hellhound chuckled. "I shoulda known."

While they talked, I turned on my phone and discovered a voicemail. The number was unlisted and the message was brief. "*It's Detective Constable Tan. Please call me as soon as you get this.*" The timestamp was an hour and a half old.

As I lowered the phone from my ear, Kane gave me a quizzical look.

"It's Tan," I said, hitting the speed dial. "Probably wants to go over some questions for the kidnappers..." I trailed off, listening to the ringtone on the other end.

"Tan."

"Hi, it's Aydan. I'm sorry I missed your call earlier. I was at the hospital with LaVonda."

"No problem. Is Ms. Rainey still hospitalized?"

"No, she was released around five o'clock and we brought her back to our hotel."

"Which hotel?"

I told him the hotel name and our room arrangements.

"And is Ms. Rainey with you now?"

Sudden trepidation made my reply come out sounding a bit more tentative than I'd intended. "Um, yes..."

"Good. Don't let her out of your sight. I'll be there in five minutes." He hung up.

"Oh," I said to dead air. "Shit."

"What?" Kane snapped.

"Um... Tan's on his way. I think he has some questions for LaVonda."

Hellhound tensed.

Holt's eyebrows rose. "Well, this should be interesting."

"LaVonda," Kane prompted. "Did you hear what Aydan said?"

She turned, looking startled. "Oh. No, I'm sorry, I wasn't listening."

"A police officer is coming to ask you some questions. He'll likely take your statement about your kidnapping, but he may also want to ask you some questions about your past and that bag of money. Do you want to have a lawyer present while he does that?"

She frowned. "Why would I? I haven't done anything wrong."

Hellhound and I exchanged a dumbfounded glance. Not a hint of hesitation in her answer. No indication at all that she was lying.

Kane blinked. "Are you sure?"

"Of course."

"All right..." Kane said slowly. "Just remember that you don't have to answer his questions if you don't want to. And you can always stop and request a lawyer if things get complicated."

LaVonda's frown deepened. "You sound as though you think I've done something bad. It's not illegal to get kidnapped, is it?"

"No..." Kane looked as though he might say something else, but I gave him a tiny headshake and he fell silent.

I had spotted Holt's intent expression. So far Kane had done nothing more than remind LaVonda of her rights. But if he said anything that might be construed as counselling her to lie...

"So..." I changed the subject with the only inane comment I could think of on short notice. "LaVonda, would you like a glass of water or anything?"

"No, thank you."

An awkward silence fell.

LaVonda went back to petting Princess.

"Aydan, if you give me your keys, I'll go and park your vehicle," Kane offered.

"Thanks." I handed them over.

Hellhound squinted at Holt. "Guess you're stayin' here with Aydan, right?" His contemptuous tone made Holt redden, but he didn't rise to the bait.

"Yep." Holt tossed his keys to Hellhound. "Park mine, too, would you?" He made the request sound like the bored command of a celebrity to a lowly valet.

Hellhound gave him a look that would have made any normal man shrivel, but Kane snagged his arm before he could retort.

"Good idea," Kane said as he steered Hellhound toward the door. "LaVonda will be well-protected if you're both here."

The two of them left, and Holt and I pretended absorption in our phones. Kane and Hellhound returned in short order, and we all stood in uncomfortable silence.

Tan's rap at the door was almost a relief. I let him in and introduced Holt, then stepped back to let him get on with it.

Tan glanced around at the semicircle of silent people surrounding him. Kane stood in a relaxed parade rest, wearing his cop face. Hellhound glowered with his arms crossed over his chest. Holt was back to his alpha-male posture, arms akimbo, steely eyes alert.

I preferred not to think about what Tan saw when he looked at me. An ill-advised glance in a mirror at the mall had revealed a weary old hag with pasty skin, an ugly reddened abrasion on her forehead, and bags under her eyes big enough to accommodate a picnic lunch for an army platoon. If my posture was telegraphing anything, it was 'Help, I'm about to fall down and won't be able to get up'.

"Would any of you like to wait outside?" Tan asked.

"We're stayin'." Hellhound's reply was as unyielding as granite.

Tan shrugged and took a seat in the chair facing LaVonda. "Ms. Rainey, I'm Detective Constable Tan. Would you please walk me through everything that happened to you?"

"I... don't know exactly what happened." LaVonda gave him an apologetic look. "I remember checking into the hotel. I ordered room service and had a shower. My food was delivered and I watched the waiter walk away through the peephole in the door. When I opened the door to get my tray, a man jumped out of the room across the hall and pushed me back into my room. After that... I don't remember. I have hazy recollections, like dreams. They had me tied up. I think someone slapped me, maybe more than once. But I... I'm sorry, I just don't know. My only definite memory is waking up in the hospital."

"The doc in Emergency said they roofied her," Hellhound contributed.

Tan nodded acknowledgement of the comment. "Ms. Rainey, would you be able to identify the man who attacked you if you saw him again?"

"N-No... I don't think so."

"Is there anything else you can tell me? Do you remember any sounds, or smells? Even vague impressions?"

LaVonda shook her head.

Tan's mouth twisted with resignation. "If you remember anything else, please call and let me know immediately. Any memories that you have now might continue to fade as the drug wears off, so it's important to tell us everything you can remember." He handed her his card.

As she nodded and accepted it, he added, "I have some other questions for you, too."

She met his eyes, looking calm and unafraid. "Okay."

"Where did you get that bag of money?"

A faint wrinkle appeared between her brows. "It's mine. It was the only thing we saved from the apartment fire, besides my purse and Princess. Didn't I tell you that, when I was hospitalized the first time? I was confused for a while, but I'm sure someone asked me about the money."

"It was probably the constable who was guarding you," Tan said. "Would you please tell me again?"

"It's fees I saved from my psychic clients over the years. They prefer to pay in cash." Her gaze was level, her tone honest and convincing.

I didn't even dare glance at Hellhound.

"It's interesting that you say you acquired it over the years," Tan said, going directly for the jugular. "Because when the money was inventoried at the P.O. it was all old bills, from thirty years ago and earlier."

LaVonda smiled. "Yes, it's surprising how many people keep cash for years and years, under their mattresses and in coffee cans buried in the back yard. Some of the money I've received has been very old."

"I'd think you should have some newer bills by now, though," Tan persisted. "You're still operating your business, aren't you?"

"Yes, I am; and you're right, only my older money is in the bag." She sounded unperturbed.

"That's a lot of money." Tan's shark-like gaze bored into her. "Where did you get it?"

"In the early years, just after I was discovered as a psychic, I got a lot of quiet publicity among some very big Hollywood stars. As you can imagine, their privacy is important to them. They offered me generous fees for my predictions, and all in cash."

God, she was convincing. I couldn't believe this was the same woman who had stammered out her fake story earlier, unable to maintain eye contact with us.

She held Tan's gaze effortlessly, her voice calm and confident as she went on, "I'm sure you know by now about my past. After I got off the street and recovered from my addictions, I craved security. I hoarded all the money I made in the early days, except for what I paid in taxes; and I spent what I needed from my most recent fees. And I just kept doing that, out of habit, I guess. I still spend my new money and keep the old."

She sounded so plausible. I knew damn well it was all lies, and still I almost believed her.

Tan gave her the hard silent scrutiny that had turned my

knees to jelly, but LaVonda only sat awaiting his next question, apparently unaffected.

"Do you remember when Bradley Percival Montmorency was killed?" he asked.

"I know he was killed around the time that I got off the street, but I have permanent gaps in my memory from years of abusing drugs, and also from a very severe assault that I experienced around that time." She shrugged. "And it was thirty years ago. Nobody's memory is that good."

Tan frowned at her again. "You were questioned in connection with his murder."

She frowned back, the picture of honest confusion. "I don't remember that. Was it when I was in the hospital in Winnipeg?"

"Yes."

LaVonda nodded, her face clearing. "That explains why I don't remember it. I'd had some head injuries..." She touched her lumpy cheekbone. "...and I had quite a few broken bones so I was on morphine." She gave Tan a faint rueful smile. "Between that and the withdrawal symptoms from street drugs, I remember almost nothing."

"Why were you beaten up?"

"I don't know. I can't even remember being beaten. I only have hazy memories of being in the hospital for a long time."

"At the time, you gave a statement to the police describing the incident."

She sighed. "If you say so. I can't remember now. As I said, I have a lot of memory gaps."

Stalemate. God, she was good.

"A lot of money disappeared around the time of Montmorency's murder," Tan tried again. "Cash in smaller bills, just like the money in your bag."

LaVonda drew herself up. "Are you accusing me of stealing?"

"I'm just asking questions. There were a lot of loose ends in that murder case."

"I'm afraid I can't tell you anything that would help," LaVonda replied with perfect composure. "I don't remember much from that time, but I'm quite sure I didn't have a bag of cash with me in the hospital. And if I'd had it when the police were called to the scene of my assault, surely it would have been documented...?"

She made the statement into a question, and Tan nodded.

"But you knew Montmorency, didn't you?" he asked.

"Yes. Most addicts did."

"And did you ever see him with a bag of money?"

LaVonda frowned. "I don't remember. As I said, my memory of that time is very poor. He certainly always had money; he was a drug dealer. But I can't imagine that he would have carried around a bag of money. That wouldn't be very safe, would it?"

"If your memory is that poor, maybe you killed him and took his money, and you just don't remember." Tan's knife-edged voice made me suppress a shiver.

LaVonda remained unmoved. "I earned that money as a psychic after I got off the street, and my income tax records with the Canada Revenue Agency prove it. And if I was questioned by the police at the time and they didn't arrest me, they obviously believed I was innocent."

"Okay," Tan said patiently. "So if you had nothing to do with Montmorency's murder and you didn't steal any money, can you explain why Richard Fitzgerald, the man whose money was stolen, is apparently trying to kidnap you now and drag you back to Winnipeg to face him?"

"Richard Fitzgerald?" LaVonda looked startled for the first time. "He wasn't one of the kidnappers. Or... was he? Am I forgetting because of the drugs they gave me?"

"No, he wasn't one of the kidnappers. But the men who kidnapped you all work for him." Tan went in for the kill. "So you admit you know Richard Fitzgerald."

"Yes," LaVonda said reluctantly.

My heart thumped painfully. Oh, LaVonda, you were doing so well until now...

"And why do you think Mr. Fitzgerald would go to the trouble of kidnapping you, only days after your true identity was revealed?" Tan leaned forward, obviously thinking he was on the verge of getting a confession. "It sounds to me as though he's seeking revenge for something."

"Well..." LaVonda hesitated. "If I had to guess, I would suspect it's because he had a sexual relationship with me for two years, starting when I was thirteen. He probably wants to cover that up."

CHAPTER 39

I couldn't tell whether the sharp inhalation had come from Holt or Kane, or maybe both. Tan spun to face us, and I did my best to look shocked at LaVonda's revelation.

Our expressions must have been appropriate, because Tan turned back to LaVonda.

"Do you have any proof to back up your accusation against Mr. Fitzgerald?" he asked. "It's not too late to press charges against him."

"No, of course there's no proof." LaVonda gave him a bitter smile. "I was thirteen. I had been sexually abused in a foster home since I was eleven. As far as I knew, it was normal for adult men to have sex with young girls. It was forty years ago, and Mr. Fitzgerald was an important man. Even if I had told somebody then, I probably would have been punished for lying."

Even though Tan's shark eyes tried to hide his feelings, I could see the pain of a good cop who'd watched the system fail too many times.

"Would anyone else remember that time in your life?" he asked. "Neighbours? Friends? Teachers?"

"He had me living in an apartment for two years, but the neighbours all turned a blind eye. I probably wasn't the first girl he'd had there, and I know I wasn't the last. But you'd never be able to find those people now. And I didn't go to school much. The work was too easy and I was bored. I didn't have friends, and the teachers mostly yelled at me because I caused trouble in class."

"They shoulda seen ya needed help!" Hellhound burst out. "An' how the hell did the foster parents explain it when ya didn't show up for school?"

"They said I'd run away," she said. "And I did. Anything was better than living there. The police found me and brought me back, and I ran away again every time. After a while, the Rutherfords just told my teachers that I was sick. The teachers were glad to accept that so they didn't have to deal with me."

"But they shoulda-"

Tan gently interrupted Arnie's protest. "Ms. Rainey, you should still file charges. If there's an investigation, they might be able to uncover witnesses, even now. And if there were other girls, too..."

"No." LaVonda's tone was flat and final. "He'll find me and kill me long before it ever goes to court. You don't know how powerful he is. I'm going to stay here tonight because I'm too exhausted to move, but tomorrow I'll disappear again. It's the only way I'll survive."

"You need to stay," Tan insisted. "We'll need your testimony to convict your kidnappers."

"I'm not pressing charges." Her gaze met his. "Even if they got convicted, they wouldn't get more than a slap on the wrist. But I'll be killed if I stay."

A short silence fell.

Tan broke it with a tired exhalation. "Why don't you get some rest and make a decision tomorrow? You have my number. Call me tomorrow and let me know."

She nodded without meeting his eyes. Her unspoken response was clear. As soon as Tan went out the door, his card was going in the garbage.

"Thank you for your time." Tan rose as though he'd aged ten years, then turned back to her. "I brought your cell phone. We checked it for fingerprints but only found yours." He handed it over to LaVonda and then addressed me. "We'll still go ahead with the interviews, likely around nineteen-thirty. Do you still want to observe?"

"Yes," Kane answered for me.

"Any specific questions you want me to ask?"

Kane and I exchanged a glance. He didn't supply any ideas, so I said, "No, we'll leave it up to you. If we think of anything in the meantime I'll call you."

Giving us a resigned nod, Tan let himself out.

As soon as the door closed behind him, Hellhound fixed Holt with a hard stare. "Step outside. We gotta have a fam'ly talk."

Holt stiffened, and I tried to defuse the tension by moving toward the door. "Come on, let's give them a few minutes."

As Kane and Holt followed my lead, Hellhound spoke again. "Aydan, stay." We turned to stare at him, and his chin rose defiantly. "She's fam'ly."

I glanced at Kane in time to see his expression close off into his impassive cop face, but the storm-grey of his eyes reflected his hurt. After decades of brotherhood, Arnie had just shut him out.

"Sorry, Cap," Arnie added hurriedly. "You're fam'ly, too, it's just... it's... we gotta talk about... woman stuff. Y'know?"

Kane nodded. "It's all right." He moved toward the door again, but Holt planted his feet, frowning.

"Go on, Greg," I prompted, hoping he'd maintain his cover in front of LaVonda. "We're safe here. Nobody's going to get in or out of this room without you knowing."

He crossed to the window, parting the heavy draperies a crack and poking his head through. Closing them again, he turned. "The window opens, and it's big enough for a person to get through."

He was looking for an excuse to stay and eavesdrop on our conversation, the stubborn bastard.

"We're on the fourth fuckin' floor," Hellhound snapped, apparently at the end of his patience. "Nobody knows we're here, an' even if they did, it's a sheer wall. Nobody's gettin' in, an' we sure as hell ain't jumpin' out." He didn't mention rappelling this time.

Holt hesitated. "Okay. But if anything happens, I'm holding you responsible, Kelly."

It wasn't hard to figure out his true meaning: 'You'd better not screw me over.'

I shrugged. "Same old, same old."

"We'll be right outside the door." Holt gave us a final intimidating glare, and he and Kane left.

Holding Princess like a security blanket, LaVonda gave Arnie a confused look. "Woman stuff? What do you mean? It's taken years of therapy to overcome, but I'm not ashamed of being raped. And I just told them about it anyway."

Hellhound scowled. "Aydan, sit down. Ya look like you're gonna keel over." He ushered me over to the chair Tan had vacated, then retraced his steps and turned on the TV, lowering the volume to a murmur that would conceal our voices.

I nodded at the vacant chair beside me. "You should sit, too."

He gave me a warning glance that clearly said 'shut up'.

I gave him the stink-eye in return, accompanied by a tiny

inclination of my chin toward LaVonda to let him know that if he didn't obey, I'd blab about the bullet-induced bruise he hadn't mentioned to her.

"Blackmail," he muttered as he brushed by me and sat. He leaned forward slowly, resting his elbows on his knees and letting out a slow breath that probably hurt a lot. "So, LaVonda," he said gently. "It's okay, ya can tell us the real story now."

She gave him a brief startled glance before studying her toes. "That was the real story."

"Bullshit," Hellhound replied. "We know ya overheard Montmorency tellin' James he was gonna kill ya, so ya killed him first an' took the money an' ran. James caught ya an' beat the hell outta ya, but ya didn't tell him where you hid the money. An' when ya got outta the hospital, ya grabbed the cash an' disappeared, an' ya been launderin' the money through your psychic business ever since. I dunno how ya managed to lie like a pro to that cop, 'cause ya were always a shitty liar. Look me in the eye, now, an' tell me I'm wrong."

She straightened indignantly and met his eyes. "How could you even..." Her gaze veered away. "Of course you're wrong."

"Kath." His voice was gentle. "It's too late to lie about it. Ya already told us the truth, while ya were roofied."

"I didn't!" Her fingers clenched in Princess's fur, earning a mew of protest. "Oh, sweetie, I'm sorry..." She comforted the cat absently, staring wide-eyed at Hellhound. "I *didn't!*"

"Yeah, ya did. Ya prob'ly don't remember tellin' us 'cause a' the drugs, but how else would I know all that shit?"

"Ohmigod." She buried her face in shaking hands and her voice came out in a thin quaver. "Did James tell you? Who else knows?"

"Nobody knows. I told the ambulance guys ya weren't makin' sense, so they wouldn't'a thought anythin' of it even if ya talked in the ambulance. An' one of us was with ya the whole time ya were in the hospital an' ya never said anythin'." He took her hand. "An' James ain't gonna tell anybody, ever. He's dead."

"*What?*"

"Yeah, I told ya that while ya were roofied, too. James is dead," Arnie repeated. "The ol' man's dead, too. You're safe from both of 'em."

"Oh, thank God!" LaVonda slumped, her eyes filling. "But... it doesn't matter now. I'm a murderer and a thief. I'm going to prison."

"No, ya ain't. Ya didn't do anythin' wrong. It ain't illegal to kill in self-defence; an' nobody ever reported any money gettin' stolen. Tan's just fishin' 'cause there were rumours about money. We're the only ones that know what really happened." Hellhound glanced at me, entreaty in his eyes. "An' we ain't tellin'."

My guts clenched. If only LaVonda hadn't benefited from Montmorency's death, things might be different. But the money made it look like premeditated murder.

Hell, maybe it had been. She had lied so smoothly to Tan, and even when she was drugged she hadn't actually said she'd killed in self-defence.

If I covered this up and Holt or Dermott found out...

"LaVonda, why don't you tell us the whole story now?" I said gently, hoping to buy time. "How did you end up killing Bradley Montmorency?"

"First of all," Hellhound interjected, "How'd ya lie so well to that cop? Ya never could look me in the eye an' lie when we were kids, an' ya still can't."

She sighed. "No, I never could lie to you. But lying to anybody else?" Her shoulders rose and fell in a resigned shrug. "I was an abused child, a teenage runaway, a drug addict, and a prostitute. Lying to the police is as natural to me as breathing."

"So ya lied to Kane about your agoraphobia."

"Not really." LaVonda gave him a shaky smile. "The best lies include some truth. I have generalized anxiety disorder, which can be caused by childhood trauma, changes in brain chemistry from drug abuse, brain damage from head injuries..."

"An' by spendin' mosta your life waitin' for somebody to show up an' kill ya," Arnie pointed out.

"That, too," she agreed with a wry twist of her lips. "I was telling the truth when I said I hadn't left my apartment in eight years and I'm intensely anxious outside; but it's not really agoraphobia. It's just easier to call it that because it's a one-word explanation that everyone understands."

"Okay, so tell us what happened with Montmorency," he encouraged.

She blew out a breath, closing her eyes.

Arnie reached over and tapped her knee. "Come on, now, look me in the eye."

Her eyes flew open and she met his gaze squarely. "I won't lie to you. Not anymore." She stroked Princess as if gathering her strength.

"I was high," she began quietly. "As always. I stayed high as much as I could. It helped me... forget."

Pain filled Arnie's face and he took her hand and held it.

"Bradley never let me have enough drugs," LaVonda went on dispassionately. "He liked to watch me suffer. He liked to know that I'd do anything, literally *anything*, to get another fix. So we were in a party house out by the University of Manitoba. It was around four o'clock in the morning and everybody had left except Bradley and me. I was coming down from the high, starting to hurt. Not bad yet, but it was coming. I begged him for another fix. He laughed."

Her gaze went distant, but she didn't look away from Arnie's steady eye contact. "He always laughed. It always gave him a hard-on..." She hesitated as if reading the misery in Arnie's eyes. "Never mind that part. After I did what he wanted, he was slapping me around like he always did. Not hard enough to seriously injure me, just slapping me hard in... tender places. Laughing. Telling me how I was garbage, and one of these days he'd kill me slowly just to hear me scream."

She gently detached her hand from Arnie's grip and rubbed some circulation back into her whitened skin.

He blanched. "Aw, shit, I'm sorry. I didn't mean to-"

"It's okay. I know this is hard for you to hear. Are you really sure you want to know?"

Arnie set his jaw. "Yeah."

LaVonda sighed. "Anyway, that's how it always went. I knew it would be hours before he let me have any more drugs. He was as high as a kite, but he wouldn't let me have any. Then James called. He was high, too. They started talking about snuff films, all the ones they'd seen lately and how the girls had been killed. Bradley was..." She made a graphic jacking-off gesture. "Excited. He had been trying to convince James to make a snuff film for quite a while. He said they could make a lot of money. James had always held back, but this time..." She shrugged. "When Bradley got off the phone, I knew. He took out his knife..."

My knuckles popped, and the jolt of pain reminded me that my hands were knotted together, every muscle in my body rigid with horror. I drew a slow breath and eased it out, but it didn't help.

LaVonda's chillingly emotionless voice went on, "I was so sick. Hurting so much. I just wanted the pain to end. I went limp and just lay there. He was sliding the knife over my body, telling me all the places he was going to cut me as soon as James got there with the camera. And I realized it wasn't going to end, not for hours. And I just... I couldn't. Couldn't take any more pain."

Her voice went completely flat. "The next time he looked down to watch himself masturbate, I grabbed the knife out of his hand and stabbed him." A small grim smile quirked her mouth. "Lucky I'd learned about the jugular vein in school."

Her smile went away and the robotic voice resumed. "There was blood everywhere. But I was naked, so it didn't matter. I got in the shower and washed it off. My clothes were on the other side of the room and they didn't have any blood on them. I got dressed and grabbed Bradley's stash. I almost shot up right then and there, but I was straight enough to realize that I had to get out before James arrived. I was on my way out when I remembered the bag of money Bradley was supposed to deliver to Mr. Fitzgerald in the morning."

Her lips twisted. "I don't remember how far I lugged that heavy bag down the street before I suddenly realized I was rich."

Her smile softened and her eyes focused on her brother. "You were eighteen, in the army and far away. You were safe, and I could finally be free. All I had to do was get someplace where James could never find me. So I hailed a cab." Her smile widened. "A cab. Imagine having enough money for a luxury like that. I had the driver take me to the bus depot, and I bought a ticket for the next bus that was leaving. I don't remember where it was going. I didn't care."

Arnie nodded. "Yeah, ya didn't hafta give your name in those days so James wouldn't'a been able to track ya."

LaVonda's smile faded. "That's what should have happened. But the bus wasn't leaving for another half an hour, and I was an addict. Bradley's drugs were calling to me." She shivered. "Screaming at me, by then. I needed a fix like I needed my next breath. But I was afraid to carry all that money around when I was high, so I put it in one of the storage lockers..."

She surfaced from her narrative with a shaky laugh. "Those were the days. You could put whatever you wanted into a storage locker at the bus depot and just walk away with the key."

Falling silent, she petted Princess with shaking hands.

"I'm sorry to make ya think about all this shit again," Arnie said softly.

"It's okay. I..." LaVonda hesitated. "It's... doing me good to tell you. I've held it in so long. Anyway..." She drew a deep breath. "I went into the bathroom and shot up, and it felt so... the relief was incredible. I was on top of the world. I was rich. I was free. I had drugs. I was high, so high. I loved the whole world. I decided to find somebody to party with, but even through my haze I knew I had to make sure my money stayed safe. So I put the key in..." She hesitated, her eye contact with Arnie wavering for the first time. "...in a... personal place... that had provided me with my living for quite a while."

He flushed, but forced a chuckle. "An' that's somethin'

ya never wanna hear from your sister."

LaVonda tried to smile, but it fell flat. "And then I went out into the bus depot. And James was there. He had easily figured out that if I'd killed Bradley and stolen the money, I'd try to leave town. I don't remember much after that. I don't know whether he dragged me out or somehow convinced me to leave with him. It was just lucky for me that he was high, too. If he'd been thinking straight, he would have taken me somewhere private and finished the job, but he just dragged me into the nearest alley and started beating me. Someone heard me screaming and called the police."

"So when you arrived at the hospital..." My voice came out in a croak as though I hadn't spoken for days. I cleared my throat. "You were so badly injured. They must have checked to see if you'd been raped, and then they would have found the key. Surely the police would have looked in the locker."

"I had been in the hospital quite a few times before." Her lips twisted with dark humour. "Occupational hazard. One of the nurses was..." She hesitated. "Not exactly a friend, but a kind woman who had always taken a personal interest in me. Tried to get me off drugs, off the street. It was just luck that she was working that night. I gave her the key and told her everything I owned was in that locker. She picked up the bag and kept it for me. I don't think she looked inside, but if she did, she never told. And the day before I was supposed to be released from the hospital, she arranged to smuggle me out of the hospital and into a women's shelter."

Her smile turned wintry. "That was James's second mistake. He had been sitting by my bedside, playing the concerned brother. Threatening me when nobody was listening. I knew I was dead as soon as I left the hospital. But for the first time in ten years, the drugs were out of my system and I could think clearly." Her smile flattened. "Both my arms were broken. I couldn't do anything *but* think."

"That fuckin' asshole," Arnie muttered. "Wish I'd killed him myself."

"I'm glad you didn't." LaVonda touched his cheek. "You're no murderer."

Pain flared in his eyes, and I reached over and took his hand.

Fortunately LaVonda didn't notice. Her gaze was turned inward as she went on, "Lying there in the hospital day after day, I made a plan. I promised myself that I would leave the street behind forever. And for the first time... I asked for help."

She swallowed. "And I got it. I won't tell you the names of the people who helped me, but there were several who helped me change my name, get therapy, and eventually get out of Winnipeg when I was strong enough."

"Did ya settle here in Regina right away?" Arnie asked.

"No, I moved around. Afraid to stay in one place. Finally I felt safe enough to settle in Regina, and I met a few people." She gave him a ghost of a smile. "That's where the part about my friend calling me psychic came from. That really happened. The rest... was lies. You're right, I set up the fake psychic business and laundered the money. For a while I lived an almost-normal life, but one day I spotted a man who looked like one of Richard Fitzgerald's enforcers. That was the last day I ever left my apartment. I took up blogging to maintain some semblance of social contact." Her lips trembled. "And you know how that ended."

"Don't worry, you're gonna be okay." Arnie reached over

to squeeze her hand. "We'll find ya new place-"

"No." One word, flat and final.

He blinked and tried again. "I know you're scared, but-"

"No," LaVonda repeated. "I'm not going to risk your life as well as mine. I've always been prepared for the day that I had to move on. Everything I need is in my purse, ready to go. Tomorrow I'll take on a new identity and vanish, and you have to promise not to follow me. It's been wonderful to see you, but it can't happen again."

Arnie jerked forward, gripping her hand. "Ya don't hafta protect me anymore! I'm a grown man. I can take care a' myself, an' I can take care a' you, too. I learned a few things in the army, ya know."

She placed her other hand tenderly over his. "I'm not questioning your courage or abilities. But unless the army somehow made you bulletproof and immortal, you can't stand against Richard Fitzgerald. You've already put yourself at risk by helping me."

He shook his head stubbornly but as he began to speak again, LaVonda placed Princess on the bed and fell to her knees beside Arnie's chair.

"Arnie, I'm begging you." Her voice shook. "Please. I've never asked you for anything, ever, but I'm begging you now. Just do this one thing for me."

He stared at her, anguish twisting his face. "Kath, I can't. I can't walk away knowin' you'll be runnin' for the rest a' your life. Knowin' they might find ya again an' there'll be nobody to help ya."

"Please." She folded his hand between hers and gazed up at him, tears trickling down her cheeks. "Arnie, *please*. If you love me... if you *ever* loved me... please let me go."

I saw the exact moment his heart broke.

His shoulders slumped, his body curling in on itself as if a giant piece had been torn from his chest.

"Awright," he said hoarsely. "Just... promise you'll say goodbye. Don't just run away again."

"I'll say goodbye." Her voice was so choked it was barely audible.

CHAPTER 40

LaVonda rested her forehead briefly against Arnie's knee, then rose as though it took the last of her strength.

"Will you take Princess for me?" she quavered. "Keep her safe?"

"I'll keep her safe." Arnie's voice was raw.

"Thank you."

Silence descended while brother and sister stared into each other's eyes. Storing each other in memory for the rest of the lifetime they wouldn't get to share.

Arnie drew an unsteady breath and rose. "Ya look wiped. We'll let ya get some sleep. Ya gonna be okay by yourself, or ya want some company? I can sit with ya..." He glanced at me, seeking permission with his eyes. "Or Aydan can, if you'd rather have a woman."

"No. Thank you, but I'd rather be alone." LaVonda gave us a sad smile. "It's what I'm used to."

"Awright. See ya in the mornin'." His voice was level, but his eyes begged the question.

"I'll see you in the morning," LaVonda said, meeting his gaze squarely. "I promise."

"Thanks."

He opened his arms tentatively, and she threw hers around him in a hug so fierce he winced. They stood wrapped in the embrace for only a few moments before LaVonda drew away.

"I love you," she whispered.

"I love ya, too. G'night." Arnie turned for the door quickly, as if to hide his suffering.

"Good night, LaVonda," I echoed, and hurried after him.

I caught up a few paces from the door and his arm came across my shoulders, heavy with the weight of his grief.

When we stepped out into the hallway, Kane and Holt were standing in identical parade rests, one on each side of the door.

Despite the bleakness in his eyes, Arnie attempted a joke. "An' that ain't conspicuous at all. Think ya could make it look any more like you're guardin' somebody?"

Kane eyed him with concern, clearly not fooled.

Before he could speak, Arnie went on, "Come on, let's get Aydan somethin' to eat before she passes out."

"Who's going to guard this door?" Holt demanded. "Wherever Kelly goes, I go, so that means one of you has to do guard duty."

"I'll stay here," Kane volunteered.

"Nah, I'll stay," Hellhound rasped. "I ain't hungry. I ate at the hospital."

"That was hours ago," I said. "You need to eat."

He grunted. "Later. Go on, you three. You'll get more outta that fancy restaurant than me. I'll just grab some shit from the vendin' machine before ya go. Be right back." He turned and strode away before we could argue.

When he returned a few minutes later carrying several bags of chips and a drink, I tried again. "What can we bring you from the restaurant?"

"Nothin'. Hurry up, now. Arlene Widdenback's gotta meet her contact, an' then ya hafta be at the cop shop in an hour an' a half. Holt, gimme your cardkey so I can watch from inside your room. Don't need to advertise that we're here."

Holt lowered his voice. "I've got a little surveillance cam in there, wired to the fisheye. It's got a motion sensor on it, so it'll ping if anything moves out here." He handed over his cardkey.

"I'm going to leave my vest in my room," Kane said quietly. "I don't feel like wearing my parka the whole time we're eating."

"Good idea," I agreed, and detoured into the room assigned to Hellhound and me.

Stripping off my bulletproof vest, I indulged in a stretch and blissful scratching of all the places on my back and ribs that I hadn't been able to get to all day. My left side was tender from the impact of my jump through the van window, but it would have been a lot worse if I hadn't been wearing my vest.

After being crammed under Kevlar all day, my sweatshirt looked as if I'd slept in it. I yanked it off and substituted a slim-fitting zip-up fleece sweater instead.

Heading for the door, I paused with my hand on the doorknob. Despite the relief of removing the vest, I felt naked leaving the room without it.

What if we were attacked?

Maybe I should put it back on.

No, don't be stupid. Kane didn't think it was necessary.

I'd be fine.

I squared my shoulders and stepped out into the corridor.

"*That's* your idea of dressing for dinner?" Resplendent in a fresh dress shirt and expensive-looking slacks, Holt gave me a contemptuous up-and-down.

I returned an equally contemptuous 'up' of my middle finger.

"Children, behave," Kane admonished. He had changed into an open-collared black shirt perfectly tailored to his spectacular shoulders and taut midriff, but his relaxed-fit jeans reassured me that I wasn't too under-dressed.

Damn, he looked good.

Somehow I managed to keep my gaze above his neck while we rode down in the elevator.

When I got my first look at the restaurant, I quailed.

It was beautiful, sparkling with tasteful Christmas decorations. Smartly-dressed waitstaff, intimate lighting, romantic music...

And I was going to have to look at Holt the whole time.

"I can't," I blurted.

"What's wrong?" Kane gave me a puzzled look, and I caught a hint of disappointment in his eyes. "Don't you like the restaurant?"

"It looks wonderful," I assured him. "I just..."

Words failed me. Holt might be a jerk sometimes and we constantly needled each other, but I didn't want to say anything genuinely hurtful.

"Suck it up, Kelly," Holt snapped. "Nobody cares how you're dressed. You two get a table. I'm going to eat at the bar where I can watch the hockey game and keep an eye on you at the same time. I've got a clear view of the whole restaurant from there."

I tried to hide my relief, but I wasn't sure I'd succeeded. I did my best to sound cranky. "Fine."

Holt turned and strode to the bar, and Kane and I approached the smiling maître d'.

After we were seated and had been presented with the

menus, Kane leaned close to murmur, "You look fine. I hope you don't feel uncomfortable here."

I smothered an unladylike guffaw and settled for a sardonic grin. "That was just Holt, projecting. You know what a clotheshorse he is. I never even thought of how I was dressed until he mentioned it."

Kane's worried look eased into a smile. "That's one of the things I love about you. You're completely unselfconscious. Confident in yourself." The pucker between his eyebrows returned. "So what was wrong? Why did you say 'I can't'?"

I leaned closer and turned my head so Holt couldn't read my lips.

Kane leaned in, too, putting my face only inches from his cheek. My unconscious inhalation rewarded me with the spicy gun-oil-and-leather scent that was Kane's alone. God, the man smelled good enough to eat.

And he was. I'd never forget how good he tasted...

Somehow I managed to keep from tracing the shell of his ear with the tip of my tongue.

After a single lust-paralyzed instant, I got my voice working. "It's such a romantic restaurant. Everything is so perfect. And all I could think of was that I was going to have to spend the whole meal looking at Holt."

Kane burst out laughing.

"And then I couldn't think of a polite way to explain," I added, giving in to giggles myself.

Kane's laughter subsided into a grin. "You just made my day."

"And Holt just made mine. Some people bring joy when they arrive; others when they leave."

I leaned back in the chair and transferred my attention

to the menu, hoping to distract myself from the urge to take Kane's hand. To slide my fingertips up the corded forearm revealed by his casually rolled-up sleeves, and seek out the curves and dips of the luscious bicep under that soft-looking fabric...

"What do you think?" Kane asked, indicated the menu. "According to the online reviews, the Italian dishes are supposed to be really good, but there are lots of other options."

I shook myself back to reality and skimmed the menu. "Wow. I'm afraid to take my attention off my surroundings long enough to read this whole tome."

The tension that had been momentarily broken by our laughter returned full force, and I shot a wary glance around the restaurant. It was sparsely populated on Christmas Eve, but any of the people here could be an assassin...

"...Aydan?"

I twitched at the sound of Kane's voice. "Sorry. What did you say?"

"I asked if you had decided on your food yet. We don't have to rush, but we can't dawdle, either."

I scanned the menu again, but the words swam before my tired eyes.

"Do you need your reading glasses?" Kane prompted.

I laid down the menu with a sigh. "My eyes aren't the problem. My brain has quit. Would you please pick something for me? I'm too tired to think right now, much less make a decision."

"What do you feel like eating?" As the question left his mouth, he caught my despairing expression and his lips curved up. "Forget I asked. I'll get you something nice."

"Thank you. And maybe we can get one of those

gourmet burgers to go. I know Arnie doesn't feel like eating, but he'll be starving as soon as he smells a burger."

"That's a good idea."

The waiter returned and Kane ordered our meal. When we were alone again, I relaxed into my chair with a sigh of pure gratitude. "You're brilliant. How did you know that pasta with cream sauce is my comfort food?"

He smiled. "Isn't it everyone's? I was torn between the seafood linguine and the gorgonzola gnocchi, but even though I know you like blue cheese, it seemed a bit too challenging tonight."

"And you were so right. Any other night I'd love the gorgonzola, but tonight seafood linguine sounds like heaven on earth."

"Good, I'm glad." Kane hesitated, sobering. "You and Arnie looked really shaken when you came out of LaVonda's room. Do you want to talk about it?"

All the horror flooded back, along with queasy guilt and fear over keeping LaVonda's secret.

If Kane knew LaVonda had murdered Montmorency and stolen the drug money, would he understand and agree that she had suffered enough?

Or would he feel compelled to do things by the book, as he had for all of his stellar law-enforcement career?

I was pretty sure he'd side with Arnie and LaVonda and me.

But if I was wrong...

Kane was watching me patiently. Giving me space.

"I, um..." My voice came out in a croak. "It was pretty awful. But I... it's not my story to tell." The tiny flash of hurt in his eyes prompted me to add, "I think Arnie's trying to protect you. I don't think he would have wanted me to be there, either, but I'd already heard most of it earlier, when LaVonda was drugged and didn't realize what she was saying."

My throat thickened and I took Kane's hand. "It's breaking his heart, John." I swallowed hard, fighting back tears. "It was so much worse than he ever imagined. And now he's going to have to let her go. He'll never see her again. Never get to make any good memories to cover up the awfulness."

"I'm sorry it's that bad." Kane's warm grip comforted my hand. "And I'm sorry you have to experience the pain with him." His voice softened. "Let me help carry the load. Pain shared is pain halved."

"No. It's not." I met his eyes, trying to make him understand. "This kind of pain... nothing reduces it. Sharing it only makes more people suffer."

Kane sighed. "I know you believe that." His thumb made gentle, soothing passes across the back of my hand. "And I know Arnie does, too, and I understand why you both feel that way. But, Aydan..." He looked deeply into my eyes. "You've never tried it. You'll do anything to prevent other people from being hurt, but you've never trusted anyone enough to share your own pain."

I stared at him, fear slamming my emotional walls into place.

"It's like an abscess," Kane said quietly. "If it's never opened, it can never heal."

I pulled my hand away, pretending to adjust the napkin on my lap. He let out a small breath, and the hurt in his eyes clenched my heart.

"I'm sorry," we said at the same time.

"No, don't apologize," Kane said. "I'm sorry for

pressuring you."

"You weren't." I took his hand again. "I'm sorry for my knee-jerk reaction. I know you're probably right." I drew a deep breath and let it out slowly, fighting my fear of vulnerability. "It's just that... when the abscess comes from a stab wound in the first place, it's really damn hard to believe that sticking another knife in it is going to make it better."

Kane winced. "That's a very effective explanation. And... very graphic." He gave me a mischievous grin as the waiter approached with our plates. "Now I'm rethinking my choice of that juicy red marinara sauce."

I relaxed and returned his smile. "If I actually believed that, I'd apologize again."

He chuckled. "No need."

After delivering our meals and offering cracked black pepper and freshly grated parmesan, the waiter withdrew. My first creamy, succulent mouthful made me moan with bliss.

"Oh... my... God. This is so good!"

"I'm glad to bring you some pleasure at last."

His apparently-unintentional double entendre struck us both at the same time. I felt my eyes widen as heat rolled through me, and his pupils dilated in return. When he spoke again, his voice was a deep rumble that vibrated every nerve in my body.

"Now there was a Freudian slip."

"If ever there was one," I agreed in a voice that was a little too breathy.

"What I meant was, you've been through so much lately, and it's nice to see you relax and enjoy something."

"Oh, okay." I gave him a look from under my lashes. "If that's all it was."

Shit, why was I flirting with him? Idiot.

His smile heated. "Oh, that's not all it was. I have a lot more than that for you."

Yes, he certainly did. Quite a few hot hard inches more, according to my traitorously vivid memory. I sucked in an involuntary breath and came very close to inhaling a scallop.

When I had finished coughing and dabbing my streaming eyes and nose, I croaked, "Maybe seafood linguine wasn't such a great choice after all. Next time, get me something that doesn't contain slippery orbs the exact size of my airway."

"Are you sure you're all right?" Kane was still hovering on the edge of his chair, poised to jump up and give me the Heimlich Manoeuvre.

"I'm fine except for my dignity. It was just pronounced dead at the scene."

He settled back in his chair and picked up his fork again with a smile. "Dignity is overrated."

"Apparently it is for me." I changed the subject. "So, have you talked to Daniel today?"

The twinkle died in Kane's eyes. "I spoke to him this afternoon, but only for a few minutes. They had to leave for the final rehearsal for his Sunday School pageant. He's playing a shepherd."

My heart clutched. "Oh, no! You're missing his Christmas Eve pageant?"

Kane's jaw firmed. "Yes, but Dad will video it for me." He let out a breath. "Aydan, I'm not trying to shut you out, but I really don't want to talk about it just now. Can we talk about more pleasant things?"

"Of course." Wishing I could ease his pain, I took his hand and summoned a teasing grin. "I've got you figured out. You just want me to flirt with you some more."

He made a creditable attempt at a smile. "It's all part of my Machiavellian scheme to seduce you."

"Well, it's working."

We bantered and flirted for the rest of the short meal, but our exchange felt hollow. It was a relief when Kane said, "I guess we'd better get going."

After a short wrangle over the bill we agreed to split it. The waiter arrived with the credit card machine and Hellhound's burger fresh from the kitchen, and a few minutes later Holt joined us as we left the restaurant.

I had expected snide comments about our flirtatious body language during dinner, but Holt maintained a dour silence while we strode to the elevator.

With a small contraction of my heart, I wondered how he must have felt, sitting alone in a hotel bar on Christmas Eve and watching us together. Maybe he had intentionally distanced himself so he wouldn't have to think about what he was missing. If all his friends and family were in Toronto, Christmas must be a lonely time for him.

"How was the game?" I asked.

"Sucked."

He said no more, and I let it be.

CHAPTER 41

When we rounded the corner on the fourth floor, Hellhound stepped out of Holt's room and stood waiting for us.

"We brought you a burger," I said, offering him the bag.

His smile did nothing to ease the darkness in his eyes. "Thanks, darlin'. That smells great."

I glanced at LaVonda's door. "Shit, I never thought to bring anything back for LaVonda. She must be starving."

"Nah, she ordered room service."

Holt jerked his chin at his room. "Go in. Let's call Arlene Widdenback's prospect." We followed him inside, and he added, "I talked to the analyst-on-call, and they haven't got anything new. Set up the meet at the Tim Horton's out by the Walmart on Victoria Avenue, at seven o'clock. That only gives him half an hour to get there, but we can be there in ten so we'll have a chance to set up. If he can't make it then, tell him it'll have to be a lot later tonight or else tomorrow. And tell him you've only got ten minutes."

Praying I wouldn't screw up Holt's simple instructions in front of everybody, I dialled.

"Ted Walker."

"Meet me in the Tim Horton's by the Walmart on Victoria Avenue at seven. I only have ten minutes."

"That will be fine." Walker hung up.

"All right, let's move," Holt said.

"Good luck, darlin'." Hellhound held me close for a moment. "Be safe." I hugged him in silence, since my voice seemed to have stopped working.

After a short trip to our rooms to don our bulletproof vests and parkas, we reconvened in the hallway.

In the elevator, Holt said, "Kane, take point out to the parking lot. I'll cover our six. You two drive out first and I'll follow a little way back so I can watch for tails. Then I'll go directly to the Tim's and set up surveillance from outside while you drive around until the meeting time. Kane, you're a known associate of Arlene Widdenback, so you can go in with her as the muscle." He jutted his jaw at Kane as if preparing for an argument.

"Good plan," Kane agreed. "Let's go."

I had thought my adrenal glands had nothing left to give, but I'd been wrong. Traversing the dark parking lot felt like walking through a hostile zone, every car hiding a potential enemy and every sound a threat. Each shapeless hooded figure increased my anxiety. Could they be secretly observing us, reporting our movements to Fitzgerald's men? There were a lot of shapeless hooded figures in the depths of a Saskatchewan winter. We'd never know until it was too late.

What if Fitzgerald had brought in an army this time? What if they attacked LaVonda and Arnie while we were gone?

My heart hurt for LaVonda and the suffering she had experienced, but my selfish fear was all for Arnie. What if we returned from the police station to find his bullet-ravaged body-

"*What?*" Kane's tense whisper made me stifle a yelp. "What did you see?" he demanded.

Heart pounding, I focused on his alert expression. "N-Nothing."

"Why did you stop?"

God, I'd been so absorbed in my worries that I'd trailed to halt outside the passenger door of the rental car. Kane and Holt scanned the parking lot, poised for action.

I let out a breath. "Sorry. Everything's fine. I was just... thinking."

"Well, think in the fucking car," Holt snapped. "We thought you'd seen something."

"N-No..." In an attempt to salvage at least a tiny bit of pride, I hurriedly added, "I was just looking at our room windows. Arnie said there was a sheer drop; and there is under LaVonda's and John's rooms. But there's part of the hotel roof under Arnie's window."

Both men measured it with their gaze.

"Probably not a threat," Kane said. "It's still two storeys down. And nobody knows we're here. I was careful when I booked the rooms; and your evasive pattern was very thorough on the way here."

I wasn't sure whether he was serious or poking fun at my vague wanderings, so I settled for a noncommittal nod.

"Hellhound would be thrilled if somebody broke in through his window," Holt said. "I bet he'd love an excuse to beat the shit out of somebody right now. I would, if LaVonda was my sister." He jerked his chin at the car. "Come on, let's go. I'm freezing my ass off, and we don't have much time."

When we were on the road, I extended my Glock to Kane. "Here, you need to be armed."

He shook his head. "No, keep it. In the first place, I don't have a permit for it; and in the second place, you're as good a shot as I am but my martial arts skills are better than yours. If there's conflict in a public place, I'd rather do it hand-to-hand and leave bullets as a last resort."

"Take the trank pistol, then," I argued. "You should have some kind of distance weapon. I'm thinking Arlene Widdenback might bring you as a visible display of muscle, but she'd make you sit somewhere out of earshot. You'll be too far away for hand-to-hand if it goes to hell fast."

Kane shot me a frown before returning his attention to the road. "I don't like it, but you're probably right. Especially since the last time we played 'Arlene Widdenback and Consort', we didn't part on particularly amicable terms."

Heat rose in my cheeks as I relived the explosive rough sex and breakup we'd staged for our enemies' listening bug. "Um. Right."

My burner vibrated and adrenaline spiked into my veins. "Shit, I hope he's not cancelling." I hit the Accept button. "What?"

"It's Holt. I'm in place. Everything looks clear. Keep this line open."

"Okay, thanks."

I glanced at my watch. Twenty minutes to showtime.

It was going to be a hell of a long twenty minutes.

We drove in silence for nearly fifteen minutes before Kane turned onto Victoria Avenue. Holt spoke over the open connection, startling me. "I think he's here. A guy just went in, bought two coffees, and sat down at a table by himself. About six feet, one-eighty, looks like he's in his mid-thirties. Black cargo pants, black parka, black military-style boots. He was wearing a black tuque but he took it off when he sat down. Short blond hair, military cut. I can't tell if he's armed under that parka, but I'm guessing so. And he moves like an athlete. This guy is definitely a threat."

I sighed. "Great. I was hoping for old, weak, and nervous."

Like me.

By the time we pulled into the Tim Horton's parking lot at six-fifty-nine, my heart was thumping and I was seriously considering telling Kane and Holt to abort.

God, what if this guy attacked me and Kane got killed? Daniel would never recover from the loss.

But if I backed out, Dermott would be furious and I'd probably end up on charges of insubordination. And so would Holt. I hadn't been able to hear Dermott's end of the conversation, but Holt's angry reaction had given me a pretty good idea of what had been said.

Kane parked and turned off the car. "Ready?"

"No." The word popped out before I could stop it.

He gave me worried scrutiny. "We can abort."

He wouldn't think any less of me if I chickened out. Neither would Holt, although he'd never let me hear the end of it.

But, dammit, *I* would think less of me.

"Let's go." My voice came out hard and level, and I got out of the car and strode toward the door before I could change my mind. "Holt, I'm putting the phone in my pocket now," I added, and did so.

The sound of the car door closing and the hurried squeak of footsteps on snow alerted me to Kane's reassuring presence. A moment later he came abreast of me, then strode ahead to hold the door.

Playing Arlene Widdenback to the hilt, I didn't give him a glance. Striding into the restaurant with my head high, I spotted the man Holt had described. We made eye contact, and he inclined his chin toward the coffee cup sitting opposite him.

Without waiting for Kane to catch up, I went over to the table. The man rose as I approached, and I mentally rehearsed the fast smooth motion that would whisk my Glock out of my pocket and into action.

"Arlene Widdenback?" he inquired in that strangely bland voice. When I nodded, he said, "Ted Walker." He didn't offer to shake hands, which suited me just fine.

I snapped an evaluating glance over him.

Most people wouldn't give Walker a second look. He had average features and wore a neutral expression that matched his toneless voice. Completely forgettable.

Except for the way he moved. That readiness in his posture, that sense of a deadly machine about to swing into action...

He was evaluating me, too. I didn't want to know what he saw.

Kane loomed behind me, and I gave him a jerk of my chin and kept my voice hard. "Sit over there."

Kane let out a surly grunt and scowled his way over to the table I'd indicated, a few yards away and out of earshot.

I sat down at Walker's table, and he took his seat, too.

"Thank you for the coffee," I said coldly. I didn't touch it.

"You're welcome. We're both busy people, so I'll get right to the point. It has come to my employer's attention that you recently demonstrated one of your specialized business products." Walker eyed me meaningfully.

What the hell was he talking about? I kept my expression impassive while my exhausted brain ground through my actions over the past few days.

"This morning, in fact," he prompted.

Comprehension arrived in an icy deluge.

Fuck, the kidnappers had told their lawyer about how I'd fired into their vehicle and they'd passed out. Ted Walker's 'employer' was Fitzgerald, digging for information about the tranquilizer pistol.

"And?" I inquired, keeping my tone disinterested.

"And my employer might be interested in purchasing some stock, if we can come to a suitable arrangement." A bland smile appeared on Walker's unremarkable features. "Your demonstration was quite impressive, but we would require full technical specifications, along with pricing and delivery information."

I channelled every office-supply salesperson I'd ever encountered. Who knew bookkeeping would provide such a helpful background for dealing in illegal weapons?

With a small superior smile, I replied, "There wasn't time for a full rundown of all the features in today's demonstration. I'm sure you and your employer will be impressed by the product's full range of capabilities. And pricing and delivery would depend on the quantities you ordered."

"Of course," he agreed politely. "When can we get a full demo and specifications?"

"I'll be in touch. Can I reach you at the number you used before?" He nodded, and I glanced at my watch and rose, adding, "Thank you for your interest."

If he was going to make a move, it would be now.

When he stood up as well, it took all my will not to grab for my Glock. Kane was already on his feet and moving toward us.

Walker didn't attack; just remained standing with oddly old-fashioned manners.

Prompted by the devil, I leaned closer and murmured, "Give my regards to Richard Fitzgerald."

Walker was good. Almost no reaction, but I caught his fractional intake of breath. His bland smile returned. "I'm sorry, I don't know who you're talking about."

I gave him a pointy-toothed smile. "My mistake."

I sailed out, head high, with Kane trailing in my wake.

CHAPTER 42

Safely back in our car, I fumbled my bug detector out with shaking hands while Kane drove out of the parking lot.

"All clear," I announced.

My pocket spoke with Holt's muffled voice. "Did Walker react when you poked him about Fitzgerald? I couldn't tell from where I was watching."

I took the phone out of my pocket. "He reacted, but he hid it well. He knew exactly who I was talking about."

"I couldn't hear your conversation," Kane said. "What did you say?"

I recounted the short exchange and he stared through the windshield, frowning thoughtfully.

"What were you hoping to accomplish by asking about Fitzgerald?" he asked.

My heart sank. I'd screwed up. I should have kept my mouth shut.

"I just wanted to see if he'd react," I muttered.

"Hm." Kane frowned at the windshield some more. "So we don't know whether Fitzgerald really is his employer or he was reacting to a competitor's name."

"I guess not."

"Still, it was interesting," Holt said. "I wish we could tail him now and find out what he does next. But he's still drinking his coffee, and it's more important to make sure we're clear. I'm going to fall back and follow you to watch for tails again. When you get to the police station, get parked and wait for me to come to your car. We'll walk to the station in the same order we left the hotel: Kane first, then Aydan, then me."

The police interviews were a complete bust. The lawyer kept such a tight rein that the only concrete answers Tan got were the kidnappers' names and addresses; which we'd already damn well known.

As we plodded toward the exit an hour and a half later, the slump of Kane's and Holt's shoulders telegraphed the same despair I felt.

"Stay alert," Kane reminded us. "If I were working for Fitzgerald, I'd be waiting at the police station and hoping LaVonda would come to identify her attackers. When they see us, Fitzgerald's men will follow us for sure. This is their best chance to recapture her."

Holt responded with a wolfish grin. "It's our best chance, too. I'm *hoping* they follow us." His action-hero attitude made me want to creep into the nearest bed, curl up in a quivering ball, and pull the covers over my head.

Instead I reminded myself that, unlike me, he wasn't operating on only a few hours of sleep after a trauma-filled week. I could forgive myself for feeling like a coward as long as I didn't act like one.

I straightened my aching back and concentrated on focusing my tired eyes on my surroundings as we stepped out into the street.

The cold darkness seemed more threatening than ever. My back itched as though the red dot of a laser sight was dancing between my shoulderblades, and I glanced repeatedly around us without spotting anything out of place. As we hustled to our vehicles, Kane and Holt seemed extra-vigilant, too.

Kane lowered his voice. "I'm going to drive an evasive pattern for a while."

Holt nodded. "Roger that."

Shivering in the passenger seat a few minutes later, I activated my bug detector. "All clear," I said, showing Kane the reassuring green glow.

He spared a glance from the road with a smile. "I'm glad you have that."

"Me, too," I agreed, wondering why it didn't make me feel any better. I still felt as though somebody was watching me.

After a silent and convoluted drive, Kane finally spoke. "Call Holt. See if he thinks we're in the clear."

I obeyed, putting the phone on speaker.

"Holt," he snapped after only one ring.

"It's Aydan, and I've got you on speaker," I replied. "Are we clear?"

"I haven't spotted any tails," he replied, but his tone lacked its usual Holt-The-Magnificent certainty.

"I've got a bad feeling," Kane said.

I let out a breath. "Good. I do, too, but I thought I was just being paranoid."

Holt barked out a laugh. "You are. It's part of the job. My gut's telling me that we're missing something, too."

"But we've been driving for quite a while and I haven't seen anything," Kane pointed out. "And Aydan checked for tracking devices on our vehicle and it scanned clear."

"Same here," Holt agreed. "So what have we missed?"

Kane shifted his shoulders as though trying to dislodge

the same uncomfortable prickle I'd felt earlier. "There has to be something. Three experienced agents don't get antsy for no reason."

I silently corrected that to 'two experienced agents', but didn't comment.

"Let's walk it back," Holt said. "Where are our weak points?"

"One of the kidnappers spotted Aydan and Hellhound with LaVonda at the apartment fire," Kane said. "And even though Aydan's face wasn't fully visible in the newspaper, she would still be identifiable. Then I was spotted leaving the hospital with LaVonda, and they got a look at this rental car. Aydan and Hellhound might have been spotted leaving the police station in their rental car. But their car is out of commission now."

I took up the thread. "At least two of the kidnappers followed Arnie from the drop zone and got a good look at him when they shot him. When we left our old hotel we were watching for tails so we're pretty sure we weren't followed to Home Depot, but the kidnappers would have seen the Home Depot logo on the truck when we spilled the load of two-by-fours. And they saw my face when I tranked them."

"Afterward, they probably made the connection between the Home Depot truck and Hellhound's Home Depot van behind them," Kane added. "So that information has likely been passed on to their successors by now. And they obviously identified Aydan as Arlene Widdenback from that newspaper article."

"Then there's the hospital tonight," Holt put in. "That's a no-brainer. They would have known LaVonda would be taken there, and they had enough time to get people in place. And all our vehicles were in the hospital parking lot. Easy to identify."

"But we didn't spot a tail on the way back from the hospital," Kane objected. "And we had enough personnel and took enough time to be sure of it." He blew out a breath. "Maybe it's that Home Depot van that's bothering me. It's easy to spot. They'd know we'd be staying at a hotel tonight, and it's not a big city. If they simply drove around checking all the hotel lots..."

My guts clenched. "Let's get back to the hotel and move the van to a different parking lot."

Kane accelerated. "No, we'll leave all the vehicles there. Aydan and Holt, we'll move you and LaVonda to a different hotel and you can guard her there. Hellhound and I will stay in the original hotel as decoys." A grim smile sharpened his voice. "And as an ambush."

"Roger that." Holt disconnected.

"Aydan, start calling hotels," Kane commanded.

By the time we turned into the hotel parking lot, I'd found vacancies at another hotel and my heart was doing a ragged tap-dance.

What if my earlier thoughts had been a premonition? What if Arnie was lying dead right now?

The well-upholstered peace of the hotel lobby offered only scant reassurance. The last batch of kidnappers had been slick and unobtrusive. The next assassin up the food chain would be even more professional.

As the elevator doors closed behind us, I identified the source of my discomfort.

"There's something else that's been bothering me," I said quietly.

"What?" Holt and Kane asked in unison.

"Any time I start wondering what's coming next, I keep

thinking 'assassin'. Maybe it's Walker. I got that vibe from him."

Kane nodded. "That would make sense. A man like Fitzgerald who's been the head of a crime family for over thirty years... he won't want to attract attention. He's already made two botched attempts. If he's as smart as I think, he'll sacrifice his desire for revenge and do damage control."

"I got a few photos of Walker, but they're pretty long-range," Holt said. "I've sent them off to the Department and we'll see if they get any facial-recognition hits."

"We should get Arnie to look at them, too," I said. "Just in case he recognizes Walker."

"You think he's a sniper?" Holt inquired. "Planning to take LaVonda out along with any witnesses, then grab the money and run?"

Kane shook his head. "That would attract even more attention. Fitzgerald might just bide his time. Keep somebody watching LaVonda until the heat dies down and then stage a mugging or home invasion, some commonplace act of violence that isn't likely to be traced back to him. That would be a smarter strategy."

"So the question is..." I said as the elevator doors opened. "...is he smart enough to let go of his vendetta, even temporarily? If he was going to play it safe, he should have backed off after the grenade launcher guys made such a big splash."

"Maybe something's changed and he's got nothing to lose," Holt said as we strode down the corridor. "Somebody else threatening to take over the Family? Or maybe he's got some incurable disease? Getting senile? After all, he's in his seventies."

Kane shot him a frown. "Seventies are hardly dotage.

Dad will be turning eighty this year. He's as sharp as ever and he still does his 5BX daily."

"I thought 5BX was for the Air Force," Holt observed.

"It was originally, but-"

Kane broke off as we rounded the corner.

The door to Holt's room stood open.

CHAPTER 43

I was sprinting on tiptoe before I even realized it, Glock clenched in my hand. Kane and Holt dashed alongside, our rapid footfalls muted by the carpet.

A few yards from the door Kane caught my arm, slowing me while Holt darted ahead to put his back to the wall beside the door, weapon at the ready. He jerked his thumb at himself, then toward the room.

I had barely returned a nod when he pivoted and lunged inside. Right behind him, my Glock traversed the empty room to freeze at the closed bathroom door.

Oh God, please don't let Arnie's lifeblood be draining away in the bathtub...

Holt checked around the bed in two fast steps, then dove back to take position beside the bathroom door. I did the same on the other side, placing my hand lightly on the door handle.

Holt gave a sharp nod.

Heart hammering, I yanked the handle and shoved the door open, leading with my gun and lunging sideways into a crouch to clear the way for Holt.

Hellhound spun from the toilet, already diving toward us in an attack despite the half-mast position of his pants.

We all pulled up short, yelping '*Fuck!*' in three-part harmony.

"Christ, I didn't need to see that," Holt snapped, turning

away from Hellhound's dangling equipment. "Why did you leave the fucking door open?"

"I was takin' a leak," Hellhound explained somewhat redundantly as we all stowed our respective weapons and he zipped up. "I left the door open so I could move fast if I had to. Plus, I figured if anybody came pokin' around in the hallway, they'd check out an open room first."

Holt shook his head and went out, giving Kane a quiet 'all clear'.

I slid my arms around Arnie and leaned into him, shaking from head to toe. "I'm so glad you're okay."

"I'm fine." He chuckled. "But hell, the look on your face when ya came through that door? I damn near shit. Remind me never to piss ya off." He pressed a whiskery kiss to my forehead. "Now that I don't hafta worry about missin' anythin' in the hallway, d'ya mind steppin' out so I can finish the job?"

"Oh. Sure." I gave him one last squeeze, avoiding his bruised midsection. "Come to LaVonda's room when you're done. We have a Plan B."

"'Kay."

I left, closing the door behind me. "He'll be with us in a minute," I told Kane and Holt.

Holt gave a theatrical shudder. "God, I can't believe you sleep with that."

"Oh, did it make you feel inadequate?" I asked sweetly. "Don't worry, I got an email just the other day that promised it could enlarge your-"

"Shut up."

"I could forward it to you."

"You could stick it up your ass and rotate." Holt smirked. "Except you'd enjoy that."

"Stop. You two give me a headache," Kane interrupted with perfect timing. My tired brain was fresh out of smartass rejoinders.

By tacit agreement, we stood in the hallway to wait for Hellhound. When he joined us a few minutes later, he surveyed our faces. "What's happenin'?"

"Do you know this guy?" Holt demanded, handing Hellhound his phone. "He's going by the name of Ted Walker."

Hellhound studied the grainy image for a moment. "Nope. Never seen him before." He handed the phone back. "Was that all ya wanted?"

"No. We might be compromised," Kane said. "We're going to relocate LaVonda to a different hotel. Aydan and Holt will stay with her. You and I will stay here in case there's any action."

"Compromised? How?" Hellhound threw a sharp glance around the empty hallway.

"We don't know for sure," Kane cautioned. "But all three of us..." He indicated Holt and me with a nod. "...are feeling uneasy about that bright orange Home Depot van. It's too easy to spot."

"Good thinkin'." Hellhound stepped over and tapped on LaVonda's door. "It's Arnie an' the gang," he called softly. "Can we come in?"

No reply.

Fear contorted his face for an instant before he controlled the expression. His next attempt was a sharp rap. "It's Arnie," he called a little louder. "Open up, okay?"

Still no answer.

My guts twisted. If something had happened to LaVonda in the few short moments he'd been in the bathroom, he'd never forgive himself.

He was raising his fist to knock again when Kane gripped his wrist and gave him a headshake. Pulling out a cardkey, Kane raised it and shot us a look.

Holt drew his gun. This time I chose the tranquilizer pistol, and Kane gave me an approving nod.

With my heart pounding painfully, I took my position beside the door.

Holt laid his hand on the handle and jerked his chin at Kane.

The cardkey zipped in and out.

The instant the light turned green Holt burst through the door and I followed. The lights flashed on courtesy of Kane or Hellhound; I didn't see which.

LaVonda bolted up in bed with a shriek, clutching the covers to her. Princess bounded away and vanished into her carrier.

"What-what?" LaVonda babbled.

"Sorry," Holt said, holstering his gun. "When you didn't answer-"

"*What?*"

As I holstered my pistol with shaking hands, LaVonda pulled an earplug out of her ear and repeated, "What?"

"Sorry," Holt said again. "We knocked on the door but you didn't answer. We thought something was wrong."

"Oh..." She made a helpless gesture somewhere between patting her chest and fanning her face. "Oh. Y-You... I... oh." She hugged the covers, trembling.

Hellhound swung the door quietly shut behind us, and Kane took control of the situation. "We're very sorry to disturb you, but we've decided to move you to a different hotel."

"Wh-What? Why?"

"This one may be compromised."

"B-But... you said we were safe here..." She glanced helplessly around the room as if expecting armed attackers to leap out of nowhere. Which, as far as she was concerned, they just had. Poor woman.

"We don't think there's any immediate threat," Kane reassured her. "But we want to relocate you just in case."

In a truly impressive display of control, LaVonda pulled herself together. "What threat do you think there might be?"

"We're afraid Fitzgerald's men might identify the Home Depot van we left in the parking lot."

She frowned. "So move the van to a different hotel."

"We thought of that," Kane replied. "But if they've already spotted it, it would be too late. It's better if we move you and let them think we're still here."

"What do you think they might do?" LaVonda glanced at the tightly-drawn draperies. "It's a big hotel. They can't figure out which rooms we're in, can they?"

"Likely not," Kane said. "I used a different name when I booked the rooms."

"So what's the worst they could do?" Lavonda asked. "If they've already spotted the van and they plan to ambush us when we leave, they'll do that no matter when we go. If they haven't spotted the van yet, then moving it solves the problem. I don't see the point of leaving now."

"The point is to get you to safety," Kane said patiently.

"And I've just pointed out that either I'm already safe here, or else I'll be attacked when I leave, no matter when that might be." Her chin rose. "I'm not going. I'm exhausted, I'm not dressed, and I refuse to *get* dressed, get packed, and go out to be attacked in the dark and the cold. If

I'm going to be attacked, I'll do it in broad daylight after a decent night's sleep."

"But-"

"No." There was that flat final tone again. "I'm staying here. And if you try to force me to leave, I'll cause a huge ruckus and have you all arrested for trying to kidnap me."

"Aw, come on, Kath," Arnie cajoled. "We wouldn't do this if we didn't think it was important. It ain't gonna be a big deal; we can help ya-"

"No." Her voice was gentler, but just as definite. "I know you're trying to help, but don't you see, Arnie? I just... just... can't. Not tonight. Tomorrow I'll be on the run again, and I'll do whatever I have to, but... just let me have tonight. Please."

We all turned to him.

Anguish twisted his face, and I knew he'd decided.

"Awright," he said quietly. "Sleep tight, then. We'll watch over ya."

"Thank you. You have no idea what that means to me." Her gratitude made my heartstrings quiver in sympathy. She made eye contact with each of us in turn. "Thank you for protecting me. This will be the last night that I'll sleep soundly for a very long time." Her lips rose in a faint smile. "And I'll be wearing my earplugs, so if you need to contact me, please call my cell phone. I always keep it beside me, and I'll feel the vibration. It will be a lot easier on all of our nerves." She recited the number for Holt's benefit, and he stored it in his phone.

"We'll let ya get some sleep, then." Arnie gave her a smile that looked as though it cost more than he had to give. "G'night."

"Good night."

We withdrew.

As the door closed behind us, I let out a long breath and sagged against the wall. "Okay, I'm done. If one more thing happens tonight, I'm going to have a heart attack and drop dead on the spot."

"You look like the walking dead now," Holt pointed out tactlessly. "Go and lie down before you fall down. You're no damn good for anything when you're this tired."

"She covered your back pretty damn good just now," Hellhound growled. "So watch your mouth."

Holt's jaw jutted, but before he could reply Kane stepped in as peacemaker.

"Let's wrap this up," he said. "Hellhound and I will move the van."

"Okay," I mumbled around a gaping yawn.

I was fumbling the cardkey for our room out of my waist pouch when Hellhound spoke.

"Uh, Aydan... d'ya mind bunkin' with Kane tonight?"

I gaped at him, shocked at the rejection; but as I looked into his tormented eyes my initial flash of hurt washed away in a tidal wave of worry.

Putting my arm around him, I drew him a few paces away from the other two and lowered my voice. "Arnie, what's wrong?"

"Sorry," he muttered. "I ain't tryin' to hurt ya, but I just... I need some time to myself."

"I'm not hurt," I promised.

A few moments ago that would have been a lie, but not anymore. I could see how much he was suffering.

"I'm just worried about you," I added gently. "I know it's going to be a rough night. I won't talk to you if that's what you want, but I could just... be there with you."

He wrapped his arms around me and rested his forehead on mine, closing his eyes. "Thanks, darlin'. That really means a lot to me, but... I just gotta do this. Ya know what I'm like. I'm gonna be up mosta the night playin' my guitar. Go bunk with Kane, an' at least you'll get some sleep. Ya need it."

"Never mind me. Do what *you* need for a change."

"This's what I need." He drew back, his hands warm on my shoulders, his eyes pleading. "Do this for me? Please?"

"Of course, if that's what you want. I'll just grab my stuff." I hesitated. "I guess I should ask John if it's okay with him first."

Arnie gave me a bittersweet smile. "It'll be okay. He's facin' Christmas without his kid. He needs ya tonight."

My heart clenched. As usual, he was putting everyone else first.

"Go on." Arnie gave me a gentle nudge. "Ask him."

Not wanting to leave him, I turned to look at Kane and raised my voice just enough for him to hear. "Is it okay if I bunk with you?"

"Of course," he said, but concern furrowed his brow. "Here's the spare cardkey." He came over and handed it to me, frowning at Hellhound. Lowering his voice, he added, "Are you sure about this, Arnie? You've been through a lot lately."

Hellhound raised his chin. "Yeah. That's why I need some time to myself."

"All right." Kane sounded as dubious as I felt. "Let's go and move that van, then."

As he strode off down the hall, I whispered in Arnie's ear. "Are you sure?"

"Yeah." He hesitated, drawing away a few inches to

study my face worriedly. "Ya know I love ya, right?"

"I know. I love you, too." I kissed him. "And I'm here for you. If you change your mind, just call me. Any time of the night."

He kissed me back. "Thanks, darlin'. I will."

He wouldn't.

I knew it as I watched him walk away.

CHAPTER 44

When I emerged from Hellhound's room carrying my backpack, Holt stood in his doorway, smirking.

"Doing the walk of shame?" he needled.

"Bite me." I plodded wearily past and let myself into Kane's room.

As the door closed behind me, I gulped. The two queen beds I had expected weren't there. Instead, a king-sized bed flaunted itself in the middle of the room.

Of course. What had I expected? The other three rooms had king-sized beds, too. Kane must have had to pay a premium to get this block of rooms together.

But as usual, I had no nightwear with me. Slipping into a separate bed would have been awkward enough, but sharing a bed?

"Get over it," I said aloud. "It's not like he's never seen you naked."

And that was the problem. How could I keep my distance, with an almost-naked Kane lying in all his muscular glory only an arms-reach away?

"Fuck it," I muttered, and headed for the bathroom. "I'm too tired to do anything, anyway."

Despite my best attempts to believe the lie, certain traitorous parts of my body tingled awake.

Fortunately, the soothing routine of preparing for bed took over. By the time I padded barefoot out of the bathroom wearing my longest T-shirt and my most modest thong underwear, my only remaining desire was to creep into bed.

Recalling that Kane preferred the left side, I slid under the covers on the right. A small moan of exhausted bliss escaped as my head sank into the soft pillow.

"Aydan, it's all right. It's just me."

I blinked awake to see Kane standing just inside the door, hands spread away from his body in a non-threatening posture. The lights were still blazing. I was sitting bolt upright in bed, the covers around my waist and my Glock levelled at him.

To my relief, my finger was extended in ready position, not on the trigger.

"Sorry." I let out a breath and stowed the gun under my pillow again. "I guess I fell asleep."

"It's all right." He smiled as he moved into the room, turning off the vestibule light. "You might be tired, but there's nothing wrong with your reflexes."

I grimaced. "Too bad my reflexes don't remember where I am until I'm drawing down on the good guys."

"Better that than sleeping through a visit from the bad guys."

"I guess that depends which end of the gun you're on."

He chuckled. "It's fine. Don't worry about it." Sobering, he studied me. "I know you're only here as a favour to Arnie, and I don't want to make this awkward. Will you be all right sleeping in the same bed with me?"

My face heated. "Sure. As long as you're okay with it."

"I'll share a bed with you any time I have the

opportunity." The depth of his voice sent a shiver down my spine. "But it didn't go so well for you last time, as I recall."

"Are you kidding? Last time was really damn hot."

Laugh lines crinkled around his eyes, but Kane shook his head. "I'm not counting that last time at Harchman's. We were on a mission, and you were fine because you knew that's all it was. But when you were living at my house as my fiancée..."

Somehow I managed not to shudder, recalling the panic and desperation of being confined by his arms, his house, his life.

His love.

"But we worked through that." I was proud that my voice came out sounding calm and reasonable. "Neither of us was ready for it at the time. As long as I know we're both on the same page now, I'll be fine."

Kane sat down on the edge of the bed, watching me with those penetrating grey eyes. "And just to be clear... which page is that?"

"We're friends." My voice cracked a little, and I cleared my throat. "With benefits, sometimes." I summoned a smile. "Probably not tonight, though. If I don't get some sleep soon, I'm going to throw up. That might be a bit of a mood-killer."

He smiled. "I can only imagine how exhausted you are. Don't worry about a thing. Everything is fine between you and me, and Holt will be on guard all night so you don't have to sleep with one eye open." He rose and turned off all the lights except the one on his side of the bed. "Go back to sleep. I'll just be a minute."

The bathroom door closed quietly behind him and I squeezed my eyes shut, trying not to listen to the bathroom noises. Funny how I could snicker with perfect comfort at Hellhound's rip-roaring farts, but the sound of Kane peeing made me squirm with embarrassment.

When he emerged a few minutes later my eyes popped open in spite of myself.

"I thought you'd be asleep by now." He stripped off his shirt, revealing the spectacular upper body I had revisited in many a steamy dream.

As he unbuttoned his pants, my mouth went dry. "Um... not yet..."

He glanced up as he dropped his jeans, catching me staring with undisguised appreciation at his well-filled hip-hugging black briefs.

What the hell, he knew exactly what he was doing to me.

I grinned. "I didn't want to miss the show."

"Are you flirting again?" He returned the grin as he slid under the covers.

"Well, if you have to ask, then the obvious answer is 'not very well'."

Kane chuckled and extended his arm. "Cuddle?"

The thought of lying warm and safe in his embrace...

I was already squirming over to his side of the bed, my body making the decision before my tired brain could apply any better judgement.

"Just for a while," I mumbled against the hard heat of his chest. "But don't be hurt if I go back to my side of the bed. I can't sleep if I can't move freely."

"That might have been good to know last April."

I tensed, but his comment had contained only good-natured teasing.

Relaxing, I teased back. "I would have told you, but I didn't want to lose my air of mystery and intrigue." He chuckled, and I added, "Sorry."

His hand glided lightly over my back, the warm caress turning my muscles to jelly. "You don't have anything to apologize for. I love you the way you are. Just relax and do whatever feels good."

Now there was a loaded invitation.

Before I could consider all the tantalizing possibilities, sleep claimed me.

I bolted upright in the darkness, gun in hand.

"What was that?" I hissed.

Kane was already rolling out of bed. "I don't know."

I scrambled out as well and hurried to the door. A peek through the fisheye lens showed only an empty corridor.

Heart thumping, I eased the door open, feeling the heat of Kane's body behind me.

On my naked butt cheeks. 'Modest' was a relative term when it came to thongs.

"Here." Kane draped one of the hotel dressing gowns over my shoulders.

"Thanks." I put it on and slipped out into the hallway, gripping my gun inside the capacious pocket of the robe and scanning the empty corridor.

Kane followed, donning a second robe, and I whispered, "Why isn't Holt out here?"

He shrugged and shook his head.

As we crept closer, Holt's door swung open and he frowned out at us. "What are you doing?"

"I heard something loud. Didn't you?" I demanded.

Holt gave me a long-suffering look. "Somebody closed their door down the hallway." He cocked a thumb toward the other end. "They didn't even slam it. Did you really think I'd miss something like that?"

I let out a breath. "No, but-"

"Well, if you're going to jump out of bed every time somebody farts, maybe you should keep watch," he groused. "I wouldn't mind sleeping."

"Cry me a river. This was your idea, not mine."

As we spoke, Kane and I had drawn closer so we could keep our voices down. In the silence of the sleeping hallway, faint music emanated from Hellhound's room.

I glanced at my watch, and Kane and I exchanged a look.

"Four AM." I sighed. "He's really upset."

"Maybe we should check on him," Kane suggested.

"Yeah..." I replied uncertainly. "He said he wanted to be left alone, though..."

We crossed the hall, and the music resolved into one of the blues tunes Arnie often played. His sexy raspy voice sang along with the guitar, teasing and entreating.

My knuckles were raised to tap on the door when cold realization struck me.

He never sang when he was upset. He didn't even play recognizable songs, only dark melodies of his own making accompanied by wordless humming.

A memory-flash paralyzed me.

Arnie's voice: *'She's never gonna be safe. Fitzgerald's gonna hunt her 'til the day he dies.'*

The darkness in his eyes.

'I just gotta do this.'

And he hadn't looked me in the eye when he had said he'd be up all night playing his guitar.

Suddenly I knew with absolute certainty: He wasn't there.

The Killer had gone to stalk his prey. And by now, he would have just completed the six-hour drive to Richard Fitzgerald's house in Winnipeg.

"Aydan?" Kane's worried voice jerked me back to the present. "Are you having second thoughts?"

My hand was still suspended in midair.

I lowered it, frantically sorting and discarding options.

"Um... yeah." I turned to face Kane, not even trying to hide the conflict I was feeling. "Arnie's never asked me to leave him alone before. I kind of think... it would be shitty to bother him."

Kane sighed. "You're probably right." He put his arm around my shoulders and turned me back toward his room. "We'll let him be, for now. We can check on him in the morning."

Back in the warm quiet of our room, I kissed Kane goodnight again and squirmed back to my side of the bed. Staring wide-eyed into the darkness, I listened to his breathing slow and deepen.

Should I tell him?

But what good would it do? Arnie was far beyond our help now. Not even a fighter jet could get us there in time.

And if anyone else found out...

My blood chilled. This was premeditated murder, plain and simple. No mitigating factors at all. If anyone else found out, Arnie would go to prison for life.

If he survived.

Oh, God. Arnie was alone in an enemy stronghold.

Despite his decades of experience and his reputation as the man who always got his kill, my stomach knotted with cold fear. His usual jobs were backed by a top-notch team. They had reconnaissance, up-to-the-minute intel, night vision, infrared; a host of advantages.

Tonight Arnie had nothing but his climbing gear.

And I was willing to bet he'd left at least one of his ropes dangling out his hotel room window.

Tension wound up in my shoulders. What if Holt decided to patrol the outside of the hotel? What if a security guard or some late-arriving guest spotted the rope?

But all those fears paled beside my biggest terror. How could one unarmed man prevail against the security of an established crime lord?

I didn't doubt Arnie's skill and determination, but he'd had a blunt-force wound, very little sleep, and a huge emotional trauma on top of it all. Add a six-hour drive across pitch-black prairie in the deadly winter cold, and he'd be dangerously depleted.

And he was facing a challenge that would be nearly impossible even if he was at his peak.

Oh, God, no. He couldn't be doing this. I had to be wrong.

But I knew I wasn't.

CHAPTER 45

The glowing numerals of the clock radio taunted my gritty eyes.

5:20 AM.

Unable to relax, I shifted from one side to my back to my other side, moving slowly so as not to disturb Kane's slumber.

It was stupid to lie awake worrying. There was nothing I could do.

When would someone discover that Arnie wasn't in his room? If Kane and Holt both believed he had still been awake at four AM, surely they wouldn't knock on his door early.

But checkout time was eleven-thirty, and LaVonda was leaving today. She would knock on his door before then to say goodbye, and he wouldn't be there.

And even if by some miracle he did make it back before checkout time, he'd be climbing into his room in broad daylight, in full view of the parking lot. There was no way he could avoid getting caught, and then he'd go to prison for the rest of his life.

Over and over, I did the math and came up with the same hopeless answer.

Six hours there. Only an hour to single-handedly

infiltrate an unfamiliar building, eliminate his well-guarded target, and get out. Six hours back. Thirteen hours, minimum; and he hadn't left until after ten PM last night.

He couldn't do it.

My aching stomach clenched as a new thought intruded.

Maybe he hadn't planned to come back.

Maybe LaVonda's revelations had pushed him over the edge, stirring up his own horrible childhood memories and driving him into a dark spiral of self-destructive hatred for what he had become.

His worried expression hovered behind my eyes. *Ya know I love ya, right?*

Oh, God, no.

He had been saying goodbye.

A whimper escaped me.

"Aydan?" Kane was instantly awake, reaching across the wide gulf of mattress to touch my shoulder. "It's all right, it's just a dream."

If only it was.

"I'm o-"

The lie caught in my throat.

I wasn't even close to okay.

Arnie, lost forever. LaVonda, living in fear for the rest of her life. Kane, missing his first Christmas with Daniel. Holt, scrutinizing my every move while Dermott lurked in the background like a malevolent spectre. If Arnie's or LaVonda's crimes came to light, I was facing life imprisonment.

I tried again to say something reassuring, but the only thing that came out of my mouth was a hiccup of misery.

"Aydan?" Kane moved closer, warm hands cupping my shoulders. "Wake up. You're dreaming."

I should have stayed with Arnie. I should have known he needed me tonight. I should have...

A sob wrenched free.

"Shhh, Aydan, it's all right. Shhh..." Kane's arms came around me, holding me close.

I fought back the tears and clung to him, rigid with fear and fatigue, bone-crushing sorrow and bitter regret.

"Shhh. It's all right." He rocked me, stroking my hair and pressing kisses to my temple. "It's all right, it was only a dream..."

At last exhaustion won and I went limp in Kane's arms.

I couldn't face him. And I couldn't explain.

"It's all right," he comforted softly, still stroking my hair. "You're safe. It was only a dream. Go back to sleep. I won't let anything happen to you. It's all right..."

Worn out by despair, I let his murmured reassurances carry me away to a place darker than sleep.

Warm arms surrounded me and I cuddled into the safety of Arnie's embrace. So comfortable...

Something was wrong.

My eyes popped open. Tension slammed into my body at the sight of Kane's strong square features on the pillow inches away.

"Everything's all right," he said softly. "You're safe."

Sick reality swamped me. *Nothing* was all right.

"Aydan." Kane stroked my cheek, frowning. "I think you're still dreaming. Wake up. Everything's all right."

With an effort of will, I forced my rigid muscles to relax. "Oh..." I sucked in a shaky breath and let it out slowly. "Good morning." I glanced around the dim room, noting the glow around the draperies. My heart plummeted. "It is morning, isn't it?"

"Yes." He smiled. "It's nine AM. Merry Christmas."

"Oh." My spirits sank even lower, but I forced myself to smile back. "Merry Christmas."

"Waking up with you in my arms is a better Christmas gift than I was expecting. You didn't try to escape in the night."

Guilt added itself to the queasy mess in my stomach. How sad was it that he couldn't even count on a simple thing like human contact from me?

"I'm turning over a new leaf." I kissed him, holding onto my smile. "Are you impressed?"

"Very." His deep morning voice sent shivers down my spine.

I realized our legs were entwined, our bodies pressed together. And he was considerably more than impressed. He was damn impressive.

As the thought registered, Kane drew away just enough to break contact with his erection.

"We should probably relieve Holt," he said. "And wake Arnie."

Ice filled my veins. Even if Arnie had survived and was returning, it had only been eleven hours. He needed more time.

"Let him sleep." I tried for a light tone, but the words came out sounding more urgent than I'd intended.

Kane drew back, bringing his puzzled frown into clearer focus. "I thought he'd want to get up so he could spend as much time as possible with LaVonda before she leaves."

"Who knows if LaVonda's even up?" I forced a smile. "If she's a morning-hater like Arnie, she won't roll out of bed until ten minutes before checkout time."

"That's true..." Kane studied me quizzically. "I get the feeling that you're stalling for some reason."

Adrenaline scorched my veins.

I raised my eyebrows, pasting on a teasing smile. "Is that a fact?" Squirming closer to make body contact again, I whispered, "Why do you suppose I'd do that?"

He sucked in a small breath as I moved against him. His voice deepened. "Well, I could flatter myself with a theory."

"Mmhmm?" I nibbled kisses along the rough sandpaper of his jaw. "What might that be?"

"My theory is..."

I ran my hand down his back to fondle his iron-hard ass and he groaned, his arms tightening around me.

"...you must be flirting again," he finished hoarsely.

"Hm. Imagine that." My hand coasted over his hip and down his thigh. Letting my fingertips trail upward, I purred against his lips. "Am I getting any better at it?"

"Ahhh... No... I don't think so." His voice was a hungry rasp as he tilted his hips to allow me better access. "I think you need a lot more practice."

"Oh." I stuck out my bottom lip, feigning disappointment as I brushed feather-light caresses over the bulging front of his underwear. "Do you know anybody who could teach me?"

His mouth crashed down on mine.

"I'll teach you," he growled against my lips. His hand slid down my back, dragging hungrily over my ass. "That thong has been driving me wild all night," he muttered as he pulled my knee up over his hip. "And the way you've been bouncing around under this T-shirt..." His hand moved up my body.

I winced at the sudden pressure on my tender ribs.

Kane's hand flew off me and he bolted up on one elbow to frown down at me. "You're hurt. You weren't being modest with the T-shirt; you were hiding an injury."

"I'm fine." I reached up to kiss him. "Come back here."

He resisted my pull. "No. Take off your shirt."

"Well, if you insist." Giving him my sexiest smile, I peeled off the T-shirt.

He turned his back.

I couldn't quite keep the shock and hurt out of my voice. "That wasn't quite the reaction I'd-" He turned on the bedside lamp and I flinched and threw a hand over my eyes. "Jeez!" Peering between my fingers, I added, "Was that really necessary?"

His frown had deepened. "Aydan, when are you going to stop lying to me?"

Oh God, he knew. Somehow he'd figured it out.

"Wh-What do you mean?" I quavered.

"You're not fine." His fingertips traced a light path over my ribs. "That's a nasty bruise. Why would you hide that from me? I could have hurt you."

"Oh." A giggle of giddy relief bubbled from my lips. "That's nothing."

"Aydan, it's not nothing. You're black and blue."

I squinted down at the darkened area. "It's just a bruise. I didn't even think of it until you touched it. My whole body hurts, so it didn't really stand out."

Kane sighed, reaching over to turn out the light again before resuming his place beside me. Sliding a gentle arm around me, he said, "If your whole body hurts, that's something you should mention to a man who's on the verge..." His voice deepened. "...of devouring you whole."

I shivered and pulled him closer. "So start devouring."

"I don't want to hurt you."

"See, this is why I lie."

He chuckled, but the sound was rueful. "Aydan, when are you going to learn that you don't have to endure pain to please other people? Now..." His lips found mine in a soft kiss. "Does this hurt?"

"Mmm." I pressed against him, my hands roving over the hard bulges of his luscious biceps. "Nope."

"Good." Deepening the kiss, he slid his hand up to massage the aching muscles of my neck and shoulder. "How's this?" he murmured against my lips.

"Ohmigod." Letting out a moan of bliss, I leaned back against the pressure of his fingers. "Oh, that feels so good."

He trailed tiny kisses across my jaw and down the side of my neck, switching to electric nibbles on the muscle his massage had just eased.

I hooked my knee over him again and made firm contact with that glorious erection. My hips rocked, friction flaring into heat.

Kane groaned, his arm encircling my shoulders while his other hand slid down between us. Easing gently past my ribs, his strong fingers delved inside my underwear, unerringly finding the perfect spot as his lips met mine again.

I gasped into his mouth as he stroked me, generating lightning bolts of sensation. When he withdrew his hand I whimpered a protest, but he was only tugging the elastic down. I lifted my hips and kicked off the thong.

Easing me onto my back, he propped himself on one elbow while his hand coasted back into position. Hot and firm, his fingers found a rhythm that made my hips jerk, begging for more.

He sprinkled kisses along my collarbone, then teasingly around my breast.

"God... John..." My words came out in a breathy moans as I clutched the hard muscles of his shoulders.

His mouth found my nipple, sucking and scraping lightly with his teeth.

I bucked under the shock of pleasure and a mindless cry wrenched from my lips. His fingers never stopped stroking, driving me wild with urgency.

"Ohmigod... *John...*" Barely conscious of my rising voice, I rocked feverishly against his hand. "*I... need...*" Muscles rigid, I strained toward the pinnacle that was close, so close...

For a heart-stopping instant his hand withdrew and a desperate wordless cry tore from my throat.

Then his finger entered me, the pad of his thumb taking over the stroking.

Smooth-slide-rough-friction-oh-my-G-

Waves of mindless pleasure swept me up, higher and higher until I exploded into ecstasy.

Drunk on sensation, I pulled Kane down, devouring his mouth, raking my hands down the hard ridges of his back muscles, tearing at the briefs he still wore.

"Aydan..." His single hoarse word lost itself in my mouth as he pulled me to him with one arm, kissing me ravenously while his other hand helped me push the briefs off.

His magnificent erection jammed against my thigh and sob of desperate need escaped me.

Pushing Kane onto his back, I swung astride him, blind with lust. My shaking fingers wrapped around his length, guiding him-

"Wait," he gasped. "Condom..."

"*Hurry.*" I slid down his body, taking him into my mouth and sucking hard.

"*Aydan...* Ahh... *God...*" His hand fisted in my hair as I added some hand action. "Slow... down..." His words didn't match the hungry thrust of his hips, driving up to meet me stroke for stroke.

Panting, I raised my head to watch the clench of his corrugated abs, the taut bulge of his biceps, the sinewy ripple of his forearm as he clutched the sheet in his fist. His chest rose and fell in rapid gasps, his eyes black in the dimness.

"Condom," he repeated hoarsely, releasing his grip on my hair and the sheet.

"*Where?*" My voice vibrated with desperation.

He reached under his pillow, emerging with the all-important packet. He tore it open with shaking hands and sheathed himself not a moment too soon.

I poised myself above him, then sank down.

Slowly...

So...

Slowly...

Watching the tension build in his body.

Feeling him fill me, deeper and deeper...

For a single moment we were still, staring into each other's eyes, our rapid breathing the only sound in the room.

The only sound in the entire world.

I moved first.

Long... slow... rise. Almost to the tip.

Luxurious... slide... down...

Kane groaned, his fingers digging into my hips. "God... Aydan..." His chiselled abs flexed as though he was fighting to hold himself back. "Please... *now!*"

The hoarse entreaty sent a rush of heat through me. I clenched around him. Rocked up...

Every nerve came alive in a rush.

I drove down on him, burying him as deep as he could go.

A wordless growl escaped him and his hips thrust up. I rode him hard, abandoning control as he urged me faster. *Harder...*

His hands cupped my breasts, palms stimulating my nipples, feeding my hunger while I ground against him.

One of his hands coasted lower, sliding between us, that rough thumb pad moving firmly right *there-*

My spine arched, my body seizing in an orgasm so fierce the room dissolved around me, leaving only my disembodied voice pleading for *more-harder* even though I was the one on top...

Somehow I was on my back, Kane's body hard against me, harder inside me.

Abandoning myself to the storm, I wrapped my legs around him, urging him deeper, raking my nails across his back.

The waves built again, flinging me higher, filling my body beyond its limits, unstoppable pressure building...

"*Aydan...*"

His raw gasp detonated my orgasm, brilliant as a nuclear explosion. Blind and deaf, pure energy, I soared aloft in millions of shattered fragments, blazing like a supernova.

CHAPTER 46

My return to earth was slow, floating mindlessly down only to be tossed upward again, over and over in slowly-ebbing swells of ecstasy.

At last I dragged my eyes open.

Kane was still on top of me, his arms vibrating as he held his weight on elbows and knees. The sound of our panting filled the room.

Sudden concern seized me. I had been so caught up in my own pleasure...

I stroked a tentative hand down his back. "Are you... did you, um..."

He let out a half-laugh, half-groan, and rolled off me to collapse on his back, grinning at the ceiling. "Oh, I did. Believe me, I did. I think my brain exploded." He turned his smile toward me. "Among other things."

"Good." I flopped over and pillowed my head on his shoulder, draping my arm across his chest. "I'm glad I'm not the only one who had a near-death experience. I'm pretty sure I heard angels singing. Or more likely they were cheering. Probably doing The Wave, too."

Kane's lips pressed against my hair and a chuckle rumbled under my hand. "At the risk of sounding shallow... if I had known this would be my compensation for missing Christmas with Daniel, it would have been a slightly less painful decision."

My heart contracted. "I'm sorry you missed Christmas."

"Me, too." His chest rose and fell. "But there will be other Christmases. This, with you..." I could hear the smile in his voice. "I'm hoping it wasn't a once-in-a-lifetime experience, but it definitely felt like it. This is the first time I've ever gotten to spend an entire night with you and wake up holding you in my arms without any doubts or regrets. To lie here in the afterglow without worrying that you'll try to drive me away again or wondering about your motives."

He must have felt the tension slam back into my body.

He hurriedly added, "Don't worry, I don't have any expectations. I'm just enjoying being here, in the moment."

A moment that I'd created with ulterior motives.

Sickening guilt twisted my stomach. When he found out, as he would very soon, he would be terribly hurt. And probably furious with me.

And rightfully so.

"Oh, no." Kane's arm tightened around me. "You're panicking again, aren't you?"

"No, of course not." The lie slipped out with practiced ease. "I was just-"

My phone vibrated, and I scrambled out of his embrace with relief. "I have to get that."

The sight of Holt's number made my guts clench.

"Kelly," I snapped.

Holt's voice was hard. "Richard Fitzgerald was murdered last night in his mansion in Winnipeg, and Hellhound did it. Get your ass over here, *now*, and bring the key to his room." He disconnected.

I froze.

Paralyzed with the phone still pressed to my ear. Unable to breathe.

"Aydan, what's wrong?" Kane was on his feet, gazing down at me worriedly.

I opened my mouth, but the pain prevented any sound from escaping.

"Aydan!" Kane gripped my shoulders, giving me a little shake. "Talk to me. *What is it?*"

At last I dragged in a breath that tore my lungs like rusty nails. "It's..." I swallowed. Squeezed my eyes shut, fighting for control. "That was Holt. He said..."

I still couldn't catch my breath.

Another shallow, agonizing inhalation.

"H-He said Richard Fitzgerald was murdered last night and..." My voice faded to a papery whisper. "Arnie did it."

Kane jerked back. "*What?* That's impossible. It's a six-hour drive to Winnipeg, and he was in his room at four AM; we both heard him..." His voice faded. "But you wouldn't let me check on him..."

He studied me, grey eyes going as cold as frozen carbon dioxide as he read the guilt that was surely written all over my face.

When he spoke again, his voice was steel-hard. "That was one of his recordings, playing on his phone. And you knew. You were covering for him." Pain and fury filled his face as he jabbed a vicious finger at the ravaged bed. "That's all this was." His voice was a raw wound. "Just a lie. To keep me distracted. To buy him time."

"No." My denial came out feeble.

Guilty as hell.

Sudden fury filled me, stiffening my spine.

"No, goddammit!" My voice snapped out like a whip. "I *didn't* damn well know! If I'd known, I never would have left his room. I never would have left him alone, not even for an instant!" Tears clogged my throat and I spun away from Kane, wrapping my arms around my body in a futile attempt to hold myself together. "I *should* have known, fuck me for the fucking idiot I am! *I should have fucking known...*"

"Oh, Aydan." Kane's arms came around me from behind. "I'm so sorry. I shouldn't have... I'm sorry."

I pulled away, unable to take his comfort without breaking down completely. "It doesn't matter." I grabbed my backpack and headed for the bathroom. "I have to go. Holt wants the key to Arnie's room."

"Aydan, I'm sorry..."

I closed the door on his voice.

I didn't look in the mirror while I threw on some clothes and yanked the brush through my hair.

When I came out a couple of minutes later Kane was dressed, but his short dark hair was rumpled as though he'd been raking his fingers through it over and over.

"Aydan, I'm sorry," he said again.

"It's okay. We'll talk later." I gripped his arms, staring up into his anguished eyes. "Right now I need you to..." I trailed off.

What could he do?

What could anybody do?

"I just... need you." I flung my arms around him in a fierce desperate hug, then pulled away before he could hold me. "Come on."

When we emerged into the hallway, Holt was pacing impatiently outside his room.

"What the hell took you?" he demanded.

"Clothes," I said shortly. "What happened?"

"Get in here." He jerked his chin at his room.

We followed him inside and he closed the door, taking

up a position next to his camera so he could continue to monitor the hallway. Kane and I stood tensely, waiting.

"Whittle called," Holt said. "The Winnipeg police phoned her because she'd been checking with them about Fitzgerald's courier vehicles and they knew it was part of her case. They found Fitzgerald murdered in his bed in Winnipeg around eight AM this morning; probable time of death around three AM. Broken neck, no sign of a struggle, no sign of forced entry, nobody else was hurt, nobody heard or saw anything, no fingerprints or physical evidence. Hellhound's usual clean professional job."

"But what about Arnie?" The question burst out of me even though I didn't want to know the answer.

"Well, obviously he did it."

"What do you mean 'obviously'?" Kane demanded. "Did they apprehend him at the scene?"

Holt gave him a contemptuous look. "Of course not. But we all know damn well he did it."

I sucked in a breath that tasted of desperate hope. "You *asshole!* You made it sound like they'd caught him in the act! He couldn't have done it. He was here at three AM. We all heard him playing his guitar and singing at four. And it takes six hours to drive to Winnipeg, and he and John were moving the van at ten o'clock last night. That only leaves five hours to the time of death. He couldn't have done it," I repeated as though I could make it true through sheer force of will.

"Nice try, Kelly," Holt said scornfully. "Ever heard of speeding? If somebody drove at one-sixty-five instead of one-ten, that trip would only take four hours. He could have been there by two AM."

My heart plummeted. It hadn't occurred to me to

recalculate the time based on Hellhound's lead foot.

Holt gave us a triumphant look. "And you know damn well that what we heard last night was a recording."

"No, we *don't* know that," Kane retorted, looking remarkably indignant for a man who had come to that exact conclusion only minutes before. "I heard Arnie singing and playing his guitar. There's no mistaking his voice."

"Yeah, nice try for you, too," Holt taunted. "News flash, Kane: Even professional vocalists don't sing for six hours straight. And anyway, I banged on his door right before I called you, and he's not in there."

I nearly doubled over the gut-punch.

Holt's victorious expression faded. "Look, I don't like it any better than you do. Fitzgerald deserved a whole lot worse than that, but it's still premeditated murder. Hellhound made his choice, but you..." He gave me a pointed look. "...don't have to pay for it. I haven't said anything to Whittle yet because Hellhound's background is classified; and so far, you and I have just been discussing this case. But starting now, if you try to hinder my investigation, they'll be looking at you for accessory-after-the-fact." He scowled. "Or maybe a conspirator, if you knew what he was going to do and didn't say anything."

"She didn't know," Kane said. "I saw her face when she got your phone call. She had no idea."

"Says her boyfriend, reeking of fresh sex. Now *there's* a reliable witness." Holt held out his hand. "Give me the cardkey, Kelly."

Numb with pain, I laid it in his palm.

"Let's go." He led the way out of the room.

The few steps between Holt's room and Arnie's felt like a marathon.

As Holt poised the cardkey at the reader, he shot us a look. "You two stay out here. You don't want any questions about whether you tampered with evidence."

Kane's arm came around my shoulders as I swallowed hard and managed a faint nod.

"We'll observe from the doorway," Kane said firmly.

Holt shrugged acquiescence.

The card slipped in and out. The *swish-click* sounded like the fall of a guillotine blade.

Holt stepped inside, flipping on the vestibule light with his elbow. Kane and I crowded behind him, Kane holding the door open.

The room was dim and silent, the draperies tightly drawn. Arnie's guitar leaned forlornly against the chair beside his small duffel bag, and my heart clenched. Would they let him have his guitar in prison? He would die without his music...

Holt strode forward.

An animal roar split the air and a huge figure bowled Holt over. The two men hit the floor hard, snarling and scuffling.

My trank pistol was already in my hand and seeking a target when I recognized Hellhound's raw-throated rasp.

"*What the everlovin' fuck?*"

"*Arnie!*" I dove into the melee. "Arnie! Arnie, omigod..."

"Back off, Kelly!" Holt was on his feet, his gun drawn, but I couldn't have released my hold on Arnie even if my life had depended on it.

"Arnie!" Kneeling beside him, I ran my hands frantically over his arms and chest, barely believing he was there and safe.

"Hey, darlin'," he said mildly. "What the fuckin' hell's goin' on? Why'd ya bust in on me?"

"Why didn't you answer your door earlier?" Holt demanded.

"When?" Hellhound frowned up at him. "I didn't hear any knockin'."

"Twenty minutes ago."

I thought I felt a tiny relaxation of Arnie's muscles.

Maybe I had imagined it.

Maybe not.

"I was sleepin'," he growled. "I ain't a fuckin' mornin' person."

Kane let the door swing closed behind him as Holt turned on the lamp and glowered down at us. "*Back away, Kelly.* Remember what I said about tampering with evidence?"

"But he's here," I protested. "You said he wasn't here. He's innocent."

"Of course he's fucking here," Holt snapped. "Where else would he go? He was probably climbing in his window at seven-thirty while it was still dark enough to get away with it."

"Whoa, what the hell are ya talkin' about?" Hellhound demanded. "Somebody wanna clue me in here?"

"First I want you to put on some fucking pants." Holt picked up the crumpled pair of jeans that lay on the floor beside the bed. After emptying the pockets onto the night table, he threw the jeans at Hellhound. "And hurry up about it. If I have to look at your junk one more time, I'm going to puke."

Hellhound rose and faced Holt, scratching his balls luxuriously and not-so-coincidentally flapping his dick in

Holt's direction. "Ya bust into my room at the ass-crack a' dawn, ya take what comes with that." Hellhound yawned and stretched theatrically before making his way back to the bed and sprawling on his back, arms tucked behind his head and legs spread wide. "I'm pretty comfortable like this. An' it's my room, so..." He scratched again, making the gesture as obscene as humanly possible. "...enjoy."

"Asshole," Holt snapped.

A dangerous grin spread across Hellhound's bearded features. "That sounded like a request."

"No, *don't!*" Kane spoke too late.

Hellhound had already sprung to his knees and mooned Holt thoroughly, spreading his ass cheeks with both hands and leering upside-down between his knees.

Holt's knuckles whitened on his pistol. "Arnold Helmand, I'm arresting you for murder. You have the right to retain and instruct counsel without delay. You may call any lawyer you wish..."

CHAPTER 47

"*Murder?* What the *fuck!*" Hellhound was right-side-up again, staring open-mouthed at Holt.

"You killed Richard Fitzgerald." Holt's voice was hard. "Around ten PM last night you set up a recording to play on a continuous loop on your phone so we'd think you were still here. You climbed out your window and drove to Winnipeg at about a hundred and sixty-five kilometres per hour, arriving there around two AM. By three AM, you had broken into Richard Fitzgerald's house and killed him. You then drove back here, climbed back in your window, turned off your recording, and went to bed."

"What the fuckin' hell have ya been smokin'?" Hellhound demanded. "That ain't even possible. Ya know what kinda resources an op like that takes. An' you're sayin' I planned it out all by myself in a coupla hours with no intel at all, an' then I somehow got in an' did the job an' got out, all in an hour? With no support? I'm good, but I ain't that good. I was here all night. I sat up playin' my guitar, an' then I went to bed."

"Oh, really?" Holt inquired. "Must have been an uncomfortable bed. Hard on your knuckles. And your face."

Hellhound fingered a cut in his cheek that hadn't been there twelve hours ago. His complexion bore the greyish cast of utter exhaustion, and for the first time I noticed that his knuckles were swollen, the skin split and torn. His rings were gone.

My heart plummeted.

"Yeah," Hellhound said with a grimace. "It was a pretty shitty night. Took me forever to get to sleep, an' then I had a buncha nightmares. Woke up punchin'. Busted a glass on the bedside table an' I nailed the headboard pretty good." He jerked his chin toward the head of the bed. "There's prob'ly still some knuckle skin on there. I picked up mosta the broken glass but I missed a piece on my pillow. Cut my face when I lay down again. Damn lucky I didn't lose an eye."

"Broke a glass, eh?" Holt scowled at him. "Where is it?"

"Garbage."

Keeping a suspicious eye on Hellhound, Holt sidled over to the garbage container and picked it up. The silvery clink of broken glass accompanied the movement, and he glanced at the contents without expression.

Putting the can back down, he fixed Hellhound with his steely gaze. "If you cut your face on your pillow, why is there no blood on the pillowcase?"

Hellhound shrugged. "I sat up pretty damn quick. Ya know how a clean cut like that doesn't start gushin' right away."

"You must have cleaned yourself up, though. So where are the bloody tissues?"

"Flushed 'em."

"Where are your fancy rings?"

"Bathroom. Took 'em off 'cause my fingers swelled up after I punched the headboard."

The two men locked eyes.

Holt raised a cynical eyebrow. "They're scrubbed clean, I suppose."

Hellhound shrugged. "I bled on 'em. Hadta clean 'em off."

"I bet if I looked in your duffel bag, I'd find climbing gear," Holt persisted.

My blood chilled.

Hellhound snorted. "No fuckin' bet. Cops already gave me hell for it, long before this happened." He straightened, satisfaction dawning on his face. "So Fitzgerald's toast. Fuckin' A. About time somebody offed that asshole."

"Arnie, maybe you shouldn't..." I began.

"Hell, darlin', I ain't gonna pretend. Everybody's gotta know I'd be happy to see that fucker dead." He nodded contemptuously at Holt. "Inspector Clouseau here wouldn't be all fuckin' fired up otherwise."

Holt's jaw stiffened at the reference to the bumbling fictional detective. He strode across the room and threw the draperies wide.

Hellhound winced. "Christ, d'ya mind?"

Holt peered out the window, then turned and spoke with biting sarcasm. "That's funny, somebody's been on the roof right under your window."

I moved toward the window, but stopped when Holt gave me a warning look. My fists clenched with the need to yell and defy him, but dammit, he was right. I couldn't help Arnie by interfering with Holt's investigation. I'd only get locked up myself.

Hellhound rose and ambled over to the window, apparently unconcerned by the fact that his nudity would be clearly visible from the parking lot. Merry Porno-Christmas, everybody.

After a cursory glance outside, he yawned and returned to the bed. "I don't see any footprints out there."

"No actual footprints, but that area of the snow has been disturbed," Holt countered. "And I bet I'll find your footprints on the ground near that corner, too."

Hellhound gave him a level look. "Bet ya won't."

"Why? Because you covered them up?"

Hellhound shrugged. "'Cause you're makin' all this shit up. An' I'm gettin' fuckin' sick of it. Why don't ya go see if ya can find some actual evidence? If ya do, let me know. 'Til then, I got some sleep to catch up on." He lay back on the bed and pulled up the covers, closing his eyes. "G'night."

"Let me see your phone," Holt snapped.

"Right there." Hellhound spoke without opening his eyes, cocking a thumb at the table where his phone sat plugged into its charger.

"I can see it's right there, asshole," Holt snarled. "I mean, I want to see the contents of your phone."

"Ya got a warrant?"

"You want to make this a formal investigation?" Holt countered nastily.

Hellhound opened one weary eye. "Ya mean, instead a' plain old harassment?" When Holt just gave him a steely glare, Hellhound sighed and sat up. "What d'ya wanna see?"

"Your playlists."

"Fine. Hand it over here."

Holt unplugged the phone, eyeing it briefly. "Pretty low battery, if it was plugged in all night."

Hellhound shrugged. "It wasn't. I plugged it in right before I went to bed."

"And when was that?" Holt gave him a narrow-eyed look.

"Dunno. I'd been up mosta the night, an' I crashed. It was still dark out, that's all I know."

"I bet it was." Holt handed him the phone. "Show me your playlists."

With a sigh, Hellhound tapped and scrolled. "There ya go." He handed the device back to Holt.

Holt scowled at the screen. "How many fucking playlists have you got, anyway?"

Hellhound shrugged. "Dunno. Lots. It's what I do."

"What's the name of the one that contains your own music?" Holt demanded.

My heart thudded anxiously. Would Arnie lie? Had he already deleted the playlist? If Holt seized the phone as evidence, they could find the deleted files...

"There's a bunch of 'em," Hellhound replied casually. "'Eddy's Live' has jam sessions with me an' whoever else was around. 'Moanin' an' Wailin'' has a coupla albums I did with another guy called Waylon, about ten years ago-"

"Just you," Holt interrupted. "Singing and playing. No live audience."

A lascivious grin spread across Hellhound's face. "That'd be 'Gettin' It On'. Chicks like it for a soundtrack. If ya know what I mean." He waggled his eyebrows as if unaware that he was destroying his own alibi.

But then again, that was exactly how he'd act if he was innocent...

"This has gone far enough," Kane said firmly. "Arnie, you should stop talking now and call a lawyer."

"Why?" Holt challenged. "You think he did it?"

"I think you're far too eager to use circumstantial evidence to jump to an erroneous conclusion," Kane replied coolly. "And I won't stand by and watch my brother get railroaded. If you're going to do this, you'll do it by the book."

Holt lowered his voice. "Look, shithead, there's more than one ass on the line here. If he actually did kill Fitzgerald, either he left enough evidence behind to convict him, or he didn't. If he did, the police will find him eventually and he'll go down no matter what I do. If he didn't, everything's fine. But if it turns out he did, and we..." He indicated himself and me with tense gesture. "...didn't investigate thoroughly enough to find it, Dermott will nail our asses to the wall. And there's no fucking way I'm going to prison because some fucking idiot didn't do a good enough job of covering his tracks."

"I ain't a fuckin' idiot," Hellhound said mildly.

"We'll see about that." Holt glared at him. "Where did you leave the van?"

"Same place as we left it last night."

"So you admit you drove it to Winnipeg."

Hellhound gave him a contemptuous look. "Nah, I mean it's right where we left it last night, an' that's the last time I was in it. Here." He grabbed the keys from the nightstand and tossed them to Holt. "Check it out. If I'd driven it for half the night, it'd still be warm."

"At this temperature?" Holt shook his head. "It's been parked for at least two hours by now. It'll be frozen solid again."

"Suit yourself." Hellhound lay back in bed again. "You're the one that wanted to be thorough."

Holt scowled. "I'll check it. And I'll check the odometer reading against the rental sheet at Home Depot."

"Knock yourself out," Hellhound said without opening his eyes.

I relaxed fractionally. He hadn't used the van.

Holt turned to Kane. "I'm going to need the keys to your

rental, too."

I tensed all over again. Hellhound had to have gotten there somehow. If he'd taken Kane's car...

Hellhound didn't twitch; just lay there with his eyes closed, apparently near sleep.

"You can look at my rental," Kane said cautiously. "But I'll go with you to check both vehicles. And I'll be photographing them to make sure there are no... misunderstandings."

"Fine," Holt snapped, and gave the mattress a kick. "Get up, you lazy bastard. We're going to look at the vehicles."

Hellhound opened his eyes. "Who's we?"

"All four of us. Kane wants to observe, I can't leave Kelly, and I'm sure as hell not leaving you here by yourself to destroy evidence."

"Not happenin'. Somebody's gotta stay with LaVonda." Hellhound propped himself up on his elbows with a frown. "An' nobody's watchin' her right now."

"She's fine. We've only been in here a few minutes."

Hellhound rolled off the bed and yanked on his jeans and the wrinkled T-shirt that had been balled up under them. "Come on, we gotta make sure she's okay. We don't want her wakin' up an' comin' to look for us, an' gettin' grabbed all over again."

Was he stalling? Oh, God, had he used Kane's rental car to drive to Winnipeg? The keys had been in Kane's pocket, but there had been a second set...

Holt's gaze sharpened as though he was thinking the same thing. "She'll be fine for a few minutes. We're going to look at the vehicles. Right now."

Hellhound turned, fists on hips.

Holt's six feet of muscle looked puny facing that much

bulk and suppressed anger. Holt straightened into his alpha-male posture, but it didn't help much.

"Thought ya said your orders were to look after LaVonda an' Aydan," Hellhound said evenly. "But it sounds to me like ya got somethin' else goin' on. Wonder if the chain a' command might be interested in knowin' what it is."

Holt stiffened. "Are you threatening me?"

Hellhound let out a grim chuckle. "Only if you're threatened by the truth. What d'ya say, Holt? Should we go check on LaVonda now?"

"Asshole," Holt muttered.

"I'll take that for a 'yes'." Hellhound headed for the door.

"Hurt your ankle in bed, too?" Holt asked.

My heart froze. I had been hoping he wouldn't notice the limp Arnie had been doing his best to conceal.

"Nah, but thanks for askin'," Hellhound said sarcastically as he pulled the door open. "I slipped on the ice when we were comin' back from parkin' the van last night."

Holt rounded on Kane. "Is that true?"

Kane shrugged easily, the quintessential James Bond. "How would I know? We took separate vehicles to the other hotel and I picked him up right beside the van, so I didn't see him walking much. Plus, I was..." His gaze flicked to me, the corner of his mouth rising in a small satisfied smile. "...preoccupied with other thoughts."

Holt hissed out a breath of irritation and followed as we left the room and went next door to LaVonda's.

Hellhound knocked on the door, then gave a rueful shake of his head. "She'll have her earplugs in. Kane, ya got your phone? Mine's still in my room."

Kane nodded, taking out his phone. He dialled the number and we waited while the ringtone came tinnily through the earpiece of his phone.

Ring. Ring. Ring.

No sound or movement inside the room.

My mouth went dry.

Arnie's fists clenched, his shoulders bunching.

Ring.

Ring.

Ring.

Ring.

Arnie snapped.

Hammering on the door with clenched fists, he bellowed, "*KATH! KATHY!*" His raw-throated cries held the naked anguish of a man who had sacrificed everything.

For nothing.

"*KATH!*" The door shivered under his onslaught.

Kane stepped forward, moving him gently aside. "Let me," he said, and took out the cardkey.

Barely able to breathe, I put my arms around Arnie. His chest heaved with hoarse panting that was almost sobs, his entire body trembling as Kane slipped the cardkey into the lock and swung open the door.

Princess peered timidly around the corner of the neatly-made bed.

No LaVonda.

The pink parka and new suitcase were gone.

CHAPTER 48

We checked the room like sleepwalkers in a nightmare.

No note. No clothes, no toiletries. LaVonda had packed and vanished as though she had never been there. The only items remaining in the room were Princess's food, litter box, and toys, bought from the love of Arnie's heart before it had been utterly destroyed.

Arnie turned to Holt. "When did she leave?" Four simple words, harsh with pain.

Holt's steely gaze wavered, then dropped to study his feet. "Around eight-thirty. She's long gone."

Arnie slumped into the chair, staring blindly at the bed.

"Was it worth it?" Holt asked quietly.

"Yeah." Arnie's voice was a monotone. "Wherever she is, at least I know she's alive."

"And you made sure she'll be safe," Holt said understandingly.

Fear ripped through me. He was trying to trap Arnie.

Kane and I spoke at the same time. "*Don't-*"

We were too late.

The Killer raised his head, staring Holt straight in the eye. "I did fuckin' *nothin'.*" Self-loathing filled his voice. "I showed up here thinkin' I was gonna protect her, an' I did fuckin' *nothin'.* She lost everythin' she owned an' got kidnapped. No wonder she fuckin' ran."

"But you made sure she'd be safe wherever she went,"

Holt persisted.

Hellhound stood. Took a menacing step toward Holt.

"Arnie..." I grabbed his arm, knowing it was pointless. If he attacked, my restraining grip would have no more effect than a flea on his sleeve.

"Listen, dipshit," The Killer said in a voice that froze me to the bone even though he wasn't talking to me. The fires of eternal torment flickered in the depths of his dark gaze as he stared into Holt's eyes from close range. "I already told ya I couldn't'a done Fitzgerald. If ya don't believe me, then fine. Go ahead an' try an' pin it on me. But if ya think I'm that good at what I do, ya might wanna think about that." His voice dropped to a gravel-crushing rasp. "Think real fuckin' hard."

Holt swallowed audibly.

"Now get the hell out before I throw ya out," Hellhound grated. "I'll stay here while ya check over my room for *evidence*." He spat the word with contempt.

Holt backed away a step before catching himself and straightening into his Holt-The-Magnificent posture. "Fine. Remember, I've got the camera trained on this room so I'll know if you leave."

"Out." Hellhound's single word was spine-chilling.

"I'll stay with him." I sent an uncertain glance up at Hellhound. "If you want me."

His stony expression softened. "Yeah."

"I can't let her-" Holt began, but Kane interrupted.

"If Aydan's safety is your only concern, you know she'll be fine here. She's a top agent, she's armed, we're right next door, and the room is under surveillance." His glacial gaze swept Holt. "But if you have another motive..."

"Would you shut the fuck up!" Holt snapped. "Stop

treating me like the fucking enemy here. I'm trying to cover all our asses!" He eyed Hellhound without warmth. "Or at least as many as I can."

Kane acknowledged that with an inclination of his chin. "Then let's start covering. These two are fine here. Let's go."

Holt hesitated, then glared at me. "If you do anything stupid..." He turned and stalked out without completing the threat.

Kane followed, gripping Arnie's shoulder in a wordless show of support as he went by.

When the door closed behind them, Arnie dropped into the chair and sank his head into his hands.

Unable to offer any comfort at all, I stood beside him, rubbing slow circles on his back. As if sensing his distress, Princess wove between his ankles, emitting worried meows.

He didn't seem to notice.

After a moment he rose. "I'm goin' back to bed."

He stripped off his T-shirt and dropped his pants, then crawled between the sheets. Turning his back to me, he pulled the covers up to his ears.

I stood uselessly for a moment, then turned off the lights and lay down behind him, spooning his back and cuddling him close.

He lay rigid, his carefully-controlled breathing the only sign of his tears.

I held him in silence until his body eased into sleep.

About twenty minutes later, a tap at the door heralded Kane's quiet voice. "Aydan?"

Arnie didn't stir.

I rolled off the bed and hurried to the door on tiptoe. Opening it a crack, I eyed Kane and Holt in the hallway.

Kane shot a worried glance beyond me at the darkened

room. "How is he?"

"Not good. But at least he's asleep now."

Kane sighed. "I guess that's the best we can hope for. Holt's finished with his room and we're going to check the vehicles now." He hesitated. "Have you thought about... going back to Calgary?"

I grimaced. "I didn't want to bring it up just yet. But we'll have to make a decision soon. We have to check out in an hour, if we're going to."

Kane nodded. "I checked with the airline, and there are seats available on the next flight. It leaves at one-thirty and gets in at about two-twenty. I think we should just book the tickets. It will be easier for him if he doesn't have to make the decision." His shoulders rose and fell in resignation. "And if he doesn't want to go yet, it's easy to cancel."

"You should go anyway," I said. "Book your seat. I'll book for Arnie and me. He bought my ticket out here, so I'll buy his and we'll be square. Oh, and could you call the airline and arrange for Princess to fly with us? I don't want to wake Arnie by talking on the phone."

"All right." Kane glanced at Holt. "We'll be back soon. This shouldn't take long." The last sentence had a distinct overtone of 'this had *better* not take long'.

They left, and I returned to my vigil.

Princess had appropriated the warm spot where I had lain, blinking up at me from a cozy nest in the blankets against the small of Arnie's back. Not wanting to disturb either of them, I perched in the chair to do my worrying.

I was almost certain that The Killer had dealt with Richard Fitzgerald. Assassination was an occupational hazard for a crime lord so there were probably a lot of other suspects; but the timing and sheer professionalism of the job had Hellhound's signature all over it.

I suppressed a groan.

What if Hellhound had taken Kane's rental car? The odometer would show an extra twelve hundred kilometres that Kane hadn't had time to drive.

Oh, God. After all Arnie had been through, it would be too cruel for him to go to prison.

And even worse than the thought of losing him forever was the knowledge that in prison, he would lose himself. The gentle good-natured musician I knew would be completely subsumed by The Killer.

I couldn't think about it. Pulling out my phone, I booked our airline tickets, then returned to worrying.

Only fifteen minutes later, another tap at the door roused me from my miserable reverie.

"Uh?" Hellhound rolled over, blinking.

"That'll be John and Greg," I said as I headed for the door. "They finished searching your room and went to check the cars."

"Huh." He hauled himself up to lean against the headboard. "Might as well let 'em in."

I peeked out the peephole, then opened the door to Kane and Holt.

"He's awake," I said, and stepped aside so they could pass.

Princess took one look at the large scary men invading her domain and scurried into her carrier. Hellhound eyed them impassively.

"Both the vehicles were stone-cold and the odometers didn't show any extra mileage," Holt said. "And it's snowing now, so if there were any footprints in the snow around here, they're gone." He didn't sound displeased. A small smile played at the corner of his mouth as he regarded Hellhound. "So, do you want to tell me how you got there?"

Hellhound grunted. "Flapped my arms an' flew, what d'ya think?"

"Good enough," Holt said. "I'm done with this. I had the analysts check all the car rental agencies, and none of them had rentals last night that fit your profile. They checked buses, private aircraft, and charter flights out of the airport. If you did do it, there's no evidence at this end." His eyes narrowed. "So unless you left some DNA or something behind at the scene and the Winnipeg police match it up to you, you're probably in the clear."

I tried not to sag with relief.

Hellhound shrugged. "Told ya." He turned to Kane. "Time for ya to go home. I'll stay here an' return the van to Home Depot tomorrow."

"Shit, I forgot about that," I said. "I already booked us tickets on the one-thirty-"

"Never mind," Holt interrupted. "I still have to coordinate with Whittle and tie up some loose ends, and I don't have any plans in Calgary anyway. The three of you go home, and I'll stay and take the van back tomorrow."

We all regarded him with suspicion.

He threw up both hands in a gesture of surrender. "What? It's my good deed for the day, okay?"

Somehow I doubted that; but maybe I was wrong. Sometimes he was a decent guy. I should cut him some slack.

"Awright," Hellhound said wearily. "Holt, if ya don't wanna see my junk again, you're prob'ly gonna wanna leave."

Holt scowled at me. "I'm still under orders to protect you. I'll wait outside while you pack. You'll ride with me to the airport and I'll escort you directly to security while Kane returns his rental car."

I nodded dumbly.

Our packing was a quiet and sober affair. Kane made another attempt to apologize but I waved him off, unable to deal with any more emotional crap.

After checking out at the front desk, Holt stopped us near the hotel's lobby doors. "Stay alert," he cautioned. "Kane and I checked the area when we went out to the cars and we didn't see any threats, but that doesn't mean there aren't any."

"It prob'ly does," Hellhound mumbled, sounding barely alive. "We're prob'ly in the clear."

"Still." Kane glanced at him, his gaze evaluating. "You stay here with Aydan. Holt and I will bring the cars around. It'll be safer for Aydan."

I let that pass without comment, knowing Kane was trying to save steps for Arnie's injured ankle.

We made a tense but uneventful trip to the airport. Outside the security screening area, Holt fixed me with his usual superior smirk. "Think you can make it through security and into the boarding lounge all by yourself? Or should I escort you through and wait with you? After all, you've still got a couple of hours before your flight. Big place like this, who knows what could happen?" He waved a sarcastic hand at the interior of the tiny airport.

Too tired and miserable to rise to his bait, I mumbled, "Whatever."

Holt looked a little disappointed by my lack of opposition. "Okay. Go on through, then."

I nodded and trudged off to the special screening area.

John and Arnie met me in the boarding lounge a few

minutes later. Arnie set Princess's carrier beside his feet before slouching into a seat and sinking his chin onto his chest.

My stomach growled, and I offered, "I'm going to grab something to eat. Can I get you guys anything?"

"Not hungry," Hellhound said without opening his eyes. "Wake me up when it's time to board."

"I'll sit with you," Kane volunteered. "Aydan, you go ahead."

I headed for the Tim Horton's. Despite Arnie's disinterest, I got sandwiches for all of us and carried them back to the other two.

Kane thanked me and dug in immediately. Arnie dragged his eyes open with a gruff, "Thanks, darlin', but ya didn't hafta do that." Still, his sandwich disappeared in short order.

Afterward, he closed his eyes again.

Kane and I sat in silence while the long minutes ticked away.

My mind wouldn't let go of LaVonda's betrayal.

How could she do that? How could she look into the eyes of the brother she claimed to love, see his love shining back at her, and choose to hurt him so deeply? She could have stuck around a few lousy minutes longer and said goodbye, the bitch.

And now she would never know what he'd done to protect her.

Well, fine. Maybe she deserved to live in fear for the rest of her miserable life.

My phone vibrated, shaking me out of my vindictive thoughts.

A glance at the call display made my stomach twist.

Holt.

Oh, God. Now what?

I jumped up and hurried away so as not to wake Arnie. Hitting the Talk button, I snapped, "Kelly."

"Meet me outside, in the pickup zone at the north entrance."

"You just made a big deal about getting me through security. Why don't you come up here?" I demanded.

"You've still got an hour before your flight. Get your ass down here." He disconnected.

Swearing under my breath, I hurried down the escalator and jogged to the end of the airport.

Outside, I spotted Holt's alpha-male posture without difficulty, and he waved me toward his rental car. I trotted over, then froze, gaping the woman in the pink parka sitting in the passenger seat.

LaVonda looked intensely anxious, pale and clutching her purse with trembling hands.

As I opened my mouth to say who-knew-what, Holt flung up a hand. "Before you say anything, let me explain."

He looked anxious, too.

"Talk."   My voice came out completely devoid of expression.

"Hang on."   He opened the passenger door and spoke gently. "LaVonda, I need to talk to Aydan in private for a few minutes. Go on into the airport."

She nodded, a convulsive jerk of her chin, and got out. Holt extracted her new suitcase from the trunk and she towed it into the building.

As I lowered myself into the passenger seat, Holt hurried around to the driver's side. "Close the door," he said. "It's fucking cold out there."

I obeyed mechanically.

"LaVonda didn't leave," he said rapidly. "I moved her to a different floor. I lied to her. Told her Hellhound knew what was happening and he'd meet her later. That's why she didn't leave a note. And I told her not to answer any incoming calls on her phone unless they were from me."

"I'm going to fucking kill you," I said flatly.

"First let me explain. Then you can kill me."

I glared at him, but refrained from pulling out my Glock and giving him a lead suppository.

He lowered his voice. "Look, I know what I put you and Hellhound through, and I'm sorry. But I had to make absolutely sure there wasn't any evidence against him and he wasn't going to let anything slip." Holt glanced around us, lowering his voice even more despite the fact that we were cocooned inside the car. "We all know damn well he did it, but this way I can tell Dermott I checked under every rock; and he can't push it any further. Even if the Winnipeg police find something that connects Hellhound later, our asses are covered. Everything by the book."

He glanced at the death-glare I was still giving him, and scowled. "*Your* ass is covered. And I risked my career and a life in prison for it. You're welcome."

First and foremost, he'd been covering his own ass. But he *had* covered mine, too.

"Thanks," I growled grudgingly. "Why the hell didn't you tell us about LaVonda as soon as you realized Arnie wasn't going to admit anything? Do you have any idea how much he's suffering right now?"

Holt made a frustrated gesture. "It's not all about him, you know. LaVonda has a right to her privacy. Her own life. From where I sat, it looked as though she'd been trying like hell to get away from him. I had to be sure of what she wanted, and it was damn hard to tell. She's so dead-set on protecting her little brother, she wasn't going to go anywhere near him until I finally told her nobody would be coming after her." He hesitated. "That's one brave lady."

I let out a small breath, ashamed of my earlier condemnation. "Yeah, she is."

Holt grimaced. "Too bad I lied to her."

My heart sank. "Oh, God. What did you tell her?"

"I told her Fitzgerald's dead, her kidnappers are all dead, and the rest of the world thinks she's dead, so she's safe."

"*What?*" I gaped at him. "Why would you tell her the kidnappers are dead?"

He smirked. "That wasn't the lie. Whittle told me earlier. They were all shot, execution style. Bodies dumped in the industrial area up north. Don't have a time of death yet, but they must have been killed soon after they were released by the police. The assassin probably picked them up from the station, pretending to be an ally."

I tensed. "You're not going to accuse Arnie of that, too, are you?"

"Not unless he managed to smuggle a firearm through airport security."

"No," I said with certainty, and changed the subject. "So if the part about the kidnappers wasn't a lie, what did you lie about?"

Holt let out a breath, his mouth flattening. "That she's safe. I really have no fucking idea. Yeah, Fitzgerald's dead and so are all the guys that tried to grab her, but we don't know who offed the kidnappers. Whoever it is, he's top of the food chain, and he may not know Fitzgerald's dead so he might still be operating on his original instructions." He scowled. "And even if he does know Fitzgerald's dead, some of these assholes have a fucked-up code of honour. He might go after LaVonda just because it's part of the contract and he always fulfills his contract."

I groaned. "Great. So now she's got a stone-cold killer on her tail."

"And so do we, probably. A guy like that wouldn't leave any loose ends."

"Oh, for *shit's* sake." I sank my head into my hands.

"But there is some good news."

I emerged cautiously from the shelter of my hands. "I could really use some."

"The assassin doesn't seem to have made the connection with our hotel, so I'm pretty sure I got LaVonda clear for now." Holt grimaced. "I just spent the last half hour parading around outside the hotel wearing her pink parka and carrying her old duffel bag. If he was going to make a move, he would have. That's the other reason I didn't call right away. How shitty would it be if I phoned and said it's all sunshine and rainbows, and then she got shot on the way to the airport?"

"You did *what?*" I stared at him. "You fucking idiot! You didn't have any backup! What if he'd shot you?"

Holt shrugged. "I was wearing my vest."

"And that'll really help when he takes the head shot. This guy's a fucking *professional!* You idiot!"

"Whatever. Anyway, I'm trying to tell you she's safe... ish. And she needs a place to go. I told her Calgary was a nice city."

I stared at him. "You hate Calgary. You hate any place that's not Toronto."

"So, I lied. She wants to have a life with her brother, and

if the assassin's still after her, it's safest for her to be around people who can protect her." His steely gaze faltered for the first time, and he turned to stare out the windshield. "I booked her a seat on your flight. If you explain to Hellhound that it was all my fault, everything should be okay between them."

For a moment, I could only stare at his craggy profile.

"You're such an asshole," I said, and leaned over to hug him.

After a twitch that told me he was probably expecting an assault instead, he patted my arm awkwardly. "Get going. You'll want to talk to Hellhound before LaVonda shows up."

"Right. Thanks." I gave him a smile. "For everything."

"No problem."

As I got out of the car, he leaned across the console. "Hey, Kelly."

"Yeah?"

"Merry Christmas."

CHAPTER 49

Inside the airport, LaVonda had checked her bag and was waiting in the security lineup.

I gave her a wave and split off to the special screening area, emerging quickly since the security personnel remembered me from earlier.

As I hurried into the boarding lounge, Kane looked up, his brow clearing. "Aydan! I was afraid something had happened. What was that phone call?"

I gave him a 'wait-a-minute' gesture and sat down beside Arnie, gently taking his hand.

He started, his eyes popping open. "Oh. Hey, darlin'. Is it time to board?"

"Not quite yet. I have something really important to tell you. Are you awake?"

He sat up, his gaze sharpening. "What's wrong?"

"Nothing's wrong. Holt screwed us over."

Hellhound let out a contemptuous snort, but I could see the worry in his eyes. "That's nothin' new. What'd he do this time?"

"He lied about LaVonda. She didn't leave without saying goodbye."

He bolted upright, then winced, his hand going protectively to his midsection. "What happened? Is she okay?"

"She's okay. He moved her to a different floor to protect

her, and he didn't tell you because he was trying to get you to admit..."

Conscious that we were in public, I didn't finish the sentence. "And he lied to her, too," I went on. "He told her you knew where she was, and you were going to meet her later. That's why she went with him. She thought you knew. She wouldn't have left without saying goodbye."

He blinked at me in silence, hope dawning on his face. "So she's... safe? An' she didn't run away?"

"Yeah." I squeezed his hand. "And she's here."

"H-Here?" He gazed blankly around us. "Like, here in the airport?"

"She has a seat on our flight. She wants to live in Calgary. If you want her there."

His face came alive, a glorious sunrise displacing the clouds of pain and fatigue. "Yeah! *Hell*, yeah! Where-" He spotted the pink parka and sprang to his feet. "*KATH!*"

Then he was running, dodging around other passengers who froze at the sight of two hundred and fifty pounds of certain death hurtling toward them.

Brother and sister met in the middle, embracing each other hard, laughing and crying in equal measure. At last they returned to where Kane and I sat, both of them beaming.

"I'm so glad," I said simply, and hugged them both.

Kane did the same, holding LaVonda tenderly and pounding Hellhound on the back with fierce joy.

LaVonda lowered her voice, still smiling at Arnie. "You're really going to have to get used to calling me LaVonda..." She paused, her smile brightening. "Actually, never mind. LaVonda Rainey is dead. I have to change my name anyway. I think... I'll be Kathy again." Her eyes brimmed. "Not Kathy Helmand." The tears trickled down to meet her smile. "A new Kathy, with a fresh start."

A tentative touch on my sleeve made me twitch.

"Ma'am..." The uniformed boarding attendant smiled. "Your flight has been called. I think you're our last four passengers, so if you'd like to board now, we'll try to get away a bit early."

I swallowed the giant lump in my throat. "Thanks. We'll be right there."

Safely aloft, I let my aching muscles relax at last.

Kane glanced over with a smile. "What was the big sigh for?"

"Sheer relief." Nodding toward where Arnie and Kathy sat together a few rows ahead of us, I added, "And happiness. They've been through so much. Just for the next couple of hours, they can relax and be completely safe. It was so nice of the airline to let us move so they could sit together and we could, too."

Kane nodded, but his smile faded rapidly into a frown. "What do you mean, 'just for the next couple of hours'?"

I sighed again. Not happiness this time.

"The assassin is still at large." Keeping my voice low, I passed on the information Holt had given me.

"Holt is so damn reckless," Kane growled. "If he'd been killed and Kathy had been taken, we never would have known until it was far too late."

"His heart was in the right place," I said. "Even if his head was up his ass."

Kane laughed. "That's as succinct as it is accurate." Sobering, he added, "And speaking of 'head up ass'... I'm so sorry for jumping to such a stupid and hurtful conclusion this morning. I should have trusted you, and more to the point, I should never have said those terrible things. I can't even expect you to forgive me. I just want you to know how very sorry I am."

My stomach clenched. "Thank you for your apology, and you're completely forgiven because it wasn't a stupid conclusion at all. It was perfectly logical, and..." My throat tightened as though trying to prevent me from saying any more.

But he deserved to know.

I forced the words out. "...it was partly true. I honestly didn't know what Arnie was going to do when we went to bed. But I realized it at four AM. I knew he wasn't there, and I was pretty damn sure where he'd gone and why. And... I didn't tell you." I couldn't meet his eyes. "I'm sorry."

"Why didn't you tell me?" Kane asked softly.

I dug my nails into my palms. Be honest with him. He deserves that.

"There were... a couple of reasons," I began hesitantly. "Mainly, I knew it was too late to do anything about it. It had been six hours since we'd seen him, and it's a six-hour drive to Winnipeg."

"Unless you're Hellhound," Kane put in. "Then it's a lot less."

"Yeah." I sighed. "I'd forgotten about that. So it was *really* too late. But I didn't know for sure, and there wasn't any way to be certain unless we broke into his room. I just didn't see any point in upsetting you."

"And you had to protect him." Kane's voice was even quieter, making me strain to hear him over the noise of the jet engine. "And you didn't trust me to protect him, too."

Oh, God. Why did it always come down to this?

I steeled myself. "You're right..."

His tiny movement betrayed his stab of pain, but when I forced myself to meet his eyes, he was wearing his impassive cop face.

Taking his hand, I went on, "...and you're wrong. I trust you more than almost anyone else in the world."

"Anyone except Arnie." Kane's voice was tinged with resignation. "You trust him absolutely."

I sighed. "I trust him as much as I'm capable of trusting anyone, which is still pretty piss-poor." Fighting my way past the fear of exposing my feelings, I added, "Arnie and I... we... I don't know." I stared at the seatback in front of me. "I guess... We don't have your... certainty. That ability to uphold the law even when it's clearly not..."

I blew out a breath. "I'm sorry. I'm not explaining this well." I turned to meet his troubled gaze and lowered my voice so the engine noise would conceal my words from everyone but Kane. "I don't want to hurt you, but I'm just going to have to be blunt here. You've spent years in law enforcement and you've made a lot of sacrifices for it. And last night, I couldn't trust you to *not* uphold the law. To *not* try to prevent Fitzgerald's murder. You couldn't save both him and Arnie. You would have had to choose."

My throat closed. Holding eye contact with an effort, I forced myself to choke out the shameful words. "I... made the choice without a second thought."

Kane sat in silence, his expression shuttered. He turned away to stare at Arnie and Kathy, their heads together in animated conversation. He was shutting me out, and no wonder.

I was worse than a common criminal.

I was a crooked cop.

Somehow I managed not to fold over the pain in my chest. Swallowing hard, I leaned my head back and closed my eyes. Just another hour, and then I could get off this plane and drive away...

"I understand." Kane's voice startled my eyes open again. He was regarding me seriously, but his grey eyes were clear. "In your place, I would have done the same."

My jaw dropped. "You would?"

"Yes. It was too late to save Fitzgerald, and there were no legal grounds to enter Arnie's room. We both heard him playing and singing, and we recognized his voice so we had no reason to believe he wasn't there." He gave me a twisted smile. "And we still don't. There isn't a scrap of evidence against him."

"But... you're Mr. By-The-Book. You always have been."

Ghosts rose in his eyes. "Not as much as you think, although I tried. But we have gone by the book in this case. Holt made sure of it. And..." He held my gaze. "I don't see how Arnie could have done it. Even though he could theoretically have driven to Winnipeg and back within the timeframe, it's a long hard drive at dangerous speeds, under dangerous conditions. And it's just not plausible that he could have infiltrated a well-guarded residence without any prior intel, done the job, and gotten out again without getting caught; all in only an hour. The chance of success is almost zero. Even a top agent wouldn't attempt it."

Cautious hope buoyed my heart. "So... you don't think he did it?"

Kane hesitated. "I don't see how he could have," he repeated.

His evasive reply answered my question. I slumped in

my seat.

"And you're right," Kane added gently. "I spent years in law enforcement, but..." He glanced again at Arnie and Kathy, the corners of his mouth easing. Returning his gaze to me, he finished, "These days, I'm more concerned with justice."

As we made our way toward the baggage claim area in the Calgary Airport, I glanced at Hellhound and Kathy a few paces ahead of us and leaned closer to Kane to murmur.

"When I can get Arnie alone for a few minutes, I'll tell him about the assassin. I'll leave it up to him whether he wants to break the news to Kathy."

"Good idea," Kane agreed. "He may not want to add to her anxiety just yet."

At the baggage carousel we caught up with the other two, and Kane said, "I called Dad this morning to let him know when we'd be arriving, and he wants us all to meet him over at my new house." His eyes crinkled in a smile. "Knowing Dad, he's up to something. I hope you can both come."

"B-Both of us?" Kathy huddled close to Arnie's shoulder, pale and trembling again. Considering what she'd been through, she was holding up amazingly well. Holt was right. Brave lady.

"Yes, of course," Kane said. "He'll be glad to see you. He remembers you..."

He trailed off as she shrank back, her expression closing down. "I... I don't think I'd better," she said quietly. "I..." Her chest rose and fell in a stifled sob and she turned away, her words barely audible. "I can't face him."

Arnie's arm came protectively around her. "Ya got

nothin' to be ashamed of," he rasped. "Nothin'. Everybody failed ya back then. It ain't your fault."

"No," she said in a small voice. "Mr. and Mrs. Kane didn't fail me. They tried to help. But I..." She spoke to the floor. "I fought them. I was rude to them. I... taunted them and swore at them. I did everything I could to push them away. I was so..."

Kane took her hand. "You were a severely troubled teen, for completely understandable reasons. Your behaviour was normal for a child in your situation, and my parents knew it. That's why they kept trying to help. But in the end..." His voice roughened. "The Rutherfords complained to Social Services, and they had to back off."

"That was my fault," Kathy mumbled. "I shouldn't have told the Rutherfords."

"Kathy, none of it was your fault. You were a child. You should have been protected, and you weren't. There was nothing you could have done differently. And Dad would be overjoyed if he got to meet you now and see you safe and healthy."

"An' strong," Arnie added, tightening his arm around her. "An' brave. Come on, Kath, it'd really mean a lot to Dad Kane. An' me."

Her face lifted, the first rays of hope brightening her eyes. "You call him 'Dad'?"

"He's my dad," Arnie said firmly. "In every way 'cept one. Our ol' man was just a fuckin' sperm donor."

With our bags in hand, we headed for the parkade. I caught Kane's eye and tilted my head toward Hellhound.

Kane gave me a tiny nod. Kathy was gazing around

anxiously, but Hellhound was more alert than I had realized.

He frowned a question at me, and I raised my voice so Kathy could hear. "Arnie, I think some of my stuff ended up in your luggage. I'm parked on the third level. If you don't mind bringing your bag up, we can sort it out there."

"Sure," he agreed. "Cap, d'ya wanna take my keys an' get Kath an' Princess settled in my SUV? I'm in short-term parkin' on the main level." He pointed as we crossed to the parkade. "Right there."

"That's going to cost you," Kane observed as Hellhound handed him the keys.

"Worth every dime," Hellhound assured him. As we strode off toward the stairwell, he lowered his voice. "What's wrong?"

"Nothing." I hesitated. "At least not right this minute. I hope. Come on, let's talk in my car."

He shot me a worried look. "'Kay."

CHAPTER 50

Sitting in my car a few minutes later, I began, "Holt lied to Kathy about how safe she is."

I spun out the tale of Holt's deception and foolhardy courage, and the ominous portent of the three executed kidnappers. As I finished the story I sighed, feeling the weight of fear descending on me all over again. "And the worst part is, we have no idea who the assassin is, or whether he's still trying to fulfill his contract. He could be just gunning for Kathy; or he might be gunning for all of us. And he's a top-of-the-food-chain professional. We'll all have to watch our backs, and we'll especially have to watch Kathy's back."

Hellhound stared through the windshield, his expression troubled.

"John and I will leave it up to you whether to tell Kathy or not," I added.

His frown deepened but he said nothing.

"Arnie," I said softly. "Talk to me. What's wrong?"

He sat in silence for a few more seconds, his fingers knotting together as though he was wrestling with a decision.

Then he faced me with a fake smile that belied the torment in his eyes. "Nothin'. Everythin's fine, darlin'."

My heart twisted. He was hating himself again. Believing that he was nothing more than a soulless killing machine that should be locked away from society.

"Arnie..." I began.

He shook his head, his face smoothing into The Killer's remote expression. "Let it go, darlin'. Everythin's fine."

I glanced around the parkade. Nobody was within visual range. Reaching into my waist pouch, I pulled out my bug detector and activated it.

Showing Arnie the reassuring green light, I murmured, "It's okay, you can talk to me. I know you're beating yourself up about killing Fitzgerald, but you knew the police could never protect Kathy, so you did what had to be done." Anger glowed deep in my belly. "And he damn well deserved it."

"Nobody deserves to be murdered." Hellhound's tone was distant as he repeated Constable Tan's words.

I sighed. "That's not the point. Whether they deserve to or not, some people *have* to die to protect society. Richard Fitzgerald had been committing God-knows-what crimes without any repercussions for decades. The police couldn't stop him, and neither could his enemies. You made the world a safer place for a lot of people."

Hellhound scowled. "Why the hell are ya so damn sure I killed him? You're as bad as Holt."

Misgiving shook me.

What if I was wrong? What if I was accusing an innocent man of a terrible crime? No wonder he was upset.

But there it was again. That tiny twitch of his eyes. That unwillingness to meet my gaze.

"Arnie, you promised not to lie to me," I reminded him softly.

He flinched. "I'm tryin' to protect ya," he grated. "Just let it be, okay?"

"Protect me from what? Holt did a full investigation and found no evidence against you. Dermott isn't in your chain of command so he can't make waves even if he suspects you. You're in the clear, Arnie. There's nothing to protect me from."

"Aydan," he growled through clenched teeth. "You're an agent. Every fuckin' year, ya gotta requalify with a lie detector test. A fuckin' *infallible* lie detector. An' if they ask ya..." He didn't finish the sentence.

My guts clenched. I'd forgotten about that.

I fell back in my seat with a defeated sigh. "Well, then, you might as well talk to me, because I'm already completely fucked. If they ask me, I'll fail."

His brow furrowed. "Why?"

"Because I know without a doubt that you climbed out your window last night, went to Winnipeg, murdered Richard Fitzgerald, came back and climbed into your room, manufactured a story and faked some evidence to divert suspicion, and then went to bed and pretended you were innocent."

"Ya can't know that." Hellhound's voice was flat.

"Yes, I can. Holt's only guessing, but I *know*. Because I know you." I reached over to touch his cheek, looking deeply into his eyes. "You never sing actual songs when you're upset. And I recognized that recording." I gave him a half-smile. "I've heard the 'Gettin' It On' playlist a time or two."

For a long moment, I thought he'd try to brazen it out.

Then he sagged in his seat with a sigh that erased The Killer's remote façade, leaving his expression exhausted and heartsick. "Fuck, Aydan, I'm sorry."

"It's okay. You did the right thing. Don't beat yourself up."

He gave me a twisted smile. "I ain't. Not the way you're thinkin', anyway. If I'd'a lost control an' killed him on impulse I'd be beatin' myself up; but the only difference between what I did last night an' what I've done for the last coupla decades is that this time I didn't get an order to do it. I ain't happy about takin' the law into my own hands; but I ain't sorry, either." His voice went rough with emotion. "I'm just... Christ, Aydan, I'm so fuckin' sorry I dragged ya into this. I thought I could get away with ya none the wiser, but I shoulda fuckin' known better." He sank his head into his hands. "I said I wouldn't shove ya under a bus to save Kath, but that's exactly what I did."

"No, you didn't."

He jerked his head up to glare at me. "Yeah, I fuckin' did. There's no way ya can fool that lie detector, an' as soon's they find out ya knew..." He trailed off, his shoulders squaring. "Okay, it ain't too late to fix this. Just call Holt an' tell him I slipped up an' confessed to ya. Let him arrest me. They won't get a conviction. I made damn sure there ain't any evidence."

"Arnie, no! I'm not going to do that!"

"Ya hafta! It's the only way you're gonna stay outta prison!"

All my fear and frustration erupted in a full-throated bellow. "*NO! Just fucking NO!*" As he began to argue again, I got my voice and temper under control and interrupted, "It wouldn't change anything anyway. Because I already covered up another murder for you."

He froze, open-mouthed, as comprehension flared in his eyes.

"The ol' man," he said quietly. "Fuck. I told ya we shoulda called the cops back then."

"Too late now." I gave him a smile, hoping I looked confident. "But it's okay. You're worrying for nothing. I passed my requalification after that coverup. They use a different set of questions for me, so it didn't come up." As he eyed me uncertainly, I added, "So, out with it. If you're not upset about killing Fitzgerald, then what's bothering you?"

Arnie grimaced. "It was partly just that I hated lyin' to ya when we'd promised 'no lies'. Sorry. But I hadta do it to protect ya." He sighed. "Hadta try, anyway. Fuck. That fuckin' playlist. It was the best I could do." He sank lower in the seat, staring at his boots. "An' I didn't figure it'd really matter in the end. Didn't think I'd be comin' back."

I reached over and took his hand, needing to touch him. My voice wobbled as I said, "That's what I figured."

"I'm sorry, darlin'."

"It's okay. I'm so glad you're here and safe, but I wouldn't have blamed you if... things didn't go well."

He smiled. "I love ya. Have I told ya that lately?"

"I love you, too."

He raised my hand to his lips and kissed it. "I can't figure out why ya do, but I'm sure glad." Still holding my hand warmly clasped in his, he added, "An' here's the other thing I wanted to tell ya, but couldn't unless I spilled the whole story: Ya don't hafta worry about the assassin. They prob'ly won't find his body 'til spring."

I gaped at him.

After a moment of voiceless shock, I demanded, "What the hell? You killed Fitzgerald *and* the assassin, and you still managed to stay under the radar? How? Tell me the whole story!"

"Remember when I told ya I was goin' down to the hospital cafeteria for a sandwich?" I nodded and he went on, "Instead, I walked to that car rental place a few blocks away from the hospital."

"You rented another car! I wondered how you'd gotten there..." I trailed off as a sickening thought hit me. "Did you use your Al Hamlin ID? Holt said he'd checked the car agencies..."

"Yeah, I used Al Hamlin."

My heart froze. If anyone dug just a little deeper, his whole alibi would unravel.

Oh, God, no...

Hellhound went on, "I told 'em I needed to pick up the car after hours, so we did the paperwork an' they gave me the keys; an' I left the car on the lot an' walked back to the hospital. I knew I was takin' a chance, but the whole thing was such a fuckin' longshot anyway. Ya know how much prep goes into my usual jobs; an' there I was with my ass hangin' out in the breeze, no intel, no gear, no nothin'. I figured, best case, I'd get to Winnipeg an' take out Fitzgerald before his guards offed me."

"But you could have waited," I argued. "We could have protected Kathy for a few more days and you could have taken more time to prepare."

"I didn't dare. Look how much had already gone wrong."

I sighed. "Yeah, I guess."

He gave a rueful shrug. "Plus, I wasn't really thinkin' straight. So last night I was waitin' for a good time to go out the window, an' I'm watchin' this car runnin' in the parkin' lot. Exhaust goin' up in a big cloud. I figured somebody was just warmin' it up, an' then they'd pull out."

"But they didn't," I guessed.

"Nah. The car shut down, but nobody got out. By this time it's after ten-thirty, an' I'm gettin' antsy. But I didn't trust that fuckin' car. So I waited. An' sure enough, the car starts up again. Runs for a while, an' then shuts down again."

My blood chilled. "The assassin. He'd already killed the three kidnappers, and he'd spotted the Home Depot van earlier so he was just waiting for us to come out."

"I didn't know he'd killed the kidnappers then, but I figured it was somebody layin' for Kath. So as soon's I got a good chance, I went out the window an' sneaked up on the car. An' damn if it wasn't one a' Fitzgerald's cars. Helluva nice Beemer sedan, windows all tinted black. An' I'm thinkin', fuck me, could I be lucky enough that Fitzgerald came to me?" He grimaced. "I wasn't that lucky. It was that Walker guy."

"Shit, I was right about him. He had a creepy vibe." I stroked a fingertip over Hellhound's bruised knuckles. "Is that where you got injured?"

"Yeah. Guess he didn't wanna attract attention with gunshots, so he took me on. He was good." Hellhound bared his teeth in a chilling non-smile. "But I was mad."

His voice lost all expression as The Killer took over the story. "So I killed him. I was gonna call an' tell ya, but then I realized I had the perfect cover. Didn't need the rental; I had a fast car that nobody'd think to trace, an' even better, the guy was a fuckin' assassin. Everythin' I needed was right there. Gloves, booties, coveralls, the whole shit-a-ree. So I dumped the body in the back seat an' hauled ass."

"In the *back seat*?" I demanded. "And you were fifty kilometres over the speed limit? If you'd gotten stopped for speeding, the police would have spotted the dead guy right away!"

Hellhound shrugged. "A dead guy in the back seat's easier to explain than a dead guy in the trunk. If I got stopped, I was gonna tell 'em I found this guy beat up real bad by the side a' the road an' I was rushin' him to the hospital."

I shook my head, marvelling at his audacity. "You do realize that the police would have asked for your driver's license and registration? Your rescue story wouldn't have held up when they found out you were driving a stolen car."

"Yeah, but I took it easy 'til I was outta Regina, an' then dumped the body out on the prairie. An' I took his ID. I figured if I got stopped later an' the cops checked with Fitzgerald when they found out it was his car, he might vouch for Walker."

"Still, that was a hell of a risk."

Hellhound let out a grim chuckle. "The whole thing was a hell of a risk. But I didn't get stopped. An' Fitzgerald's address was already programmed into the nav system as 'home', so when I got into Winnipeg I went straight there. An' then..." He grinned. "Ask me how many horseshoes I got wedged up my ass."

"How many?" I obliged.

"'Bout six horses' worth. I was gonna cruise past an' case the joint; but as soon's I got close, the gate opened automatically. None a' the guards even blinked. I drove on up to the attached garage an' hit the door opener. Drove in an' parked right beside two other cars just like the one I was drivin'. The house keys were on the key ring. There were a shitpile a' cameras an' guards outside, but none inside."

I shook my head. "That's more than six horses' worth. More like a twelve-horse hitch. So you did the job, got back in the car, and drove away with nobody the wiser."

"Yep. If the guards point any fingers, it'll be at Walker. An' far's anybody knows, he did Fitzgerald an' then vanished. I ditched the disposables in a dumpster on the other side a'

Winnipeg. Drove back to Regina an' left the car unlocked downtown with the keys in the ignition. By now, it's been stolen or towed."

"But they'll find Walker's weapons and gear if they check the car at the impound lot."

Hellhound shrugged. "Not my problem. There's nothin' to connect me to that car."

I sagged in the seat, letting out a long breath. "So Kathy's safe. And there's no evidence against you."

"Yeah. We're all good." He smiled. "But Arlene Widdenback's arms deal prob'ly just went south."

I threw my arms around him, hugging him awkwardly across the console while I kissed him.

He kissed me back tenderly. "Thanks for all ya did, darlin'. I owe ya."

"No, you don't. You've covered my ass often enough." I gave him one last squeeze before letting him go. "I guess you'd better get back to your SUV."

"Yeah." Arnie's voice was deep with satisfaction. "Kathy's waitin' for me."

As I drove out of the parkade into the cold winter sun, I couldn't help checking obsessively behind me for tails.

Fitzgerald was dead. Walker was dead. We were safe, dammit.

Nevertheless, my gaze strayed to my rearview mirrors over and over.

By the time I stopped in front of Kane's newly-purchased bungalow, I was almost certain we hadn't been followed. Arnie and Kathy were already parked, and Kane pulled up behind me as I turned off my car.

I let out a breath. If Kane had come directly home, it meant he hadn't spotted a tail, either.

As I got out of the car, he strode up beside me.

"The assassin is dead," I said quietly. "It was Walker. We're clear."

"*What?* How-" Kane interrupted himself. "Never mind, I don't want to know." He hesitated. "Are you sure?"

"Positive." I glanced around us reflexively. "But... I still can't relax."

Kane linked his arms gently around me. "That's understandable. But this time you really are being paranoid." He pressed his lips to my forehead. "Relax. It's over and everyone is safe. I was on high alert all the way here, and I didn't see anything suspicious."

Leaning into him, I released my tension on a long breath. "Neither did I." I put on a smile as Arnie and Kathy came over. "Well, let's go and see what your Dad's up to."

Kane smiled and inclined his head subtly toward the house. "I think he has an accomplice. I can see I'll have to instruct Daniel in unobtrusive spycraft."

I grinned, watching the blinds part, then fall back into place, then part again at the eye level of an eager seven-year-old. "Go on, then, Dad; don't keep him in suspense," I teased.

CHAPTER 51

Kane chuckled and we went up the walk toward his house together, followed by Arnie and Kathy.

Kane swung the door open, stepping inside to call, "Hello, this house!"

"*Daddy-Daddy-Daddy!*" Daniel rocketed around the corner, flinging his arms around Kane's legs before bouncing away again, too wound up to maintain the hug for more than a few seconds. "Surprise, Daddy, Merry Surprise Christmas!" Daniel jumped up and down, beaming. "We got a tree and we got a turkey and we got-"

His words dissolved into a squeal of glee as Kane swooped him off his feet, tossing him in the air and catching him in a hug with a noisy smacking kiss on the top of his head.

"Are you surprised, Daddy, are you surprised?" Daniel demanded.

"I'm very surprised," Kane confirmed, grinning as he took in the Christmas tree standing slightly askew and obviously decorated by small enthusiastic hands. The living room furniture from his condo had been arranged in a rough grouping around the tree, and the scent of roasting turkey filled the air.

Doug Kane emerged from the kitchen, his face alight with a smile that folded the wrinkles deep around his eyes and mouth. "My boys!" he exclaimed, pulling first Arnie and then John into a hug. "And my girls." He hugged me warmly, then turned to Kathy, who was trying to hide behind Arnie with her gaze downcast.

"Kathy," he said softly. "My poor child. It's wonderful to see you healthy at last." He folded her into his arms.

She pressed her face into his shoulder and her voice came out in a sob. "I'm sorry."

"Oh, sweetheart, don't be sorry." His voice shook. "Be proud. You made it all on your own." He gripped her shoulders, his grey gaze searching her face. "And I know you're still strong enough to make it on your own, if you want to. Just remember that you don't have to. You have a family who loves you and wants to help."

"Th-Thank you." She managed a watery smile, and I turned away to dab at the moisture in the corners of my eyes.

"So what's this about a turkey?" Kane asked jovially, releasing us from the emotional moment.

"We got a turkey, Daddy!" Daniel squirmed down from Kane's arms and tugged him toward the kitchen. "Come on, we need help."

Kane's father chuckled as we followed them around the corner into the kitchen. "Welcome to chaos," he quipped, waving a hand at the piles of boxes in various stages of unpacking.

Cookware and utensils littered the countertops, but a small stack of plates and some cutlery on the table promised a more-or-less civilized dining experience.

"We managed to find the turkey roaster," Doug went on. "And we wrangled the turkey into it, but we didn't start until after you'd called this morning. Dinner will be a bit later than usual, maybe around seven. I hope."

Kane's lips turned up as he surveyed the mess. "You've

worked miracles in only a day. And is that your famous homemade stuffing I smell?"

"I helped make the stuffing, Daddy," Daniel informed him.

Kane's smile widened. "I'm sure you were a big help."

"And we've got cranberry sauce, and..." Daniel's voice took on a minor key. "Vegetables."

"I think we've got everything we need to make a proper dinner," Doug said. "All we need is the chef to pull it together." He grinned at Kane. "I hope you're up to the challenge."

Kane grinned back. "I'm sure we'll manage."

While they spoke, Daniel sidled over to Doug.

"Grampa." Daniel tugged Doug's sleeve. "Grampa!"

"Yes, Daniel?"

Daniel tugged again, going up on his tiptoes as Doug stooped. Even behind Daniel's concealing hand, his whisper was clearly audible. "Is it time yet?"

The laugh lines creased Doug's face. "Yes, I think it's time."

"*Presents!*" Daniel spun and raced down the hall, his "*Yay!*" receding rapidly.

"Let's go, folks." Doug herded us toward the living room. "We have to go and sit by the Christmas tree now."

As we took our seats, Kane lowered his voice. "Dad, what's going on? I thought you were going to give Daniel my presents on Christmas Eve, when he and Alicia always do theirs."

Doug's eyes twinkled as Daniel rounded the corner, dragging a moving dolly laden with brightly-wrapped parcels. "Daniel and I talked it over and he decided he'd rather wait until you came home. Isn't that right, Daniel?"

"That's right, Grampa!" Daniel parked the dolly with a flourish in front of Kane's chair, beaming. "Merry Surprise Christmas, Daddy! Look what I got you!" He dove into the pile and extracted a haphazardly wrapped package plastered with enough tape to secure a dozen gifts. "Open it, open it!"

Blinking rapidly, Kane accepted the parcel as though it was the most valuable thing he'd ever received.

As Daniel leaned in, quivering with excitement, Kane wrapped an arm around him and raised the package to his ear. Assuming a thoughtful expression, he shook it.

"Hmm. It sounds like... paper." Daniel giggled, and Kane continued to draw out the suspense, sniffing the parcel thoroughly. "It smells like... paper." He palpated it, turning it over and around. "It feels like..."

By now Daniel was bouncing up and down. "Open it, Daddy! Open it and see!"

As if he hadn't heard, Kane continued, "...paper. Hmm. I wonder if I should open it?"

"YES!" we all chorused.

Grinning, he began to pick painstakingly at the corner of the first piece of tape.

Doug rose, laughing. "I can't take it anymore. Here." He extracted a small jackknife from his pocket and handed it over. "If we're going to take twenty minutes to open every gift, we'll be here all night."

Kane capitulated, slitting the paper and peeking inside.

"Do you like it, Daddy, do you like it?" Daniel vibrated beside his chair, gazing up with eager eyes. "I bought it with my very own money!"

Kane reached into the package, pulling out a dollar-store keychain bearing a fake-gold fob that spelled out '*#1 Dad*'.

He hugged Daniel. "It's the best present I've ever

gotten." His voice was choked, his eyes full.

"Yay!" Innocently oblivious to his father's emotion, Daniel whirled back to the pile of gifts. "Grampa, I got one for you, too!"

Smiling, Doug accepted the gift. A few moments later '*#1 Grandpa*' was revealed, and Doug gave Daniel a hug. "Thank you. I'll put my keys on it right now."

Turning back to the pile, Daniel extracted a piece of paper and hurried over to Hellhound. "I drew a picture for you, Uncle Arnie! Do you like it?"

"Yeah, I like it," Hellhound confirmed, grinning. "Look, everybody, it's Hooker." He turned the paper toward us, displaying a crayoned drawing of a brown four-legged creature. The pointed ears hinted at feline ancestry, but the broad tail looked more like a beaver than a cat. Hellhound turned back to Daniel. "Ya even remembered his fluffy tail. Thanks, kiddo. I'll hang it up as soon's I get home."

Daniel accepted the praise with the poise of an accomplished artist, flinging his arms around Hellhound for a moment before returning to the pile. "Auntie Aydan, this is for you!"

He skipped over bearing another crayoned drawing. A smile spread across my face at the sight of a stick person with long bright-red hair beside a blue blob supported by two black blobs. Underneath, painstakingly crayoned letters spelled out '*1966 Corvette Stingray*'.

"Grampa helped with the spelling," Daniel confided. "And I drew a wrench, too, so you can fix it." He pointed to a blob at the end of one of the stick figure's arms.

"Thank you, Daniel." Feeling awkward, I hesitated, but Daniel threw his arms around me anyway. I hugged him back. "I'm going to hang it up in my garage, right by my

Corvette." Displaying it to the others, I added, "How cool is this?"

As murmurs of approbation surrounded him, Daniel wheeled back to the pile. "Auntie Kathy, I drew this for you." He hurried over to Kathy, whose eyes filled when she accepted the paper. Daniel gazed up at her earnestly. "Grampa said you were lost for a long time. I got kidnapped. It was really scary. I cried, too, but Daddy says it's okay to cry. But you're safe now so I drew you safe in front of Daddy's house with me and Daddy and Grampa and Uncle Arnie and Auntie Aydan."

"Thank you, sweetheart." Kathy cuddled him close, laying her cheek on the top of his head. "It's beautiful. And I'm sorry, but I don't have a present for you."

"Yes, you do," Doug interjected hurriedly. "You must have forgotten. It's right here, remember?" He pulled a small package out of the pile. "And here's one from Uncle Arnie, and Auntie Aydan, too. Do you want to open them now, Daniel?"

"Yes!"

As Daniel scurried over, I mouthed 'Thank you' to Doug, who threw me a wink and a smile.

The small packages turned out to be miniature cars, inexpensive but valuable to us nonetheless.

As Daniel dove gleefully into the rest of the pile, I leaned back in my chair and watched Kane. He had eyes only for Daniel's delight in his gifts, completely immersed in the magic.

When the last of the packages had been torn open and noisily celebrated, Doug frowned at the empty moving dolly, feigning puzzlement.

"I think there's something missing here, Daniel. I don't

see anything that Santa brought you."

Daniel gazed up at him, obviously confused. "Santa's presents are at Mommy's house."

"But Santa comes to Daddy's house, too," Doug assured him. "Maybe he left your presents somewhere else in the house because we didn't have the Christmas tree up yet. I'm sure I saw a big fat stocking around here somewhere. Now let me think... where did I see it?"

He pretended to ponder as Daniel's eyes grew rounder and rounder.

"I think I remember now!" Doug exclaimed. "Come on, everybody, let's see if we can find some more presents."

He headed for the hallway with Daniel at his heels, Kane following close behind. I poked my head around the corner in time to see Doug open the door to the linen closet.

"Well, would you look at that," he said.

Daniel let out an ear-piercing whoop. "Santa came! Santa came! Daddy, look! Santa came!"

Kane stooped to share the marvel with Daniel, then straightened to give 'Santa' Doug a hug that clearly communicated the fullness of gratitude in his heart.

"Daddy." Daniel's voice was thoughtful. "Santa came to Mommy's house yesterday and your house today. Do you think he'll do it next year, too? 'Cause if he does, then maybe you and Mommy wouldn't have to be angry so much."

Kane cleared his throat, crouching to hug Daniel. "I'm sure he'll do the same next year," he said huskily. "Santa always knows how to make things turn out right."

Daniel's face lit up. "Yay! Merry Surprise Christmas every year!" As he tugged Kane back to the closet to admire the spoils, I eased back a pace to enjoy the tableau.

Kane bending down to share Daniel's excitement, both

their faces alight while Doug beamed at them.

Arnie and Kathy standing close together, Kathy smiling widely at her first real family Christmas.

Arnie's attention was all on Kathy, joy glowing in his face despite his obvious exhaustion.

As I watched, he glanced at me and held out his arm invitingly. I came over and tucked myself into the embrace, slipping my arm around him in turn. Holding me close to his side, he leaned down to press his lips to my temple and whisper, "Merry Christmas, darlin'."

Relaxing at last, I hugged him a little tighter and whispered back.

"Merry Christmas."

Book 16 is available!

Visit my Books page at dianehenders.com/books for progress
updates and announcements.

A Request

Thanks for reading!

If you enjoyed this book, I'd really appreciate it if you'd take a moment to review it online.

Here are some suggestions for the "star" ratings:
Five stars: Loved the book and can hardly wait for the next one.
Four stars: Liked the book and plan to read the next one.
Three stars: The book was okay. Might read the next one.
Two stars: Didn't like the book. Probably won't read the next one.
One star: Hated the book. Would never read another in the series.

You can help prospective readers by writing a few sentences about what you liked or disliked about the book.

Thanks for taking the time to do a review!

About Me

Before I started writing fiction, I had a checkered career: technical writer, computer geek, and interior designer. I'm good at two out of three of those. Fortunately, I had the sense to quit the one I sucked at (interior design).

When my mid-life crisis hit, I took up muay thai and started writing thrillers featuring a middle-aged female protagonist. ('Walter Mitty', you say? Nope, never heard of him.)

Writing and kicking the hell out of stuff seemed more productive than more typical mid-life-crisis activities like getting a divorce, buying a Harley Crossbones, and cruising across the country picking up men in sleazy bars; especially since it's winter most months of the year here in Canada.

It's much more comfortable to sit at my computer. And Harleys are expensive. Come to think of it, so are beer and gasoline.

Oh, and I still love my husband. There's that. So I stuck with the writing.

Diane Henders

And here's my "professional" bio, in case you need something more suitable for mixed company:

Diane Henders is the Kindle best-selling author of the NEVER SAY SPY series: Sexy thrillers packed with tension, laughs, profanity, and sometimes warm fuzzies.

The first book in the series, NEVER SAY SPY, has had over 450,000 downloads to date, and stayed on Kindle's 'Women Sleuths' Top 100 list for 60 consecutive months.

Diane enjoys target shooting, gardening, auto mechanics, painting (art, not walls), music, and martial arts; and loves food and drink almost as much as she loves her husband. They live in the wilds of British Columbia, Canada, where they get all the adrenaline rush they could ever want by growing fruit trees in bear country.

Want to know what else is roiling around in the cesspit of my mind? Drop by my blog and website at dianehenders.com, check out the extras, and don't forget to leave a comment in the guest book to say hi – I love hearing from you! Or you can connect with me on Facebook at:
https://www.facebook.com/authordianehenders.
See you there!